BUFFALO DUST

MEL A ROWE

Also by Mel A ROWE

ELSIE CREEK SERIES:

The ART of DUST

DIAMOND in the DUST

CAKED in DUST

XMAS DUST

MUSTER in the DUST

ROLLED in DUST

WRITTEN in DUST

DOCTORING DUST

BUFFALO DUST

OASIS OF THE OUTBACK DUOLOGY:

The Station, Volume One

The Station, Volume Two

STANDALONE STORIES:

Avoiding the Pity Party

Unplanned Party

The Football Whisperer

Winter's Walk

Run Beautiful Run

The Sister Trip

Receive exclusive insights, and news on upcoming releases
by joining: https://melarowe.com/newsletter/

COPYRIGHT

***Caveat: As a courtesy, since there may be some sparse language choices in this story that may represent an obstacle for the reader, I am offering this warning. Please note this language and cultural references are purely for fictional purposes only and not designed to offend any individual persons, culture, or religions implied.*

The following is written in Australian English

I consider the ELSIE CREEK SERIES a love
letter to the unique individuals that continue to
shape the Northern Territory into a truly
amazing part of Australia.

My dad would've loved it.

One

Being crushed and covered in buffalo drool was not how Jordi had planned to enjoy her day. But getting licked in the face by a massive, overbearing black beast was outright detestable. The full-grown water buffalo, wearing pink ribbons around its horns like a schoolgirl in braids, had her trapped against her van. Its wet nose sniffed in her hair and in her ear, causing her to cringe all over.

'Cecil. Back off!' The powerful male voice was commanding, as a stocky shoulder pushed against the hefty buffalo. 'You must be carrying something Cecil likes, because he's normally a softie.'

'Y-you don't live here, do you?' Of all the flower deliveries, it had to be Luke who got to play her hot hero, forcing Jordi to busily brush herself down, trying to look presentable.

'I do.' He narrowed his brown eyes at her, the colour of brown sugar sprinkled over a chocolate sundae. Along with that lopsided grin, that made up the man. Luke. AKA Bottle Shop Luke, AKA Bottle Shop Boy—who most certainly wasn't a boy.

'Well, if it isn't the flower girl, eh?' He raked his fingers through his thick hair, the colour of rich cherry wood and deep saddle leather, highlighted with a few streaks kissed by the sun.

She scoffed at him. 'You know my name is Jordi, and I'm

a *florist*, not a flower girl.'

'You don't think I know that, Angelfish?' His lopsided grin widened. 'But I think Cecil has a crush on you, with that sweet tooth he has for flowers. And *he's* the one who calls you flower girl.'

'Sure he does. He's not going to hump my leg like a dog, is he?' Once again, she was forced back against her van to get away from the buffalo's flaring nostrils.

'Come on, Cecil, be a gentleman.' Luke shouldered the buffalo the way a handler pulls back on a dog. 'Why are you here, Jordi?'

'I'm trying to do my job. I've got a delivery for an Esther Bennett. Is that your girlfriend?' A question that regularly plagued her mind.

Luke grimaced, crossing muscular arms over a very toned torso that was ripped without being too buff. 'No. My surname is Bennett and Esther's my grandmother. Who is sending my grandmother flowers?'

His grandmother. *Phew.*

Just standing this close to the guy had her mouth watering she couldn't look at him, with her fingers fumbling on the door handle before pulling open the van's side door a little too hard.

'Hey, will that beast eat my flower arrangements?' She put herself between the bulky beast with flaring nostrils and her van, surprised at how she suddenly had a backbone. Or was that because Luke was here?

'Have you got something in there to distract Cecil, like bait does on a fishing line? Cecil loves daisies. He'll love you forever if you feed him daisies.'

'I do …' She rummaged around in her van, the cool air a stark contrast to the outback's heat.

Flicking the lids on the styrofoam boxes that kept her flowers fresh, she searched for the herbaceously fragrant daisies that reminded her of flourishing spring garden beds— unlike the red dust bowl that made up this property.

'Here, you feed it.' She held out a bunch of daisies to the

mega-handsome guy, who frowned at them like she was handing him a head of dried-up broccoli.

'No, you can feed him.'

'It's your pet. I'm just here to deliver the flowers.' *And leave.*

'Everyone does it.' Luke stepped forward with determination brimming in his sugary-sweet brown eyes, but his cologne was a jaw-dropping fabulous fragrance. For a female who basked daily in floral aromas, never had vanilla, leather, and denim with a fine weave of lavender and bitter almond, blended so magnificently on a man. It deserved its own floral category and class.

'They're your flowers, so you do the honours.' Luke's grip was warm and strong, but gentle, even though he was practically dragging her along like a caveman claiming his bride.

'What are you doing?' She tried to pull herself free, hating anyone touching her.

'Chill, my little angelfish. Cecil's just a big puppy. The little kids are always feeding Cecil at the school, so trust me when I say that he will not harm you ... Hmm, I'd better tell the school principal to limit his tucker, Cecil's really putting on the beef.' Luke's lopsided grin was charming and boyish all at the same time. He had a glow about him, topped with an intense focus, as if she was the only person in the paddock, when normally people looked at the flowers she was holding, not her. Come on, who remembered the face of their last delivery driver?

He held her trembling hand, which barely gripped the daisy stems that were thrust under that big black nose. She winced as fear brushed over her tingling scalp and down her spine when it opened its huge mouth. She saw teeth!

'Easy does it ...' Luke held her there, his chest to her back to stop her bolting. Clamping her eyes shut in fear of losing fingers, she felt nothing, just a tug on the stems.

She cracked an eyelid to peek at the buffalo chomping on the flowers like a cow. A very, very big cow. Its dark eyes rolled with delight, as its long flickering tongue swiped its lips before taking another dainty bite of the daisies the way a person would eat at a restaurant, savouring every morsel of their feast.

'There, not that bad, eh?' Luke let go of her wrist, to tenderly pat the buffalo's glossy coat. 'You'll be besties before you know it, if you keep feeding Cecil like that.'

Jordi shrugged, feeling every bit the awkward nerd for her fear of feeding a water buffalo.

Hang on a second—this was her bread and butter that was now dusting the black lips of a horned beast.

There went her profit margins for the day.

Suddenly remembering her deadline, Jordi dusted her hands and turned to scoop up the vibrant orange floral arrangement from her van. She read the name from the small card. 'This is for Esther Bennett. Is she around?'

'Should be.' Luke peeked at the card saying *Happy Birthday* and frowned. 'Jumpin' baitfish.' He dragged out his phone. 'Silly alarm didn't work.'

'Let me guess, you forgot it's your grandmother's birthday.' She'd seen it countless times. It was all part of the job, delivering handfuls of joy to the world.

'Hey, I set a reminder on my phone.' He held up the small screen to prove it.

'When?'

'Last year, when I forgot back then.'

She giggled at his boyish shrug and that charming smile that did wonders to her swirling belly of buzzing bees.

'Who else are you delivering to today?'

'Um ... A Pamela Hopkins. Do you know her? Works at the school.'

'New teacher, dating a cowboy.' He shrugged, poking his nose inside the van to read the cards that were carefully attached to assorted flower arrangements. He always did that. 'Who else?' He tapped on the large pink orchid display.

'Hey, that's private.' She tried to block him. 'That's like reading someone's mail.'

He pointed at one of the arrangements inside her van. 'I see that's for Marie Pederson. She works in the council office.'

'She's not home. Hey, do you know where I could find her? Her orchid display is far too good to leave frying at the front door of her house.'

'Marie lives in the council office from nine until four, Monday to Friday, and sees me every Friday at exactly ten past four for her weekly supply of chardonnay.'

'Makes sense then.' Especially when the large card and the special balloon said: *congratulations for twenty years on the job.*

'So, my little angelfish, are you gonna save my day?'

'Excuse me?' There was nothing angelic about her. But this was side-hustling Luke, the bottle shop manager from the Elsie Creek Pub, who'd talk you into buying buckets of water while sitting beside a river!

'Sell me something you've got floating in that van, so I can give it to Gran.'

'I'm not some mobile flower shop. I don't sell, I deliver.' Her sister did the selling.

Again, Luke peeked into her van. 'Do you sleep in here, too?' He pointed at her rolled-up swag, arching an eyebrow at her with concern.

'The resorts aren't cheap in Kakadu during the tourist season.' It was her busiest time on the road, doing her seasonal rural run. It was her kind of heaven, well away from people, customers, and responsibilities that did not involve feeding water buffaloes and drooling at Luke who was giving her a pleading look.

Flamin' flora!

Why did she have to give in to him. Every. Single. Time.

She climbed into the back of her van and rummaged through the foam boxes, where delicate floral aromas washed over her. 'Is it a big birthday for your grandmother?'

Luke rubbed the back of his neck, shifting his boot to rest on her van's step. His presence was far too big for their shared space. 'Esther's over eighty. So, I'd imagine every birthday is big, don't you think?'

It was a struggle to forget all about Aphrodite's Adonis blocking her doorway and focus on the flowers. With a few pieces plucked here and there, a wrap of cellophane and a twist of ribbon and wire—which she always kept on hand for floral emergencies—she held out her latest creation. 'Will this do? It's even got some esters, which are part of the Aster family.' The bouquet had purple esters and pompom daisies, with the drama of purple irises accentuating the purple kale, and a lavender tinted banksia as the jewel in the crown. It came together with flat grey eucalyptus leaves to create a rustic blend of colour, texture, and aroma. It was blooming marvellous.

Luke's eyes widened, as did his smile, stepping back from the van holding the flowers like a trophy. 'Gran's going to love these. Her favourite colour is purple.'

'Did you know there's an *Esther rose*, and an *Esther Read* daisy—but I think that variety is toxic to dogs and cats, which might not be too kind to buffaloes?'

'I can't believe you did that in five minutes.' Luke now held two flower arrangements, while trying to keep his back to the buffalo, who was lifting its head for a sniff. 'Do you always carry that much stock with you?'

'You caught me at the start of my run, so you're lucky I could make that arrangement for your grandmother.' Climbing out of her van, Jordi brushed down the purple petals from her long-sleeved work shirt, as water splats and tiny leaves scattered down her jeans. Normally she didn't arrange flowers in the back of her van either, not when dressed for deliveries. Normally she'd shove the flowers in people's faces and leave.

But Luke had a habit of leaning against her window demanding a chat every time she drove through the bottle shop asking for directions to properties not found on any digital map.

'Hey, listen, if you ever want to make yourself a quick buck for the bait bucket, you could drop off a few posies at the bottle shop.'

Jordi scoffed, pulling down her shirt's sleeves to cover her hands. 'Why? The pub sells booze, not flowers.'

'I'll sell them to a few customers. It'll be perfect for the Friday home-time rush, for those fellas to keep their wives happy before they run away fishing for the weekend. I know I can sell them.'

A police siren whooped in the air, making her jump.

By the front gate red dust stirred as an elderly woman, in a sky-blue Cinderella-style ball gown, drove her ride-on lawnmower past the *Anaborro Downs* sign and down the driveway. Her tiara sparkled in the sun as she waved at them, with the police car following her.

'Just great ...' Luke scrubbed a hand over his face as if to wipe away the incoming nightmare.

'Who's that?'

'My gran. Here, hold these.' He thrust the two flower arrangements back into her arms.

'Why?'

'Because I think Gran is about to get arrested. Again!'

Two

Luke arched his eyebrows at the latest spectacle coming down the driveway in her ball gown. 'Gran, please tell me you're not getting arrested again?'

'Are you for real?' Jordi giggled, attempting to hide behind the two bunches of flowers she held for him. As far as he was concerned, she didn't smile enough.

'It's what Gran does. She loves being the centre of attention.'

'Hoorah, my lovelies.' Gran waved in the air like some inept fairy godmother who'd conjured a police escort, with her pale purply-grey hair swept back, and her sparkly tiara as bright as her smile. 'Look who I found.' She pointed at the police vehicle.

Senior Constable Porter climbed out of the four-wheel drive police ute. 'Esther, a ride-on mower is not a car. You can't take it to town.'

'Your boss stole my licence, so what else can I use? I had to go to the school. It's my reading day.'

Luke turned off the mower, so he wouldn't have to shout over the engine. 'No, Gran, tomorrow is your reading day. Friday.'

'Well, that explains why they weren't ready for me.'

Luke helped his grandmother off the ride-on mower. 'I told you I would drive you into town.'

'Pfft. I can drive just fine. It's the stupid rules they're changing all the time that's the problem. I doubt even you, Porter, could keep up.' Esther pointed a purple fingernail at the cop. 'You look much better now your boss is back from holidays—not so stressed out.'

'I never thought I'd be so happy to have Marcus back. I'm over doing paperwork, rosters, and reports for a while.' From the front seat of the police vehicle, Porter removed a tray of coffees and a folded flyer.

'I can see that, if you've got time to deliver coffee and junk mail.' Straightening up her tiara, Esther turned around, the diamantes on the skirts of her ball gown sparkling under the sun. 'Luke, did you finally bring home a girl for me to meet?'

Jordi went bright red, choking out a cough.

It made Luke chuckle, especially when Jordi scowled at him, shoving the flowers back in his face. She'd been dropping by the bottle shop for about a year now, and normally he couldn't get a stammering boo from the shy woman, so this was a huge improvement.

'Gran, this is Jordi. She delivered your flowers.' He held out the two bouquets to his grandmother.

'What's the occasion?' Esther gushed at her flowers as if she was the star on a Broadway show.

'It's your birthday.'

'No, it's not. That's next week.'

'It's today, Esther.' Porter handed Luke a coffee. 'It's the only reason why I didn't arrest you for dangerous driving in an unregistered vehicle while unlicensed.'

'Well, happy birthday to me, then. Who are the flowers from?'

'I'm guessing from Mum and Dad.' Some kind of orange olive branch, no doubt.

'You can throw those out.' Esther scowled, pushing the purple posy at him.

'Easy, Gran, I gave you the purple bunch. I just watched Jordi make them.' And there it was, another smile, only this time there was pride in Jordi's aqua eyes, the same colour of the river reflecting a summer sky.

Jordi tucked wisps of her soft hair behind her dainty ear, her hair brushing past her shoulders in soft waves—not brown, not blonde, but a sandy beige and pretty.

It's just a pity she was always so shy, hunching her shoulders and pulling down her shirt sleeves over her hands.

'Fine, I'll throw the other flowers out then.' Gran raised the orange flower bouquet as if to toss them across the paddock.

Jordi gasped, staggering back as if Esther had elbowed her in the mouth.

'Don't say that, Gran. Not while the florist is standing right next to you.'

'It's not you, petal, it's the sender.' Esther went to pat Jordi, who flinched as if scalded by his grandmother's touch. 'I'd never shoot the messenger. Not that I can anyway, because the pesky police took my guns and my gun licence too.' She scowled at Porter.

'You were threatening to shoot that real estate agent.'

'He was trespassing.'

'I'm going now. Happy birthday, Esther.' Jordi rushed for her van.

Luke opened the driver's door for Jordi. 'Do me a favour, and think about selling some of your flowers in the bottle shop, eh? I'll even hit you up for a weekly order of daisies for a certain buffalo, too.' He moved sideways, blocking the beast that was leaning over his shoulder to follow Jordi. Not that he could blame Cecil, because Jordi smelt like a field of flowers, tempting him to lean in and inhale deeply.

'So, it'll be a side-hustle as a way to feed your buffalo for free?' She arched an eyebrow at him.

'Hey, I'll make sure you get a share of the profits.' He didn't mind a hustle or four.

'I'll think about it.'

'Jordi, you can come back anytime. I'll make you dinner.' Esther then wagged her finger at Luke. 'I don't care what you say, young man, women are allowed. Luke never brings his dates home.'

'Gran, you don't need to broadcast any Bennett business to the world.' He rolled his eyes at the family mantra, while waving at Jordi driving away in her van.

But Jordi wasn't like that. She wasn't some one-night stand. He treated her differently because he knew she was fragile.

'I must take these flowers inside. Thank you for my gift, Luke.' Esther kissed his cheek.

He smiled softly. 'Happy birthday, Gran.'

'I'll let you put the ride-on mower away.' With arms full of flowers, she gave a well-practised side kick to shift the poufy skirt of her ball gown. It's hem barely skimmed over the red dust driveway as she headed for the house.

'Gran, why are you wearing two different boots?'

'Am I?' She lifted the hem of her ball gown. 'So I am.'

'Did you forget where you put them?' Like she'd forgotten the most important date on her calendar?

But then he'd forgotten her birthday too.

'I'll put the kettle on, and I'll make a birthday cake for lunch. Come on, Cecil, I've got a birthday treat for you, too.'

'Where did you find her?' Luke asked Porter, sipping on his coffee.

'Zipping along the bike paths behind the school. She just barrelled across the road, right in front of me. Good thing I was doing less than walking speed.'

'I've hidden the keys to all the other vehicles, I guess I'll be adding the mower to the mix.' He was used to their pet water buffalo, Cecil, wandering the roads to town. The problem was Gran was going walkabout now, too.

'This might cheer you up.' Porter held out the flyer.

'Did you get this from the post office?'

'I avoid the post office these days.'

It was a touchy subject to mention the postmistress around Porter. To be honest, Tess did dick his best mate around.

'No freaking way.' Luke's eyes widened as he read the

flyer. 'They're finally bringing the Million-dollar Barra here?' Australia's richest fishing competition was coming to Elsie Creek.

'I thought you'd like that. They'll be announcing it today. The mayor came into work to let us know. Marcus is spewing because he has to redo the police rosters. He wants me working on the boat for the Elsie Creek Barra Classic.'

'We're meant to do that fishing competition together as a team.'

'Sucks for me, too. But with that million-dollar barra flapping its gills in our backyard, we'll have every man and his dingo showing up for the Classic.'

'The river is going to be clogged with coastal cowboys.'

'But you'll have home-ground advantage.' Porter tapped on the flyer. 'Which means you can win some big bucks this year, along with the credibility to start your own fishing tour company.'

'It suddenly feels like it's *my* birthday.' Luke smiled down at the page. It didn't last long, as he handed the flyer back to Porter. 'I can't.'

'Why not?'

The front door of the house opened, allowing jazz music to filter through the air, where Esther threw the orange floral arrangement onto the lawn to feed the water buffalo.

Cecil, who'd been chasing a butterfly, skipped over to the flowers like a wobbly puppy.

'I've got to watch over Gran.' She was forgetting things. It was a bad sign, especially when Esther loved her birthdays, normally celebrating from dawn.

'Who used to keep an eye on Esther?'

'Iris.' He pointed at the neighbouring property.

'I'm sorry about Iris,' said Porter.

'Me too.' Luke narrowed his eyes at the dead fields that led to the fence line, where the once well-trodden track between the two properties was already fading. Before her passing Iris had sold the place, but so far there was no sign of their mysterious new neighbours.

He wiped over his mouth, re-reading the flyer while tasting the temptation of winning a million smackeroos — leaving him with one big obstacle … 'Who do you know who'd want to granny-sit an uncontrollable octogenarian?'

Three

Through the van's windscreen, the gorgeous countryside was like a front row seat in a fancy cinema. She loved this area of the Northern Territory outback, with its rustic reds and sunburnt ochres through to the mix of black soil plains, dotted with gigantic ant mounds and clusters of boulders so smooth they looked like giant dinosaur eggs.

The drive always cleared her mind as the outback unveiled itself around each sweeping turn where the asphalt rolled like a black ribbon under an oceanic sky. But it was also the stunning range of gums, banksias, and other flourishing native trees, highlighted by an abundant display of wildflowers dotting the area like paint across a canvas.

He never paid me! The thought made her sit straighter behind her steering wheel.

Not only did she feed a perfectly decent bunch of daisies to Luke's pet buffalo—that she could still smell on her shirt—but Luke never paid her for the flowers he'd given his grandmother. That was two bunches of flowers he'd scored for free. 'What a hustler.'

Should she turn around and go get her money?

Yeah—nah. The heat flared in her face for daring to think such a thing. Besides, she had a delivery schedule to keep.

On the side of the road, among the red soils and wildflowers, stood the road sign announcing her approach to Elsie Creek. It was the start of the same string of billboard signs advertising the local supermarket, a beer brand advertising the pub, and another for the hardware store. Last was the tall *fire risk sign* clearly showing they were under a fire ban—which was common for the tail end of the dry season. She'd passed those roadside signs so many times, she didn't really notice them anymore. But they all displayed the distance to Elsie Creek like a countdown: *fifteen kilometres. Ten Kilometres. Five kilometres.*

Usually, with each passing sign, she'd wriggle in her seat, swallowing the nervous anticipation while fighting her desire to see Luke again, where she'd fake a lack of knowledge to ask him for directions. But she'd just seen Luke at his house.

The town's roofs were showing in between the gaps of the smooth sloping hills in the distance when her phone rang. It was her sister.

Jordi pressed the hands-free button. 'Hi, Nat.'

'Hey, where are you?' Her sister's voice was clear over the car speakers.

'Elsie Creek.'

'Listen, Jordi, um, I'm just going to come out and say it …' Natalie took a deep breath and spoke fast. 'Mitchell has been given a shot at a promotion to his dream job.'

'That's brilliant news.' Jordi liked her brother-in-law, Mitchell, who absolutely doted on her big sister, Natalie. 'Give Mitchell my congratulations.'

'Mitchell hasn't got it yet, but his chances are good. Like, really good, because his boss sent him home with the application form to complete and everything.' Natalie exhaled heavily, as if to calm her excitement. 'But, you see, my darling husband is hesitating, which is why I'm calling you.'

'Why?'

'This promotion is to another air force base, down south.'

The van's tyres crunched and popped on the crusty red gravel as Jordi pulled over and parked her van among the sparse scattering of wildflowers on the side of the road. Through her windscreen she had a grand view of an enormous blue sky, with only a few fluffy peony-shaped clouds on the horizon.

'Are you there, Jordi?'

'So you'll be moving away ...' *Leaving me.*

'We're lucky we've stayed this long. Mitchell knocked back the last transfer when Mum and Dad passed.'

'I didn't know that.'

'We weren't ready then. I know I wasn't. But now ...' Nat again inhaled sharply. 'I want you to buy out my share of the shop.'

'*Stalks and Stems* is a family business. Not a sole operator.'

'Or we can sell the house *and* the shop, then you can come with us.'

'Do you even know where Mitchell is getting posted?'

'No. But Mitchell has been working up to this for a long time. He deserves this. And I'll be supporting him, no matter where he goes.'

Jordi winced at her big sister's firm words.

'I'm sorry to dump this on you while you're on the road, but I just found out myself, and I wanted to give you as much warning as possible.'

Jordi forced a smile, trying to feel some kind of cheer in a situation that just sucked. 'I'm happy for Mitchell. I really am. Tell him I'll have my fingers crossed.'

'Good. Mitchell will be happy to hear you said that.'

Jordi wasn't happy about it, but she couldn't be selfish either. 'Look, I've got to keep going. I don't like driving in the dark.'

'Sure, drive safe. And think about what I said about selling up. A change might be good for all of us.'

How could this happen when her world had finally become stable again—only for that red flowery carpet to get ripped out from underneath her?

How could she manage the florist shop on her own when she avoided the shopfront?

It wasn't that long ago their customers would screw their faces up in disgust and children would point at her, as they'd flee the store in horror just from the sight of her.

Public shaming used to be a daily occurrence, that she'd learned to avoid the public at all costs—which meant hiding in the back of the store or doing deliveries. People only saw the flowers, never the delivery driver who hid under her cap and sunglasses to not scare them off with her ugliness.

But did she dare face the alternative of leaving, following the only family she had left, and leaving the horrors of her past behind?

Four

'Gran? What are you doing?' Luke approached Esther at the wire fence. Dressed in black, her tiara was swapped for a black hat, and a matching lacy parasol to shade her from the sun. 'I've been looking for you everywhere.'

'They're moving in.' Esther pointed at the two removalist trucks parked out front of Iris's old house.

'Don't gawk like that, Gran. I'm pretty sure you told me it was rude to point during my childhood.'

'Those rules are excused today. I'm standing on Bennett land, and we've been here for generations. They're the invaders.'

'Iris originally came from Western Australia.'

'And lived in that house for over seventy years. That made her a local.' Esther shoulders sank as heavily as her sigh. His grandmother was still mourning her friend, and today's event didn't help much either.

'Come on, you don't want to be late.' Luke escorted his grandmother to his ute, and soon they were on the road to town.

'The supermarket's sign is looking faded.' Esther pointed at the roadside sign they passed. 'You'd think the mayor would do something about his own sign. It could do with some pizzazz.'

'Why? No one sees them. We all know where the supermarket is.'

'But it looks so dull, compared to the pub's sign. Does

that beer company pay the publican for that?' Esther pointed at the second billboard that dominated the side of the road.

'I'm pretty sure my boss gets some sort of kickback for advertising their beer brand.'

'Does it make people buy that brand of beer?'

He chuckled low. 'You don't mess with a man's beer — unless it's free, then they'll try anything. Although, they are drinking Alex's beer.' And he was happy to hustle for Alex and support the local brewer.

Maybe he should suggest Alex put his unique Elsie Creek beer brand on the pub's billboards that were strategically placed at various entrance points leading into town.

But he hadn't seen Alex in a while, even though he just lived down the road. They used to hang out all the time, back in school, with Timothy Kirby from Rigby Downs making up the other part of their pack. But those guys were busy these days, with their new partners, living their own lives — especially Alex with the new baby.

Luke turned down the main street of Elsie Creek. From the passenger seat Esther waved at people like she was the Queen of England.

'Have you got your phone on you?'

'In my bag.' Esther patted the large carpetbag that she'd had for a decade, or two.

Elsie Creek wasn't that big a town, with the pub on the left corner with the train station on his right, near the post office, the craft store and the hairdresser's. On the other side stood the hardware store, the supermarket, and a few smaller shops, recognising everyone who walked its streets.

'I don't see Cecil anywhere.' Esther swivelled around in the passenger seat.

'He'd be at the school.' Luke pointed at the clock on the dashboard. 'It's recess time. Should I call the school principal to put a limit on Cecil's feeding times? He's starting to look like a beer barrel.' Because they'd given up trying to lock up the escape artist.

Esther shrugged, her smile gone as she faced the road. 'It

won't make any difference. The children will always feed Cecil, no matter what the grown-ups say. Cecil will stop when he's full.'

'Except when it comes to flowers. Cecil would roll in them, if he could.'

This time she cracked a grin, with a tiny spark in her eyes. 'Cecil did seem to love that florist yesterday. What was her name?'

'Jordi. It's short for Jordin. Jordin Watkins.' The timid florist with the shy smile, who'd tuck her hair behind her ears, as her cheeks glowed, whenever she'd talk to him. It was even better when her eyes would swim with curiosity, as her kissable lips tugged into a smile he wanted to lean in and taste.

But with Jordi that was a line he could never cross.

It'd been a privilege to watch her get bolder every time she'd visit him. So much so that it had become his mission to get her to talk, to open up more, hoping for one of her wide smiles that truly shone in her eyes.

He couldn't stop thinking about yesterday's surprise visit at his home, where she'd displayed her creative flair and talent by whipping up a fancy bouquet of flowers in a matter of minutes. It was the first time he'd seen her pride hold back the demons that seemed to haunt her.

It was Friday. Would Jordi still visit him today to ask for directions? Or would he be lucky enough to catch her when she delivered her flowers for the pub?

With the railway line on their right, they passed the stockyards full of cattle, shuffling in the red dust to create a haze that stained the sun.

'I see it's train day.' Esther pointed at the cattle yards. 'Which means you'll be busy at work.'

'Just another day at the office.' Judging by the number of road trains and utes filling the car park, the pub was going to be flat out as soon as that train left the station. 'Have you turned on your phone?'

'No one calls me.'

'I do.'

'You forget, sweetheart, I come from an era that didn't have mobile phones. They're so annoying.'

'I just want you safe, Gran.' With the airfield on their left, he turned right onto the skinny road. Crossing the train tracks, the road wove around the small hill where the town's church sat. 'Want me to come with you?'

'Did you know Harvey Morris?'

'I had nothing to do with him. He didn't drink.' Luke nodded in greeting to a few people who were regular customers at the bottle shop. The rest were his grandmother's friends. It was practically the same crowd of people who'd gathered here only a month ago.

'Harvey stopped doing stuff, saying he was too old for this and too old for that ...' Esther scowled as she unscrewed the top of her hip flask and took a deep swig. The volatile aroma of Esther's particular whisky brand had a distinct cereal-like wood and winey blend, reminding him of those balmy Sunday evenings when people would gather around Gran's grand piano to sing or share tall stories long into the night.

He opened Esther's door and helped her out. She straightened her black dress, put on her hat, opening her lace parasol.

Luke grabbed her wreath from the box on the ute's rear tray. 'I see you put Mum and Dad's flowers to use.' Esther had repurposed the orange bouquet, adding some natives to the flowers that Jordi seemed so proud of yesterday.

'I only put in the flowers not safe for Cecil to eat. Don't worry, sweetheart, your flowers are sitting on my kitchen table, next to Iris's letter from the lawyer.'

'When are you going to read that letter? It's been a month, Gran.'

'I'm not ready yet.'

It had surprised them when the local lawyer, Otis, requested their presence at the reading of Iris's will. The nasally droning voice of the lawyer had put him to sleep, until Esther thumped him in the chest. At first, waking up confused, he'd assumed Otis was kicking them out, so he could lace his tea with brandy and settle in to watch *Days of Our Lives*, because everyone knew Otis hadn't missed an episode in ten years.

But Luke awoke to hear that Iris, their gentle, elderly neighbour, was loaded and had donated some money to the local bush hospital, and to the ranger's new animal sanctuary. Last on the list was the *secret sister project*, where the lawyer handed Esther a sealed envelope that she stared at as tears trickled down her cheeks.

That same envelope sat on Esther's kitchen table, still sealed since the day she'd brought it home. It was keeping Esther stuck in a constant state of mourning, dulling that mischievous sparkle in her eyes that was a big part of her true smile.

'Did you speak to Mum and Dad, yesterday? I heard the house phone ringing.'

'Well, why didn't you answer it?'

The silence was as long as their family feud.

'I've got to get to work. I'll take my break when you want me to drive you home, so call me.' He held out her large wreath. 'Please tell me you've switched on your phone?'

Esther shrugged.

'Let me check.' He swapped the wreath for her carpetbag. He dug out her phone and, once it buzzed to life in his hands, turned up the volume. 'Remember, call me and I'll come and collect you.'

'I'm quite capable of finding my own way home.' She popped a mint, before reaching up to kiss his cheek. Her warm aroma reminded him of a fluffy vanilla marshmallow, with a prickly and spicy peppering of liquorice as Esther's favourite perfume, saved for special occasions. Sadly, these days those special occasions were attending funerals.

He narrowed his eyes at his grandmother. She worried him. Even though Esther did her best to hide her grief, he knew there was a deep level of sadness hidden behind her smile and shiny tiaras. Her smile had been slipping these past six months, obsessed with funerals, rewriting obituaries, and making funeral wreaths. It wasn't healthy.

Scrubbing his palms over his face, he climbed back into the ute. He had bills to pay and a job to do, and his grandmother was a grown woman who knew he was just down the road if she needed him.

Even though he felt like a parent leaving his child on their first play date, Esther was with her friends—even if their numbers were dwindling—who'd hopefully help Esther regain her thirst for life.

When he should be asking where was *his* thirst for life, where was his smile, his drive? Because he'd lost all that well over a year ago.

Five

Jordi steered her van towards the small church, loaded with floral wreaths for some guy named Harvey. He wasn't as popular as Iris, where Jordi's van had been jam-packed full of wreaths that day.

Jordi parked at the rear of the small church, where the funeral director was waiting to greet her.

'Thanks for doing this, Jordi. So sorry for the rush, the family changed their mind at the last minute.'

'All good. Thanks for thinking of us.' There was no point in complaining about last-minute changes. After all, it was her business, *if* she took on the family floristry. Never mind that she was secretly hoping her brother-in-law didn't get the promotion, then her sister could stay, and life could be blissfully normal and free from this fear of change hanging over her head.

Jordi followed the funeral director inside the small church and helped arrange the wreaths around the casket. Even though she'd done this a thousand times too many, forcefully reminding herself that she was just decorating a prop, nothing more, it still made her sad.

'I know you.' It was Esther, in a stylish hat that reminded her of a scene from her mother's favourite movie, *Breakfast at Tiffany's*, complete with the pearls, and lace gloves to match her lacy parasol.

'No ball gown and tiara, Esther?'

'Not today. Funeral drab, I'm afraid. Where do you think my wreath should go? I'd hate for it to clash with the others.'

Jordi arched an eyebrow at the wreath of healthy grey eucalyptus leaves and stunning orange flowers. 'It's beautifully done, Esther. Particularly the orange ranunculus. I didn't know they grew in the outback.' Nor the rare orange calla lily that sat beside the coffee break roses. Those particular flower varieties had to be flown *in* to the Northern Territory, where she stood alongside the other florists waiting at Darwin airport for their freight of flowers.

'I don't grow the flowers, silly.' Esther shared a short giggle. 'I had the sweetest young thing deliver them to me.'

'Didn't you like them?' Jordi's voice squeaked, forcing her to clear her throat. Remembering her mother's wise words that *not everyone liked flowers*. But then her father's wise words of *don't trust anyone who doesn't like flowers*. Her dad would know.

'Oh, petal, I just loved them. I just didn't like who they were from.'

'You said that yesterday. So, why—'

'Fob 'em off at a funeral.' Bobbing her eyebrows up and down, Esther's grin was full of mischief. 'If you want to know the story, you'll have to come and sit with me.' Hooking her arm through Jordi's, Esther dragged her to the wooden pews.

'I can't stay.' Hating people touching her, she tugged her arm free to brush down the sleeves to cover her hands.

Esther patted the empty seat beside her. 'Sit. Harvey won't mind.'

'Who?'

'Harvey is the guy we're burying.'

Oops.

Jordi sat on the edge of the hard wooden pew. The air was thick and heavy, as if the room was pressing in from all sides, highlighting the closed coffin at the front. 'I should go.'

'You can't spare five minutes?'

'Not at a funeral. It feels wrong.' She shivered, eyeing the nearest exit.

'You'll be fine.' Esther fanned herself with the program. 'So how do you know my grandson?'

'I don't. Well, only from the bottle shop.' She was just a customer to Luke, who only tried to hustle her into buying booze.

'So, you're a big drinker, then?'

'No.' Jordi rarely drank, only driving through the bottle shop to perve on Luke. No, wait, that was to ask for directions. *Ugh*, she was pathetic, because Luke was a popular guy, and she was the beast kept in the back room of a florist shop.

'I don't mind a tipple or five.' Like a naughty schoolgirl, Esther flashed her hipflask hidden inside her large, old-fashioned carpetbag. 'You must know Luke. He looks at you differently.'

Most people looked at her differently, before fleeing in the other direction. 'I don't think so. I hardly know the guy.' Jordi choked out a laugh. Quickly dropping her head at her poor manners for daring to laugh at a funeral.

'But I've known Luke all his life … And I knew Harvey too.' Esther gazed at the sparse crowd spread out among the pews.

The mood grew heavier, as the still air mingled with assorted perfumes, cold wood, and musty paper from the bibles being flicked open. Jordi wriggled in her seat. She hated funerals at the best of times. 'I can't be here.'

'I said it was okay.'

'I just can't.' Jordi went to leave, but Esther clutched her hand. Her breath became short and rushed as if the air was thick and suffocating, as her heart hammered so hard it was echoing in her ears. Was this a panic attack? 'I've got to go. I've got flowers to deliver. They can't stay in that van long without the AC running.'

'Well, count me in.' With her retro Audrey Hepburn–style pumps click-clacking across the floorboards, Esther was quite the scene-stealer. Necks craned, people swivelled, and whispers followed them as they left the church.

Jordi could feel their stares, like those women who'd bolt from their florist shop in fear of catching some deadly disease from her. Why couldn't her skin be as thick as the scars she desperately tried to hide and give her the power to ignore them all?

Once outside, under the glare of the outback sun, only then Jordi could breathe easier.

'So, where are we going, petal?' Esther popped open her lacy parasol to shade herself.

'You should go back inside.'

'No. I'm riding with you today.' Esther peeked inside the van's passenger window, twirling her lace parasol like a vintage schoolgirl skipping school for the day.

'I'm working. Aren't you meant to be attending this funeral?'

'Sure, I could grace these people with my presence. And Harvey was a wonderful man, he truly was.' Esther paused, bowing her head for a moment of silence, only to lift her chin and crinkle her nose as if smelling something rotten. 'But I can't stand his wife, the widow. Plus, this is my second funeral in a month, with the same group of people talking about the same things: the weather, farming, whose health is failing, or who *died*.' Esther took a step closer; her perfume was light like vanilla marshmallows and sweet liquorice with a hint of mint. 'Besides causing a delicious scandal for those inside,' she said, nodding at the church, 'I need to do something fun, or my poor grandson will worry himself to death over my welfare.'

'Who said what I did was fun?' Jordi pointed to the empty hearse.

'We'll make it fun.' Esther opened the van's passenger door and climbed inside before Jordi could stop her. 'Let's go. Time waits for no one.'

Six

'I love your job, petal.' Esther skipped back to the van, where Jordi waited behind the steering wheel. 'I knew there was a reason for hijacking your passenger seat today.'

Jordi laughed at Esther's energetic joy. It was infectious.

'Where to now?' Esther pulled down her seatbelt as Jordi leaned over to help clip it into place.

'One more delivery before the pub. It's just down the road from your place.' Even if her delivery run was taking twice as long, it had been nice sharing it with someone.

'Oh, a neighbour. Which one?'

'Quentin Lawsten.'

Esther thoughtfully tapped her chin. 'I don't know the name. Who are the flowers from?'

'Connor Symes.' Then she spilled as if talking her sister over the flowers they'd make and the stories behind them. 'He's telling her how much he loves her. It's so romantic.' Jordi loved this part of her job, witnessing those truly romantic moments, where flowers were used as a symbol of love. She always drove away from those deliveries smiling. Then realised what she'd said. 'Hey, you won't tell anyone about who they're from and stuff. It's meant to be confidential.'

'All good, petal, just treat me like a co-worker. But the Symes family, I know.' She tapped on her chin. 'Oh, you mean Que. She's with Connor. You don't mess with Connor, he's a military hot shot who shot the man who shot Cecil when he was trying to shoot Que.'

'What?' Jordi's eyebrows rose.

'It's all good.' Esther waved her hand as if shooing away a slow fly. 'Que is the one who writes on Cecil's back in the mornings. I have Que to thank for the glossy polish on Cecil's coat. She makes an organic blend of chalk and oil that's just marvellous on Cecil's skin.'

'Why do you let people graffiti your pet buffalo?' Jordi had seen Cecil wandering the roads advertising events in town like the craft store's candle-making classes, or letting everyone know toilet paper was on special at the local supermarket.

'Cecil is more of the town's pet than mine. He's such an escape artist, it's impossible keeping him locked up on the property. He especially loves the children feeding him at the school … Can we just pop in home for a minute? I need a hand with something.'

'Sure.' Jordi steered down the dirt driveway, past the stone wall with the bold brass plate proclaiming *Anaborro Downs* at the entrance. 'What does Anaborro mean?'

'Anaborro is the Aboriginal word for buffalo. And the Bennetts, my family, were professional buffalo hunters.'

'For real?'

'That house,' said Esther, pointing to the spacious, colonial-style house. 'My grandfather called it *the Lodge*.'

'Sounds fancy.' And it looked fancy, with its large windows symmetrically placed on either side of the double front doors filled with detailed stained glass. Delicate cast-iron filigree lace decorated the eaves of the deep verandah. A corrugated roof, combined with wooden cyclone shutters for the windows, gave the place an elegant heritage appearance.

'Oh, it was. The Lodge was a place for rich men, and other big-game hunters, eager for their chance to hunt wild buffalo in the outback. Many may have heard of America's Buffalo Bill, but in the Territory, it was my grandfather, Robin Bennett, who was known as Bison-eye Bennett. There were many great Australian poets who wrote about my grandfather and the buffalo hunt.'

'I didn't know Buffalo hunting was such a lucrative thing,' Jordi said as she helped Esther out of the van.

'It was, and still is in certain circles. This way, petal, we won't be long.' Esther led them up the wide stone steps to the cool, shady verandahs. 'We don't want to keep you from your job. And I like your job.'

'What do you need my help with?'

'To move these.' Esther pointed to the set of Seville-style wicker armchairs. They were the epitome of outdoor luxury, nestled beneath a massive staghorn fern growing against the wall. Nearby, assorted ferns hung from baskets, while clusters of flowering begonias and giant peace lilies helped create an elegant atmosphere for a cool and comfortable place to sit.

'I'm surprised you can grow these flowering plants with a flower-eating buffalo on the premises.'

'Cecil doesn't like them, so I'm lucky. Now, I want to put those two wicker chairs over by that tree.' Esther pointed.

'What tree?' The yard was filled with nothing but crusty sunburnt soils.

'The neighbour's tree, by the fence. Come along, petal. We can load them into your van and drive over.'

'Why don't you get Luke to do it? He's got the ute.'

'Why? When you're here.'

With the chairs packed, they drove over the lumpy dry dirt that sent puffs of red dust to swirl in the humid air. Cutting across the paddock, she noted there was irrigation in place, but the soil was like compacted concrete, showing signs of farming land, long neglected.

As Jordi unloaded the wicker chairs, Esther shuffled them in the dirt. Red dust sprinkled over her black shoes, spreading along the hem of her black skirt. She fluffed up the cushions, propped up her parasol, and sat facing the fence. 'Ah, yes. This will do. It's a good spot to enjoy the view.'

There was nothing out here.

'Down there, we have a lovely little lake in the back.'

Esther pointed at the sunburnt dirt paddock that spread like a ruined hallway runner. 'It used to be full of lotus flowers. You would've liked it. Talking about liquids ...' She opened her carpetbag and removed her hipflask. Esther took a sip, inhaling sharply at the liquor as she screwed the lid back on. 'Take a seat, petal, consider this our afternoon tea break.'

'In that case ...' The chair creaked as Jordi gripped the white rattan arms, her body surrendering into the gently undulating curves of the expertly hand-woven chair. This luxurious chair didn't suit this spot under the sparse shade from the towering ghost gum where the slight breeze shifted a fine silt of red dust. 'Why are we facing the neighbours?'

'They're moving in.' While slowly twirling her parasol, Esther nodded at the removalist carrying goods from the truck to the house.

'Isn't this a bit like spying?' The white chairs on red dirt made them stand out.

'We're on Bennett land.'

'But to watch the neighbours, when your house is much prettier.'

'It is.' Esther craned her neck back at the house.

'How did your family become hunters?'

'Professional hunters, petal.'

'Must have been a good thing, considering how beautiful that house is.'

'Well, back in the eighteen hundreds, the first settlers brought buffalo in for meat, which soon became a big money enterprise for the Bennetts, who played a big part in the Northern Territory's history.' Esther twirled her parasol, while watching the various household goods being carted from the truck.

'How?' Jordi sank deeper into the comfy chair. All she needed was a tall glass of ice water, and one of those fancy wicker fans and she was set.

'Every dry season, we'd fling open the doors to the Lodge and welcome the many rich hunters who'd travel from all over the globe for their chance at scoring a buffalo.'

'Did you hunt?'

'Since I was a small girl. But I also helped my mother clean the rooms and make these amazing feasts that filled our dining room table, playing our parts as the ladies of the Lodge. It was such fun listening to the bull-catchers' stories of their close shaves, and the guests who'd sing around the piano celebrating the success of the hunt.' She softly frowned at the neighbour's property, where the removalists were carting a group of couches on their trolleys. 'How many couches do you count?'

'Four.' Jordi arched her eyebrows at the four deep brown leather couches. She didn't even own one. 'So, your family were hunters?'

'Always. My father, husband, and my son Walden were all professional hunters. It was their job. Sadly, a buffalo rammed my husband's vehicle against a tree. Terrence wasn't a Bennett, he was a Caddell. He let me keep the Bennett surname.' She coyly grinned as she leaned over and said, 'It was quite the scandal at the time that I stayed a Bennett.' She sat higher, straightening her black dress. 'Terrence understood. He was a good man.'

'I'm sorry for your loss.'

'It's a sad side effect when you hunt such large and dangerous prey, I'm afraid. And us Bennett's have had plenty of close calls in the day. One of my uncles got speared by their horns, another trampled, and my father got maimed. He died before they could get him to the hospital. After that, my son closed the Lodge to visitors, sadly, stopping the stories and celebrations of those victorious from their hunt.' Esther sighed heavily, her shoulders slumping.

'Are you talking about Luke's father?' And here she was sitting in a luxurious chair at Luke's house and the guy was nowhere to be seen.

Esther nodded. 'Walden married Violet. She was this city girl who kept harping on at Walden about how hunting buffalo was so dangerous.'

'It sounds like it is.'

'It's nowhere near as bad as being a crocodile wrangler. But the silly thing was, Violet was attracted to Walden because of the whole rugged hunter persona. My son was a man's man, and so fierce, with a deadeye just like his grandfather.' Esther slowly shook her head. 'Walden became a farmer only because he promised his newly pregnant wife, Violet, that he'd only hunt for family.'

'That's nice he did that for her.'

'You'd think his wife would be happy. But nooo because Violet would get so mad when Walden would take Luke hunting. But that's the way the Bennetts have always been, and we always had our freezers full of fish and meat.'

'Walden doesn't live here now, does he? Because he sent you those flowers.' And this farming land was nothing but a desert of dust.

'Southern coast of Queensland. Violet's family is there. They want me to go there, too.' Esther shared a soft wistful smile over the property that truly meant more to her than red dirt and a fence line. 'Every single day I'm grateful to my wonderful grandson that I get to stay here. I'm terrified at the thought of leaving. I saw how sad poor Iris was when she was told she couldn't go home—I don't want that. This is my home. I'm honestly one of the lucky ones to have lived in the same place all my life. Why move?'

The thought of moving was also terrifying for Jordi, it made her stomach squeeze with hot bile.

'Don't you want to be with your family?' Jordi had always been close to her sister, and they'd grown closer ever since their parents had passed. She didn't know how she'd cope without Natalie being nearby, or Mitchell to play the big brother.

'The southern winters will only flare up my arthritis, and they have pollen alerts that'll trigger my sinusitis. Then I'd be leaving my friends. Not to mention my responsibilities to the school. If I was to parade around in my ball gown and gum boots, down south, they'd threaten to lock me up in a loony bin. Most of all, I have a certain water buffalo to look after. Can you picture Cecil strolling through suburbia?'

Jordi grinned. 'Have you always had pet buffaloes?'

'Never. Come on, my family were professional buffalo hunters. My grandfather would roll over in his grave.' Again, Esther shared a girlish giggle. 'But Cecil is special. I'll tell you his story one day. Do you drink cocktails?'

Jordi shrugged, watching the removalists struggle with yet another fancy-looking couch. This one was black leather.

'How many couches is that now?'

'Five.'

'Hmm … Iris had one. We never used it because Iris used to make these amazing cocktails with her home-grown pineapples that were the perfect accompaniment for watching the sunset in her back garden.' Esther pointed to the neighbour's house, where rows of pineapples were sunburnt and withered. 'Cecil would visit Iris every morning and night to make sure she was okay, and I'd pop over daily for a cuppa.' Esther sighed heavily, her bent elbow resting on the arm of the wicker chair to rest her chin on her hand. 'Sadly, Iris tripped on her back steps during the big rains and broke her hip, they never let her out of the hospital after that. Iris was ninety-two. And I'm eighty-four. Harvey, today, he was only in his seventies … Time just sucks.'

Jordi gently patted Esther's hand.

Esther cupped Jordi's hand and gave it a tender squeeze.

'I have to go.' Jordi pulled her hand free, tucking her sleeve down to cover it. 'I can't leave those flowers sitting in the sun for long.'

'Not without me, young lady.' Esther got up from her chair.

'Do you want me to take your chairs back?'

'No. They'll be fine there. I'm not done with that lot.' She scowled at the removalists running in and out with tall lamps, some weird sculptures, and rolls and rolls of mats. There was a lot of stuff filling those two trucks.

It was a stark reminder that in the not-too-distant future Jordi may to be moving house, or her entire life. She wasn't ready for that.

Seven

ow well behind schedule, from Esther happily chatting to everyone at every delivery stop, Jordi had lost her chance of finding a nice camping spot before dark and was contemplating the long drive back.

'How can I get your job?' Esther asked from the passenger seat.

'Being a florist?' Jordi checked her GPS, as she steered them down the wide dirt road, coming onto the bitumen.

'No, the delivery driver bit. The way people's faces light up when they see flowers, it's like you're spreading cheer and joy to people. You should wear a costume. Like a cow or a fairy.'

A snort-laugh escaped Jordi. 'No. But, you're right, the part about giving flowers to people is fun.' The way their eyes would shine from the surprise gave flowers such power. It was the best part of her job.

'Is it your florist shop?'

'Family business. Mum was a florist and Dad was a policeman learning how to grow flowers.'

'A policeman growing flowers?'

'Odd, I know. To see Dad with his enormous hands working on flowers looked odd, but he said it was the best stress relief for him. I helped him turn our five-acre block into a place to grow flowers.'

'Are you a farmer? Or a florist?'

'Both. Well, I'd been working in the florist shop making

up flower posies for the supermarkets back when I was in primary school. And on Valentine's Day or Mother's Day it was severe family time where we'd all be working non-stop making and delivering flower arrangements all over town.' She grinned at the memory. 'Then one day, Dad came home with this big cake and some champagne, with Mum all rosy cheeked and full of cheer to present my sister and I with our trade certificates based on our years of experience.' That was the day her entire family sat around the kitchen table eagerly talking about the future of the family business.

'So, you studied nothing else in school?'

'I'd studied to become a commercial cut flower producer. A floriculturist.'

'A flower farmer?'

Jordi nodded. 'After growing for years on my parent's block, I was planning to go halves with Dad and invest in a larger property. I'd even drawn up the plans, including the planting and harvesting cycles to suit the Australian flower trade, and everything.'

'What happened?'

'My parents passed away.' Jordi winced at the side mirror reflecting the empty outback highway. 'It changed everything.'

'Do you still live at your parent's house, the family home?'

'My sister lives there with her husband…' But all those flowers she'd planted with her father were long gone. 'Who knows how long we'll be keeping the shop for.'

'What do you mean?'

'My brother-in-law is applying for a promotion. And Mitchell is the nicest guy who truly deserves it, it's just that he's in the air force—'

'And he may get posted elsewhere?'

Jordi nodded, her hands tightening on the steering wheel. 'Mitchell has to go through the interview process first. But he's confident he'll get it. So much so that my sister's offered to sell her share of the house and store to me.'

'Do you want that?'

'I don't know what I want.' She bit her lip at the words that had spilled freely.

'What were you planning to do before your parents passed?'

'I was going to grow tropical and native flowers. I have plenty of contacts to supply to the flower markets down south.'

'Orchids?'

'No. Heliconia varieties, hardy bromeliads, curcumas and those colourful hidden or surprise gingers, and a lot of natives. The type of stock that doesn't need shade houses but are perfect for lapping up the Northern Territory climate. I have—did have—a market ready to sell down south, faster than I could grow it.'

'Why didn't you?'

She shrugged. It felt wrong doing it without her family.

'Do you like the florist shop?'

'I'm not good with people.'

'You're fine with me.'

'I like you. Even though you hijacked your spot in this car.' She gave the colourful octogenarian a side smile. 'I just don't do general public.'

'Why not?'

No way was she going to share her horror story. 'I'm not designed for retail. I'm a behind-the-scenes kind of person, which is why I do the deliveries. While you deserve your own stage show.'

Esther laughed with her chin held high. 'Life's too short to be shy, petal.'

Shyness was Jordi's shield. 'So, what do you do, Esther, besides being the lady of the Lodge?'

'I'm a retired teacher. I volunteer once a week in the school library to read to the children.'

'That's why you wear ball gowns?'

'It's fabulous fun. You should come. The littlies love getting dressed up, and they get so excited about stories being read to them. Friday is the highlight of my week—but I saw them yesterday, because today …' Esther brushed off some lint from her black funeral clothes. 'I used to do so much more, but with Iris gone, and that pesky policeman taking my driver's licence, I'm trapped at home. Especially when it wasn't my fault. It was those silly roos that ran across the road in front of me, making me swerve.'

'They can't take your licence for dodging the wildlife on the roads. I do it all the time.'

'I agree. Just not in my case, when all I did was bump into this itty-bitty fence and dragged it home with me. It was so small, I didn't even know I'd done it. I just thought the roads were extra dusty that day.'

Jordi giggled behind her hand.

'I was so preoccupied. I didn't even see the police lights from that pesky police sergeant.'

'Porter?'

'No, Porter's boss, Marcus. I'd only noticed him after I got stuck in my driveway from the fencing posts, hooking up with the front gate, and there was Marcus—who I'd taught to read, mind you—lecturing me as he unravelled some of that fence so I could get into the yard. That's when I realised the fence was a bit longer than I thought. Have you met him?'

'No.' How big was the fence?

'Marcus is a big-big man with arms on him like a beefcake. He used to be one of my favourite students when he was a small boy. But now, he's a dick! He took my licence, and he took my guns away, too. For a Bennett to lose their hunting rifles is a scandal to the Bennett legacy. My father, and his father, and his father's father would roll over in their graves that I'd lost their guns.'

'How could you not notice that you were dragging along a fence?'

'I'd just been told one of my closest friends couldn't go home from the hospital. I was a little distracted. She'd been confined to the hospice wing and told she only had a few months to live and was selling her home … Iris passed away a month ago.' The shine dulled in Esther's smile.

'I'm sorry.'

'Iris was eighteen, and a new bride, when she moved in next door. The day Iris moved in, I gave her a bunch of flowers from my mother and asked her if she'd come to my tenth birthday party with her new husband.'

'Did she?'

'And every year after that for over seventy years … Except this year's birthday.' Again, Esther shared another soft sigh as she stared out the window. 'Iris was a part of my family. She was a bridesmaid at my wedding and the godmother to my son. She was like a sister to me …'

The hum of the van's engine was almost hypnotic, as the wire fence ran beside them, with scatterings of white Brahmans grazing in red dust plains that highlighted the silver-leafed melaleucas.

'What was the original plan you had with your family's florist shop, before they …'

'I was going to supply the shop, and the marketplace, with native flowers. I'd work in the back of the shop with Dad, doing our commercial contracts, taking turns to do the deliveries. Mum and my sister, Natalie, were the ones who loved talking to customers.'

'Like Luke. He'd talk a buffalo out of his hide if he could. But he knows you, there's something there.' Esther wiggled her finger at Jordi.

Esther was imagining it, because Luke only hustled Jordi out of her money for booze and now flowers.

And, for the second time that day, Jordi drove past the supermarket's sign followed by the larger billboard for the pub, then the hardware store, with the smaller sign welcoming people to Elsie Creek.

'Do you think those road signs need a makeover?' Esther pointed at them.

'I don't notice them anymore.'

'Exactly. If people are using them to advertise their stores, they should jump out at you. Right? Yet, they lack a certain pizzazz.'

'I've never considered the life of a roadside sign.' They shared a small laugh as the road rolled towards town.

'Do you think I should run the florist shop?'

Esther narrowed her brown eyes, the same colour as Luke's, except hers were surrounded by the many laugh lines of someone who'd walked this earth a long time. 'I think you should run the store. You can always hire someone to manage the front of the shop so you can avoid the customers.'

'That's a good idea. We have a lady who helps out now.' Jordi sat higher in her seat. 'Do you think I could do it?'

'What are you afraid of?'

'Failing.' Especially that fear of disappointing her parents.

She slumped behind the steering wheel, burdened with the fear that the family's legacy they'd meant to grow together was now being scattered like flower seeds lost to the wind.

'Do you know what the worst kind of failure is, petal?'

Jordi shrugged.

'The worst kind of failure is not trying. Because when you get to sit back in your eighties like I am, you'll be regretting that you didn't try.'

Eight

'What do you mean, a white van?' Luke gripped his phone tighter while talking to the town's priest. 'I watched my grandmother walk inside the church to attend the funeral.'

'She was here, but then she left.'

'With who?'

'I have no idea. Esther didn't even stay for the service.'

The last time anyone had mentioned a white van to Luke was when the ranger was looking for poachers.

He ended the call and raked fingers through his hair, as he paced the bottle shop's concrete driveway, tempted to jump into his nearby ute and start searching. But where would he go?

After his call to Esther's phone went unanswered, he scrolled through his phone, searching for a number and hit dial. It was picked up after the second ring. 'Porter, where are you?'

'Sitting on the highway, playing with the speed gun for the Friday home-time rush. You?'

'Gran's gone missing.'

'Since when?'

'About five hours ago, apparently. I delivered Gran to the funeral, where she was last seen being driven away in a white van. Have you seen any white vans?'

'I did. It was heading out of town when I was heading in to work.'

'Which way. Who was it?'

'Sorry, I didn't take any notice.'

'So, where is my grandmother?'

The bottle shop bell dinged, warning of an incoming car. He turned to face a white van, with his grandmother in the passenger seat. 'Don't worry, Porter, she just showed up.'

'Whose van is it?'

'The flower girl's. I'll talk to you later.'

'Hoorah, honey.' Esther eagerly waved through the open window.

Twitchy with anger, Luke ripped open the passenger door. 'I've been sick with worry about you. I called your phone and you didn't answer. I practically abused the priest and was about to send Porter out on a police chase for this white van.'

'We've been having the best time, sweetheart. I just need to borrow the loo.' Esther patted his cheek before skipping past, leaving him to scowl at the closing staff door. He felt like he'd aged in seconds.

From the back of the van Jordi carried a bucket of flowers.

'You!' The anger flared like hot lava in his veins as he pointed at Jordi. 'What do you think you're doing, pinching my grandmother like that?'

'Hey! Esther hijacked *me*.'

It was his turn to flinch like he'd been slapped because this was Jordi. Sweet, sensitive, and super-shy Jordi who rarely spoke. And it also sounded like something Esther would do. 'How does that work, when you were driving?'

'Esther climbed onto the passenger seat and refused to get out.'

'You could have called me.'

'Esther's a grown woman. I'm not her babysitter. What are you stressing about?'

'Because I didn't know where she was.' He clenched his jaw and began pacing. 'Even though Esther is my grandmother, some days she's like a rebellious teenager.'

'I noticed.' Jordi giggled. It was a sweet giggle, stopping all his anger just from the power of one of her rare yet pretty smiles.

But then he remembered he was meant to be mad at her. 'So where have you been with *my* grandmother?'

'Doing flower deliveries. It's what I do.' Jordi put down the bucket of assorted orchids to drop her hands on her hips and match his frown.

'I thought you delivered your flowers yesterday?' Because she normally did her deliveries on Fridays. If he was lucky, he'd see her on Saturday, too.

'Because I had that special request for your grandmother's flowers yesterday, I split up my run. Today's funeral must have stirred up sentiment in this town because I've been delivering flowers all day.' She crossed her arms over her chest. Her scowl wasn't pretty when he preferred her smiling.

'Oh …'

'Oh, really? That's it.' She arched an eyebrow at him.

His lips tugged into a smirk as her anger deepened.

'What about an apology?'

'For what?'

She stabbed at the air between them. 'What about a thank you?'

'For what?' He had to admire her fire. It was so much better than her shyness.

Again, she stabbed the air with her finger. He was tempted to snap at it with his teeth. 'You still owe me for those flowers you fed your pet buffalo and the ones you gave to Esther to save your butt for forgetting it was her birthday.'

He stepped back, raising his open palms in surrender. She was right. 'Sorry. Thanks. And how much do I owe you?' He dragged out his wallet from his jeans pocket.

'Jeez, you could at least sound sincere.' The sarcasm rolled off her tongue. 'Don't worry about it.'

'Eh?' Now she was confusing him.

'For the record, I had a great time hanging out with your grandmother.'

'You did?' He narrowed his eyes at her.

'Esther is a lot of fun.'

Hello, my sweet-smelling little angelfish. 'Would you be interested in granny-sitting?'

'Excuse me?'

'I want to take part in this local fishing competition, but I need someone to watch over Gran.'

'Isn't Esther a bit old for a babysitter?'

'I'm doing it to keep Gran safe, and normally I'd ask the neighbour, Iris, but ...' He sighed, sliding his hands into the front pockets of his jeans.

'Esther told me about Iris. She sounded like a nice lady.' Sympathy shone off her like a freaking Christmas angel on top of the tree, especially the way the sunlight streamed inside the drive-thru making her hair shine, and her eyes sparkle.

'Iris was the best neighbour. Well, the only neighbour I've had my entire life. She was close with my grandmother.'

'Esther told me.'

'Sadly, Gran's been a handful ever since Iris went to hospital and she lost her driver's licence. It got worse when the lawyer at Iris's will reading handed Gran this envelope — that she still hasn't opened. It sits there on the kitchen table fuelling her mourning, or depression, or whatever it is that Gran's going through. I don't know what to do with her or how to make her happy again.' *Whoa! Where did that come from?* He roughly raked his fingers through his hair, realising what he'd just done. He'd aired the drama of his family business, Bennett Business, and he never did that. 'I'm sorry.'

'And that's a more sincere apology than the one you gave me earlier.'

He matched her soft grin, only to narrow his eyes at her. 'Hey, you're not going to broadcast what I just said, are you?'

She shrugged her slender shoulders. 'Who am I going to tell?'

'That's right, you don't live here. Where do you live? Not in that van, I hope?'

'Outside of Darwin.'

'Long way.'

'I like the drive.'

'You should've been a truck driver.'

'I like flowers, and my van.' She hugged herself as that layer of shyness draped over her like a smothering cocoon. 'Were you for real about selling flowers in here?' She craned her slender neck to look around the bottle shop where he spent his days.

The bottle shop was basically a shed added to the side of the pub, wide enough for two trucks to duck under the open roller doors, to park inside. Along one side there was a wall of glass-door fridges and a counter with a cash register that stood near the door to the coldroom. At the far end was the connecting door that led to the pub, where his grandmother had disappeared.

'I'll put your flowers next to the cash register.' He tapped the counter he'd lean on most days of the week. 'It's the best place for them.'

'Why?'

'Because every customer keeps their eyes on the cash register, especially when they're expecting change or their credit cards back.'

'What do you get out of it, if I gave you some flowers?' She narrowed those pretty eyes at him, wrinkling her nose that highlighted her scattering of freckles. On closer inspection, they weren't freckles at all but skin blemishes.

Under his scrutiny, Jordi dropped her head, pulling down the sleeves of her shirt to tuck her hands inside the cuffs.

'You set the price, wholesale of course. I'll make my cut from that. It's just business. I do it for other farmers.' He pointed to the rack of eggs and assorted fruit and vegetables.

'I can do that.' She gave an affirmative nod, only to scuff a shoe across the concrete. 'Hey, do you know of any part-time work going around here?'

He tilted his head at her. 'Why? Is the flower business having a tough time these days?'

'I'm thinking of venturing out with the store and need to increase my cashflow.'

'What are you doing tonight?'

Her frown shifted in so many ways. 'Er, why?'

'The boss lady is short-handed.' He tossed his thumb back to the pub where his grandmother still hadn't come back — she was probably dancing on the tables in the front bar by now.

'I don't do bar work. Dealing with people is not my thing.'

'The kitchen's looking for help. You'll even score a free feed out of it.' Which would give him time to convince the flower girl to become his granny-sitter.

'Um ...' Jordi peeked back at the road that gave a clear view of the sun hanging low in the sky. 'I should drive home.'

'Don't worry, Gran has plenty of room for you to stay at the Lodge.' Letting Gran think Jordi was a guest would work for his granny-sitting scheme.

'Come on, I'll take you to the boss lady. I'm assuming these flowers are for the pub's dining room?' He scooped up her flower bucket, then gently put his arm around her shoulders, but she flinched, and he dropped his arm. 'Sorry. Forgot.'

'Forgot what?' She looked at him with horror, stepping well away as if he'd burned her.

'I forget my boundaries with people.' Not quite what he'd meant, but he couldn't tell her the truth. 'The kitchen is this way.'

Nine

Hair tied back, with a scarf wrapped around her neck, Jordi wore thick gloves protecting her hands from the scalding water, as the sweat trickled down her back.

She'd never been shy about getting her hands dirty, but she'd never worked in a commercial kitchen before. And the Elsie Creek pub kitchen was far more modern than she'd expected, with stainless-steel benches, industrial ovens, rows of gas burners, and a large hotplate and grill. That was the chef Lenny's domain, where they were separated by a long serving bench with heat lights that ran down the centre of the room.

On this side of the dividing bench was Jordi's area. It's where she manned the commercial dishwasher. It was a simple process of rinsing off dishes in the two deep sinks before loading them in the dishwasher. When the tray was full, she'd slide it into the dishwasher and slam down the heavy door, leaving it to rumble in the background. A few minutes later she'd open the door and let the steam work wonders on her skin's pores, as the dishes air-dried before she packed them away. Then do it all over again.

'Here, you try this treat.' Lenny's husky voice had an Eastern European accent to it.

Lenny put a plate on the end of the aluminium bench near the screen door that allowed the cool evening breeze to flow through. He dragged over a stool. 'Pop yourself down there for a bit.'

'Really?'

'You are due a meal break, and you said you liked pasta. So, here you go …' He even swiped over the seat with his tea towel. 'If you don't like my cooking, we can't be friends.'

She giggled as she sat on the stool. The combination of bacon and garlicky-cream scents blended with the many food aromas filling the pub's kitchen. The aromas were constantly changing from frying onions, to searing steaks, rich wine sauces and gravies, to vibrant lemons squeezed over thick fillets of barramundi.

'Now, it's time for the entertainment to begin.' Lenny fiddled with a set of audio speakers that rested above the main island bench. 'You finish eating, then I'll teach you how to make a salad.'

'For what?'

'People. It's easy, my little cake crumb.'

She nearly choked on her fettucine at the nickname.

'Now, shh …' Lenny put his finger over his lips. 'We listen about the town's gossip while we get my fishing tips for the week. I like fossicking for gold and float the boat occasionally to get the line wet. Do you fish?'

'No. Is this town big enough for a radio station?' Not that she'd know anyone to gossip about.

'Pirate podcast.'

She twirled the creamy fettucine with her fork. 'A what?'

'It's a pre-recorded podcast called *Dramas from the Dinghy* that the local community radio broadcasts once a week.'

'A fishing show?' How blooming boring.

'It's run by two larrikins, who tell us what's biting, where to go, and who's up to no good.' Lenny chuckled as he winked. 'They release an episode every Friday night at six pm, just before the dinner rush.'

'I thought that was the dinner rush?' She pointed to the stack of order chits Lenny had stabbed onto the spike with glee whenever he'd finished cooking a meal. A lot of those meals she had to wrap, cutting her fingers on the edges of the industrial strength aluminium foil that was similar to a papercut. There had to be a better way to wrap takeaway meals than this?

'No, my little cake crumb, that was the regular Friday home-time rush. We still have the train day rush to contend with. Shh—it's on.'

As Lenny worked on the orders, the speakers crackled with the voices of two middle-aged men yakking about fishing tides. Jordi didn't listen, too busy devouring the flavoursome pasta dish. Even once her stomach was full, she just couldn't waste a single noodle. Lenny could cook. Which explained why the kitchen was so busy.

'*Today we're sad to announce that we're about to be flooded with coastal cowboys,*' came one of the radio hosts over the speakers. '*The invaders are coming. I repeat, the invaders are coming, my fair friends of Elsie Creek. So, lock up your daughters and let the hounds loose.*'

'That's Tidal Tom,' said Lenny, flipping burgers on the hotplate. 'The other fella who helps host the show is the reel rascal, River Ron.'

Jordi tried to smile, but the fishing puns were a bit on the nose.

'*That's right,*' said River Ron, with his deep ocker accent and husky tone, '*the bigwigs are letting loose one of those tagged pretties worth one million dollars into our local waterways.*'

Everything stopped. The noise in the hallway that carried from the pub's front bar went silent. Even Lenny stopped flipping the burgers on the sizzling hotplate.

Was this the fishing competition Luke had mentioned earlier, while trying to convince Jordi to granny-sit? A million dollars to catch a fish? Who did that?!

'Turn that up, will ya?' Grey-haired Billy stood in the doorway, lifting his trouser suspenders higher up his shoulders.

'That's the pub's yardie, Billy. He lives here, like I do,' Lenny explained to Jordi, as he placed a plate of steak and veggies in front of the older man. 'Billy, this is Jordi.'

'I know who the flower girl is.' Billy playfully winked at

Jordi as he stood closer to the speakers and started carving up his plate of food.

'I forget, you've been delivering flowers to our dining room how long now?'

'A year.' Wow, it'd been a year since she'd been well enough to work full time again. Now here she was contemplating managing the family florist shop. Her sister had been doing it on her own for six months before Jordi came back, and it was a job they'd both been doing since they were kids.

She could do it. Right?

Jordi had savings earmarked for the property she had been planning to buy with her parents, and she could use that to take over the family store instead. Or did she get a business loan? Or should she learn how to fish and go after that million-dollar fish herself?

The voices from the middle-aged podcasters seemed to echo through the pub, breaking through her thoughts. *'That's right, fishos, not only are we puttin' up with the grey nomads clogging up our highways with their crawlin' caravans doing less than the speed limit,'* said Tidal Tom with a snorty-nose laugh.

'We'll have them jamming up our boat ramps and waterways. So, those who want to enter the Elsie Creek Barra Classic, get your entries in today.' River Ron's husky voice sounded like a long-time smoker who'd just come back from screaming at a heavy-metal rock concert all night.

'Pick your spots, work out a strategy for them arm stretches, and stock up on the rubbers, jigs, and hard bodies. Because we've got perfect tides for the classic and we're expecting a record number of competitive anglers muscling in on our turf.'

'Let's hope they put a cap on the number of those competitors. Otherwise, we'll have a lot of hotheads on the waters who may spill overboard.'

'Which brings us to our croc report, River Ron. Are you gonna do the ramble?'

'Listen, Tom, you want me to change your name from Tidal Tom to Tattler Tom?' It was obvious they were teasing each

other, as the men chuckled on the air, with Lenny and Billy doing the same in the kitchen.

'He's a reel rascal that River Ron.' Billy's ruddy cheeks were rosy as he adjusted his fancy fedora.

'*Fine, allow me then ...*' Some paper rustled and then the sounds of a typewriter tapped away, as if giving an old-fashioned news report.

With Billy in his suspenders, and Lenny beside him both listening hard, it reminded Jordi of the Golden Age of Radio. The days when families gathered around the radios to listen to radio plays, detective serials, soap operas, quiz shows, sports events and news. Yet these guys were doing it for a radio show about fishing.

'*It's nesting time, peoples, and according to our local croc wrangler, there are six nests belonging to the harem of that colossal beast we all know as King, the body-builder's version of a saltwater crocodile that lurks around Goat Island. It's just been confirmed by our illustrious park ranger, the ranga you don't want to mess with, to watch out for that saltie and his pretties, plus the many more we don't know about,*' said River Ron.

His offsider, Tom, continued the pace like a team over the air, '*So, unless you want your boat bashed by one of those armour-plated prehistoric ice crushers, we advise you skip trolling through this region. As for the barge report ...*'

A gong was smashed in the background, and it was Ron's turn to speak. '*Golden snapper are flush on the sandbar by the mouth of Elsie Creek. Bait fish are leading those marvellous Mangrove Jacks higher upstream near the boat ramp, so it's worth the gamble to put something new on the plate this weekend. And the Alpha Angler of the Week goes to John Frazier for sucking up to his wife with a special flower delivery.*'

Jordi's ears perked up at the mention of flower delivery. Surprised she recognised the name of Frazier too.

'*What did you do, John? That's what we'd like to know?*' asked Tom, his nasally laugh mimicked by Lenny, the chef, slapping steaks on the sizzling hotplate.

'*And the rest of the hot gossip and scandals for this week is ...*

The new teacher Pamela has hooked herself a cowboy. Although he's chosen to remain nameless, everyone knows it wasn't Cowboy Freaking Craig this time.'

'I won that bet.' Billy raised his thumb in the air, the other tucked into his suspenders as he rocked on his heels.

'Shh, will ya?' Lenny frowned at Billy as he fiddled with the volume on his speakers.

'Ya speakers are nearly cactus.'

'They're fine if you don't yak so much.'

'*Welcome back to Detective Senior Sergeant Marcus Moore,'* said River Ron's husky voice over the airways. '*The town's top cop has finally given up his chances of being the next world surfing champion in Bali. But we all know the reason for returning home from his honeymoon is that his new bride is starting her next book. Which means Policeman Porter can stop going grey from the stress.'*

'*I swear that Policeman Porter aged overnight, sucking sour lemons with his morning coffee,'* said Tidal Tom.

The two men laughed over the radio. Again, their laugher was mimicked by Lenny and Billy in the kitchen, but it also seemed to carry down the corridor from the bar. It was as if the entire pub was listening.

Through the kitchen's screen door, Jordi had a view of the bottle shop, where Luke leaned against the side of a ute with a couple of cowboys, patting their cattle dogs that sat in the back tray. Just like Lenny and Billy in the kitchen, they were listening to the fishing show through the ute's speakers.

Jordi didn't know who these people were and had never been fishing. But these two men, hosting the *Dramas from the Dinghy*, were having a fat time, mimicking the ebb and flow of two mates sharing a conversation as if on a boat. Playing an assortment of music, adding weird and wonderful voice effects to their reports, while taking the mickey out of each other. But they were also educating people on fishing laws, while offering tips to take home a prize catch. In the end they'd created a polished podcast that had everyone stopping what they were doing to listen.

'To end the show, we'd like to tip our favourite fishing caps and raise a frothy to Marie Pederson for her twenty years of service at the Elsie Creek council office.'

'Wow, twenty years, huh?' Tidal Tom said. 'Reckon we'll be doin' this in twenty years?'

'Lookin' at your ugly mug every week? Who knows? But we'll brave the beasts that lurk in our waters, scrambling the mudflats to climb into our tinnies to drop another episode next week. So, remember, fishos, share your stories, or a happy snap of your catch, and any gossip or news to share by emailing us at Dramas from the Dinghy. Hoo roo until next week, fishos …'

'This is Tidal Tom and the reel rascal, River Ron, signing off.'

And then there was silence, that seemed oddly loud in a pub for a Friday night.

It didn't last long when the jukebox cranked out country-rock music as the voices of many men rose. From the bottle shop, Luke got busy delivering cartons of beer to various cars, utes, and trucks, as the barmaids and waitresses started rushing to the kitchen with their orders.

'Did you know the Million-dollar Barra is coming to town, Boss Lady?' Billy tipped his hat to Samantha, the publican, carrying in a stack of dirty dishes from the front bar.

'Of course, she did,' said Lenny. 'Nothing happens in town without Samantha knowing first.'

'Guess we'll be busy, huh?'

'We will.' Samantha put her stack of dishes on the sink and helped Jordi sort through them. 'The bar staff are taking room bookings now. Lenny, do we need to book more kitchen staff for the Classic? I'm thinking of getting a band and doing something in the beer garden that weekend?'

'Can we keep my little cake crumb?' Lenny pointed his spatula at Jordi.

Hosing off the empty plates, Jordi felt the heat creep all the way to her ears. 'You know that's kinda weird, right?' Jordi couldn't believe she'd said that out loud, slapping a hand over her mouth.

Lenny shrugged, holding his shoulders high while meekly scrunching up his apron. 'I don't mean nothing by it.'

He was so sweet about it, she gave him a shy smile and half shrug, considering the guy was her supervisor, and they'd been having fun all night.

'Nah, she's the flower girl, not cake crumb,' said Billy with another wry wink. 'And that's me done for the day. Night all.' With a thumb flick of his suspenders, he was out the door, climbing the internal stairs to the pub's residential area. It's where Jordi put one of her flower arrangements at the top of the stairs to greet their guests.

'What do you say, Jordi?' Samantha washed her hands in the sink.

Jordi hesitated, because technically Samantha was her customer, and now her boss.

'You usually cruise though on the same days, delivering flowers to my restaurant. I haven't been able to find a part-time kitchen hand, not since Lucy ran away to live with the new fire chief. And Lenny likes you.'

'It couldn't be permanent.' But if she was going to buy her sister out, she'd need every penny. Plus, it had been fun hanging out with Lenny in the kitchen. 'Let me finish my first shift and we'll see.'

Besides, her dad always had two jobs, one for the police and the other for the family business and seemed to cope. She could, too.

'Come see me, when you're done.' Samantha nodded. 'I'll be restocking the coldroom if anyone needs me. Want me to take this to the bar?' She scooped up the plates of food, reading the docket.

'Thank you, Boss Lady.' Lenny bowed at the publican, who'd only be a few years older than Jordi. 'Jordi, can you take this plate to Luke? It's his tucker for the night. Then I'll show you how to make salads as pretty as your flower arrangements.'

'Sure.' She removed her kitchen gloves and picked up the plate of steak and vegetables. If she did come back, she'd bring her own apron and tools.

'Take five while you're out there,' said Lenny. 'Lord knows I do with my nicotine addiction. Please tell Luke I need more red wine for the kitchen.'

'Sure.' It would give her a chance to negotiate the granny-sitting and flower-selling deals, which meant talking to the handsome hustler who'd effortlessly talked her into doing this job as a kitchen hand.

She pushed on the creaky screen door, the cool air refreshing on her clammy skin. Craning her neck up at the stars that were so deep, it was as if the Milky Way was draping over her like a cloak.

Yet each step across the dusty and dark yard to the bottle shop seemed like she was walking the plank.

Come on, it was just Luke. A nice guy who only saw her as a potential granny-sitter. Nothing more.

Pity she didn't think of him as just a potential customer, torturing herself because there was no way Luke, or any man for that matter, would touch her. After all, she was damaged goods.

Ten

The Friday night flow of traffic through the bottle shop was constant, keeping Luke busy. Until the fire chief's fancy emergency vehicle rolled to a stop, where behind the steering wheel sat the new fire chief that Luke had managed to avoid. In the passenger seat was Rigsy, who used to live next door to the pub in the unofficial Elsie Creek Inn.

'Rigsy, to what do I owe the pleasure, mate?' Luke jovially shook Rigsy's hand. 'It's been a while.'

'Too long, mate.' Rigsy poked up the brim of his sweat-stained Akubra, shading his eyes. 'I've been busy. I'm just in town for train day and to help Jax.'

'And you still find the time to volunteer for the firies?' He pointed to Rigsy's volunteer fireman T-shirt.

'You should come back and join us.'

Luke hesitated.

'Hey, I'm Jax.' The new fire chief held out his hand.

'Luke.' He shook the fire chief's hand, whose muscular arms were covered in some serious tribal ink, giving off a mean vibe. 'What can I do for you fellas?'

'We're stocking up for the volunteer fireman's barbecue tomorrow. It's a recruitment drive, hoping to get a few more volunteers,' said Jax. 'Were you a volunteer?'

'It's because of Luke I joined up.' Rigsy patted Luke's shoulder.

'I did no such thing. Got a list of drinks?'

'Here.' Jax held out a piece of paper.

'Cool. I'll get the trolley. Open the truck for me.' Luke

ducked inside the coldroom, but their voices carried through the open doorway.

'Was your mate, Luke, a volunteer?'

'Luke was the second-in-command of your station, Chief.'

'Luke's a fireman?'

'He was acting fire chief whenever the old chief's wife got sick, and they went down south for medical treatment.'

Luke couldn't stack the cartons quick enough, to get them the out the door. He hated being reminded of his past like that. Didn't they think he could hear them through the open door?

'You know, Luke's got almost as many medals as you, Chief, one for saving this town from a bushfire, and his years of service. But then one day Luke quits the firies, stopped farming, stopped hanging out with his mates, and started working here as the bottle shop manager.' Rigsy sighed heavily. 'It's a pity because Luke used to play a big part in Elsie Creek's fire management, he'd make your job a helluva lot easier.'

'How so?' Jax asked Rigsy.

'The old fire chief, and the old park ranger used to get Luke to help them plan the burn-offs with minimal effort for maximum effect, because he knew the area so well.'

'And he has this knowledge because...'

'Luke's one of the Bennetts. They're big game hunters who've been hunting this region since forever. Heck, Luke has probably walked every inch of this region ten times over before he could shave.' Rigsy sniffed hard, his voice lowered as he said, 'Luke is also a damned good firefighter, Chief. The rest of the vollies will tell you, too. Hey, next time you're sparring with our town's top cop, ask Marcus to tell you about Luke. He might tell you the whole story.'

'Here we go, fellas.' Luke bustled through with the trolley loaded with boxes for the Fire Chief's truck.

'Are you sure you don't want to come back and volunteer, Luke?' asked Rigsy.

'I'm flat out at home, and here.' His grandmother was

keeping him busy, now tucked up safely at home. He hoped.

Luke then caught a faint aroma coming from the kitchen, but underneath it was the scent of assorted flowers. He spun around to search the shadows beyond the doorway. 'Jordi? What are you doing hiding out there?'

'I brought your dinner.' She held out the plate the same way she delivered her flowers.

How long had she been standing there?

'We'll leave you to it,' said Jax with a nod.

'Have a good night.' Luke gave them a customary wave like he did with every customer, then arched an eyebrow at Jordi. 'You, get out of the shade. You don't want to get star burnt.'

'What?' Her giggle made him smile. 'This is for you.'

'Thank you. I'm famished.' He took the meal, dragging over his stool behind the counter. Taking the cutlery, his fingers brushed against her soft skin.

But she ducked her head. A brush of red dusted over her cheeks, while she tucked her hands into her sleeves.

'How are you doing in the kitchen?'

'It's fun. Lenny's a nice guy.' She scuffed the heel of her boot against the concrete step.

'Normally, Lenny is a grouchy prick to new people.'

'He calls me his *little cake crumb*.' She rolled her eyes, but they were shining with amusement. 'What is his accent?'

'Hungarian. He's a chef with a couple of Michelin stars to his name.'

'What's he doing out here, if he's that good a chef?'

Luke shrugged. 'Lenny was widowed. Quit everything, sold his restaurant, his home, and travelled to the other side of the world to fossick for gold in the outback. Not that he's found too much, because this job pays for his smokes and rum, which makes him a grouchy prick first thing in the morning. But if Lenny is calling you his little cake crumb, he must like you.'

'Lenny reminds me of the way my dad's friends would tease us …' Her smile fell as she pulled at the sleeves of her shirt. 'Where is Esther?'

'Home. Just so you know, Esther's excited you're staying over tonight.' It had been a while since he'd seen Esther so happy, talking all about her day with Jordi and eagerly planning Jordi's stay. Making her the perfect granny-sitter if he could only get Jordi to say yes.

'I can't put Esther out like that. I have my swag in the van.'

'Or you can have a soft bed, hot shower, and Gran will make you breakfast. She loves entertaining. Trust me, she wants this. Besides, I'm not letting you drive back this late, not when there's plenty of room at the Lodge.' He wasn't going to let her talk her way out of it either. He wanted her safe.

He then winced, rubbing the back of his neck. 'And I'm sorry for snapping at you earlier.'

'You were just being protective of your grandmother, I get it. I'd be the same if my grandmother went off with some stranger.'

'You're not a stranger.'

'Huh?'

He had to stop doing that, feeling like he knew her. 'We're co-employees now. And you bring me food.'

'Talking about supervisors, Lenny's asked for some more red wine.'

'Sure. Just so you know, I could've sold a dozen bunches of your flowers tonight. Why not bring in half-a-dozen next week, as a trial.' He knew she was a timid thing, who'd surprised him by taking on the kitchen duties without any complaints.

'I can do that.' Her nod was firm, but there was a different spark in her eyes.

'I'll get that red.' His finger ran along the wine rack as the bell rang alerting him to an incoming car. He frowned at the beefed-up black four-wheel drive towing a sleek black boat called the *Barra Wrangler*.

'Just my luck to have this coastal cowboy rock up.' He

scowled at the cretin behind the wheel.

'Who's that?'

'Dom. Dominic Donnelly. A world-class cretin you need to steer clear of.' He pulled a bottle of red wine off the shelf and scribbled a note for the register.

'Cretin, huh? You shouldn't put yourself down like that, Luke.' Dom sneered at Luke as he strolled up to the counter, adjusting his white cowboy hat. 'Hello, sweetheart? Where did you spring from?'

'Leave her alone.' Luke dumped the bottle of red hard on the counter like a hammer.

'Mm-hmmm ...' Dom took a deep sniff at Jordi. 'Don't you smell like a world of flowers?'

Jordi cringed, stepping away from Dom.

Luke saw red. 'I said, leave her alone.' He clapped a heavy hand on Dom's shoulder, putting himself between Dom and Jordi. 'Back off, cowboy. You hear me? This one is off limits.'

Dom stepped back, wearing that cocky grin that begged for Luke to wipe it away with his fists. 'Don't think you can scare me any, bottle shop boy. But I think you forgot to include your girlfriend in on the joke.'

Luke turned to discover Jordi was fleeing back to the kitchen. 'Look at what you did, arsehole.' He shoved Dom hard in the chest. 'You know, the people who tolerate you on a daily basis deserve bravery awards, especially since you've doubled up on that much stupidity a brain-eating zombie would starve around you.'

Dom stepped in closer, both the same height and weight. Luke could take him, with his hands squeezed into fists, desperate to dance over this cretin's face.

'Watch yourself, snowflake—or I'll make you famous as an extra in some hospital soapie as the guy who plays dead.'

'Do we have a problem here, fellas?' At the far end of the driveway stood Porter, closing the door of his police car. He casually strolled into the bottle shop, hooking his thumb into his police vest, with the keys swinging off his chunky police belt that held his handgun in its holster.

'Nothing to see here, officer. Just a friendly chat, is all.' Dom took a step back.

'What do you want?' Luke's voice was low and edgy, with a trigger so tight it'd snap.

'Carton of beer and two bags of ice. Go fetch, boy, and if you're nice, I'll give you a tip.' Dom waved his hundred-dollar bill at Luke like a king to a slave.

Luke snatched the cash and went in search of the hottest beer carton and the softest ice that'd melt in no time.

'Did you hear they announced the Million-dollar Barra as part of the Classic this year?' Dom spoke to Porter, leaning against his sleek, top-of-the-line barra boat, perfect for the rivers.

If only Luke had that sort of cash, he'd have a boat just like it.

Porter plucked a soda can from the drinks fridge and counted his change at the counter. 'I did. Are you entering?'

Dom laughed, one of those irritating laughs that always made Luke's skin crawl. It tempted him to pop the lid on a dozen beers to spill inside the cretin's car.

'I'll be winning, is what you should be saying.' Dom patted his boat. 'I'm going out this weekend to work on my fishing strategy. I'll be picking my possies before the tourists show up.'

'You are a tourist.' Luke dumped the beer and ice in the back tray of Dom's beefy ute, with his voice low and loaded with warning. 'Now be a good little tourist and flock off to where you and your kind belong and stay there.'

But Dom only grinned with a set of teeth so white they'd glow in the dark. 'With service like that, mate, you know I'll be back.' Dom opened his driver's door. 'And do yourself a favour, Luke, forget about entering the Elsie Creek Classic, you'll just get in my way. Say hello to the flower girl for me. I'll get her number the next time I see her.' He tapped his hat with an evil laugh before climbing into the car.

Luke gritted his teeth, watching the lights of Dom's boat

trailer disappear down the road.

'Why do you let Dom get under your skin like that?' Porter cracked open his can of soft drink.

Luke rubbed rough hands over his face as if to scrub away the memory. 'I honestly don't know.' Maybe it was Rigsy bringing up the junk from his past he'd been trying to forget, or that Jordi had been upset that he'd lost his cool.

Normally Luke would cheer on other people whenever they caught a fish on the river, and he'd happily chinwag with anyone, but with Dom. It. Was. War.

Yet he frowned harder at himself when his eyes landed on the bottle of red wine left standing on the counter. He hadn't meant to scare off Jordi. She was fragile as it was.

How could he make it up to her, especially when he needed her to granny-sit so he could concentrate on the fishing competition? If he scored that million-dollar fish, he'd never have to deal with cretins like Dom again. He could finally have a life.

Eleven

The smell of grilling bacon weaved through the house as Jordi woke on a bed with soft pillows under an even softer quilt, as if made entirely of heavenly soft feathers. The bed was enormous, but the room was gigantic, with polished wooden floorboards, antique wooden dressers, and a set of double French doors that gave an incredible view of the countryside. She was a guest at the Lodge.

The floorboards were cool under her feet, the runners soft down the corridor that was lined with black and white historical images. She passed a large dining room with its highly polished table that could easily seat twenty people.

At the end, the hall opened to a large room where the sun shone through the walls of louvred windows. Assorted couches and comfy armchairs were arranged in various areas for easy entertaining, complete with a polished bar that stood at one end and a glossy grand piano commanding the centre of the room.

On the main interior wall, a massive set of buffalo horns towered over vintage shotguns, spears, and didgeridoos, with more historical images lining the walls. Jordi could feel the history, almost hearing the whispers of the stories told or the songs sung around that piano in a time when social media didn't exist with the associated need to be picture perfect for the camera, in a time when those smiles in the grainy black-and-white images shone amongst their sweat and dirt, as a testimony to the glorious adventure of a hunt.

The most adventurous thing Jordi did was pack her van

and do flower deliveries.

'Morning, petal. Sleep well?' Esther stood in the doorway wearing a yellow apron and a sparkly tiara.

'I had the best sleep.' She stretched with a yawn, feeling like she could sleep another ten hours. It had been that good.

'Come on, I've got your brekkie ready. Walden will be in shortly.'

'Who?'

'Who did I say?' Esther adjusted her tiara.

'Walden.' Why was Esther wearing a tiara for breakfast?

'Oh, I meant Luke.'

Last night, Jordi had expected Luke to gallantly walk her to the door or something romantically stupid like that. But all he did was check on his grandmother, check the dials on the stove, then mumble goodnight as he walked out the back door to leave her alone in a big house with Esther snoring in her reclining chair beside her pet buffalo.

Seriously, they kept a buffalo in the house! In the lounge room, which was nothing like the grand sitting room, where concertina doors were purposefully designed to allow their pet buffalo to walk in and out with its wide horns. That's what Luke had mumbled as he gave her a quick tour from the back doorway, in the kind of rehearsed speech of someone wanting to get their shift over and done with.

It was obvious Luke was only being nice to her because he wanted her to granny-sit Esther for the fishing competition. Nothing more.

'Sit, young lady.'

Sunlight brightened the large kitchen with its shelves stacked with jars of assorted fruit and vegetable preserves. It was like stepping into a different era, with the kitchen table set for three with polished cutlery, side plates, and assorted jams jars on their own silver tray. There was even a dainty butter dish resting among the matching cups and saucers, with Esther's purple birthday flowers beautifully arranged in a large teapot. The table setting was better than any she'd seen in any of the resorts she'd delivered flowers to.

It reminded her of Sunday breakfasts, helping Natalie decorate their kitchen table with flowers, tablecloths, and napkins. Other families may have their Sunday dinners as their weekly family get-togethers, but in her family it was always a fancy Sunday breakfast, where they'd feast on eggs, toast, fresh fruit, crispy bacon, warm fluffy muffins, and various other delicacies. Sunday breakfast was their family time, the only time they could guarantee her father could be there no matter what shift he had at the police station.

Jordi couldn't remember the last time she'd had a Sunday breakfast, let alone eaten at the table with her sister. With Natalie leaving, how many Sunday breakfasts did they have left? 'I should hit the road.'

'You won't make business hours this morning.'

'My sister hires help for Saturdays.' Maybe her potential staff to help Jordi watch the store.

Cleaning his boots on the mat, Luke entered through the back door. 'Morning, Gran.' He kissed Esther's cheek.

'Morning, my darling boy. Breakfast is ready.'

Where was her good morning? Huh? All she got was a nod.

Sitting opposite Jordi, Luke flicked open the napkin he placed on his lap. 'Care to explain why there are two wicker chairs sitting along the fence line this morning, Gran?'

'Jordi did it.'

'What?' She glared at Esther. It was better than looking at Luke, with his damp tousled hair, smooth chin, deep tan, smelling of soap and that sweet combination of leather, denim, and vanilla spice.

'Oh, really?' He arched an eyebrow at Jordi, dragging his bowl closer, to then scoop out some peaches from the jar, that were so fragrantly sweet they reminded her of summer. He then added a scoop of creamy yoghurt and topped it off with a sprinkle of toasted granola.

'Don't blame me, I'm just a visitor.' Except she didn't have a fat wallet or a need to hunt for things like the past guests of the Lodge. Although hunting for her keys for a fast getaway would be a good start.

'We thought it was a pleasant spot to check out the neighbour's furniture. They have five couches, you know.' Esther put a basket of toast on the table.

'We have seven, if you count the wicker couches on the verandah.' Luke pointed his spoon at the large doorway that led to the sitting room with its grand piano.

'You do?' Jordi didn't know anyone who owned that many couches, let alone a grand piano. Its colossal size and shiny exterior dominated the attention of everyone, even hers while in another room.

'So, we do. Which means I have ample furniture to create a new sitting garden. This is your plate, petal.' Esther put a plate of bacon and eggs in front of Jordi, then took away Luke's empty bowl.

'It looks lovely, Esther.' Jordi hesitated, pulling the sleeves down on her shirt to cover her wrists before reaching for the cutlery.

'Don't wait for me.' Esther plonked her teapot in the middle like a protective barrier of sorts.

'So, when do you need to be back at work?' Luke twisted the pepper mill over his plate of bacon and eggs.

'Tomorrow. I like to cruise back, do a load of laundry, clean out my van before starting the week ahead.' Finally, she found the courage to reach for the pepper mill that now sat beside the purple flowers. 'I like how you put these flowers in the teapot, Esther. It's a brilliant touch.' They could use something like that in the store.

'My grandson gave me those flowers.' Esther's smile was as bright as the sparkling tiara that caught the morning sunlight, reflecting a rainbow of colours across the kitchen walls.

Luke cheekily bobbed his eyebrows up and down at Jordi, his way of acknowledging that she'd saved his butt for forgetting Esther's birthday. That he never paid for.

Perhaps she should have accepted the money if she hadn't been so huffy with him earlier.

Esther joined them at the table. 'So, what does a florist do? I don't know the business side, only the delivery side—now that was fun.'

Her work wasn't that glamorous. 'I meet the plane at midnight for freight. Then with the fresh stock, I'll create the assorted flower arrangements, then start the supermarket deliveries at daybreak.' She gave a few grinds of the black pepper to sprinkle like black dots over the egg whites and golden yolk. Putting it back on the table, she noticed the official-looking envelope from a lawyer, with Esther's name on it labelled *Secret Sister Project*. Was that the letter from Iris that Luke had mentioned earlier?

'And your sister?' Esther asked.

'Natalie manages the shopfront and takes the orders.' Jordi needed to change the subject. 'I heard about your fishing competition last night.'

'Oh, me too.' Esther poured a stream of fragrant tea from the pot. 'Is it true that they've tagged a barramundi that's worth a million dollars?'

'Yes. It's become an annual event known as Australia's richest fishing competition.' Luke mumbled between mouthfuls.

'How do they do that to a fish?' Jordi asked.

'They attach this long red strip in their fins—it's painless—then release it into the wild for someone to catch. But if you catch it you have to keep the fish whole to show the judges you haven't tampered with it in any way.'

'Only the one fish?'

'They also release a heap of other tagged fish worth a few bob. Over the years lots of people have caught the ten-thousand-dollar tagged fish, and I'd read in the newspaper that this one lady hauled in a fish tagged for twenty-five thousand while arguing with her husband.'

'Has anyone caught the million-dollar fish?'

'Not yet. Plenty of people take sickies from work to go fishing in hope of catching one. But it's not that easy, because who knows if the fish will survive, when we've got sharks and crocodiles who think barra is pretty tasty. But this year is different.'

'Why?'

'Because they normally let loose the million-dollar barra, and all of those other tagged fish, closer to Darwin to bump up the tourist trade. But this year they're letting it loose in our waterways in time for the Elsie Creek Fishing Classic.'

'You're entering the Classic this year?' Esther asked Luke.

'I want to.' Over the lip of his teacup, he gave Jordi a pleading look.

'Luke and his father, Walden, won it a few times over the years. They made quite the team.' Esther then sighed, her smile swapped for a deep sadness. 'But then Walden left, and Luke's been busy.'

'Gran, it's okay.' He tenderly patted her hand.

'Why are you so keen to win this classic?' Jordi asked, considering it seemed like impossible odds.

'I want to start a fishing tour company. A legit one, instead of the cash-in-hand jobs I do on my day off.' Luke put the dainty teacup down on the matching saucer. His table manners were impeccable. 'Winning the Classic would give me instant credibility. And if I score that fish, I'll be able to get a better boat and vehicle, plus pay for the various licences I'd need to run legit fishing tours. The insurance alone is a killer in costs.'

Esther smiled at the room. 'And we can open the Lodge again.'

Luke frowned. 'No. The punters can catch the train from the southern cities, cross the road to the pub, where I'll pick them up in the morning. The publican is willing to give those punters a discount. So you won't have to clean any rooms or cook for them, Gran.'

Esther gave a deep sigh as her sad eyes lovingly roamed the room as if staring at an old friend who'd been ill for some time.

Luke gently patted his grandmother's frail hand. 'We don't need to pander to the punters anymore. Not when you're retired and can relax now. This way, all I do is take them to the boat ramp and show them a good time on the water. That's it.'

'I know nothing about fishing. Flowers, yes. Fish, meh.' Jordi picked up her teacup and sipped.

He arched an eyebrow, swallowing the last of his meal, then wiped his mouth with the napkin. 'Can you fish?'

'I've never been fishing.'

'Well, my little angelfish, we need to fix that.' He folded the napkin and dropped it on his empty plate. 'In fact, you'll be my practice run. You'll be perfect.'

'For what?' With a body full of scars, Jordi was far from perfect.

'If I'm going to run a fishing tour company, having a virgin on board to take fishing, as a practice run, will be brilliant.'

Jordi blushed to an all-time high at the word *virgin*.

'You should take Violet out today, Walden.' Esther took Luke's empty plate to the sink.

Jordi arched her eyebrows. *Who?* She silently mouthed to Luke.

'Gran, her name is Jordi, and I'm Luke.'

Again, Esther patted her tiara. 'I just said that, didn't I?'

'I can't. I have to get back.' Yet Jordi struggled to leave.

'Next week? We'll make a date. You can come with us too, Gran.'

'Oh, no. You two go play. I'm having a lady's luncheon then.' Esther pointed to her wall calendar, marked in a big circle. 'And before you ask, young man, Tess and her grandmother are coming to collect me.' Esther leaned towards Jordi and said, 'Tess is our postmistress, who should be dating Porter. But she kept chickening out and broke poor Porter's heart—especially when he got into trouble for getting his boss's new wife kidnapped.'

'What?' Jordi slow blinked a few times while trying to process that information.

'It's all good now.'

'Gran.' Luke's voice was loaded with warning.

'I know, I know. No need to broadcast Bennett business to the masses, or your best friend Porter's business. But I'll make snacks for the boat.'

'But ...' Jordi didn't do boats or fish. 'I don't know anything about fishing, and I don't have any fishing clothes. What do people wear fishing?'

'That's easily fixed. I've got some board shorts, hats, and plenty of sunscreen.' Luke gulped down his tea, got up from the table while sliding on his sunglasses that made him look effortlessly cool. 'I've got a long-sleeved fishing shirt that'll protect your skin perfectly. It'll be a great practice run for me to work out my plan for the Barra Classic. So, what do you say?'

Twelve

Middle of the week, under the shade of the back shed, Luke was servicing his boat's engine. Somewhere nearby something was yapping. It wasn't quite a bark, more like a yip. He looked out over the yard where fine red dust floated on the breeze beneath an outback sun.

His phone beeped, alerting him to an incoming text.

He looked at the name and smiled. It was from Jordi with one word: *water.*

Jordi was the most challenging female he'd ever come across. He never had to try too hard with females, but then he usually didn't care if they walked away, either. But Jordi was different. She didn't talk, dance, laugh, sing, and only ever drank one tall ice-filled glass of pink gin. That's it. She was nothing like some of the binge-drinking babes he served in the bottle shop.

He wanted to spoil Jordi, and he also wanted to convince her to help him granny-sit for the three-day fishing competition.

He pressed dial on his phone and waited for her to pick up. Was she going to ignore him?

'H-hello?' She sounded nervous over the phone.

'There must be something else you like to drink besides water. I'll have plenty of water on the boat, as it is.'

'I'm not fussy.'

He kind of wished she was. 'Well, Gran's doing the tucker. What about snacks?'

'I'm fine. Seriously, I am.'

'You're not chickening out on our fishing date?' If he could show someone who'd never fished, like Jordi, a good time, he could teach anyone. Which made Jordi his perfect test case.

Yet, this phone call felt just as awkward as if he was actually taking Jordi out on a real date.

'Um …' Jordi sounded like she was cringing, while trying to think of an excuse to end this call.

But he wasn't giving up that easily.

'Gran's baking you a cake.' It'd been a long time since he'd seen Esther excited about entertaining. 'Gran made me take her shopping for the ingredients. And she's making you supper on Friday night after the pub. Lenny can't wait for his little cake crumb to come back.'

Jordi's little laugh was sweet over the phone. 'You don't think it's kinda weird being called cake crumb?'

'Don't worry, you're not his type. It's Lenny. He'd rather drink another rum, smoke his smokes, and flip a burger than date anyone.'

The yapping continued in the distance. It was annoying, like a dripping tap echoing in a strange motel room. He peered up at the tall gum trees for a mimicking bird, while talking with Jordi on the phone. 'Have you got many deliveries in town? Will you need directions this week?'

'Umm, I do …' She shuffled through some paperwork, as the yapping continued. 'Kelly-Anne Wright has some flowers from her husband, Tony.'

'Is he in trouble?'

'Not every bunch is a *Sorry I stuffed up* bunch, you know. Some do it for anniversaries or birthdays, or just because they care. I like making anniversary ones, like those who've made thirty years.' He could hear her smile. 'Do you know the Wright's place? The GPS isn't saying much, and Google Maps only knows the highway.'

'I do. I'll draw you a mud map that you can collect from the bottle shop.' Because he looked forward to her weekly visits.

'Deal.'

Again, he smiled. 'Anyone else?'

'Only one at the hospice. I know where that is.'

'Me too.' Not that he wanted to. 'Gran used to visit Iris there every second day until she lost her licence.' Then it was when he could take her, at least twice a week.

'Esther told me she lost her licence for ripping some fence. That doesn't sound fair.'

'Angelfish, it was a hundred-foot-long fence Gran peeled back like a banana skin, dragging it down the road. It took me two days to put that fence back, with Porter helping me, so Gran didn't get charged with property damage.' He rubbed at the deep lines across his forehead. 'And this is where you tell me who else you're delivering joy to in the world?' Just like that first day she drove into his bottle shop asking for directions.

'I shouldn't.'

'Who am I going to tell.'

'Well, you might think this one is cheesy.'

'So, spill.'

'Well, we got this really cute request for flowers. My sister and I think its adorable.'

His nose crinkled. 'Do I want to know?'

'It's from Alex Landers and baby Elsie and says: *To Supermom Verily: happy first month anniversary as a family.*'

He scratched the back of his head. 'It's not that cheesy.'

'My sister was talking with Alex on the phone for over an hour. Their baby had open-heart surgery, but according to Alex, the doctor said little Elsie is healthy, happy, and sleeping through the night. But you should've heard his joy when the baby held his hand or smiled at him. The guy was gushing! Not many guys' gush.'

'That's true.' He certainly didn't gush. He also knew Alex and was struggling to picture the brewmaster as a gusher. But he really liked how Jordi was uncharacteristically chatty this morning.

'My sister and I both believe that when Natalie has a baby, her husband will be just like Alex. But in this case, Alex has every right to gush. That poor little baby, open-heart surgery after just being born, that's terrifying.'

Elsie's birth had certainly been the stuff of daytime dramas, with the entire town involved. 'Has it been a month since Elsie's birth?'

'Yes. So Alex has decided to celebrate the moment and treat each day as precious.' She went quiet for a moment.

If he could, he would have wrapped her up in his arms and held her, not saying a word, because her silence was filled with sadness. But she was hundreds of kilometres away. Plus, Jordi didn't like anyone touching her.

He then realised the yapping had stopped.

Jordi sniffed hard over the phone and shifted some more paperwork in the background. 'Then I have the usual customers, a few resorts on my way to town, the pub, the supermarket, the church for their weekly sermon and that's it.'

'You've forgotten our trial on the bottle shop sales.'

'Six bunches, right?'

'I'll leave that up to you.'

'That's not how it works. You tell me what you want, or I'll pass you to my sister for the order taking. She's good with that.'

'You're doing just fine, Angelfish. So, I know Jimbo wants one for his wife. Mean-Rene's husband, Bear, said he'll take a bunch home for sure. But don't make them like the supermarket ones, we want blokey flowers.'

Her laugh seemed to dance across the phone line, he could almost picture it. 'I'm guessing banksias and other natives.'

'Not something we can just pluck off a tree in the yard—no, wait! That's perfect. Their partners will think they did the plucking and pinching on their way home.'

'That's illegal. It's why we have commercial growers.'

'I can't see the local police arresting people over plucking flowers. Cattle rustling, illegal fishing, speeding, hunting out of season, or poaching, yes. Flowers—no.'

'I see your point.'

'I mean no disrespect to your industry.'

'My father would say the same ...' Her voice was so small.

Even if the silence was uncomfortable, he'd wait.

She exhaled heavily. 'My father was a policeman, a watch commander, who enjoyed growing flowers for Mum. He did it for stress relief and because he liked the way flowers made people smile.'

'Really?' Luke frowned, not at Jordi but at the yapping starting up again. It was irritating. But he couldn't locate the source from under the cool shade of his boatshed.

'Dad said after dealing with the bad side of life all the time, it was nice to see the good side. Having people smile at him, and not scowl at his police uniform, whenever he knocked on a person's door. He loved doing the deliveries.'

'I didn't realise there was so much power in flowers. No wonder Gran wants your job.'

There it was, another laugh that was both airy and light. It was heartwarming.

'So, has your brother-in-law got the new job yet?'

'No.' Again she shared another long sigh. 'He knows they've rung his referees, so now we're waiting to see if he's good enough for the panel interview. I hope he gets the job— but I don't. Is that wrong?'

'No, it's not.'

'You're just saying that, because you want me to granny-sit.'

'I am not. When my old man left the farm, part of me didn't want him to leave, and honestly, Dad was the same. But Mum was happy.'

'Really?'

'It's why Dad keeps asking Gran to move over there.' He roughly scrubbed nails through his hair, then put his fishing cap back on. 'I reckon Gran would say yes if they asked her to move *in* with them, and not put her in some home. But Mum won't have Gran living with them.' His mother had refused point blank, complaining it was her turn to be the lady of the house, and not Gran.

He'd never realised his mother had held so much resentment towards Esther. Which left the big bad buffalo hunter, the great Walden Bennett, stuck as the piggy in the middle trying to keep the two women he loved happy.

So now Esther refused to speak to her son and daughter-in-law.

'Esther told me how much she appreciates you letting her stay at home. She loves the Lodge, and you.'

He could just hug Jordi for saying that. It was the pat on the back he didn't know he needed.

But that annoying yapping grew more frantic.

He stepped outside and peered around the property. 'Oh, no.'

'What?'

'Gran is at it again.'

'What's she done this time?'

'She's got Cecil dragging her bathtub across the paddock.'

'Her what?'

'Gran can't climb in and out of spas and we don't have a pool, so we built her a tub with handles. It lives on its own trailer. But now she's got Cecil playing the part of an ox, dragging it to the fence line.' Cecil, the big puppy, was following Esther, with large ropes around his chest and shoulders, effortlessly dragging the tub on wheels. The dust rose as if they were ploughing the field with a white bathtub.

'Esther doesn't like your new neighbours, does she?' Jordi's soft giggle was almost melodic—if he wasn't annoyed with his grandmother so much.

'I don't know why, when she hasn't even met them yet. I've got to go. But before I do, Gran has washed one of my fishing shirts for you, she's put it on your bed in the Lodge.'

'Oh, um ... Okay.'

'So, you be safe on those roads. Text me when you're

leaving town, so I know to keep an eye out for you.'

'Hey, I know what I'm doing.'

'Gran will demand to know where you are. Welcome to the Bennett fold.' He smiled, hanging up the phone, hoping she'd be okay.

He texted her again: *'What is your drinks order that doesn't involve bananas, coz that's bad luck on boats. Be daring, Angelfish.'*

To his surprise, she sent him a meme of a woman rolling her eyes with the word *Whatever* emblazoned on it. It was hilarious. And so unexpected from the shy woman.

He really liked this side of her, wishing she'd open up more.

But that yapping became more frantic.

Only this time Cecil let out a low groan. It had Luke's attention, because Cecil rarely made any noise unless in pain.

Luke sprinted across the field. 'Gran? What's wrong with Cecil?'

'It's that rat.' Gran pointed to the fence. 'It's teasing Cecil.'

'Easy, big fella.' He patted the big neck of the black buffalo as he crouched down to the yapping, cream-coloured, four-legged creature. 'It's a pug dog.'

'That oversized rat is upsetting my Cecil.' Esther tenderly stroked the side of her buffalo.

'Gran, I think you're the one upsetting the dog. And what are you doing to poor Cecil?' He removed the ropes around the buffalo's stocky shoulders, while the pug kept yapping. It was really irritating.

'I wanted to bring my bath over here.'

'Why?'

Esther adjusted her tiara, with her chin raised in defiance. 'Well, you hid the keys to the truck, tractor, and the ride-on mower.'

'Why did you bring your tub out here?' It usually lived in her private orchid garden at the back of her room, where no one could see her. Not this open space by the neighbours.

'Shoo, rat.' She propped open her large beach umbrella and waved it towards the dog that yapped harder.

But then Cecil snorted loudly, dropping his big head down low to protect Gran, dragging his hoof in the dirt as if to charge.

'Stop that, Gran ... Easy, Cecil.' With one hand against Cecil's blunted horns, and through the gap in the wire fence he held out his other hand to the pug. 'Come on, little fella. I won't bite you, but the old lady might.'

'It's upsetting Cecil.' Esther plonked her beach umbrella into the red soil, then settled into a wicker chair. 'And it has such an annoying yap.'

The dog sniffed at his hand, then wagged its tail with a smile on his face, happy to be patted. 'There we go. He's cute—'

'For a rat.'

Luke picked up the pug with its super-soft fur, nestling into his chest as if it was used to being held. 'You'll be alright, little fella. Meet the neighbours. This is Cecil.'

Cecil's big nostrils flared as the pug whimpered, cowering into Luke's chest. 'Easy, big fella.'

With a deep level of patience and a kindness in his dark eyes, Cecil waited for the pug to make the next move. It's flat face and tiny nose wrinkled as it grew gamer, stretching its neck to sniff at the massive beast wearing pink ribbons wrapped around its blunted buffalo horns.

When the pug gave a light yap, which was a signal for Cecil to give his version of a kiss of approval, which was a lick practically from one end of the small pug to the other.

'There, all friends now.' Luke put the dog down, and it happily skittered around Cecil's hoofs, before jumping straight into Esther's lap.

'What do I do?' With hands up, Esther screwed her nose at the dog like it was some poisonous weed.

'Pat it, Gran. Be nice to your new neighbour.'

'It's tiny. The sea eagles and kites will snap it up in no time.'

'That's true ... When did the neighbours chop down their tree?' Fresh sawdust and a tree stump was all that was left of the old ghost gum, and the rows of pineapple plants were gone, leaving nothing but dirt.

'Yesterday. I remember helping Iris plant those pineapples in her yard.' Her voice rose with distress.

'Is that why you've brought the bath out here?'

'Well, if they want to see what we're doing, why not put on a show?'

Luke cringed. 'You're not, are you?' Who'd want to see an octogenarian bathing?

'My yard, I can do what I like.' With her chin raised, she patted the pug. 'What do I do about this rat?' Under the umbrella's shade, the pug got comfy in Esther's lap, as Cecil groaned to sit beside Gran for an ear rub in the red dusty paddock.

'Coco! COCO …' A male voice hollered across the field. *'Oh, for the love of vodka and blueberries, come here, you pudgy pug!'*

'Over here.' Luke waved from the fence line.

'Don't do that.' Gran hissed.

'Why not?'

'What if they're nice? I can't play my mind games then.'

Luke shook his head, with a chuckle low and deep.

'Hello, I'm—'

'Felix from Sydney, right?' Luke recognised the guy, dressed in linen pants like a Sydneysider about to do lunch at some yacht club.

'Well, if it isn't Bottle Shop Luke. Is this your place?'

'It's the family home.' Even if his name was on the mortgage, Anaborro Downs was home to all Bennetts.

Gran cleared her throat.

'This is my grandmother, Esther Bennett.'

Sitting like a queen in her wicker chair, her tiara twinkling, Esther held up the pug with its shiny black nose and flat face. 'You can have your rat back.'

Luke passed the pug over the fence. 'You'd want to be careful with your dog, something that small and the scavenger birds will snap him up.'

'And the snakes, and the dingoes. He's croc bait is what he is.'

'Gran, be nice.'

'Hmph. Why? They destroyed Iris's garden. I'm going back inside.' She stood from her chair, with Cecil moaning to his feet to follow.

'Sorry, mate. Normally Gran's a good sort. She just misses Iris, who used to own your house.' He nodded at Esther, holding on to Cecil's horns to help her navigate across the dusty field.

Gran may have a point; it was one thing dealing with people through work, it was another to have a new neighbour. His first one ever. 'I thought you lived in Sydney.'

'After house-sitting for Wren and Marcus for so long, when I returned to Sydney I just kept thinking of Elsie Creek and Wren. So I snapped up this place.' Felix hoisted Coco higher in his arms. 'And, to be honest, I fell in love with the horse statue at the local museum that Homeless Hank made.'

'Not the life-size horse made of assorted junk metal?' It was the largest sculpture in the town's tiny museum.

'That's the one. I just couldn't bear to let it go. Sadly, the freight was going to be a killer, plus there was just no room for it when I live upstairs in my nightclub.'

Luke smirked with amusement. 'So, you bought the house for a horse statue?'

'I know, it's crazy, but that's the fun of it.' Felix gave a cheeky grin, with his shoulders held high. 'What can I say, Elsie Creek, in all her quirkiness, has got under my skin.'

'So, you don't like pineapples? Because Iris had some super sweet varieties.'

'I couldn't keep the pineapples because my partner's allergic to them and I was worried their spikes would harm Coco.'

'Do you plan on becoming a farmer?' The thought of noisy farming machinery might be an issue, considering he slept during the day.

'No.' Felix sniggered, as he looked over his yard. 'I just

want to admire it. Where I'm from, you could fit my entire suburb on this one block of land. I love it. Don't worry, I'll be busy working at the Sandfly, plus helping my new-found friend Kat do some marketing to promote the town's local museum, in between setting up my new house—if I can keep Coco inside. You're such a rascal, Coco.' He hugged his dog.

Luke noted the time on his watch. 'I've got to head to work. Well, welcome to the neighbourhood.' Let's hope his gran behaved and didn't start some feud with the new neighbours—it was bad enough with the feud still simmering with his folks.

Thirteen

From the second Jordi had entered the pub's kitchen that evening there had been a constant stream of takeaway meal orders. Her years of working with cellophane and wrapping flowers had become advantageous in her speed for packing and wrapping the various takeaway meal orders, and for her second week on the job, she was ready for the Friday home-time rush.

Customers collected their takeaway orders at the kitchen's back door, with Luke busily serving the constant stream of vehicles through the bottle shop. There were groups of cowboys in utes keen to make the trek home to their cattle stations, while others went camping. Along with the truck drivers radioing-in their dinner orders, where their assorted trucks lined the highway outside of the pub. The home-time rush reminded her of the Valentine's Day and Mother's Day flower arrangement creation and sales crammed into less than two hours.

And then it was all over. For the moment.

'Well done, my little cake crumb. Now, we make a treat for you …' Lenny showed her how to create a bouquet of roses from strawberries! Plump, vibrant red strawberries, with their lush green leafy bases, were intricately carved and held upright by long barbecue skewers in a jar, looking like a dozen long-stemmed, red roses. Jordi couldn't stop admiring them.

'Am I in time for dinner and a show?' Billy hoisted one of his trouser suspenders higher onto his shoulder with a box tucked under his other arm.

'Serving it up now,' said Lenny, manning the grill. 'Pepper sauce?'

'Always. Look, I even got you a pressie.' Billy plonked the box on the counter and removed a set of speakers. 'One of the Triple Js accidentally knocked his old speaker into the pot of crabs. So, the Flynn brothers got us shock resistant waterproof jobbies. Luke recommended 'em. He's got one on his boat. Where I hear you're going fishing tomorrow for the first time, flower girl.'

Jordi shrugged. 'Luke talked me into it. How do I get out of it?'

'You don't. You'll have the best time with Luke. I always do. At least he catches fish, not like some smoking chimney stacks I know.' Billy slyly winked at Jordi as he set up the new speakers.

'Here, fill that mouth with food, you old fool.' Lenny grumbled at Billy, putting his plate of steak and vegetables in front of the grey-haired yardie.

Then it was just like last week with the pirate podcast, *Dramas from the Dinghy*, with their cheesy intro music loud and clear over the new speakers. The jukebox was silenced, and a hush came over the pub as they all seemed to bow their heads to listen to the radio.

Tidal Tom started the show bantering with his offsider, the reel rascal, River Ron. *'Only one week to go to the Barra Classic. So, my fellow fishos, the Elsie Creek mayor is pleased to announce all spaces are full.'*

'Overfull if you ask me. We've got flamin' eighty boats out there flooding our waterways next weekend. Eighty. The Elsie Creek Classic has never had that many.'

'As the mayor will tell you, it's good for the town. And with a million bucks up for grabs, I'd bet you a bunch of flippin' fins there will be a stack more boats showing up for their shot, with a whole load of shenanigans happenin' on board.'

'And this is where we get to play big bad gropers. The town's top cop has warned us he'll be increasing the number of breathos

and radars on the road. But he'll also be doing random breath testing on the water, as well as checking on your catches to ensure the legal bag limits and fish size rules are followed. So, don't give them fellas in uniform a hard time—'

'Even if we all want to drop that pesky speed gun into the river and let it troll for any underwater racing.'

'—it's for our safety.'

'Look at us being all grown up. Is this what adulthood looks like?' Tom chortled deeply.

River Ron had the husky laugh of a middle-aged smoker. 'Back to what's happening with the Barra Classic ...' The sound of paper shuffling could be heard over the speakers, giving the impression of an old-school news report. 'The local volunteer fire crew will be playing harbourmasters on our one and only little boat ramp, so be patient when launching your boats that weekend. The park ranger will also be patrolling the river systems to ensure the wildlife remains unharmed, and she has the right to check your catches too, fellas, so play nice. The good news is her partner, the Hot Doc, will be part of the ranger's crew, making himself available in case of any watery emergencies during the Barra Classic. Who else is crashing this barra party, Tom?'

'There will be plenty of competition marshals trolling the waters with a camera crew. And as a request from the mayor, please no flashing your posterior for the cameras, boys. We want a clean race—'

'Or get your bums bleached for posterity pics.'

Billy almost choked on his piece of steak, as hearty laughter bounced along the hallway coming from the front bar.

'And now let us pause from casting our lines in the water, to bow our heads for a moment,' River Ron said in a sombre tone.

'Wait, I'll take my lucky fishing hat off for this.'

'Listen up, fishos, we have our very first message from God!'

Angelic musical harps started playing, it had Jordi look up from the sinks in search of that sound.

'The publican herself has emailed us that the pub's rooms are fully booked out. She asks that everyone please stop hassling her bar *staff for rooms, as there is a waiting list longer than the distance between two neap tides. But she said the king of the kitchen, Lenny—'*

'Oi! That's me!' At the hotplate, Lenny gleefully waved his egg flipper in the air.

'Is having one of his legendary spit roasts for the afterparty held in the pub's beer garden. There will also be a live band and everyone is welcome. Lastly, for those punters who wish to put their names forward to see if Karma will predict the winner, speak to the pub's yardie, Billy.'

'And that's me!' Billy grinned, with gravy dripping off his forkful of mashed spuds.

'As we all know, Karma is on a restricted diet. The publican has informed us that Karma will only be jumping at the end of the first full day of competition. And not before. So please,' implored Tidal Tom, *'no feeding the ferocious man-eater for tips on where to find that million-dollar fish, fellas.'*

'Well, now you've shared that fin-tastic idea, they may have to beef up the security around the pub's pet crocodile,' said River Ron.

'Which brings us to the Croc Report for this week ...'

Jordi zoned out, using the fancy kitchen slicer to cut up more salad vegetables for the dinner rush.

'... and now for the gossip, rumours, and scandals rocking the town of Elsie Creek, I'll hand over to the honourable Tidal Tom for the honours.'

'Why thank you, River Ron, that's reel nice of you.'

Jordi rolled her eyes over the fishing puns, but Lenny and Billy didn't seem to mind it.

'First up, we'd like to send a hook-line-and sinkin' shoutout to Kelly-Anne and Tony Wright celebrating their thirtieth anniversary.'

'Yeah, mate, what's the secret to marriage you've got goin' on to last thirty years? Us fishos could do with an inside tip on keeping the little woman happy, so we can spend more time on the water.'

'Talking about happy families, I want everyone who is listening out there to please raise your glasses in the air to congratulate our

local brewmaster, Alex, and our retired Olympian, and softball coach, Verily, for their baby daughter Elsie. That little girl just scored a clean bill of health and has survived her first month after her open-heart surgery. So here's to little Elsie.'

'Cheers.' As the two men clinked their cups over the stereo speakers, the hearty chorus echoed loud from various areas of the pub.

Even Lenny and Billy raised their coffee mugs in a salute to the baby.

Jordi's heart just bloomed with a warmth that they'd do such a thing, a town all behind a couple and their baby. Also surprised that she knew who the podcast hosts were talking about, because she'd delivered flowers to Verily earlier today and got to meet little Elsie.

As the podcast continued, the screen door opened, and Luke put his empty plate on the sink beside Jordi. 'Hey, we sold out already.'

'Sold out of what?'

He gave her a lopsided grin, with amusement shining in his eyes. 'All of your flowers are gone.'

'Already? They liked the blokey flowers?' She'd been stressing for days over the assignment. Hitting up her brother-in-law, Mitchell, for his feedback on what was considered blokey-type flowers.

'Yep. And this is your share of the profits to help go towards your store.' Luke slid the cash into her apron pocket.

'Really?' So how much had the hustler made for himself?

'You should double the order for next week.'

'But ...' She'd only done six, and it was a full bucket of flowers that normally never sold in their store because—dare she say it—they looked too masculine for flowers. 'You know it's the stuff I see on the side of the roads, all the time.'

'Which is perfect,' he said with a sly wink. 'Like I said, Angelfish, it's all about knowing your market and the local blokes love the idea.'

She narrowed her eyes at him. 'What else did you sell besides beer?'

'I've sold out of jerky and the Havershom's homemade goat cheese. Do you reckon we should make up some hampers? I saw your fancy wrapping for the takeaway meals, we could expand on that.'

'For what?'

'I dunno? Something they could take home to their family for Fridays. I'll work on the wine and snacks, you come up with the flowers, and them fancy takeaway containers, and cutlery.'

'You know, we do gift baskets in the florist shop.'

'Yeah … Nah.' He shook his head. 'I dunno. Would they be suitable for this place?'

'Umm …' They were hampers for newborns, baby showers, new brides, get well hampers and pampering gift baskets perfect for those who liked their flowers, but were more suited for their feminine clientele. 'Probably not if your clientele liked the blokey flowers.'

'Hey, if I can sell car park spaces at the vacant lot next door for the barra classic, we can sell flowers and finger food to the fancy fishos.' He leaned against the doorjamb near her sinks, the laugh lines around his eyes highlighting the mischievous shine in his eyes.

'You sold car park spaces, in a paddock?' She pointed out the darkened window that showed nothing but flat open terrain. 'To fishing boats?'

'Angelfish …' His deepening voice had her skin bristling with electricity. 'Those barra boats belonging to the professional anglers are worth fifty K each, then you add the engines, trailers, safety gear, fishing gear, and you're looking at a complete beast worth well over two hundred grand that doesn't come with car alarms.'

'I never knew that.' She licked her lips at how beautifully the colour of cinnamon blended with the brown sugar sprinkles that made up the colour of his eyes.

'Not that long ago, during the treasure hunt, my old boat got pinched from this pub, so I know what it means to keep a boat secure.'

'I'm so sorry to hear that.'

'It's cool. I got it back in one piece.'

'Oi, car.' Billy pointed to the screen door that gave them a clear view of a ute entering the bright lights of the bottle shop.

Luke peered through the screen door. 'Gotta go. Don't forget, Gran's made you supper, and she's got your room ready at the Lodge.' Luke dashed out the door, and she leaned over to watch Luke's sexy swagger back to the bottle shop.

'And last of all, fishos, the flower girl is taking to the water,' came the husky voice over the radio.

'Hey, that's you.' Billy pointed at Jordi as she wheeled around to face the two men in the kitchen.

'Huh?' Jordi tugged at her shirt to cool down from her close encounter with Luke. 'They must be talking about some other flower girl—it's a common title for weddings.'

'Shhh.' Lenny waved his spatula at them.

'Be on the lookout for Midgie, who is taking his middle daughter Jennie out on the water for her first go at casting in the wild. We've also got the moaning miner, Batty, taking that new teacher out on a fishing date—so it's obvious that cowboy must've lucked out last week. But the flower girl is the pub's new pot scrubber—so be nice, you boys in the pub or Lenny will have your heads—'

'I will. You're my cake crumb now.'

'Do you know how weird that sounds.' Where did she suddenly get the mouth on her, giving cheek to Billy and now Lenny? She hadn't been this chatty in a long time.

'Only in fun, my friend. You're not my type. I'm gay.'

'Oh.' She blinked a few times, while Billy shrugged as if it was another day in the office.

'Bottle Shop Luke of The Barra Bandit fame is taking the virgin of the waters, the flower girl, fishing ...'

'I'm a virgin what?' Her tongue was suddenly on an uncontrollable roll, speaking without thinking.

'It means you've never been fishing before. Is that true?'

Billy asked. 'Luke told me he was taking you out as a test to see if he could run a fishing charter company for real. That lad's taken plenty of people out over the years, but to find a fishing virgin in this region is rare. That's makes you famous, kiddo.'

Jordi wanted to hide her head and never show her face in town again.

Through the open window she scowled at Luke waving at her with a cheesy grin, being patted on the back by a customer as if he'd won the lottery.

How rude. Was she some game to Luke?

What was his deal? Especially when he didn't like his life made public, and now it was being splashed all over the airwaves for everyone in this small town to hear. Or was that because he was using her to advertise his future fishing business?

It still didn't make it right, not when she'd been trying so hard to hide, and now she was being thrust under the town's spotlight as a virgin! It was the one place she'd desperately tried to avoid—and that was being seen.

Fourteen

The following morning Jordi was dragged out of the world's most comfortable bed before it was even daylight, to face the wilderness where man-eating crocodiles roamed. *Yikes.*

Jordi didn't do fishing. She didn't do hobbies or sports. She was happy just doing her job, making floral arrangement to brighten people's lives and then move on. That was it. Not this.

But everyone at the pub knew all about it, with Lenny giving her tips on what lure to use, Billy telling her what bait to try, and Esther waiting up last night to share her many tales of fishing trips.

'There she is. Come along, petal. Luke's waiting.' With a different sparkling tiara tucked into her soft purply-white hair, Esther hooked her arm through Jordi's where she hovered by the kitchen doorway. 'Luke likes to eat on the road to the fishing ramp, so I've put breakfast in the car, and all we need is you.'

In Luke's fishing shirt, which was more like a dress, it hid her back, arms and neck areas that she was most conscious of. As her thongs flipped up the dirt behind her, Esther escorted her to where Luke was working on *The Barra Bandit* sitting on the trailer.

It was a fancy boat.

That somehow sent a jolt of fear through her that she wanted to go back to bed, or get in her van and run.

'Don't you dare.' With hands on his hips, the lines on

Luke's forehead deepened. 'You're not running away from this. We have a date.'

She hiked her shoulders higher. 'I-I don't know what to expect.'

'You're just going fishing.' He shrugged like they were going to the shop for milk.

'She's scared, Walden.' Esther patted Jordi's upper arm, where she flinched from being touched.

'My name is Luke, Gran.'

'Didn't I say that?'

'Jordi, there's nothing to fear.' He grabbed her hand and brought her closer to the boat.

OMG! She was holding his hand. And this time, she didn't flinch.

'As this is my first tour with a proper first-time tourist, I'll give you the safety speech.'

'Safety is good.'

'Can you swim?'

'Yes. But it's croc country.' And it was still dark.

'Don't I know it.' He climbed up the boat trailer and onto the boat. It had a flat floor completely carpeted, with two swivel seats in the back, and a rectangular console containing a steering wheel, levers, and buttons. At the rear stood a row of rods lined up like lean car aerials, plus two massive outboard motors, black of course, that made up the rest of the boat. It was a lot bigger than she'd expected.

Under the shed's spotlight, Jordi stood on the boat trailer's wheel arch, while Luke pointed to various items like a car salesman showing off the features of his fancy boat.

'There are six life jackets on board. I've put one under each of our seats, and four in the front hatch here.' At the front of the boat, he lifted a lid. The floor had hatches everywhere, including an in-built esky, allowing for plenty of room to walk around freely.

'You can store your bag in here. It's a waterproof hatch. The captain's console also has a waterproof hatch for your phone. The oars live on either side of the boat, and this chunky orange thing is an EPIRB.' He tapped the rectangular plastic box strapped to the side of the console that made up the helm.

'A what?'

'An Emergency Position Indicating Radio Beacon. When this puppy gets activated, it sends out a signal for help. And as we're going into crocodile-infested waters, there is an inflatable life raft on board, but it's best if you swim for land as quickly as you can. And when you hit the riverbank, run inland as fast as you can, because salties sunbake on riverbanks, and can jump their entire body length free from the water.'

Jordi swallowed hard. 'Is there some sort of crocodile repellent?'

'I wish.'

Jordi jumped off the boat trailer, looking to Esther for help.

'You're scaring Jordi. And me,' said Esther.

'There's nothing to fear. The chances are pretty slim of ever getting attacked by a crocodile. The only time that happens is when someone is doing something stupid. Just be crocodile smart, simply by being wary of them at all times, and remember even if you can't see them, they can see you.' Luke effortlessly jumped off the boat to land beside her. 'My tip for you is to always sit in the boat. You'll be safe there with no chances of falling overboard. Questions?' Luke's brow lines deepened with the laugh lines softening around his eyes, worried she'd chicken out—which she wanted to do.

She hated the thought of disappointing him, when he'd gone to all this effort, texting and calling her every day this week. It was her turn to do something nice for him, so she dug deep for some sort of courage to face an unknown world. 'Will I get to steer the boat?'

His charming, lopsided grin spread. 'If you behave, I might let you. Come on, let's go. You can't catch fish from there.'

Fifteen

The sky was a mushroom pink, dotted by a colony of fruit bats heading for home. Their reflections clear in the waterway was as smooth as glass, where the boat's hull barely caused a ripple. With the breeze cool against his skin, Luke steered his favourite toy down the wide river bend. It was his favourite time of the day—sunrise on the water.

'Are you okay?' He shouted over the outboard engines.

'This is gorgeous.' For the first time, Jordi smiled so wide, it was like she'd swallowed the sun and was sending light beams into his soul. Her hair was back, with the wind showing off her pretty face, and the beauty was she hadn't even noticed that she'd pushed her sleeves up to her elbows. She finally looked free from those demons holding her back.

Damn, she was pretty.

He was proud that she'd found the courage to come. And he finally got to see her bare legs in shorts. She looked good in the smallest fishing shirt he owned, which was way too big for her. No female ever wore his shirt like this—but he liked it a lot.

His grin grew as he steered them deeper down the river where massive gum trees lined the banks, towering over clusters of spiky pandanus palms. They were broken up by thick clumps of towering native bamboo, with their soft feathery ends waving gently in the breeze.

On the edge of the estuary, where the brackish saltwater mixed with the fresh, stood an impenetrable maze of woody mangrove trees. Their dark, glossy green canopies cast shadows to block the banks, and their thick tangle of roots stood high above the water's edge, as if standing on a hundred skinny legs to keep their trunk dry.

He pulled up where the river met the mouth of a wide creek bed, pushing the boat's nose into the thick cluster of mangrove trees. 'We'll drop our first pot here, then head upstream.'

'Why am I picturing you dragging out some pot to boil water?'

He gave a hearty chortle, amused with her remark. 'Dilly pot. For mud crabs.'

'What variety are those weird-looking water trees?'

'Eh? They're just mangrove trees.' He shrugged.

'And …'

Wow, she really was a fishing virgin.

Well, if he wanted to do this as a full-time gig he'd better get used to those types of questions.

He narrowed his eyes to look at the river the way Jordi was, as if seeing it for the first time, the layers of the trees lining the banks, the water blending with the fresh air and vibrant scent of green leaves and earthy tree bark, but the way the water reflected the ginormous sky was like a mirror. His world must seem so foreign to her right now.

'Mangrove trees are an important part of the river systems.' Hoping he didn't sound like some boring school professor. 'They stop soil erosion, and their web of aerial roots create these intricate underwater forests that are home to various fish varieties, shrimps, and mud crabs. Do you like crabs?'

'I do. My dad used to get some from the markets on Saturday for Mum. He'd cook them on the wok on the barbecue at home.' The shine in her eyes dulled, and she pulled her sleeves down to tuck her hands inside the cuffs, with her legs hidden beneath the fishing shirt, as if curling into a ball to hide.

He hated how she did that.

'Well, did you know that these ugly-looking mangrove trees grow an edible fruit?' He pulled out five crab pots that folded up into rectangular boxes made of netting material. 'They call it the mangrove apple. Aboriginals use it to heal skin wounds, or to treat stomach aches. My grandfather swore by them as the best thing in case of toothaches. And we can even use it as a mosquito repellent if we run out.'

Jordi crinkled her cute nose, highlighting the tiny skin blemishes that looked like freckles. 'How would the fruit taste if it's an insect repellent?'

'They're like a sour persimmon apple, full of seeds, with this funky cheesy aftertaste.' He playfully shuddered, getting a grin out of her. 'Not the best, and they're quite pongy when you first slice them open. But they're good if you want to add something sour in a curry. Local Aboriginals used to use the mangrove timber to make canoes, paddles, spears and even boomerangs.'

'You sound like a tour guide now.'

He grinned, glad to see her relaxing again. 'Here, you can do this.' He held out the pot.

'What do I do?'

'Tie this piece of meat to the bottom of the pot. Your hands are small enough to do a better job than me. Consider it a part of the whole fishing experience.' He passed her some string. 'Put it in the centre, on the floor, so the crabs can crawl in for a feast. Make sure it's secure though, their claws are sharp and they're tough enough to drag it away.'

'I didn't realise that. So then, what do we do?'

We? He liked the way it sounded coming from her lips.

He cleared his throat, focusing on the water, checking for any lurking predators. 'Well, we drop it over the side and let it sink.'

Her strong, nimble, and lean fingers expertly tied knots in record time.

'You'd be used to tying knots with flowers?'

'I bend plenty of wire, too.'

'Good to know.'

And she was pretty.

Really pretty, the way the morning sunlight captured the layers of colour in her sandy-brown hair, but those blue eyes were soft and full of emotion.

If he was honest with himself, everything about Jordi was wonderful. Except that damned shyness smothering her like a joy-killing cloud.

'How's that?' She dropped the first pot over the side as he held on to the mangrove's skinny trunk to keep the boat in place.

He watched the pot slowly sink to the bottom. 'Brilliant. Now toss that buoy over the tree branch. It's attached to the pots, which will make it easy to find them when we come back. We'll be following this creek to the flats.'

'What's up there?'

'You'll see.'

She really knew nothing about fishing. It was like teaching a toddler to walk to make sure they didn't bump into any sharp edges. But if he wanted to do this as a business, he'd need to prove he could give punters a decent fishing experience.

He dropped the last of the crab pots into the water, the boat's engine barely rumbling as he waited for Jordi to take her seat, when another boat came roaring around the corner.

'Watch out, Jordi.' Luke pulled her towards him, as a black boat ripped past them, sending wave after wave to rock the boat from side to side. 'I've got you.' He held her to his chest, her hair so soft against his cheek, and her mixed floral aroma wove deep into his lungs. It'd almost be romantic if he wasn't scowling at the cretin in the other boat called the *Barra Wrangler*. 'Watch yourself, cretin.'

'It's your fault for getting distracted by the female,' called out Dom. 'Everyone knows it's bad luck to have a woman on a boat.' Dom then waved his cowboy hat, before roaring away.

Luke clenched his fist, gritting his teeth, keen to mess up that mongrel's face.

'What is wrong with that man?' Jordi mumbled.

'Breathing is a start. Are you okay?' He helped Jordi back into her seat.

'I'm okay. Is it true women are bad luck on boats?'

'Superstitious sailors thought so. Along with a stack of other things like bananas were bad luck to have on board. Not that I believe any of them, but their tales do amuse the tourists.'

'How does that make sense?' Jordi jutted out her chin. 'Women fish all the time. Esther told me her fishing stories last night.'

'I have no issues about women fishing. Old-time sailors used to think the mermaids would get jealous of women. Or sailors would get distracted by having a woman on board and not do their job.'

'Mermaids, huh?' She coyly grinned, stretching her neck to peer over the edge of the boat. 'What about bananas?'

'That's based more on logic. You see, bananas give off a gas that ripens any food around them. It's handy if you have rock-hard avocados, but it's bad for cargo ships.'

'How?'

'In the old sailing days of pirates and wooden galleons, the banana gases would ripen all their fruit and vegetables. It made their food stocks ferment like alcohol does, turning it into a fuel that'd start fires on their wooden ships.'

'Are you for real? '

'So the stories go. Look, I've had my mother and Gran on board, and they've caught more fish than me, even when Gran brought out her banana cake. Our family used to grow bananas commercially, so Gran was always bringing something made from bananas onboard.'

'You're kidding. That dust b—' She pushed her lips together to stop herself from speaking.

'You can say it.'

Jordi shook her head.

'*Dust bowl* is what you were going to say.' She was so freaking adorable. He couldn't stop grinning at her.

'No, I wasn't.'

'But it's true.' He rummaged through the esky for some water bottles. 'We'll need to wait for the water to settle after that idiot tore it up.' He handed her a water bottle.

'It's so pretty out here.' She sipped on her water, with her eyes keenly taking in the details.

'It's also very dangerous, because of the swamp puppies.' He pointed to the far banks, where camouflaged by the grey mud, lay a bask of crocodiles.

'How can you call a crocodile a *swamp puppy*?'

'We've got all sorts of names for them. Like you, Angelfish.' He snickered quietly.

She rolled her pretty eyes at him, with that smile growing. 'So why don't you guys grow bananas anymore?'

That wiped the smile off his face. 'The banana freckle came in.'

'That's a fungus, right?'

'It's just spots on fruit that doesn't look pretty for people in the shops. It has no impact on the fruit itself. But the government hired these over-zealous crop inspectors who came and tore down our crops, poisoned the stumps and then drove away. They even had the police there in case Dad got angry, being known as a hunter. And he was furious. We all were.' He dropped his head at the memory that was heavy in his chest. 'I watched it break my father's heart, to see all of his hard work, and his father's work, torn down by strangers. Then they sprayed the area, poisoning the soil, to then ban us from grow anything for twelve months.' He grimaced at the golden sky. 'What's worse was we didn't even have any traces of that disease. No one did in our region.' He rubbed at the bristling heat at the back of his neck. 'If that banana freckle wasn't so badly mismanaged, my dad would still be here ...'

'Can they do that? Just tear down your crops like that?'

'Under the Territory's Plant Health Act, they can. Because we were in some risk zone where they were systematically going through people's backyards and ripping up healthy plants! Even though their testing proved our crops didn't have that plant disease, and neither did anyone we knew, they still got the chop. All from some politician signing off on the decision from some air-conditioned boardroom in the city, without even consulting all the producers they were supposedly trying to protect!'

'That is so unfair.' Jordi tightened her lips into a thin line. For a florist who wanted to grow her own crops, he could see it was having an impact on her.

'Dad didn't do any farming after that. He also didn't want the responsibility of looking after punters, even though Gran was pushing to reopen the Lodge, and Mum was deadset against it.' Yet here he was, thinking about starting his own tour business, hunting for game fish.

'I'm confused. Your grandmother said your family stopped hunting because of an accident with her father getting maimed? And your father stopped hunting when your mother was pregnant with you.'

'No. My grandfather, Esther's husband, got killed by a buffalo bull while trying to protect a punter. Dad stopped taking out tourists after that, closing the Lodge. But he was still a professional hunter, who did the government contracts for animal culling in national parks and cattle stations to hunt for buffalo and pigs damaging their lands. The banana farming was always something we did, when not hunting.'

'But Esther said ...' She paused. 'She's having trouble remembering things, isn't she?'

'Gran calls me by my father's name at least once a day.'

'That's Walden?'

'Yeah. And I've heard her call you by my mother's name, Violet. Which is ironic when Gran isn't even talking to my parents.'

'Why not? They sent flowers for her birthday last week.'

He frowned. 'They want Gran in a home ... As much as I hate to admit it—I worry about Gran when I'm working.' Lately he'd worry about the octogenarian when she wasn't in his sights. 'Did you know that she's suddenly decided to take bubble baths on the fence line to scare off the neighbours?'

Her snigger burst into a laugh that bounced off the water to echo through the trees like a laughing bird. 'I saw the bathtub there.'

'Even though, she's been acting like a child, I still think my parents were too quick to consider putting Gran into a home where she doesn't know anyone.' He wiped over his mouth, as if to get rid of a horrid taste, with this fierce need to protect his grandmother. 'I'd hate to get shoved into a home just because it's convenient for the family, wouldn't you?'

She nodded, with empathetic eyes.

'Sadly, my mother is pushing for it. While Dad's feeling guilty for leaving Gran and the farm behind, for giving up. Even though I told Dad to grow something else, he didn't have the heart for it anymore.'

'Understandable if they destroyed his crops like that. I'd be gutted, too.'

He sat back, narrowing his eyes at her, because she'd somehow forced him to see these things from another point of view.

'What does your father do now?'

'He drives trucks up and down the east coast, in between fishing. And yet, Dad was one of the best buffalo hunters in the country.'

'Is he happy?'

'Huh?'

'Is you father happy?'

'I don't know.'

'Why not?'

'I've been busy...' *Avoiding them.* He rubbed at the tightness in his chest, surprised at how much he was sharing with her. 'Gran isn't talking to my parents, and when I do talk to them, they keep telling me that they want to ship Gran off to live among strangers in another state. Look, the main reason Gran is refusing to go is because she believes my parents won't even visit her with their busy work-life schedules. Especially when Dad is never there, looking for excuses to be on the road all the time.'

'Hey ...' Jordi leaned over and patted his hand, which was rare when she'd flinch at anyone touching her. But then she levelled her gaze and the intensity of her stare trapped him, taking the heat right out of him. 'You should call your father.'

'Why?'

'Because I can never ring my parents again. Believe me, there are days I wish I could. You don't know how lucky you are to still have them around.'

'They'll just lecture me about putting Gran in a home.'

'Tell them that. At least make the time for a conversation. You don't want your last words to your parents to be something you'll always regret.' She leaned back, hiding her hands in her shirt sleeves to gaze sadly over the water.

Dammit. He raked his fingers through his hair. 'You're right. I'll do it.'

She gazed up at him with such big eyes, he fought the urge to reach out and hug her.

'And I'll do it, too,' she said.

'Do what?'

'Granny-sit.'

'You little ripper.' Now he really wanted to hug her.

'On one condition?' She held up her index finger.

'What's that?'

'I have to catch a fish first.'

Sixteen

Sunburnt, sweaty, and slimy from sunscreen, Jordi was a mess. But she ignored it all, as Luke steered his boat through wide rivers to deep streams that narrowed into a creek. The constant shifting banks changed from sparse ghost gums and dry grasses to a dense tropical foliage that shielded the sun, to suddenly enter what Luke called *the flats*. An open flood plain, wider than the eye could see.

Giant pink lotus flowers, bigger than a human head, waved from thick, celery-like stems that ran deep into clear waters where tiny fish darted for the shadows. But to see an entire flood plain full of these opulent beauties had her heart soaring at the natural wonder.

The air was thick with a rich, honeyed, floral aroma with its earthy undertones hidden behind the creamy-green blend that was both sweet and herbaceously spicy all at the same time. No wonder they used the lotus fragrance as a base in so many perfumes.

'Those flowers are amazing.' And she was in her kind of heaven. She gripped the side of the boat as it floated within a bed of lotuses poking up between their wax-coated leaves larger than dinner plates.

'Well, in that case.' Luke slowed down the boat, removing the pocketknife from the holster on his belt. The silence without the engine left only the sound of trickling water, as a few birds flew past on the breeze, exposing a deep sense of peace beneath, as he flicked open the blade to cut a lotus flower free from this private paradise. 'Here.'

'They're so heavy.' With two hands, she held the flower the size of a dinosaur's egg. It took up her whole lap. 'Thank you.'

'Being a florist, I'd imagine few people would give you flowers.'

She shook her head, pursing her lips tight to stop her smile at the sheer generosity and thoughtfulness of this one simple gift. It was like her heart cracked open to let the colours of her soul free, with a lightness in her chest at what he'd done for her. It only intensified her adoration for the guy—even though she knew he'd probably end up only pitying her, to keep her at arm's length as the granny-sitter.

But in this one minuscule moment, there were no imperfections in the world, just mother nature's beauty she held in the palms of her hands.

'It's stunning. Thank you.' With her fingertip, she traced the veins along the petals' outer edges, tickling their silky-smooth insides, where its vibrant pink glowed to its sun-yellow feathery stamen that surrounded the seed pod core to make up the sacred lotus.

Luke casually cleaned his pocketknife before sliding it back into the sheath. 'We used to have our own private lotus garden. It had many varieties, even the rare blue lotus.'

What she'd give to see that. 'Is that the lake Esther mentioned?'

'More like a fancy dam.' Luke picked up a fishing rod and secured the lure on the end, then effortlessly cast it behind them as the boat slowly drifted along an unseen current. 'Dad had barra and red claw in it. We even made this small dock for our rowboat. It's where he'd teach me to swim and fish in a place free from crocodiles.'

'Sounds like fun.'

'It was.' He gave a soft smile. The lines on his forehead were gone, and his shoulders relaxed as he gazed at the water, watching the fishing line following behind the boat. It was a delicious look on him, perhaps from a fond memory. 'Some nights, Dad would take Mum out there, with bottles of wine and a basket of nibblies. He'd have me light up the candles that we'd line up along the dock. As a kid I didn't get why they'd just sit there in the dark in that rowboat to stare up at the stars. But now I do ...'

It sounded perfectly romantic. 'What happened to the dam?'

He sniffed, straightening in his seat, with one hand on the steering wheel, the other holding the rod, his brow creased. 'With no crops to water, Dad turned off the bore and it soon became a mosquito haven. We bulldozed one side of it.' He sighed, with his eyes swimming with a sadness that reflected the beauty of the world that surrounded them. 'It was the final straw for Dad, especially when he'd learned that our land had lost its value because of the banana freckle disease we never had.'

Again, he shifted in his seat, tugging on the rod to make the fishing line jig as they trolled the waters. 'It would have broken Gran's heart to sell the place, because there has always been a Bennett at Anaborro Downs. So, I bought out Dad, so he could semi-retire to Queensland and drive trucks through suburbia.' His jaw twitched as if to contain his disappointment.

'Will you ever grow anything at Anaborro Downs?'

'I'll never grow bananas again. I keep thinking I'll do something every dry season, but then the fishing is on, and I'm busy on the water or at the bottle shop. And then there's Gran ...' His brow ruffled, as he peered over his shoulder in the direction of his home.

With so many responsibilities, it was easy to understand why Luke went fishing—it was his escape.

And why not? It was beautiful out here.

Jordi swivelled in her seat, taking in the scenery. There were no buildings, no cars, no people, not even a phone tower in sight. Only an enormous sky and a sea of pink lotus flowers smack bang in the middle of the outback. She'd never realised something like this could ever exist, and had never felt more relaxed than in this moment.

'Hey, reel this in for me.' Luke held out his fishing rod to her, his attention on something on the other side of the boat.

'What are you doing?' With her lotus flower safely tucked away in the corner, she clumsily reeled in his line, damp from the water. But the reel was so smooth the way it effortlessly rolled up the nearly invisible fishing line—when suddenly the fishing lure flew free from the water.

'Watch that.' Luke used his arm to deflect the line that wrapped around the sleeve of his fishing shirt. 'There are nine hooks on this lure, hoping to get a good jag.' He untangled it off his shirt to clip the lethal hooks into the eye of the rod.

His fishing language was hard to decipher.

'Now sit there and don't move. I'm going to see if I can't get you a shot at something very few people get to experience. Consider it a part of the tour.'

How could he top this scenery alone?

She slid his rod into its holder where many others stood like a knight's jousting sticks ready for battle.

The fishing lures they used for bait were funny-looking plastic fish with weird colours, covered in spiky hooks. And Luke had two tackle boxes full of them, all with names such as hard bodies, spinners, frogs, rubbers, hardnose, divers, gutter masters, rattlers and more. He'd explained how each one was designed for a special way of swimming, jagging, running, or spinning through the water. Along with the electronic underwater sonar he called the fish finder, somehow the art of fishing was much more of a science than a sport.

At the front of the boat, Luke carefully gathered the cast net in his hands, keeping it neatly coiled, he kept a steady stance ready for action.

The veins of his muscular forearms became more pronounced as he clenched the centre point of the net in one hand. The remaining net gathered like a curtain in his other hand to drape over his strong fingers. His jaw tightened while his eyes narrowed their focus, his breathing slowed as the power of the hunter emanated in the air. Powerful. Lethal. And beautiful.

As if in her own private museum, holding her breath to admire his stature, the seconds ticked by.

Then his arms shot out in a fluid motion, propelling the net outward, to launch itself clear over the water.

The net gracefully arced through the air, its circular shape flared open the way a cream petunia spreads its petals. It fell across the water like rain, to sink and capture what was underneath.

Using its attached rope, Luke's biceps pumped as he dragged in the cast net with a cheeky grin. 'You're either going to hate me or love me, but you might want to keep your feet off the floor for a second.'

She hugged her knees, keen to see what he'd caught.

With a wash of river water, he dropped the net onto the boat's floor with a heavy thud. Something inside it wriggled and thumped on the floor. With his back to her, Luke struggled for a moment before digging around the toolbox to grab a roll of grey duct tape. The crackly shredding sound of thick tape being dragged off its roll echoed around them. 'Here.'

'No. Way.' She stood on her chair as if he'd let a mouse loose on the boat.

'It won't bite. I've taped its snout.' Just like she did with her flower deliveries, Luke held out a baby crocodile, about the size of a small dog. 'It's a snapping handbag.'

'No, that's a crocodile. Right?'

'We call it that because they make fancy shoes and bags for fancy overseas dress designers out of crocodile skin. You can hold it.'

Luke gently nudged her to sit down and placed the baby crocodile in her lap, where it settled.

Jordi tenderly ran her fingers over its skin, marvelling at the remarkable texture of small, raised, bumpy ridges that ran down its spine, where uniform oval-shaped scales interlocked with one another like a puzzle. Its colours were a blend earthy olive greens, browns, and greys to provide a carefully crafted camouflage suit. But its unique eyes were made up of a dark black iris with slit-shaped pupils. 'I can't believe something this small gets so big and deadly.'

Luke crouched beside her, keeping a steady hand on the animal. 'If this little guy sticks with his mother, she'll watch over him until he's old enough to fend for himself to become a master hunter, if he survives puberty.'

The hairs on her neck spiked as her eyes darted to the flood plains. 'Where's the mother?' She whispered.

He grinned. 'Around. She'll be starting to worry about him.'

'How? I mean, do they feel?'

'Joy, love, affection.'

'Yeah …' She swallowed.

'Sure. They fiercely look after their young. And they're sociable, too. But never forget they're very deadly creatures.'

'So, they'd have no predators.'

'This little guy has plenty. At this size they often get eaten by goannas, birds, fish, other crocodiles, and feral pigs. If he matures, he'll have to compete for his own territory and that's often a fight to the death. In the meantime, he's safe for a while with a billabong full of fish and his mum watching over him.' He gently stroked the baby crocodile. 'Want me to take a photo?'

'That's okay. I don't do social media or selfies.'

'What about to show your sister?'

'Sure. Nat would like that.' Even if she felt like a fool, she smiled, holding the baby crocodile. Then Luke removed the tape from the crocodile's snout, and she squealed in delight as they let it free, where it quickly disappeared into the water like a fish.

But the day just got better as Luke shared his knowledge of bush tucker, Dreamtime stories, tales of past fishing expeditions and of the wildlife. She really wasn't that fussed about fishing, not while on this amazing tour of a lifetime.

'Look …' He switched off the boat's engine to point at the

water. 'My dad called them river ghosts.'

'What are they?' She leaned closer to the water, which was so pristinely clear her shadow formed on the white river sand.

'Freshwater whiprays.'

A family of five whiprays floated just below the surface where water reeds grew amongst the wild lotuses. Their broad, flattened pectoral fins undulated in a wavelike motion, giving them an almost ethereal appearance of gliding underwater. It was mesmerising to watch them curiously swim around the boat, she leaned closer to not miss their silent underwater dance while Luke gently held her shoulder.

'They're beautiful.' And so peaceful to watch as they floated the way a piece of paper slowly falls in the air.

'Alice, the local park ranger, was telling me that breed of freshwater ray is only found in northern waters. Not much is known about them, but they're my lucky charm.'

'Your what?' She giggled, getting back in her seat.

'Some fishermen have their lucky lures, or lucky hats or favourite fishing shirt.' He playfully flicked at the colourful shirt she was wearing, making her smile widen.

And she didn't even flinch. Not once.

'Whenever I see one of those whiprays, I know things are going to work out. So, my little angelfish, it's time you caught a fish.'

He handed her a rod and showed her how to cast. It didn't go well. She created a bird's nest of bunched up, tangled line, choking the reel. She then got the lures snagged or lost and almost gave up.

But Luke was patient, refusing to let her quit.

Suddenly, *whack!* Something hit her line hard, like a freight train. 'WHAT IS HAPPENING!'

The reel whirled, the rod bent, and she was leaning back as if pulling on a whale.

'You're on!'

'On what? Besides standing on a rocking boat.'

'You've got a barra on the line.'

'What do I do?'

'Use your weight. Sit in the chair and put your feet on the hull, lean back and pull on the rod.' Luke guided her to her seat, putting her body into position like she was a living doll. 'Then, as you lean forward, you reel it in. Let the power of the water and your body weight work for you. If it's a barra, it'll fight you. It's what they're famous for.'

Luke never interfered. He just stood beside her, coaching her as she began reeling in whatever gargantuan underwater creature was on the end of her line.

'Are you sure it's a fish and not a sunken boat?' It was heavy, whatever it was, forcing her to put everything into the fight.

'Yeah, I'm sure.' Luke pointed to the water where a massive fish broke through the silvery surface to leap high into the air. Its body scales shone like a rainbow, flicking water off its tail to sparkle like diamonds under the sun.

'It's trying to drop the lure. Keep reeling it in. Don't lose the tension or it'll dive under rocks and snag you.' Luke's voice had a sense of urgency to it.

'How can I remember all that?' She just kept on reeling in the wet line as the fish fought harder, while her sweaty hands struggled to hold the rod.

'Well, remember this.' He leaned closer to her, pointing to the fish. 'Whenever anything splashes around in the water like that fish is doing, it attracts the crocodiles. So, unless you want to lose it, reel it in faster.'

Her muscles ached, her shoulders burned, the sweat streamed down her face, as she kept reeling in the line as fast as she could.

'Keep going, don't stop, you're wearing it out. Be sure to always keep that line taut or you'll lose it.'

She listened without responding, her hand beating the handle like it was the end of a whisk, as she pulled the line tight, the rod flexing as the fish fought constantly.

Finally, Luke picked up a landing net and scooped the silver fish from the water, landing it on the boat with a much heavier thud than the baby crocodile. It was huge. 'That's a keeper. Well done, Jordi.'

Her eyes widened at the sheer size of the beast. That she, little Jordi, managed to wrestle and reel it in from the water, was amazing.

'I did it.' Her smile full as her heartbeat pounded with the adrenaline fuelling her bloodstream, she hugged him. Then he hugged her, and the boat barely rocked beneath their feet. She'd just taken on a beast and won, and she wanted the world to know all about it.

'You should be so proud of yourself.' He kissed her forehead, and she lifted her head, matching his smile.

Only to pause.

The air filled with static electricity and time stood still, as if the world took a deep breath.

Was he going to kiss her?

On her toes, she leaned closer, getting wrapped up in his aroma of vanilla, denim and leather, and after winning a battle with the beast she wanted to kiss her hero. Wait, she was the hero here.

Luke stepped back, breaking the connection, to inspect the fish flapping on the floor of the boat. 'It's a keeper.'

She tried to hide her disappointment. Even if she always knew she'd just be a horror story in disguise when it came to men. It was better to just stay as friends and not hope for more, because there was no way someone like Luke would ever be interested in her.

She grabbed her water bottle and took a long thirsty drink to douse her desires.

'How do you tell if it's a *keeper*?' She'd heard him use that word before.

'If a barra is over the legal size limit, which is fifty-five centimetres, you get to keep it. It's a brilliant catch for your first fish.'

'What do I do with it?'

'We'll take photos and then take it home for dinner and put some in the freezer.'

'Mitchell will love it.'

'Who?' His smile faltered.

'My brother-in-law. Mitchell is always cooking fish at home.' The large fish flapped hard against the boat floor like it was tapping out a rhythm, with its streamlined body so smooth. Unlike the crocodile scales, the barramundi scales were round and somewhat iridescent, reflecting the sunlight. 'Those spikes look sharp on its fin.'

'They are.' He put his foot on the fish, dragging out his pocketknife again. He flicked open a thin needle-like blade, then with a quick flick at the fish, it became still.

'What did you do?'

'Iki jime.'

'Huh?'

'I spiked the fish brain. It's the most humane way to euthanise them, so they don't stress out from suffocation.' Once again, he cleaned his pocketknife to return it back into its sheath. 'Now, get up here and hold your prize. And you can use your new gift I bought you.'

'You bought me a present?' Romantic hope set off a warm cyclonic swirl in her belly, sending tingles across her skin. She tilted her head as he bent down to the hatch, giving her the most exquisite view of his beautiful butt.

He opened the front hatch and removed a small pouch. 'You can use it now.'

It was heavy and made of a nylon mesh pocket. She pulled back on the Velcro and a heavy metal tool landed in her hand. 'A pocketknife?' It wasn't very romantic at all.

'I like to call them a fisherman's friend. I never get into the boat without one.' He helped her open the pocketknife to the long-nosed pliers. 'You use this to hold up your fish and not get spiked by the fins, as fresh fish scales are slippery. Up you go, smile for the camera.'

At the front of the boat, she struggled to hold her first fish, which was nearly a metre long and probably weighed twenty kilos. It was heavier than the freight boxes she regularly loaded and unloaded.

But this was something different. Surrounded by the open air, with a large lagoon full of pink lotus flowers, holding her first fish.

She now understood why people went fishing. It was that hunter-gatherer instinct, that primal need to put food on the table. But it was also the connection to nature that surrounded them, and the adventure that came with it to get here. There was the challenge and the patience to focus, while relaxing at the same time, along with a sense of camaraderie shared while stuck in the confines of a boat to create a memory she'd keep for the rest of her life.

She smiled so wide her cheeks ached. She couldn't stop and didn't want to stop smiling. But it was Luke's smile that made her smile even more, filling her with pure joy and gratitude that he'd given her this moment she'd truly cherish. She'd do anything for him.

Even though Luke saw it as a business deal, he'd just cemented their granny-sitting deal.

Seventeen

'**W**here are we going now?' Jordi looked good behind the wheel of Luke's boat. Her smile had not dimmed, not once since she'd caught her fish. It was as if she'd found the thrill of the hunt, and his prize was the gift of finding her true smile. Holy mackerel, it was pretty.

'We'll swap seats.' Luke playfully tapped her cute butt as she skipped to her seat. 'Hold on.' He pushed the throttle and his boat roared to swing wide into the main river run and head upstream. 'You need to celebrate your first fish.' And he had a reason to celebrate helping a fishing virgin catch a prize.

'Out here?' She playfully scoffed as if he was on some happy drug.

It was infectious being around her when she was like this. No wonder Esther enjoyed hanging around Jordi.

'There. At Goat Island.' He nodded at a tall wooden structure, built on an island of rocks in the middle of the river, with a slim boardwalk stretching over the water to meet the land. The wall of windows reflected the sun, with its front deck offering a grand view of the river where a few fishos had gathered. He docked his boat parallel to the floating pier that shifted with the tide.

'Why are we here?'

'It's where fishos come to brag about their catches for the day. And, Angelfish, you have every right to brag.' He hauled her fish from his icebox and carried it up the stairs. 'Come on.'

She pulled down her shirtsleeves to cover her hands, brushing down her hair to hide her neck and face. He hated how she did that. Especially when her smile faltered.

'I want to see how heavy this thing is.' He led them up the gangway to the main deck. 'Hey, Two-dollar Darryl?' he called out to the Aboriginal man behind the bar. 'You might want to get that polaroid camera out, because we've got one for the Virgins' Board.'

Two-dollar Darryl eagerly greeted them, with his white teeth a stark contrast to his dark skin and grey flecks in his black curls. 'Who caught that?'

'This is Jordi's first fish on her first fishing trip.' Luke heaved Jordi's barra onto a sturdy hook for the overhead scale. It came in at a whopping thirty-two kilos.

Damn, she did good. 'Well done, Angelfish.' He even patted her shoulder, and she let him as her eyes widened at the scale holding her fish.

'I didn't think they got that big.'

'They get bigger,' he whispered into her ear, delighting in the goosebumps spreading down her neck, and the shy smile she gave him as if he'd tickled her.

'Well done, Miss. Well done.' Darryl inspected the fish, like he did every fish that came into this place. 'You've earned a shout and pic for the board. You stay there, Miss. There's a Virgin Special coming right up.'

'And a beer for the skipper, too.' Luke playfully nudged Jordi's arm as a few of the other fishos came forward to inspect the fish. 'Relax, Jordi, and celebrate.'

'What is this place?'

'The Sandfly Saloon. It's a fisherman's bar. I had my first drink here with my dad when I caught my first legitimate fish. I was seven when I drank my Virgin Special. Dad said it's the modern fisherman's form of blooding when you go on a hunt.'

He followed her gaze as she looked over the once-rustic sly saloon, where its sunburnt walls were freshly painted.

Inside there wasn't a single cobweb on the shark teeth and the large sawfish on display as if in a fisherman's museum. 'This place has had a makeover.'

She looked around, unsure. 'I'm not going to be sacrificed to some fishing god, forced to drink barra blood, am I?'

A deep belly laugh erupted from his chest. Her sense of humour was refreshingly unexpected. He'd love to see more of it.

Pity she didn't get the joke. It had to be such a different world for a florist.

'Relax, it's all in good fun.' He rubbed her lower back, hoping she would.

Darryl soon returned with a tray of shot glasses. 'Here you go, miss.'

'I shouldn't—'

'You have to, Miss. It's tradition.' Darryl put the shot glass into Jordi's hand, not giving her a choice, then passed Luke a glass, and one for himself. Clearing his throat, he solemnly said, 'May the waters bless you and your fish freezer be forever full. Well done on your first fish, Miss.' He clinked her glass and tossed his back. Luke did the same.

Poor Jordi coughed at the hard liquor. 'I'm not much of a drinker.'

If she didn't drink, then why did she keep visiting him in the bottle shop to buy booze?

With beer in hand, he leaned his hip against the wooden railing as Darryl made Jordi stand beside her fish while he took a photo with his polaroid camera.

Then Darryl dragged Jordi inside, to show her the spot she'd earned on the Virgins' Board.

Luke may have seen and felt pride many times, but it was an honour to witness the deepest pride of the unspoken kind, the one that came from the heart where words couldn't fully express it. He could see it in Jordi's upright posture and the shine in her eyes. Hell, he felt that pride swell inside his chest, swallowing down the lump in his throat with the need to suddenly break out in applause for her.

Watching Jordi's pride in seeing her face among the many men, women, children—even his own mugshot that stood among his friends, now adults—who'd come to Sandfly to celebrate their first fish, it was a moment he'd cherish. Jordi was part of the bigger picture now, making her a part of something special, which is what this town did.

But he'd done it too, the deal was set for Jordi to granny-sit so he could enter the fishing competition. And if he'd managed to help a fishing virgin, like Jordi, haul in a points-winning fish, that gave him the confidence of not only winning the Barra Classic, but he'd proved he could take anyone out fishing and show them a good time.

'Bottle Shop Luke, you're here.' Felix approached in stylish linen slacks, walking like a man on a runway in Paris and not the floorboards of the Sandfly Saloon, where most of the punters wore thongs, fishing shirts, and shorts, stinking of sweat, sunscreen, and fish.

'Hey, it's Felix from Sydney. Or should I be calling you neighbour?' He shook hands with the neighbour.

'I'm never home these days, being so busy with the preparations for this fishing competition. But Darryl did tell me how you used to visit for the blues and jazz nights. We're going to have one on the rich-fish-competition nights.'

'That sounds good.' But then he sighed. 'I can't.'

'Why not?'

'Esther, my grandmother.'

'I said I'll look after her.' Jordi stood beside him, with a touch of sunburn across her nose, bringing out her dainty scatterings of pale blemishes that didn't darken like freckles. But they were still cute.

'Jordi, this is our new neighbour, Felix.' Did he say *our*? He meant *his*. No, *ours*, because he shared the place with Esther.

'So is it true you play the piano?' Felix asked Luke.

'Play! Ha. Bottle Shop Luke and Grandma Esther would have this place rocking on jazz and blues nights,' Two-dollar Darryl said to Jordi and Felix.

Luke scoffed. 'Did not.'

'You could jam with them keys on the piano since you were a lad. No offence there, boss man. You may know show tunes, but Luke and his grandma, they'd have this place jiving with Luke playin' that piano, and his grandma singing.'

'Why did you stop?' Felix asked Luke.

'The piano lost a key and Gran struggles with the stairs.' It was too dangerous for Esther, especially on the floating deck that shifted with the incoming bow waves.

'We found that lost piano key,' said Darryl, 'which means you can come back and play.'

'I didn't know you played piano,' Jordi commented.

'Gran taught me.' Luke shrugged off the pressure to perform. He'd rather go fishing than play piano.

'Makes sense when you have a grand piano in the Lodge.'

'Nooo.' Felix's eyes were enormous. 'Do you really have a full-sized grand piano—out here?'

'It's out of tune.'

'I'll tune it.' Felix raised his hand in the air, bobbing his head up and down.

'You know, you might win Gran's approval if you did. Do you make cocktails too?' He was hoping to find a way to curb his grandmother's somewhat bitter behaviour to the new neighbour.

'Pfft. Do crocodiles bask in this river? Is the outback dust red?'

'That'd be a big yes,' said Darryl, nudging Felix. 'He makes 'em all the time. Even made us a new one called the Sandfly Shaker. You should try it, Miss.'

'Bring your grandma,' said Felix.

'You can bring her. You have road access to this place, not me.' Because no one drove through the front gate to the Peddler's property where their fence signs said: *we'll shoot first then feed you to the crocodiles before asking questions* to deter trespassers.

Old Pop Peddler had been notorious for carrying a

machete on one side of his belt, with his sawn-off shotgun swinging on his hip like a western cowboy. And Wren, the new long-lost Peddler, was now married to the town's top cop, who'd shot the last trespasser who'd dared to enter the Peddler property without permission!

Yeah, living in the Northern Territory was like living in the Wild West. But Felix was Wren's BFF, so he could drive on their property without fear.

'Play something. Please?' Jordi asked.

'I'll create a cocktail after you,' said Felix.

Luke narrowed his eyes at the pair trying to hustle the hustler. 'Name a cocktail after my grandmother, Esther, and I will.'

'Deal.' Felix nodded gleefully, but it was Jordi's nod that meant more to him.

How the heck did he get talked into this? Jordi—who never touched people—led him by the hand to the upright piano. Lifting the lid, he saw the once stained and off-white keys were now white. 'It's been a while.'

'I'll help ...' Darryl pulled out his harmonica and blasted the air with a horrid noise. A few fishermen on the deck winced, while others cheered, raising their beers.

Luke grinned, playfully slamming on the keys. All awkwardness was soon gone as his fingers glided across the keyboard to start a blues riff Darryl had taught him the first time he'd sat at the Sandfly's piano. Back then, his dad leaned against the bar beside his grandfather, celebrating the victory of Luke's first fish.

It had become common to have Two-dollar Darryl beside him, sharing the same piano stool where his legs grew longer over the years, to play tunes such as *My Heavy Heart Blues*, to the harmonica singing Daryl's favourite tune: *Lickity Split*.

It came naturally playing with Darryl, and when the last note hung in the air his fingers hovered over the black and white keys. A bead of sweat trickled down his face, and he looked up. Jordi clapped with the rest of them, but she smiled at him. Only this time, it was a different smile he'd never seen before. It was a soft smile, with glistening eyes, and all he saw was Jordi.

'Well done, Master Luke. You've still got it.' Darryl patted him heartily on the back, breaking that connection he had with Jordi.

Luke reached for his beer to wash down the feeling of foolishness for letting Jordi see him like this.

Luke only played when he had a belly full of beer, hanging around the usual fishos, who didn't care if he missed a few notes, playing until the sun rose on another day. It never mattered to his Gran, or even his mother, who would be demanding he keep playing so they could dance with his father across the floorboards of the Sandfly Saloon.

But now, with his parents on the far side of the country, the responsibilities of being an adult seemed to steal all the fun, as he noted the time. 'We'd better get back to Gran.'

Eighteen

uke was charming, fearless, adventurous, chivalrous, kind, cunning and caring, and he could play the piano. He was the perfect man.

Jordi couldn't believe he could play the piano so well, easily commanding everyone's attention at the Sandfly, as if he was some superstar of the seas. She felt like she could walk on water, not only from being beside him, but also with her photo on the Virgins' Board, while her fish was being admired by the other fishermen. And that drink Two-dollar Darryl had made her swallow shifted something inside her.

She'd always liked Luke, with a silly secret crush, and her desperate five-minute conversation fixes. Finding any excuse to talk to him in the bottle shop was enough to last her a week of wishful daydreaming that the popular guy might actually like her.

It had become an obsession.

She'd spend all week trying to find more lame excuses to drive through his bottle shop on a Friday to ask for directions to places she was already familiar with. But she did it to have him lean at her van's window, with his aroma of denim, leather and vanilla weaving around her. She'd then lean over her steering wheel to admire his confident swagger in his jeans as he'd fetch her drinks from the assorted fridges. He'd then slide them into the esky she kept among her floral arrangements, where he'd tap on the name cards of the people he knew and where to find them.

But this week it had been different.

All week, Luke kept texting or ringing her about this fishing 'date'. Strangely this part, going to a bar for a drink, actually felt like a date.

The Sandfly Saloon wasn't a swanky bar, filled with candles or dim lights to create a romantic mood. It was a fishing bar, with fishing nets lining the ceiling, and a grand view of crocodiles basking on the nearby riverbanks. A whole new world she'd never been privy to before, and she was having the best time ever—all because of Luke.

'We'll take this fish home to Gran.' Luke's biceps tightened as he lifted her fish off Sandfly's hook. 'You wait until she sees it. She'll want us to celebrate the hunt Bennett style.'

Strangely, she couldn't wait to see what Esther thought of her fish, too. 'Will we be having fish for dinner?'

'You bet. You'll have to clean and cook it, though.'

She pulled a face.

He gave a deep chuckle that made her want to smile like some goofball. 'It's all part of the process, especially your first fish. It's easy. I'll show you. We can bag up the fillets and freeze them tonight, so you can take them back to your family.'

Luke was always thinking of others. Underneath the bravado, Luke really cared about people. He wasn't just about selling booze in the bottle shop, he was selling flowers to help his customers create happy homes, or finding solutions to people's problems—like creating a safe space for people to park their boats. But he also genuinely listened to people. Luke was a motivator, a consoler, a negotiator, an organiser, and a hustler. Did that make Luke a *keeper*, too?

It was easy to see why he was so popular with this fishing crowd, that she was struggling to stop herself from falling deeply, madly, and foolishly in love with the guy.

'Wait there, I'll put this fish away first.' With the fish safely stowed on board in ice, he cleaned his hands. 'Okay, your turn.'

Ever the gentleman, Luke held her hand to help her climb

on board. She had yet to get her sea legs on a boat that shifted like a surfboard. At times, she'd worried it'd tip on its side.

Safely in her seat, she scooped up the pink lotus. She wanted to hug it like the man who'd given it to her.

'So where did you steal that fish from?' It was Dom climbing down the stairs, landing with a thud on the shifting pontoon that sloshed the water to send a scattering of ripples over the river's surface. 'Did you buy that fish from Two-dollar-Darryl?'

'Where's your prize fish to get weighed at the bar?'

'I'm saving it for the Barra Classic, where my name will be on that trophy and that million-dollar barra will buy me a new chopper to run fishing tours.' Dom slid into the driver's seat of his sleek fishing boat.

Luke's scowl was dark. 'Since when?'

'If a cowboy like you thinks he can run fishing tours, why can't I? Or is that a con to get the dates on your boat?' Dom tossed his thumb at Jordi. 'You're not the first female on his boat, and you won't be the last. So don't get too attached, sweetheart. Everyone knows Luke goes through women faster than bait used on a fleet of tuna boats.'

'Do you mind?' Luke's frown was ferocious, with fists curled at his sides.

Jordi tucked her hands into her shirt sleeves, holding her large lotus flower in her lap. She wanted to hide.

Dom was right. Luke had this easy way with women, with the reputation as a man who could sweet-talk anyone into anything. The only reason he was talking to her was because he needed a granny-sitter and to test his skills for running his fishing tour operations.

How silly of her to think he'd ever be attracted to her—or that any male would, for that matter. After all, she was the scarred beast that scared children away from her family's flower store.

On the dock, Luke unwound the boat's anchoring ropes. 'Don't listen to him, Jordi. Dom's just being a prize dick.'

Too late.

Dom laughed, backing his boat away from the dock. He then gunned his twin outboard engines to create a massive rooster's comb–sized wave. Luke ducked to miss it, but it completely washed over the top of the boat.

Jordi squealed as she stood in a rush, drenched from head to toe, with her pink lotus flung from her lap to splash into the water and sink out of sight.

'You low-life piece of scum. I'll have your head for that!' Standing on the dry dock, Luke waved his fist at Dom, who only laughed as he tapped the brim of his white cowboy hat.

Luke jumped onto the boat and rummaged around for a towel. 'Here, take this. Are you okay?'

She felt every bit the drowned rat, as the fresh water blended with the sunscreen to sting her eyes. Her high mood had sunk like her flower plunging to the deep dark shadows of the crocodile-infested river. 'Can we just go?' Dom's words had been the wake-up call she needed to not fall into some romantic fantasy over Luke. It would never happen. Not with a girl like her.

Nineteen

The Barra Bandit, safely tucked under its protective boat cover, rested on its trailer that rattled behind Luke's ute, sending a huge plume of red dust into the clear skies, covering the three towering roadside signs advertising the local stores, as they passed them heading for home.

Seated in the passenger seat, Jordi had hardly spoken since Dom had swamped her with river water. He'd seen her self-esteem, along with her smile, disappear with that sinking lotus flower he'd given her. It damned near broke his heart.

The next time he saw Dom he was going to punch that prick in the mouth for what he'd done to Jordi. No, he was going to tie that cretin behind his boat like a lump of bait and drag his sorry arse down the river where the largest swamp puppies roamed.

He raked fingers through his windblown hair to calm himself down. He'd never been so jacked-up over an incident. Normally, he'd laugh it off. But this—this was war for what Dom had done to Jordi. No one messed with his family and got away with it.

Oi, pull back on the bait, mate? Was Jordi family?

That thought made him shuffle in his seat, his grip tightening on the steering wheel, as he sneakily peeked at Jordi.

With her head leaning against the passenger window, she watched the world pass them by. Her lean legs were tanned from today, bringing out the colour of her flashy green toenail polish. He hadn't expected that of her.

Jordi kept her fingernails short and free from polish and didn't wear any form of jewellery. Normally she'd wear jeans and her work shirt buttoned to her chin, with the cuffs from the long sleeves hiding her hands.

But her heavenly soft and subtle blended scent reminded him of fields of flowers swaying gently under a summer's cool breeze. A time when ice cubes clinked against tall glasses, as you settled back in the wicker chairs scattered along the Lodge's verandah.

He liked sunrises over the waters, allowing him to reset on a new day. But he adored sunsets more. Especially those that he'd shared with Jordi—even though she didn't know it. Those moments where his shadow stretched long over the bottle shop's cemented driveway, he'd face a world of fire giving him a moment of peace. He'd spot Jordi, working at the pub's kitchen sinks, stopping to admire the sunset too, where under a colour-soaked sky it became a special spotlight that only highlighted her natural beauty. And she was flawless.

'What's that?' Jordi sat taller in the passenger seat, pointing towards the farm. 'Is that smoke?'

He leaned over the steering wheel, as his frown deepened. 'Aw, hell no. Hold on.' He gunned through the gears, racing down the dirt road. A fast corner had him sliding into the driveway of Anaborro Downs, where smoke filled the air in thick dark grey sheets.

Out of the ute, he searched for the source as billowing smoke turned black somewhere in the field. How? When he'd kept the property free from all fire hazards.

'There.' Jordi pointed across the field to the fence line. 'It's Esther, by her bathtub.'

His heart stopped, as liquid ice rushed through his veins at the sight of his grandmother waving away at the thick smoke. It was his greatest fear—his family and his home were in trouble.

'Jordi, get my grandmother out of there. I'll get the tractor.' Doing what he'd once trained so hard for, Luke ran for the shed. He jiggled through his car keys and jumped into the tractor's seat. In a matter of moments, it roared to life. With a hearty chug of diesel smoke spewing out of the exhaust stack, he flicked the lever to lift the tractor's front bucket, then drove it out of the shed.

A normal person would run from a blaze, but Luke put his foot flat on the pedal and the tractor's large tyres chewed up the paddock's soil, heading straight for the fire roaring beside his grandmother.

Twenty

Jordi was running towards Esther when a roaring flash of ferocious flames leapt high, spreading the billowing smoke around her. Jordi gasped, skidding to a stop. The heat and crackle of the flames made her walk backwards until she froze. She couldn't run. She couldn't move. She couldn't even breathe.

Blue-tipped, gold and orange flames leapt and danced several feet into the air, with its sparks spiralling higher to get lost in the thick, churning smoke. An intense heat radiated from the drum, making the surrounding air shimmer and distort from the toxic haze that was thick and acrid, making her eyes water and blur. Even with the heightened sense of danger, she still couldn't move, trapped by her fear.

Standing well away from the fire, she could still feel those flames licking across her skin, as the memory of the horrific charred smell of burning flesh scorched her sinuses. She struggled to breathe, with her heart hammering in her ears.

'*Gran, get over to Jordi.*' Luke steered the tractor across the paddock.

Somehow Luke's voice snapped her out of her trance, and she sprinted to where Esther stood, cuddling her carpetbag. 'Come on, Esther. Let's get to safety.' She dragged the elderly woman towards the ute.

'I was only heating the bath.' Esther's tiara and hair were covered in black soot that smeared across her face, as sweat streaks created track marks down her cheeks. 'It just took off on me.'

'Are you okay?' Jordi checked over Esther, who was heaving for air.

'I don't know what happened.' Esther trembled as she held Jordi's hand, hugging her carpetbag. Her wild eyes stared at the fire at the end of the field. 'Luke is going to be so mad at me. He's very particular about fires. Luke used to be a firefighter.'

'I didn't know that.' She'd just assumed he was a farmer, who went fishing and worked in a bottle shop. What made him stop?

'Esther, let's get you to the boat. There's water there.' Even though they were well away from that horrendous smoke, noxious fumes wafted from the drum, carrying an overpowering odour of burning plastic, rubber, and chemicals that made her want to gag.

Pulling out a hose that was attached to the massive water tank on the back of the tractor, Luke started spraying large forceful streams of water.

But the fire roared and hissed, its flames stubbornly resisting the onslaught of water. They flickered erratically with their orange tongues lashing out, to hiss with steam. The smoke doubled in thickness, churning swirls from black to grey as if refusing to surrender, but Luke forced it back down into the old forty-four-gallon drum.

Even as the last of the flames died down, billowing black clouds of putrid smoke poured out of the metal drum and darkened the sky.

Holding her shirt over her mouth, she feared for Luke. Digging around in the boat, she found a cloth. 'Cover your mouth and nose, Esther.'

Jordi squinted through the churning smoke as fear for Luke rose to a whole new level. Clutching on to Esther, she desperately searched the smoke to find him.

Bursting through the smoky barrier, with his T-shirt covering his nose and mouth, Luke jumped into the tractor's seat. He gunned the tractor's engine, and activated the large bucket on the front, scooping up a pile of red dirt, he dumped it over the top of the drum, the bathtub, and wicker chairs, instantly dousing the smoke. Just like that.

Everyone took a deep breath.

'Are you okay, Esther?' Jordi checked over Esther, who still wore her tiara that didn't sparkle.

'I-I-I didn't mean to.' Esther gasped for air as tears trickled down her cheeks.

'Please tell me you're okay?' Jordi checked Esther's skin. Her arms, neck and face were pink, but not burnt. But her breathing was erratic.

'*What the hell do you think you were doing, Gran?*' An angry vein ticked on Luke's temple as the dust kicked up with each stride. 'You were burning plastic. That's toxic smoke.'

'I was only burning some rubbish.'

'Why?'

'To heat the water for my bathtub.'

'It's thirty-seven degrees, Gran.' He loomed over her.

Esther hugged her carpetbag like a little child, with tears and sweat streaming down her face. But she was panting for air.

'Stop it, Luke.' Jordi pushed him away from Esther. 'Calm down. It's over.'

'Don't tell me what I can and can't do. Not when she started a fire!' He pointed at Esther.

'Luke!' Jordi gripped his shirt, forcing him to look at her. 'Esther needs to go to the hospital.'

Deep remorse washed over Luke, instantly defusing his anger. 'What?'

'You said it was toxic smoke—Esther's struggling to breathe.'

His eyes widened in horror as he stepped back.

'Come on, Esther, take deep breaths or you'll go into shock.' Jordi rubbed slow circles against Esther's back. 'Breathe in … and out. Come on, Esther, do it with me.' Even though Esther was trying, her heart rate wasn't slowing down.

It was Jordi's turn to let the fear show as she turned to Luke for help. 'Her heart rate isn't slowing down and there's a rattle in her chest.'

Esther started coughing so hard she doubled over.

'Aw, crap. Gran.' Luke held his grandmother, who was gagging.

'We'll take my van. I'll drive, you sit in the back with Esther.'

Twenty-one

'**I** shouldn't have left her alone.' Luke moaned into his palms, covering his face. His elbows rested on his knees as he sat in one of the world's most uncomfortable plastic chairs in the longest, coldest, crappiest corridor in the history of hospitals. 'I should have never left Gran alone.'

'This isn't your fault.' Jordi rubbed his back.

He'd heard that before.

Which did nothing to appease the guilt and fear he felt for Esther. The longer they waited, the more the dread filled his chest.

'I'm really making a mess of it, aren't I? Maybe Dad's right ...' He got to his feet and paced the wide corridor with its garish floor tiles filled with dots. The ceiling was the same, only with white tiles filled with more dots. What was up with all the dots? They even had dot paintings on the walls. Dots. Dots. Dots.

'About what?'

He rubbed his eyes, feeling the dust and soot against his skin. The stench of smoke reeked in his clothes. 'Maybe Gran should go into a home. But it'd break her heart.' As much as it did his. 'It'd destroy her soul.'

'Can't you hire someone to care for Esther during the day? Like a companion.'

'Dad and I were hoping Mum would take on the job. But she won't. And this war Gran has waged against the neighbours has gone beyond a joke.' He ran fingers through his coarse hair. 'You know, every night I'm checking in on her, to see she's switched off the stove. I've even converted the gas stove to one of those special electric ones that won't burn her. I've put in new taps that make it easier for her to turn them on and off, and thermostatic valves on the hot water taps so she didn't scald herself in the shower. Rails and ramps to help her with any steps. But I've also had to hide the keys to the tractors, trucks, even the ride-on lawnmower. She was okay for a bit, but I can't understand what's gotten into her lately because she's been acting like a big kid.'

'She's lonely.'

He blinked at Jordi's blunt words, bouncing off the walls to ring in his ears. 'Eh?'

'Esther's friends are dying on her. Iris is gone and she's got a new neighbour she doesn't know, as well as losing her ability to visit her friends because she's not allowed to drive anymore. For a woman who loves to socialise, you can tell she's lonely.'

He looked at Jordi. Like, really looked at her, to notice her compassion. Jordi was relating to Gran, revealing a haunting loneliness in her watery eyes.

He sighed, crumbling into his seat in defeat. 'You're right. Gran has always loved an audience. She hated it when Dad closed the Lodge to punters. But then Gran had Iris for her cocktail hour, and we'd go to the blues and jazz nights at the Sandfly, so she could sing again.'

'What does Esther have left besides you and Cecil?'

'Reading to the little kids at the school library. But that's once a week. Gran belongs to these other groups, but I can't drive her because of work.' Sure, Esther had plenty of friends to collect her, but she didn't like to bother anyone, because Bennett business was always their own, not to be broadcast to the world.

'You know, all I want is to see Esther happy and safe, yet it seems like such a battle these days. I'd pay you to stay at the Lodge, but you have work to do ...' In a job that was four hours away.

The hospital's main doors slid open and in walked a man in a crisp fireman's uniform. It was the same uniform Luke had stuffed into a box that lived in the back of his cupboard.

'Luke.' The fire chief nodded.

Dammit, could this day get any worse? Luke wiped his hands down his thighs before standing. 'Chief.'

'Jax is fine.' Jax shook hands with Luke and was introduced to Jordi. 'Take a seat. How's your grandmother?'

'She's with the doctor now.' Luke scowled at the long corridor. The last time he'd been to this hospital was with Esther when they'd come to say goodbye to Iris.

Jordi squeezed his hand. So small yet strong. His scalp prickling at the realisation of how big a thing this was for Jordi. She didn't like anyone touching her. And here she was consoling him, holding his hand.

But he had a much bigger fish to fry, namely the fire chief sitting on his other side. 'Are you here about the fire?'

Jax gave an affirmative nod.

'Gran was burning some rubbish in a drum. It was a contained fire. I put it out with water, then used the tractor to bury it with topsoil.'

'I saw that.'

Luke arched an eyebrow. 'You were quick to get out there.'

'As we're under a total fire ban, I've got a few fire spotters who call at the first sign of smoke. We can never be too careful out here.'

'Yeah, I know …' He'd seen firsthand the devastation fire could cause. This time, he squeezed Jordi's small hand, so glad she was here.

'You aren't going to fine my grandmother for starting a fire during a total fire ban, are you, Chief? Nothing got damaged, nothing got burnt. Just smoke...' Hoping with everything inside his grandmother was okay. That she'd waddle out of that examination room, adjusting her tiara while gripping her carpetbag as she rummaged around for her hipflask, yakking and smiling like she did every time he'd brought her in for her check-ups.

But this time, they'd whisked Gran away in an oxygen mask, as the doctor barked out orders, leaving Luke to stare at a closed door, with Jordi consoling him.

'No,' said Jax. 'I just had to check on the fire. It's a part of my duties, especially when someone has to come to the hospital because of a fire.'

'I understand.' It was part of the job he remembered well.

'Why do you keep a water tank on your tractor?'

'It was a sprayer we used for fertilising the bananas. I turned it into a water tank.' He might not be a fireman anymore, but he made sure they were fire safe on his property and the neighbours.

Well, wasn't that a kick in the teeth, considering his grandmother was here because of a fire!

'You maintain decent firebreaks, I'll give you that.'

Luke barely shrugged, staring at the stupid dots on the floor, but he could feel Jordi watching him.

'I read your file.'

He dropped his head, pulling his hand free from Jordi, to scrub his palms over his face.

'I might go find us a coffee.' Jordi left before he could stop her.

He leaned back, arms crossed over his chest. 'Yeah, and what did you read, Chief?'

'That you're a highly decorated firefighter who got a mention on the Queen's Australia Day list along with a Commonwealth Bravery award, where you didn't want to go to the town's awards ceremony and refused to accept the award.'

He shrugged. 'I was just doing my job.'

'That involved a two-vehicle accident on the highway, where an RV caught fire from their fridge's pilot light.'

Luke had been interviewed by the fire investigators, interrogated by the police, and had assisted various specialists. He'd sat in the coroner's court to listen to their synopsis, the cause and origin, and their detailed logical results, all neatly presented for the coroner. With a lot of technical waffle and scientifically proven evidence, they all concluded that it was an accident.

But it didn't begin to describe what he'd seen, lived, and breathed.

He lifted his heavy head to watch Jordi at the vending machine. What he'd give for her to hug him again, just like she'd hugged him on the boat, celebrating her first fish. Even though it had happened earlier today, it felt like decades ago.

'I read you suffered third-degree burns dragging the only survivor out of a burning car.'

He turned to face Jax, the frown nothing compared to the fire flaring inside his chest. 'What do you want me to say? I didn't have time to save the rest of them. Only one survived.' He'd failed on so many levels that for months afterwards he would wake up soaked in a cold sweat. It took a long, long time for those damned nightmares to stop.

And they stopped the day Jordi drove through his bottle shop that very first time, with her shy smile, asking for directions to deliver flowers. She'd been his angel and didn't even know it.

'It wasn't your fault.'

'So everyone keeps telling me.' But it didn't stop the acidic burn of guilt that ate him alive from the inside.

'You couldn't have done anything to help them,' said Jax. 'And I get it.'

Luke ruffled his forehead, as he sat back against the hard plastic chair that was as uncomfortable as this conversation.

Jax shuffled his workboots, exhaling heavily as he peered up and down the hallway before dropping the volume of his voice as he spoke. 'After years of working for the air force, I joined the city's fire department, where we spent more time attending car accidents than fighting fires. It was brutal, witnessing the carnage of what a car's metal and glass does to the human body, to families, and to the firefighters who were trying to save them.' Jax dropped a heavy hand on Luke's shoulder that was tighter than he realised. 'I'd like it if you'd come visit me sometime ...'

Luke frowned. 'Why?'

'Just to talk. I can't find anywhere in the paperwork about anyone speaking to you about the incident. Which is part of the fire chief's job.'

'The old fire chief was away. His wife was ill.' It was why the fire chief quit—for family. Luke understood that. Heaving in a lungful of air, wishing his grandmother would suddenly traipse down that corridor in her ball gown and gum boots.

'Still, someone from the department should have spoken to you about the incident. Did anyone from the fire department come and see you? Their chaplain?'

'Mate, we live four hours away from the nearest city. What do you reckon?'

'That's what I thought.' Jax lowered himself to meet Luke's eyes. 'That's why I'm offering it to you now. It's just a conversation and, hey, I'll get Lucy to make us some lunch. She's the greatest cook.'

'Why? You don't know me.'

'Because I know what it's like to have an incident stop you from being at your best, letting that burden of failure fester inside. I get it. So, hear me when I say you did everything by the book—nobody could've helped those people who died, but you went above and beyond saving the one person you could save. Otherwise, you would have never received that bravery award.'

'I'm fine.' Even though it felt like the chief had cracked open his shell to peer deep into his chest of secrets, allowing the shame of failure free to blister and infect deep into his skin.

'You're working at the bottle shop. Your farm hasn't had a crop in years. You don't hang out with your old friends—'

'We're all busy.' Surprised Jax had taken such an interest in him.

'You quit the fire department, where everyone tells me how much you used to love it, when you were the station's second-in-command, and the Territory's youngest acting fire chief.' Jax's voice deepened as he leaned in closer. 'And when most people get a bravery award they celebrate—yet you quit the job, refusing to be recognised for your efforts. Can you see the pattern here?'

'I don't have PTSD. Or trauma issues.' But the fire in his chest had him clenching his fists to stop himself from lashing out.

'I didn't say you did.' Jax didn't break eye contact. He didn't even flinch. Built of solid muscle, covered in mean-looking tribal ink, Jax was a fireman who'd take on anything. 'This is something that only first responders go through. I doubt those men in white coats have a name for it—which we all try and avoid—it's why cops drink together in bars after work. In this town, Marcus has drinks out the back of the police station and I hold weekly barbecues for volunteers where we can freely talk without judgement, sharing our situations that we can relate to.'

'What do you want?' Luke gritted down on his teeth.

'Nothing. I just want to help, especially when I can relate to your situation. Because if it hasn't already, today's incident might trigger those issues you haven't dealt with yet.'

'I just put out a fire in my yard. That's it.' But this conversation was bringing up all sorts of junk he wanted to avoid.

But he remembered Jordi freezing in fear. Her expression had been one of pure horror, while hypnotised by the flames.

He also remembered her pushing him back when he was angry. And that took courage for the timid Jordi to do something like that. It showed she wasn't scared of him— even when he was blind with rage, she'd stood up to him. But it also demonstrated how much she cared for his family.

Now, she calmly looked at the paintings that lined the hospital's corridor, the same way she inspected the photos at the Lodge. Luke wanted to stand beside Jordi and not listen to this pile of rotten bait fish spoiling the air. He wanted to hold Jordi's hand and stick to the small talk. Not this.

'Come and see me, anytime, Luke, my door is always

open.' Jax stood and held out his hand.

Luke shook it.

But Jax held it a little longer. 'I have a job vacancy at the station. Your old job, if you want it. I could do with regular days off.'

Luke was at a loss for words.

Yet, he just couldn't get past that feeling of absolute failure. It not only squeezed his chest, but it also rested heavily across his shoulders, weighing him down like a lead fishing sinker that lay forever lost at the bottom of the river. Because when he'd failed, the consequences had been catastrophic.

Twenty-two

'You can't let them keep me here.' Esther gripped the front of Luke's shirt while trying to wriggle off the bed in her hospital room.

'It's just overnight for observations, Gran.' He didn't want to leave Esther like this, not with her pleas tearing strips off his soul.

'They lie. They said that to Iris, too. And we both know she never went home again.'

Didn't that take his fears to a whole new high.

Esther pushed herself off the bed. 'I'm leaving, even if I have to walk home, young man.'

'Gran, *you started a fire!*' Luke's voice was louder than expected. He raked fingers through his hair and gave Jordi an apologetic shrug as he continued to scold his grandmother like a child. 'If we hadn't shown up, what would you have done?'

'I … I …' She sat back on the bed, holding her chest, wheezing.

'Here, the oxygen will help you breathe easier.' Jordi adjusted the oxygen straps around Esther's head. 'I know the mask is annoying, but it helps. Trust me.'

'I have to go back tonight,' Gran said from behind the mask.

'Not gonna happen, Gran, so stop arguing with me.'

'I have to. The rat's here.' She pointed to her large carpetbag, which shifted on the end of her bed.

'What rat?' Jordi peered around the room, looking ready

to jump onto the guest chair.

Gran opened the large carpetbag, letting out the cream-coloured pug, wagging its tail.

'Don't tell me you had that poor thing trapped in your bag this entire time?' Luke scooped up the pug and carried it to the sink, and let the dog eagerly lap up some water.

'The nurses gave the rat water and were playing with him while I was being x-rayed, or was that an ultrasound thingy?'

'Is that why you were taking so long getting examined? While Jordi and I were out in the hallway, worried about you?' Luke put the dog on the bed where it did circles of joy, then snuggled up to Esther. 'I don't believe this, Gran. That's dognapping.'

Jordi burst into a giggle. 'Dognapping?'

Luke struggled to keep a serious face at her cute giggle.

'No, it's not. The rat likes me.' Esther was like a five-year-old, holding the dog as if it was a living doll.

'We can't keep it,' said Luke, playing the part of the big bad parent to his grandmother.

'Why not? It sneaks over all the time.'

'Is that why you're always sitting along the fence? For the dog.'

Esther ignored him, while patting the dog. 'Don't mind Luke. He mustn't have caught any fish to be so cranky.'

'Jordi caught a whopper, Gran, and we were coming home to celebrate the hunt with you before we ended up here.'

'Where's the fish now?'

'On ice, still in the back of the boat.' Catching a glimpse of himself in the mirror, he tried to straighten up his hair that stood up from dirt and soot, while reeking of smoke and fish. He needed a shower.

'Well done, Jordi,' said Gran, ripping off the mask. 'Now I have a reason to go home because we must celebrate the hunt. It's a Bennett tradition.'

'No. You're staying here.' Luke put his hands on Esther's shoulders, forcing her gently back onto the bed, and lowered the oxygen mask over her face.

'We can celebrate tomorrow,' said Jordi. 'You need to rest up.'

'It won't be the same.' Then the oxygen mask muffled Esther's words.

'What?'

Esther pushed up the oxygen mask, letting it sit in the middle of her forehead. 'I'm sorry.' And she was full of remorse. Fidgeting with her fingers, which was rare because Esther had never been a fidgeter. As a kid, she used to slap his hands for fidgeting or not sitting still at the large dining room table at the Lodge. 'I'm sorry, Luke. It was my stupidity for taking a joke too far.'

'Yeah, well, the real joke is on you, because Felix wasn't even home.' Luke crossed his arms over his chest.

Esther arched an eyebrow at him. 'How do you know?'

'Felix was helping Two-dollar Darryl at the Sandfly, where Jordi got the Virgin Special, and her photo on the wall for her fish.'

'I also got to see Luke play the piano.' Jordi shared a shy smile, but there was pride in her eyes—for him?

'So, they've fixed the piano then?' Esther wouldn't even look at him, as she patted the pug.

'Felix told me he has a baby grand piano and has offered to tune your piano at the Lodge.' Luke gently pulled down the mask to cover Esther's mouth and nose. 'Don't you think your one-sided feud with the neighbour should be over?'

Esther smoothed down her bed as the pug snuggled up to Luke for a pat.

'We get why you did it, you're lonely.'

'I truly miss Iris. I do ...' Esther peered around the walls, licking her thin lips under the mask. 'Do you promise you'll pick me up in the morning?'

'I swear it.' Luke dragged his finger over his chest as if crossing his heart. 'I just want you safe.'

Esther sighed. 'Fine.' She pulled down the mask to let it rest under her chin. 'But I'll want a change of clothes, my hairbrush, toothbrush, and a new tiara. I've ruined my other one and I feel naked without one.' She brushed fingers through her hair, trying to fluff it up.

'I can do that.' Luke grinned with relief.

'And you must celebrate the hunt with Jordi.' She waved her finger at Jordi. 'You must, young lady. It's tradition.'

'After we drop the dog off.'

'Do you have to?' Gran hugged the pug. 'They leave the poor thing alone all day.'

'It's not your pet. When you have a water buffalo that needs feeding.' He pointed to the window showing the sunset was starting.

'Cecil will wonder where I am. Do spoil my darling boy.' She passed the pug to Luke. 'You can go now. I'm an old woman in need of rest. They're having chicken cacciatore tonight, and custard. I like a good custard.' She pulled her mask over her nose and mouth and leaned back into her nest of pillows.

Luke kissed her forehead. 'Night, Gran. I'll see you in the morning.'

At the door, he hesitated, hating to see Esther like this.

'Night, Esther. I'll watch over them.' Jordi weaved her fingers through his and gave them a squeeze. He was grateful she was there with him, as he carried the dog out the door.

Twenty-three

'What do I do?' Jordi had never put a buffalo to bed before. And Cecil wasn't your average everyday water buffalo, with pink ribbons tangled around his horns, and his black coat a mass of chalk drawings.

Luke shrugged. 'It's easy.'

'For you.' Because Cecil was huge.

'All you do is feed him first …' Luke led them to the back of the house to a cement slab area that looked like a stable of sorts, while Cecil's hooves clip-clopped behind them. 'We keep Cecil's feed locked away.' Reaching to the metal box high above the door, which reminded her of a letterbox, Luke removed a key that he used to unlock a whopping big padlock that kept a wire cage shut. Inside was feeding hay, bags of grain and assorted cleaning items like shampoos, conditioners, and brushes. There were also spools and spools of assorted coloured ribbons that hung from a metal rod. They were just like the ribbons used at her family's florist shop.

'What is this place?'

'Cecil's feeding stall.' Luke grabbed a large tub and spooned in assorted grains and hay. 'You don't have any fresh daisies in your pocket, do you?'

She rolled her eyes at him, still in her skanky fishing shirt and shorts.

Luke led the buffalo to the cement slab, with his colossal head bobbing up and down eagerly. 'Here we go, big fella.'

Luke emptied the tub into the feed trough, and Cecil snorted and sniffed with glee.

Luke slipped a harness around the buffalo's large neck as he ate, then ran fresh water into the drinking trough, before returning the tub to the cage. He pulled out a bottle of shampoo and a chunky horse brush and closed the gate with a distinct click of the lock, then returned the key to the lockbox.

'That's a bit extreme, to keep food away from an animal.' Jordi pointed to the lockbox.

'We have to, or Cecil will break in. Believe me, he's crafty. He's been known to go into the house and raid our fridges. Now this is for you.' He handed her the brush and shampoo bottle.

'And I'm to do what with this?'

'You get the once-in-a-lifetime opportunity to bathe this beautiful buffalo, while he eats.'

'Are you serious?' Was he trying to hustle her?

His grin grew wider the more she frowned at him.

'Cecil's already got a crush on you, being the flower girl. If you do this, he'll love you for life.'

'You *are* serious.'

'Hose is there, the water's warm from the tank. Oh, and he's a water buffalo, so he loves the water.'

'If Cecil loves it so much, why keep him tethered like that?'

'Because he'll wallow in the mud, like water buffaloes do. Your task is to wash all that chalk off his back.'

'Why isn't he allowed to roll?'

'Because Cecil will be too dirty to go inside Gran's house, and that's where he sleeps. Bloody pampered thing, you are ...' Luke's humour left him as he tenderly stroked the buffalo. 'Gran will be back tomorrow, Cecil. I promise.'

She felt bad for the pair of them. 'Okay, so what do I do?'

Luke's lopsided grin widened. 'Hose him off, dump some shampoo on him, lather it up then wash it off. Just like washing a black carpet of sorts. Then brush him down.

Towels up there.' Luke started walking away but stopped and looked back. 'Oh, and one more thing …'

'What?' She wasn't sure of his cocky grin growing.

'You have to walk him around the block once you're done washing him.'

'What? Why?'

'He needs to do his business. Track starts there. Cecil knows the way. Use the lead on the harness; it's just like walking a dog.'

'I don't own a dog.'

'Remember to remove the harness before he goes to bed. I'll be washing the boat.' His chuckle echoed in the air as he headed for the shed, leaving her alone with a whopping big water buffalo.

What was she meant to do?

With hands on hips, she stared at Cecil.

He raised his head from the feed trough to look at her, chewing like a cow, with flecks of grain on his chin and some hay on his cheek. But the pink ribbon around his horns were tattered and twisted and his black coat was a mass of chalk scribbles. He looked as if he'd been the main attraction at a toddler's birthday party that had ended in a food fight.

'Let's remove those ribbons first.' She unwound reams of bright pink florist ribbons from the hard bone-like curved horns that were as long as her arm.

The ribbon on his tail was an indescribable colour she didn't want to touch.

She hosed off the beast until he was dripping wet, but the chalk still stuck to his black coat in clumps.

Squirting a dollop of shampoo in her hand, she rubbed it into his sides that were covered in a mishmash of chalk colours for flowers, smiley faces, stick figures and many childlike scrawls covering his entire body.

It was going to take forever to clean that muck off.

Determined, she grabbed the shampoo, and squirted more along the beast's spine. With the nearby floor broom, she brushed his back, the same way she cleaned her van.

Cecil groaned, shifting his body the way a washing machine would shift clothes during the wash cycle. He stretched his neck, arched his back, then shuddered all over, shaking his body, flinging soap suds, and water everywhere. She was helpless to stop him.

Then he went back to eating.

Did that mean he liked it?

Covered in suds, water, and buffalo what-not, she'd only cleaned one side of the beast. 'You're lucky I like Esther, and Luke.' She was only doing this for them.

Taking a deep breath, Jordi started on the other side, standing well back this time, using the full length of the broomstick to ensure she was well out of kicking distance as she scrubbed the soap into a lather.

Again, Cecil groaned. This time deeper, with his eyes rolling back in his head. It reminded her of how her sister would moan with delight from a foot massage when they'd shout themselves a pedicure after being on their feet all day.

But when she hosed him off, she got showered again in the water spray as Cecil shook his body like a dog.

Wiping off the suds and sweat from her cheeks, she could feel buffalo hair all over her. 'I think we're done. Do you agree, Cecil?'

Cecil slurped up some water from the drinking trough. His black tongue swept across his lips, and he nodded at her as if to say he was done.

'Is this the part where you lead me around the park?' Hesitantly, she unclipped Cecil from the stall, and walked beside him as he waddled down a well-worn dirt track.

If her sister saw her now, holding the end of a thick rope tethered to a buffalo she was walking like a dog in the park, she wouldn't believe it.

Cecil's massive rump shifted from side to side in a long lazy gait. He occasionally stopped to sniff at a small wildflower or go cross-eyed at a moth hovering around his nose. His curiosity was almost childlike.

But no one warned her about the sheer mountain of muck

that piled onto the dirt when he lifted his tail.

She coughed and gagged, holding her nose to walk as far away as she could without dropping the lead.

Jordi barely held on to the lead, allowing Cecil to wander ahead of her. Until he stopped to look at her. His head bobbed up and down as if to say *hurry up and walk beside me, lady*.

'I'm coming.' Ensuring she kept her distance from those horns, they did a large loop around the Lodge. They passed various fruit trees that made up a healthy orchard. Nearby, a heavily fenced area contained a thriving vegetable garden.

A mass of pink bougainvillea climbed a trellis to a secret garden of sorts with a stunning view of the sunset. There, she paused at the sheer size of the sky that towered over them. A few long-necked brolgas flew across the horizon, as a silence seemed to fall across the land, as the skies came alive with a rich depth of colours that made the shadows stretch across the sunburnt land.

Cecil stood beside her as if to watch the last of the sinking sun disappear on the horizon. Then, with a nod, Cecil led them back to the house, where his large hoofs clip-clopped up the ramp to the verandah and he waited at the concertina doors.

Jordi pushed them open, and Cecil strolled inside. His heavy hoofs were loud on the floor until he stood before Esther's chair and sniffed. His big black eyes were so sad that she finally found the courage to pat the poor thing. 'Esther will be back tomorrow, Cecil. I promise she will.'

With his harness removed, Cecil approached the large round pillow—bigger than his body. He groaned, moaned, huffed, and shuffled until he lay down and found the perfect spot, then sighed.

And that was what it was like putting a pampered pet buffalo to bed.

Twenty-four

She was cute. Damned cute.

Luke chuckled to himself, watching Jordi wash Cecil with a broom. It was awkward, but it did the job, and Cecil seemed to like it. Even though Cecil's groans had him rushing over to find out what was wrong.

But nothing was wrong. Cecil was groaning from the pleasure.

Luke wasn't going to interfere with the broom-brushing technique Jordi had invented. He wished he'd come up with the idea himself, especially for those days when he had no idea what muck Cecil had rolled in.

But he kept watching, to ensure Jordi was okay as she walked Cecil around the block. Luke wasn't worried about Cecil, who wouldn't hurt a fly. It was Jordi he watched over.

Sure, he could have done the right thing in putting Cecil to bed himself. He'd done it plenty of times over the decades, but he wanted Jordi to try something new.

When Jordi reeled in her first fish by herself it had ignited something insider her, and the pride she found in herself was purely magical to witness. He wanted her to get out of her comfort zone and find that inner confidence he knew she had. It was Jordi who needed to believe in herself and stop hiding. Even though he was hiding on the block, watching Jordi walk Cecil, where the unlikely duo had stopped to admire the sunset together.

Something shifted inside his chest, a warmth that made his lips curve into a smile, leaning his shoulder against the tree to watch them.

Yeah, he was stalking her.

How could he not.

An hour after she'd put Cecil to bed, Luke found Jordi, with her hair damp, fresh from the shower, checking on Cecil sleeping on his bed beside his grandmother's empty chair.

The buffalo wouldn't move until morning.

'World's most spoilt buffalo, that is.'

Jordi spun around to face Luke where he leaned his shoulder against the doorjamb. 'I didn't hear you come in.'

'Come on, we've got a fish to clean.'

'You could have told me that before I had my shower.'

'It's not that bad. We'll do it down the shed.' By torchlight, they left through the back door where the skies fell over them as if draping them in a rich cloak made of starlight.

Jordi slowed down to stare up at the sky that'd make anyone dizzy with the endless layers of stars upon stars, like he used to do all the time as a kid.

Arching his neck back, Luke tried to remember when he'd last laid back and checked out the stars.

Inside the shed, they passed his favourite toy, the boat, all clean and ready to go back out again. Then through to the far wall where a row of sinks and a large aluminium bench sat near a butcher's bandsaw.

'What is this place?'

'You could call it the butcher's house.'

'Huh?'

'It's the slaughter room.'

'Ew.' She screwed up her cute nose, the lights highlighting the blemishes that looked like freckles.

'I know you're not a vegetarian, and this is a hunter's house.' He grinned at her as he rummaged around in the fridge and sorted out their drinks. Cracking open a can, he poured its contents into a tall glass of ice, he placed it on the aluminium bench in front of Jordi. 'Try that drink. You'll like that one.'

'Mojito?' Jordi sniffed before she sipped. She stood back

with the tip of her pink tongue licking her lips. 'Mint and lime?'

'It's refreshing.'

She nodded, taking another deep mouthful.

'Easy, Angelfish, that's got white rum in it.'

Again, her pretty pink tongue swiped across her lips as she peered into her glass.

That tongue of hers was unbuttoning his insides, making him swallow hard, reaching for his beer.

'Is this how you celebrate the hunt?'

He sighed, gazing up at the dark house that seemed so small under the stars. It looked lonely without the presence of a Bennett.

'If Gran was here, she'd have the lights on in the house, the music blaring, cooking up a feast, to then dance in the sitting room around the piano.' *Dammit, Gran …* He hated the thought of her being stuck in the hospital.

'So, life was one big party.'

'It used to be. Dad and Gran would party until dawn, and I'd fall asleep on the couch, or I'd use Cecil as my pillow when this place was rocking.'

'Do you miss that?'

'Honestly? … No. I like my privacy. I'm not like Gran, or my old man.'

'But you are an entertainer. The way you played piano at the Sandfly Saloon, and when you play the host of the drive-thru bottle shop.'

'Yeah, right …' He shook his head, rummaging around the bench for the metal glove and the plastic butcher's apron. 'You can put these on, please.'

Jordi slipped on the thick butcher's apron as the bright globes cast a halo effect over her damp hair. But her grin widened as she slid on the metal glove that was a few sizes too big for her. 'Are we going jousting?'

'Eh?' He paused brushing the filleting knife's blade across the sharpening steel.

She giggled while giving a sloppy wave with the glove.

'This glove reminds me of the chain mail mesh from the Knights of the Excalibur era.'

'C'mere. The reason why you're wearing that metal glove is so you don't cut yourself.' He beckoned her with his crooked finger. She'd caught a fighting barramundi in the wild, patted a baby crocodile, and bathed a buffalo, so she should be willing to get her hands dirty cleaning a fish. Right?

Twenty-five

The way Luke beckoned her with the simplicity of a crooked finger, she was helpless to resist.

Until he dragged her large fish across the bench like it was on an operating table.

'You'll cut there …' He surrounded her as he taught her to clean and fillet her fish. Once that was done, they bagged it up, sliding the thick white fillets into the nearby freezer, and then cleaned up in no time.

It reminded her of the process for creating flower posies for the supermarkets. Snipping and stripping stems, sorting flowers into groups, wiring them into place before wrapping them in cellophane and ribbon, then into a styrofoam box for transport. Leaving her to clean up her workbenches and hose down the floor.

Except Luke's close proximity, as he explained each step, set her on fire. She had to remind herself this was just a job to him, and there was nothing romantic about it all.

Besides, how could anything be romantic when filleting a fish? *Ugh.*

'Now we'll cook it.' Luke took out a deep tin plate, dropped in some flour, added salt and pepper, mixed it around with his fingers, then added the large fillets of fish. Dusting the flour off his hands, he flicked on the gas burner of the outdoor kitchen. Adding a knob of butter to the pan, he swirled it around before slapping the floury fillets into the pan.

There was no showmanship to it; everything was done quickly and efficiently.

With the benches spotless, Jordi washed her hands in the deep sink, as the music played in the background. The shed's lights were the only lights seen anywhere for miles—excluding the gazillion stars twinkling in the blackest of skies.

She dried her hands on the towel that hung near a sliding glass door where an assortment of men's boots rested on the rack. Nearby stood more fridges and a chest freezer against a coldroom wall. And on the back wall hung assorted knives, scales, and hooks, like you'd find in a butcher's shop.

'Do you still hunt?' She leaned against the bench to watch Luke cook. Only to blink at the realisation that, besides her father and brother-in-law Mitchell, no guy had ever cooked for her, certainly not like this. She fiddled with her shirt's cuffs, rubbing her foot against her ankle, trying to stand right, act cool, and stop being an awkward freak.

'Besides going with Dad, I've hunted wild pigs for the local park ranger from time to time. Alice uses the meat as bait for her crocodile cages, or for my mate's dogs. Although his dogs prefer buffalo.' Luke cut up a ripe green lime, then drizzled juice over the fish that hissed and sizzled in the pan, emitting an aroma similar to fresh mushrooms and cucumbers—the fresh fish did not smell fishy at all.

Jordi's mouth watered and her belly started rumbling with hunger. 'Do you hunt anything else?

'Geese when it's hunting season. Gran likes her geese. She makes this great pate and cold meat dish you'll beg her to make every day if she could. She also uses the feathers for Cecil's bed. Gran wastes nothing ...' His frown flickered, obviously missing Esther, as he used the spatula to flick over the fish in the sizzling pan. 'We do the odd rogue crocodile for the rangers or the police, when needed. And we have the contract for banteng.'

'What's that?'

'Wild ox. They look like domestic cattle, but smaller.

They're known as the Bali cow or the Javanese ox. They've got these wiry horns on them, kind of like a mix between a goat and a cow. Oh, and they have these white socks and white rumps that remind me of a gazelle.'

'I've never heard of them.'

'Few people have. Which is strange, considering the Northern Territory has the largest population of banteng in the world.'

'How big a herd are you talking about? Or are you making that up?'

He shook his head. But with his lopsided grin, she wasn't so sure.

'Bantengs are nearly extinct; there are only a few thousand left in the wild. Even though it's a feral pest to the region, we don't harm them.'

'But you said you hunted them.'

'With tranquiliser guns, then we carry them out of the thick monsoon jungles and put them into pens. When we have enough, we wait for the barge to transport them out of there.'

'To take them to the butchers?'

'No.' He shook his head. 'Just because we're hunters, it doesn't mean we're killers. We hunt for lots of reasons, and never waste anything, if we can help it. And with the banteng, we've been trying to repopulate them because they're considered endangered. Dad used to keep a herd on the property. Gran used to milk a few and make cheese.' He sighed, pointing to the back of the dark property.

'Why are they endangered?'

'Banteng have lost their native habitats because of deforestation, disease, being hunted for food and traditional medicine, and also game hunting. Their horns have made poaching their biggest killer in Southeast Asia.'

'So, what do you do with them when you catch them?'

'We've supplied domestic and overseas zoos, a few rodeo breeders, and a few cattle stations. I know of a few stations that use them for game hunting—which is a waste.'

'Why?'

'They're quite harmless compared to all the other wild beasts that the Northern Territory has on offer.'

'So says the buffalo hunter.'

He winked at her, shaking the frypan to evenly coat the fish in the lime-butter mixture. 'When we're hunting for banteng we take out the quads and build this big bush camp near the beach on the peninsula. It's a great trip. We spend weeks out there seeing nobody else—because you can't get in there without a permit.'

'Why not?'

'It's a national park, and they only allow half a dozen people in there at one time, it's that protected.'

'And they let you hunt there?'

'They pay us to remove some of the banteng herd to keep it manageable. Even though they're considered feral, you can see they're actually doing good for that habitat by eating the grasses that normally become fuel for bushfires. But the rangers don't want the area overpopulated and, like I said, we've been trying to help get them off the endangered list.'

She dropped her jaw in awe of the man. A hunter who saved creatures, had a pet buffalo, and was a fireman. The layers to this guy amazed her. He was so much more than a guy managing a bottle shop at the local pub.

'Come, sit and eat.' He patted the stool next to the bench. It wasn't fancy like the Lodge, with Luke serving two plates of fish, even with tubs of salad on the side.

'Are these salads from the pub?' They looked familiar to her.

'Shh, don't tell Gran.'

'But Esther loves to cook and entertain.' Every time she visited the Lodge, Esther in her sparkly tiara would happily dish up a feast.

'Gran's asleep by sunset, and I don't come in until after the bottle shop shuts.' He handed her some cutlery, put salt and pepper on the table, tossed his tea towel over his shoulder to then pause as the creases in his brow shifted.

'What's wrong?'

'It's not right.' He pointed to the tin plates of fish.

'What?'

'It's your first fish, and Gran would've dragged out the good china to set the dining room table, and served it on a silver platter, with candles and everything. I should—'

'Don't.' She grabbed his thick wrist. 'I—I live in the shed, too.'

'Excuse me?'

'I'm guessing that's your room there.' She pointed to the glass door, near the assorted boots. 'You sleep out here.'

'How did you guess?'

'You move around this area like it's your home.'

'It is. That room used to be Dad's office. I moved in there when I was a teenager.'

'Why?'

'I got sick of the parties at the Lodge, with all these old people, talking about things I wasn't interested in. Mum set me up here, where I could watch my movies or play video games and music, cleaning the guns and our hunting gear without upsetting the punters in the Lodge.' He reached for the salt shaker.

'But, didn't Porter say he took all of your guns from Esther the day I delivered Esther's birthday flowers.'

He gave a short huff. 'Gran was trying to scare off a trespasser from Iris's house. We didn't realise it was some real estate manager trying to put the house on the market.'

'How bad was it?'

'It wasn't good. Gran scared him so badly he demanded they arrest Gran. Which they did.'

'In handcuffs?'

'Hell, no. Not on my watch!' He scowled. 'Gran did lose her gun licence and had to surrender her rifles to save her butt from going to jail. Her fines were converted to community service, which she does at the school library anyhow. The shotguns up at the Lodge—'

'The ones hanging on the wall near the piano?'

He nodded. 'They've had their firing pins removed because they're antiques. They belonged to my great-great-grandfather, Bison-eye Bennett. But we do have three gun safes inside the Lodge. Two were for guests, one was for Gran. Dad and I kept our stash in the armoury out here in the shed. You get to it through my room.' Luke pointed to the glass sliding door. 'So, do you really live in a shed? I thought you lived with your sister.'

'I live in the shed at the back of the shop.'

'No way.'

Jordi shrugged as she cut at the meaty white fish that practically melted like butter on her tongue. 'This is divine.'

'Nothing beats fresh fish.'

'I never knew fish could taste like this.' The white meaty barramundi reminded her of freshwater trout, but smooth, buttery, and slightly sweet on the palate, with only a mild fishy flavour. It had her tastebuds dancing, as she eagerly loaded her fork for more.

'Jordi, that's the taste of the hunt. You caught this. That's why it tastes so much sweeter and meatier.'

She blushed and stared down at her plate. Could he be right? 'I feel like such a barbarian.'

His lips shifted into a smile, with a chuckle coming deep from his chest. 'Why? Humans have been hunting meat for a millennia. And I bet you can taste the difference, now you're eating fresh fish.'

She hated to admit it, giving him a slight nod as she took another hearty mouthful.

'You don't sleep in your van in the shed, do you?'

She shook her head, sipping her drink. 'The van is parked inside. I sleep in the old coldroom on the couch.'

'You what?' He frowned at her.

'Don't judge me.'

'But a coldroom? Like that one?' He pointed to the coldroom that stood empty in the far corner. It really was a butcher's back room, complete with a bandsaw.

'It's much bigger than that. The store used to be a

greengrocer's, which Mum refit into a florist shop. I park my van inside and do the orders.'

'So you work from home? Or is that live at work?'

'It's easier for me because I pick up the flowers from the airport at midnight. Then I go back and make the posies while it's still cool, so they don't wither in the heat and humidity. Then I load up the van and deliver them to supermarkets when their doors open at six, keeping the flowers as fresh as possible for the customers.'

'Who does the Friday and Saturday deliveries when you're out here?'

'Gladys helps in the store part time, and her husband will do the local deliveries. But I do the commercial contracts, like supermarkets, restaurants, some upmarket corporate spaces, and hotels on our client list. My sister looks after the store and we both do the online requests.'

'Do other florists deliver out here?'

'No. We're the only florist that goes beyond Darwin's outer suburbs. If any of the other florists get a request for regional areas, they'll send the order through to us, taking a small commission, of course.'

'I had no idea.'

'And I'm probably boring you.'

'No, you're not. But you still didn't tell me why you live in a shed.'

'Didn't I just explain my reason?'

'No.' His grin spread wide. 'Hey, I told you why I live in a shed, so tell me why you do, and then I'll give you the right to ask me any question you want.'

'Um …' She hesitated.

'The reason I live in the shed is it's normal for me. I keep saying I'll move back into the house, but I never do. Since I work nights at the bottle shop, I don't want to disturb Gran if I want to play music and stuff. Now, it's your turn.'

'I do it so my sister and Mitchell can have some privacy at my parent's old house. And I can get my job done so much quicker. I just get up, shower, and start working on orders while the kettle's boiling.' She lived for her work. That was it.

'You already said that. What's the real reason.'

'And …' She swallowed hard. 'The house reminds me too much that my parents aren't here anymore.'

Luke said nothing. He didn't have to. She recognised the pity in his eyes; she hated that look. But it was better than the one of horror that people had when they fled from her.

With head down, she ate in silence with only the music in the background and the silence of the countryside.

When she was finished, she put her cutlery down on her empty plate, comfortably full and satisfied. 'That was the best fish.'

'I agree.' He whisked the plates away and washed them in a jiff. 'Your turn to ask.'

'Anything?'

'Sure, ask away.'

She hesitated, biting her bottom lip.

'Jordi …' He sat opposite her at the bench, his eyes trapping hers. 'Go on. What do you want to ask me?'

She blurted it out all in one breath. 'What was the accident that made you want to stop being a fireman?' He'd be sexy in his uniform.

Luke frowned.

'I didn't mean to overhear you talking with Jax at the hospital but …' Their voices had carried down the corridor.

'Dammit.'

'I'm sorry, I shouldn't have pried. I'll go —'

He reached over and snagged her hand. 'Sit. But we'll need something stronger to drink if you want me to answer that question.'

Twenty-six

Inside his room, Luke rummaged around for some shot glasses, returning with his favourite bottle of tequila. Why did Jordi have to ask that question? She could have asked a million other questions, instead of that one!

He cut more lime on a small board, then lined up three shot glasses in front of Jordi and three for himself and poured.

'Are we having slammers? Or are those shots?'

'Tequila crudas. Give me your hand.' He manipulated her small hand to sprinkle salt on her soft skin. 'You lick the salt, swallow the shot, then suck the lime. Do it with me.'

She swallowed nervously but nodded.

'Lick, shoot, suck. Go.' They licked at the salt from the back of their hands, threw back the nip of tequila, then sucked on the lime.

He licked the salt from his lips, which mellowed out the harshness of the tequila, while the lime cut back at the bite of the salt. Plus, a decent tequila made a real difference.

Jordi's pink tongue flickered over her lush red lips, as she wiped the lime juice from her chin, giggling at herself. 'That was fun.'

'I like 'em. So does Porter.'

'Do you see him much?'

'Almost every night, now that Porter doesn't want to date anymore. He's happy doing night shift, so he swings by the bottle shop to see what I'm doing. We used to have the same days off and go fishing—before his boss, Marcus, went on leave. Come on, one more …' He held out the salt shaker.

Again, a lick of the salt, followed by the tequila, and then a suck on the lime that went down so much easier the second time around. He was impressed that Jordi did it with him, and the smile she shared for finishing it.

'Here, drink this too.' He put icy water bottles on the table. 'Even though it's decent tequila, you're not a big drinker.'

'I know.' She giggled behind her hand, almost spilling the water from her lip.

'So why do you buy booze from the bottle shop if you don't drink?'

She shrank into her shoulders like a child caught stealing from the cookie jar. 'I, um …' She played with a few stray salt crystals scattered on the bench. 'When I ask for directions, I feel rude for taking up your time and not buying anything.'

Sweet salmon cakes, she was adorable.

Until she frowned. 'Hey, you were meant to be answering my question. You're good.' She wagged her finger at him. 'Doing the shots was a distraction.'

He grinned, only for his smile to slowly fall. 'Do you really want to know?'

'Yes. Is it true what Jax said earlier that you've given up so much?'

He inhaled deeply, resting his elbow on the bench that ran between them. 'I didn't realise it until Jax said that stuff. The yard stuff,' he said, waving to the darkness. 'After watching Dad's heartbreak in losing all of our crops, I don't know if I want to go through that. And …'

'The fireman's job. I didn't even know you were a firefighter, until today.'

'Growing up, I was going to be a professional hunter like my dad. Not a fireman.'

'So, what happened?'

'I'd volunteered to be in our local bush fire unit, with Dad, when I was twelve and loved it. I'd hassle Gran every week to drive me when Dad was out hunting on the big trips. I'd been a volunteer firie for over ten years, had my various vehicle licences from working the farm, and became a team leader for the volunteers. But then one day the old fire chief and my dad came around waving this big yellow envelope with a bottle of rum, telling me I'd been accepted to do the twenty-week training course to become a full-time fireman.'

'You didn't apply?'

'My dad did, recruiting the help of the fire chief.' He chuckled, rubbing his forehead. 'But hey, I wasn't going to complain. So off I went to fireman's school, graduated, and came back to work at Elsie Creek Fire Station. Full time. It all happened so easily, so naturally, it didn't feel like a job.'

'Why didn't you stay in the job?'

'I enjoy fishing more.'

She pursed her lips together, shaking her head. 'You still could've fished like you do now, working at the bottle shop.'

He shrugged, picking up the third shot glass. He didn't even use the salt or lime, just tossed the tequila shot back straight and let it burn smoothly down his throat and through his chest. 'It's okay, you don't need to drink it.'

She sighed with relief she didn't have to. 'So it's true? You stopped a lot of things because of this accident.'

The overhead fan ticked as it stirred the air.

By the far wall, a bug tapped against the light.

He couldn't look at her, even if she was patiently waiting for an answer.

But when he did answer, it was with clear conviction, admitting it more to himself. 'They were right.'

'Where was the accident?'

'Jordi …'

'We had a deal.'

'On the Arnhem Highway,' he let the words spill. 'We were coming back from doing a controlled burn I was using as a training exercise for the volunteers, when we unexpectedly came across this vehicle accident.' He rubbed at his forehead, trying to erase the memory from his mind. 'It had just happened. There was broken glass all over the road, and I remember this spare tyre rolling right past us as smoke rose from the tyre tracks. You could smell the burning rubber ...' He wanted to stop. He had to stop. And now.

Twenty-seven

Jordi listened to Luke tell his tale. It was obvious that he didn't want to talk about it, but if he'd been keeping this bottled up for so long, she had to help. If he wasn't willing to talk to the fire chief, Jax, maybe Luke would talk to her, to help him move past the pain. And he was in pain talking to her about it, she could see it. 'Go on …'

'According to the crash investigator's report the RV was on the wrong side of the road. It was driven by an American tourist, who'd just collected it from the airport a few hours earlier, and they weren't used to driving on the left side of the road.'

'You're kidding.'

He slowly shook his head. 'The other car came round the bend and tried to move out of the way. At the same time the RV driver tried to correct itself, the two vehicles swerved and collided with each other.' He demonstrated the direction with his hands. 'The RV smashed into a massive gum tree, instantly killing the driver. The passenger, the driver's new bride, wasn't wearing a seatbelt and smashed through the front windscreen. She broke her neck in the fall. The other car …' He winced.

'Go on.' She was on the edge of her seat, as the hairs on her neck prickled.

'The other car was driving under the speed limit at about a hundred clicks. They'd hit the side of the RV, propelling them off the road. The impact and speed they were travelling caused the car to flip over, and it rolled a few times into a dry, grassy paddock before landing on its roof.'

'What did you do?'

'I jumped the fence, trying to dodge all of these cattle that were running in a stampede, stirring up the dust. That's when the first of the flames started at the RV and began chasing the spilled fuel that had come from the car ...' He reached for his beer and drank it dry.

With trembling fingers, Jordi reached for the third shot glass, tossing back the tequila, desperate to feel anything more than the numbness now in her fingers. 'Keep going.' She didn't even realise she was crying until she wiped her cheek.

'I can't.' He shook his head, pain etched across his face.

'I. Said. Keep. Going.' She gritted her teeth and glared at him. '*Finish it!*'

'One fire crew had their hoses on the RV, but their aerosol cans—maybe deodorant or hairspray—were exploding, sending sparks flying to the surrounding grasses. The teams were using fire extinguishers and sacks and were trying to stop those flames from reaching the car, or spreading into that dry paddock, which was the perfect fuel for a bush fire.'

'While you ran for the car?'

He barely nodded.

'What did you find?' Her voice a whisper, sitting on the edge of her seat.

'The steering wheel had trapped the driver. The airbag couldn't save him from the impact where the front of the car was badly crushed, and the passenger's side was worse. I was instructing my crew to drive the truck down. We were going to rip the door open, to get them out.'

'But ...'

'The flames started, and the car was on fire in a matter of seconds. You could smell the fuel.'

'And the people in the car?'

He licked his lips. 'They were begging me to get their daughter from the back seat.'

'What was she doing?'

'She was hanging upside down, in the middle of the back seat, trapped by the seatbelt. I broke the window and cut her free from the seatbelt using this very same pocketknife.' He slammed it on the bench. 'Then I dragged her the hell out of there, but she resisted all the way.'

'She wanted to save her parents.'

'I was going to go back for them, Jordi. I swear it.'

'Why didn't you? They'd still be *alive.*'

'Because the fire hit the fuel tank, and the car exploded. You were barely free from the car when we got hit with that explosion. You were already on fire, but that blast threw us both onto the road. I was desperately trying to put out the flames burning your clothes and skin. I didn't even know I was on fire myself until my crew smothered me.'

She viciously swiped the hot tears from her cheeks, the anger bitter in her throat as she struggled to swallow.

'Every single day, I wish I could have saved them.'

'Me. Too.' She scowled at him. 'I kept wondering why they didn't save my parents.'

'There wasn't time, I swear it. You were lucky to get out of there alive as it was.' He paced the floor, running fingers through his hair. 'You know, I drove to Darwin and saw you.'

'When?'

'While you were in that coma. I brought you flowers every week, until you woke. The last time I was there ...' He dropped his heavy head, his sigh even heavier. 'I was in the corridor when your sister told you you'd lost your parents. You were sobbing so loudly, demanding why we—me,' he said, tapping his fist against his chest, '—couldn't save your parents. Why did we only save you?'

The tears streamed now, as she remembered that time. It had been like waking up to a never-ending nightmare. Staring at an unrecognisable face in the mirror, trapped in a body of relentless burning pain.

His voice softened, as did his stance. 'I heard you call yourself ugly, because your hair was burnt off, your eyebrows and lashes were gone, and your back was badly scarred. You said you didn't deserve to live.'

She hadn't wanted to, not when everything hurt. Putting on clothes hurt. Human touch hurt. And later she had to endure people pointing at her, or asking if she had cancer, or why was she dressed like a mummy, wearing the protective gauze, where kids would flee from her in horror. But it only got worse when her skin looked like a shiny jelly when they removed the gauze from her face. And her scalp was too tender to wear a wig or a scarf, exposing her scarred head until her hair started growing back.

Eighteen months ago, she'd been a normal girl complaining of split ends, wondering if she should get false eyelashes done when she'd next get her eyebrows threaded, only to wake up to a nightmare.

'What happened after you got me out? I don't know anything, except waking up in hospital.' Six weeks later.

'I held you in our fire truck as we raced to meet the flying doctors at the nearest airstrip. On the plane, I sat beside you when we were medevaced to Darwin's burns unit.'

'You were burnt too?'

He nodded, lifting his shirt to show the scarring on the top of his shoulder and upper arm.

She cupped her mouth, her heart falling for him. He'd hurt himself—put himself on the line—to save her.

'I heard the medical staff discussing with the pilot that they didn't think you'd make the flight. At the hospital, the medical staff didn't think you'd make the night in the ICU. But you did, Jordi.' He held out his hand to her, palm open. 'You held my hand the entire flight all the way to the ICU, I swear you may have only held my hand that once, but I never let go, and I never gave up on you. Until you woke up ...'

'Why didn't you say anything sooner?'

'Because I failed you.' He punched at his chest. 'I didn't save your parents when you were so desperate to save them, fighting me to get to them.' He paced the floor, raking fingers through his hair. 'The nightmares were relentless, replaying over and over again, what I could've or should've done to save your parents, to save you from those burn marks that cover your back.'

She gasped, stepping back from the bench. It finally hit her: he knew about her scars. He'd known this entire time!

'But then the nightmares stopped.' His voice was low, controlled, calm even.

'When?'

'The day you drove through my bottle shop asking for directions.' He walked around the bench to face her and reached out to touch her hair, but she stepped away. 'I recognised you straight away. Your hair had grown back, and so did your eyebrows and lashes. The burns on your lips and cheeks had healed, and those blemishes, the burn scars, had become so small on your cheeks that they looked like freckles to me.'

She touched the network of raised dots scattered across her cheeks. They were burn scars, not freckles.

'But you'd keep your hair down to cover your neck. You'd roll the sleeves down to your wrists to hide the burns, and were so timid, keeping your distance in case anybody touched you. I kept waiting for you to remember me, to shout at me. Something.'

'I don't remember anything.'

'You shouldn't need to remember, Jordi, because I remember enough for the both of us.' He gently cupped her cheek. 'Jordi, I understand why you hide your skin, but you shouldn't have to. It's nothing to be ashamed of.'

Again, she stepped back from him. 'Were you only kind to me out of pity? Or because the nightmares and guilt stopped?'

He raised his chin, standing in a solid stance in front of her. 'At first. Yes. And no. I don't know ...' He raked fingers through his hair again, revealing the pain, guilt, and more.

She scowled at him.

'I remember while they treated us both at the hospital, I heard the other police speak highly of your father. The waiting room was full of cops, all waiting to hear about you.'

'I didn't know that.'

'You were in the ICU for a long time.' His eyes became glassy as he exhaled heavily. 'I'm sorry I didn't save your parents, Jordi. I truly am sorry. But what I do know is that your parents were the type of people who'd tell you to stop hiding who you are.'

'Aren't you doing the same? Hiding too? Quitting your job, your farm.'

He shook his head. 'You don't get it, I failed you. By not saving your parents or dragging you out of that car sooner, you wouldn't have to live with those scars you hate. To me, that kind of failure is the worst kind ... But seeing you today, out there fishing, your smile, and that freedom you seemed to enjoy, that was the best medicine for me. I recognised it because it's what helped me to heal, too.'

'I had a good time. I did.' Again, she took in a shaky breath. 'Back then, I stopped everything, too. Like you. Not even living in the family home.'

The lines on his brow deepened as concern shadowed his eyes. 'How can you say that? So what if you're living in a shed? I do.' He pointed to the door that led to his room.

'I was supposed to buy a block of land and become a commercial cut-flower producer. A floriculturist with all these big dreams. It's why we were out there, looking at farming land. My parents died because of me ...'

'Hey, it's not your fault, Jordi. It's not.' He pulled her to his chest, wrapping his arms around her. And she let him, when normally she let no one hold her because of her scars.

She gazed up at Luke, who'd been carrying around the guilt—over her, for her. His failings were hers. Not his.

Swallowing the thick lump in her tight throat, she licked her dry lips. His eyes followed her every move. 'I forgive you.'

He blinked furiously, stepping back from her, shaking his head as if refusing to listen.

'I forgive you, Luke.' Waiting by her bed, had that been

what he was looking for? She then stammered out. 'Thank you.'

'For what?' He grimaced at her in disgust.

'For not failing. Because you saved me.' She reached up and touched his cheek. He'd been hurting as much as she had over the same accident, and she'd never remembered him. Her hero.

She stood on her tiptoes and pressed a kiss to his jaw, then gave in to her deepest desire to kiss his lips.

'Jordi.' His hands gently cradled her face, stopping her, but one thumb tenderly brushed her cheek. 'I don't think that's a good idea.'

'It's my scars, isn't it?' She pulled back, but he gripped her arms.

'No, it's not that.'

'Well, what is it?' She licked her lips, tasting the salt from those tequila shots, which had given her the courage to try. She'd always wanted to kiss him.

With her fingertips tracing down the side of his handsome face and along his jawline, she dragged her thumb across his lips, to then press it against her tongue to taste him.

His teeth clenched as he sucked in his breath, as if resisting her.

'I don't want to hurt you.' His voice was husky — sexy even — as his lids grew heavy, his eyes darkening to a rich double espresso shot highlighting the sprinkle of brown sugar crystals.

She wasn't going to give him a choice. Crashing her lips into his, she tasted lime and tequila and a minty sweetness that blended into a delicious paradise against her tongue.

They traded kisses, back and forth. His fingers tenderly tangling in her hair, as hers scraped through his. Yet with every passing second their kiss deepened as their chests pressed against each other, until his hand slid up the back of her shirt, and she instantly tensed all over.

'Jordi, I can stop.' His breath short and sharp, as if trying to control himself.

'It's okay.'

'Can I see them?'

'Why?' Horrified, she pushed back.

'Because I want you to stop hiding them.'

She fought against her fear, struggled even. Yet, it was like her fingers belonged to someone else as she unbuttoned her shirt, pushing it off her shoulders, to stand there, never more exposed in her life. She'd done it for doctors, specialists, nurses every day for months through the various skin graft operations and bandage changes. Yet this was different.

Standing in only a bra and shorts, she turned her back to him, with nowhere to hide.

She heard his sharp inhale. It didn't surprise her. Her scars were ugly. They were a thick, lumpy, discoloured mesh of burned flesh that ran from her hips, up over her shoulders, and across her arms, spreading the way paint flicks off a brush down to her wrists. Her back was the worst.

She hugged herself. He wanted to see them, *well take a good look, buddy.*

She waited for him to tell her to put her shirt on. To walk away, or something.

Instead, he touched her. His fingertips trickled over her skin like drops of warm water. Then his lips pressed against them, as if trying to take away her pain, to heal the scars that truly did run deep, melting her with each kiss.

'Do they hurt?'

'They're getting better with time. There's still some discomfort when touched, or a sharp sting if I stretch the wrong way.' But she liked the way he touched her skin, so tenderly. But it still didn't hide what they were. 'They're ugly.' And she felt ugly, dropping her head, trapped under the heavy weight of shame.

'Do you know why I call you Angelfish?'

'Duh, you like fishing.'

'That. And because the first time I saw you, you looked like an angel who'd lost her wings. And these scars,' he said, tracing his finger over their shape, 'are shaped like angel wings to me.'

She blinked tears, swaying at the words that seemed to burrow deep into the darkest parts of her soul, the way a single white feather floats into an abyss.

'Never hide them from me.' He turned her around.

She expected to see pity, or horror in his eyes. But the look he gave her was utterly possessive. Their eyes locked, and her heart hammered a heavy rhythm as blood rushed heat through her body.

Her ragged breath matched his, as the need to find pleasure became all too overwhelming for her. She needed to have her body feel like her own again. Not some scarred horror story, but that of a female that started with his kiss that sent the ashes of her past to the wind, with his lips reviving her soul to give it wings, to beat free from the embers and rise like a phoenix.

Even with his touch so gentle, she felt a new flame under her skin, a delicious burn that mixed with desire.

The look on his face was savagely beautiful, and he wanted her. Just her.

Just as much as she wanted him.

'Take me to bed, Luke.'

He picked her up, holding her chest to his as he wrapped her legs around his waist. Their lips meshed with desperation, as if breathing for each other, and he carried her inside his room, pushing the door shut behind them.

Twenty-eight

Bliss. Luke had never truly understood the meaning of that simple word, bliss. It might not be how the dictionary would define it, but bliss seemed to be the only way to describe this feeling he had inside, as if he was floating on air. Pretty darned blissed out. All because of the beautiful woman, holding his hand, smiling at him like he was a king, as they walked down the hospital corridor.

Overnight, Luke had learned the power of forgiveness. Many had tried to tell him about forgiving himself, that he wasn't at fault for the outcome of that accident. But when Jordi had forgiven him, thanked him even, then the blessed gift of being with her and waking up to her … Bliss.

Pure. Freaking. Bliss.

'You should stay tonight, drive back in the morning.' In all honesty, he didn't want Jordi going back to Darwin at all. It was too far away.

'I've got to meet the plane tonight and start the orders for the week. And you'll be focusing on the competition. I'll be back to granny-sit on Friday.'

'Hey, if I can find someone else to look after Gran, would you like to come with me on the boat?'

'Really?'

'You'd make a cute first mate.' Ah, yes, his bliss was like a bubble full of sweet treats with Jordi as the sweetest treat any man could ever want. He dragged her closer, to swing his arm over her shoulders, to kiss the top of her soft hair and breathe in her heavenly floral scent. Bliss should be the name of her perfume, bottled just for him.

They strolled around the corner into Gran's room.

'Ready, Gran? Aw, crap.' He frowned, stopping just inside the room, as that bubble of bliss burst, scattering all that feel-good sentiment to smithereens.

'I can't freaking believe you called your father!' Gran was livid. Standing at the end of her bed, wagging her plump finger at him.

'I had to, Gran. I swore to Dad if anything happened to you, I'd make the call. Believe me, I didn't want to do it, either. But that was the deal.'

'Otherwise, I'd be tearing strips off Luke's hind if he hadn't.' Walden's deep voice cut through their argument. His beard was thick and woolly, the wrinkles around his eyes only deepened his tan, and he was still as strong as a wild bull, with a stare that could stand down a herd of charging buffalo.

'Here's your bag of clothes, Gran.' Luke held out her overnight bag. 'Tiara included.'

'You have a lot to make up for, young man. We were okay. You didn't need to get his highness off his high horse to gallop across the country to be here.' Gran snatched the bag, stomping into the bathroom and slamming the door behind her.

'I don't own any horses, Mum. Haven't done so for years.' Walden shouted at the closed door.

'Hi, Dad.'

'Son.' Walden pulled Luke into a beefy bear hug that always came with a hearty pat on the back. 'Good to see you.'

'You too.' Luke nodded at the duffel bag sitting at the end of the bed. 'Just fly in?'

'Landed at the airstrip an hour ago. I got sick of waiting for news.'

'I left you a stack of messages, telling you Gran was okay.'

'Got them. But I still wanted to be here. Who's this?' Walden nodded at Jordi hovering in the doorway.

'Dad, this is …' What did he call her? His girlfriend?

'Jordi.' She was a new woman, holding her hand out full of confidence. And he liked that look on her. Nearly as much as the way she'd looked with her hair spilled over his pillows with that blissful look in her eyes waking up to him and being with him.

Ah, yes, bliss.

Luke sighed, sliding his hands in his pockets, admiring the way the sun shone off her hair. He just couldn't stop watching her.

'I've heard some great things about you, sir.' Even if Jordi was biting her bottom lip that he liked to nibble on, she had her shirt sleeves rolled down to her wrists, and wasn't hiding her hands. Was Jordi feeling that bliss too?

'Well, you won't hear anything good now, not with my mother in the mood she's in.' Walden nodded at the closed bathroom door. 'Stubborn fool she is.'

'I can hear you! I'm old, not deaf!' Esther shouted from behind the door.

'Still a handful.' Walden chuckled. 'Listen, son, can we step out …' He tossed his thumb toward the hallway.

'I'll wait here for Esther.' Jordi moved to the bed, which left Luke to dutifully follow his father down the hallway and out into the sunshine.

'What happened?' Walden tapped his shirt pocket to pull out his sunglasses.

'I told you it was a fire.' Luke dragged his sunglasses off the brim of his favourite fishing cap. 'Gran was warring with the new neighbour. But Felix is good.' When he'd dropped the dog off last night, Felix was all over it like it was a baby. Then once Luke had explained the dog's grand adventure, Felix tried to talk Luke into doing a gig at the Sandfly.

'Dognapping, huh?' His father's lips twitched as if struggling to stop his smile.

'It seems Gran has grown attached to their dog.'

'We'll get her one, if that's what she wants. But I want her coming back with me.'

'No.' Luke frowned, crossing his arms over his chest.

'Son ...' His father dropped his large hand on his shoulder. 'Your grandmother started a fire.'

'It was in a forty-four-gallon drum, using some rubbish from the house —'

'No excuse, son. It was a toxic fire. The thing that's got me more worried is that she knows what not to burn, and she's lived out here all her life to know not to start a fire when under a total fire ban.'

His father was right. And it had niggled at him too because he'd discussed at length with Esther over what to incinerate and what went to the tip.

'Are we looking at a fine for breaching the fire ban?'

'No.'

'Good.' His father crossed his arms over his stocky chest. 'Esther's become a burden. I know she is. You don't need that, son. Not when you could do so much more with your time than look after your grandmother.'

'That's what family does, Dad.' Luke frowned at his father, who sounded just like his mother.

'I know. It's why I'm happy to have my mother at the aged care facility near me. They can monitor her with plenty of activities to keep her entertained and make sure she doesn't get arrested.'

'It won't be the same. Gran doesn't know anyone there. And Dad, Gran isn't sick. She's just her healthy, mischievous self, the same as she's always been.' But underneath something was happening to Gran. She wasn't the same and it worried him, but he didn't dare mention this to his father because it'd only give his parents the ammunition they needed to take Esther away — which is what scared her the most.

'She's forgetting things.'

'You would too if you lived as long and colourful a life like Gran has. Dad, you can hardly remember what's-it or who's-it from the pub you go fishing with.' Now he was making excuses for Esther. It was wrong.

'She's keeps calling me by my father's name.'

'And Gran keeps calling me Walden. And I think she does that because she misses you, Dad.'

Walden leaned his beefy shoulder against the wall of the hospital. 'Has she had those medical tests?'

'Yes. I did as you asked, and the doctor here ran them. Gran wanted to know, too. Her bones are strong, so no osteoporosis. And her hearing is fine—'

'We all heard that.'

'Gran doesn't have cataracts, but she uses glasses to read and watch the TV at night. She has a touch of arthritis in her knees, but still walks Cecil around the block every night before bed. If she moves to a cooler climate, she's worried her arthritis will play up like her hay fever. Despite the age spots and wrinkles she's always complaining about, Gran is a perfectly healthy eighty-four-year young woman.' But after the fire incident, he was planning on confronting her. That fire was a huge warning sign they'd be foolish to ignore because there was something wrong with Esther.

The sheer weight of his thoughts had his shoulders droop as he leaned back against the wall for support.

'Crikey, eighty-four? I couldn't remember how old she was on her last birthday. Did she get the flowers?'

'Yep. And she tossed half of them out onto the lawn to feed Cecil and the rest of them went to the funeral of a friend.'

Walden gave a deep and hearty chuckle. 'That's my mother. God love her.'

Sharing the joke, the father and son leaned against the wall and faced the view of the hospital's car park, where the main road led towards the highway. With the small outback airport on the left, its nearest neighbour was the police station. Next stood the local fire station that Luke knew very well. Opposite that sat a large vacant block of land.

'What happened to the ranger's station?' Walden pointed to the barren block.

'The house got eaten away by termites. They tore it down. The ranger's station has been moved to the back of the hospital, taking over the old doctor's house. More room. How long are you staying in town for, Dad?'

'A few days. Maybe a week, to do some fishing or something.'

'We've got that million-dollar barra happening at the moment.'

'True? I forgot the barra Classic was on this weekend.'

'Oh, really.' Luke narrowed his eyes at his father. Was this Walden's excuse to sneak away from Mum, and get a seat on the boat for the Classic? 'How is Mum?'

'Good. Told me to tell you to call her.'

'I've been busy.'

'I can see that.' He nudged Luke's side. 'She's a pretty girl, that one. Not as brassy as the others.'

'She's a keeper, Dad.' He said it without even thinking about it, but it felt right. 'Jordi's been helping with Gran, taking her on her rural runs delivering flowers. Gran loves it.'

'So why has Esther been mucking up so much?'

'Iris passed away.'

'Sorry to hear that.' His dad rubbed the back of his thick neck. 'I didn't mind Iris; she was a good neighbour who was at every one of our family events. Not like the stick-in-the-muds around us in suburbia. Always complaining about me parking the truck in the street or warming it up in the mornings. But your mother's happy. Going to yoga, and pottery classes and some other craft classes. We have her sister and her new husband over for dinner. He's a wiry fella who complains about getting papercuts in his day job.' The father and son—the rugged big-game hunters who had carried wild banteng over their shoulders out of a monsoon jungle filled with snakes, crocodiles, wild buffalo, and boars, to save an endangered species—shared a look. 'Still, it's good to know Violet's not sitting home alone, bored, while I'm out on the road.'

'Are you happy, Dad?' After this morning, while wearing those glossy rose-coloured glasses, seduced under that feel-good bubble of bliss, his answer to that question would be a *hell yeah!*

'Oh, you know, happy wife, happy life. How do you know Jordi?'

Classic deflection, Dad!

Luke could say she was a customer, or that she worked at the pub. But Jordi was more than that. 'Remember that car accident on the highway …'

'The one where you got burnt saving that girl. The reason for your bravery medal?'

He licked his lips, peering beneath his hat brim to the fire station that used to be his second home.

'That's her?' Walden pointed at the hospital's main doors.

'It was pure coincidence we met up again.' But he was eternally grateful the minute Jordi had driven back into his world.

The hospital's main doors slid open to Jordi helping Gran outside.

'Can we go now?' Gran adjusted her tiara, then rummaged around in her carpetbag. 'My hipflask is empty, and I want to see Cecil. Jordi told me Cecil refused to leave the house this morning, staying beside my chair.'

'That's rare,' said Walden, arching an eyebrow at Luke.

'I left the door open for Cecil to do his business.' But the water buffalo with his big black eyes, was sulking, big time, missing Esther. Luke could relate. 'Come on, Gran. We're in Jordi's van. Got room for you too, Dad.'

'Nope. You can stay at the pub, Walden.' Gran wagged that lethal plump finger at her grown son. 'We all know you're here to lock me away in some home, when I've got a perfectly good home now.'

Yep, one big happy family. With Gran grumbling, Dad wearing that stubborn look that said he was not yet convinced that Esther should stay, and poor Jordi stuck in the middle. It should make for an interesting ride back to the Lodge.

Twenty-nine

'Dad left.' Luke's sad sigh sounded over the phone that Jordi had balanced between her ear and shoulder while she flicked through her paperwork.

'When?' She leaned against the side of the van inside the florist's work shed.

'Gran and I dropped him off at the airstrip this morning to catch the mail plane. Dad warned us both if anything happened to Gran, she was going away.'

'Like some last warning?'

'Yep. Dad wanted to stay. You could tell he misses the place. I wouldn't have minded it, but he had to get back. He'd promised to take Mum to one of her sister's sixtieth this weekend. It's at some vineyard in the hills, accommodation already paid for and everything.'

'Sounds nice.' Romantic even, like the many red roses she'd finished preparing for the Friday date-night trade.

'So, are you set for the weekend?' She felt giddy, with her tummy swirling just at the thought of seeing Luke again. To have his lopsided grin aimed at her, and to feel his arms wrap around her as he held her against his chest, where she could just breathe and let the world completely disappear.

'I am. At the pub last night, we had our orientation and explanation of the fishing rules for the Classic. Lenny told me to tell you he misses his little cake crumb.'

'Weird ...' But her lips tugged into a grin. 'I'll be there tonight.'

'I won't be. I'll be watching Gran.'

'I've reorganised my run to swing by to collect Esther first. I'll call when I'm in range.'

'Good. I'll have her ready. Not that it'll be hard, Gran loves doing the rural run with you.'

'I enjoy doing it with her. She's fun. And she knows most of the people.'

'So, who are you delivering flowers to this week?'

'Well, I've got a stack of *thank you* flowers to deliver from some very grateful husbands fishing in the Classic. What do you do in these fishing competitions?'

'Fish. What else is there?'

'I know that. But ...' She felt so dumb asking when she could just search it online—if she wanted to. But she preferred hearing about it from Luke.

'Well, for the Elsie Creek Barra Classic, it's a three-day day fishing competition making it a long weekend. And there are two cups, one for best teams, and the other for best angler. The Elsie Creek Classic isn't as big as the barra competitions around Darwin, they can get up to a quarter of a million in cash and prizes with these big fancy trophies.'

'And the Elsie Creek Classic?'

'This year they've got some big sponsors, so there's ten thousand in cash, and some prizes from the local stores, including some sleek-looking fishing gear I wouldn't mind adding to my arsenal. But they have this old brass trophy that sits on the pub's top shelf. The winner gets their name engraved on it, and a glass one to take home. I have a few collecting dust around here, somewhere.'

Probably next to the bravery medal she'd heard about.

'We're restricted to fishing in an eighty-five-kilometre stretch of water, where the marshals and Porter will be patrolling.'

'That's a lot of river area.'

'Not really, when you've got over eighty boats vying for space. It starts just above the Elsie Creek boat ramp through to the mouth of the river, including the side creeks. But each day we can only start fishing from sunrise and must be back by sunset on the Friday and Saturday. That's when the judges tally up the weight and size of our fish catch each day, converting them into points they list on this big board at the pub. On Sunday we finish at midday, so they can announce the winners and people can pack up and get ready for work on Monday.'

'So whoever gets the highest points wins? Not the biggest fish?'

'Yep. They have different points for different fish types like saratogas and grunters, even mud crabs.'

'Do you get points for the prettiest fish? Or points for the fish with the shiniest scales?'

His chuckle only made her smile behind her fingers.

'Just fish types, size, and weight. Yesterday was more about ground rules and boat checks. A lot of those punters, new to the area, checked out the river. They'll be heading out there now …'

Jordi checked her watch. It wasn't even sunrise.

'So, when you get here, my little angelfish, I'll hit the river.'

'On your own?' She gripped her heart, unsure of him venturing into the realm of crocodiles alone.

'I go fishing on my own all the time. But my normal fishing partners are busy.'

'Who's that?'

'Dad. Even though Dad couldn't stay, we did some fishing while he was here. He helped me work out a strategy for the Classic. And Porter's busy playing policeman, patrolling the waters. But hey, I helped Dad put in these granny-cams he brought in with him, yesterday.'

'Does Esther know?'

'Dad told Gran, leaving the empty boxes on the kitchen table so she knew all about them.'

'What did Esther say?' Either it was an invasion of privacy or there really was an issue with Esther.

'She was furious. But Dad refused to tell her where he put

them, letting her know that he'd be watching if she mucked up and she'd be on the first plane to the retirement home.'

'That's cruel.'

His sigh was heavy. 'Honestly, Jordi, it'll give me peace of mind for a bit until the test results come back.'

'What test results?'

'The reason they were taking so long with Gran in the hospital after the fire, wasn't about the nurses playing with the pug, it was because the doctor was conducting a series of tests.' He took a shaky breath, his voice lowering as he said, 'Jordi, they were screening her for dementia. Not only did they do a stack of blood tests, but they were assessing Gran's skills for reading, writing, orientation and short-term memory.'

'Why didn't she say anything?'

'Gran only told me after Dad left. I'd been confronting her over the fire suggesting we may have an issue, when the cunning thing confessed all, only *after* she'd made me swear not to say anything to Dad, not until the results come back.' But his voice was loaded with worry.

'What will you do if ...' Her heart just ached for both Luke and for Esther.

'We've agreed to wait for the results, then take it from there. But I may have to consider getting her a companion, like you mentioned.' He exhaled heavily, just picturing him brushing fingers though his hair. 'So, when do you leave?'

'In about ten minutes.' The back door of the shed opened, and her sister stepped inside. A full hour and a half early for the job. 'And here comes the boss, so I'd better look busy.'

'Drive safe, beautiful. See you when I can.'

'Was that the new boyfriend?' Natalie playfully bobbed her eyebrows while carrying two takeaway coffee cups.

Jordi shrugged, putting her phone away to take her coffee. 'Morning. You're early.'

'I wanted to catch you before you left.'

'I was just about to leave, so good timing. Thanks for the coffee.' She took a sip while scribbling some notes on the clipboard, before she slid it between the seats of her van. 'I did up the floral displays for all of the online orders, the usual Friday trade, and there was a funeral request that came through late last night.'

'Whose?'

'An ex-football coach from the Darwin Buffaloes. I did his wreath up in the shape of a football. I think they'll like that one. The funeral director's collecting it around ten.'

'Good ...' Natalie dumped her bag and coffee on the nearby workbench. 'Um, listen, sis.'

Jordi arched an eyebrow at Natalie, who only called her that before sharing bad news. Was this why her sister was here so early?

'Mitchell got the job.'

She struggled to stay calm. 'When did Mitchell find out?'

'Last night. He's stoked.' So was Natalie with her excited smile growing.

'Do you know where he's getting posted?'

'Edinburgh RAAF Base. In two weeks.' Natalie dug around in her bag for her phone, to show a map on the small screen. 'The base is twenty-eight kilometres away from Adelaide, where we'll have a new house and everything.'

'And what will you do?'

'Well, I don't think I'll be working for long.' Natalie patted her lower belly and smiled a soft soothing motherly smile. The kind of smile Natalie normally gave to cute puppies and kittens, but not her stomach.

'You're pregnant?'

Natalie barely nodded, looking happy and terrified all at the same time.

'Oh my gosh!' Jordi squealed, rushing to hug her sister, truly delighted for her. 'You'll be an amazing mother and Mitchell's going to be the best dad.'

'Mitchell is over the moon. I've never seen the man so happy. I am blessed that way. But ... Listen, Jordi.' Natalie grabbed her sister's hand. 'Remember how we were going to rent out the house?'

'Yes.'

'Well, the funniest thing happened last night. We had the realtor come to inspect the house, to tell us what we could rent it out for, and he brought along a potential tenant.'

'And ...'

'The guy offered to buy the place, right then and there, saying he had the money in the bank and everything.' Natalie tossed her hands in the air.

'Was he kidding?'

'I thought so too and told him to pull his head in. But then he goes on about how he'd spent the past year searching for the perfect place for his family and was willing to sign the contract right then and there. All while the real estate agent was drooling over his commission for the quick sale.' Natalie then gripped Jordi's wrist. 'I was so stunned, I could only squeak because I'd completely lost my voice. Mitchell had to do the talking for me.'

'No way. You—speechless?' Because Natalie always did the talking, which is what made her so good when dealing with customers in their store.

'I know. But it was real.' Natalie rummaged through her bag and pulled out some paperwork from the realtor.

'What did you say?'

'Nothing. I couldn't speak, just blink. Thank goodness for my savvy husband, because Mitchell said we'd need to get an appraisal on the house first, because I haven't got a clue on what it's worth, and that we'd get back to them.'

'You've certainly had a big twenty-four hours. The baby, Mitchell's job, posting to a new house?' But selling the house wasn't a part of their plans—that was their parent's house, the family home. 'What do you want to do, Nat?'

'Sell.' Natalie didn't even hesitate.

Yet Jordi couldn't stop blinking as she tried to process all that Natalie had dumped on her. 'Why?'

'It's our way of letting go to move on from the past. Dad and Mum would be okay with that. No matter what we decide, all they'd care about was that we were happy.' Then

Natalie winced. 'We can also sell the store and really make a clean break.'

Jordi's throat tightened as she struggled to speak. 'I was going to buy your share of the family business.' *Family, sis!*

'Gladys, our part-time florist ...'

Jordi barely nodded, with her feet somehow glued to the floor while her stomach churned like sour butter.

'Gladys is going partners with her cousin, Bernice, who is a florist too. Gladys says her cousin has sold everything, and is all cashed up from her divorce, and is coming to live up here. They've offered to buy the store, take over our commercial contracts, and everything.'

'Including the rural run? Because we both know Gladys doesn't go past the Berrimah line if she can help it.'

'No. We'll have to surrender the rural run to the other stores.'

'But I built up that part of the business myself. The resorts, the—'

'Most of it's just for the tourist season. What about you going back to your dream of being a grower? Or come with me. I'd love to have you around when the baby comes. Mitchell would love you to be there, too.'

'I—I ...' Jordi struggled to think, snatching up her van keys. 'I've got to go.' She had a delivery schedule to keep.

'Think about it, Jordi. We can sell both the house and the store. It'll be a fresh start for all of us.'

'What about Luke?' Her Luke. The only guy on the planet to like her—scars and all.

'You've just started dating the guy, if you can call it dating, when his main aim seems to be to get you to babysit his grandmother.'

'Am not.' Although that last phone conversation did have her thinking her sister might be right. 'Hey, I like Esther. You would too.'

'You know better than anyone to commit yourself to someone you've just met.'

'We didn't just meet.'

'You know what I mean. For all you know, you're only attracted to him because he rescued you.'

Jordi gasped as if slapped in the face. 'That's not true.' She couldn't remember the accident or Luke saving her.

'Who knows what you'll find if you came to Adelaide. Maybe someone who's more than a guy who works in a bottle shop—'

'Luke isn't just a bottle shop manager.'

'Isn't he? Because, sis, you deserve better. Not someone who …' Natalie rubbed her nose as if trying to delicately reword her next sentence.

Jordi could guess what her sister was thinking. 'You think Luke is only with me because he's feeling guilty for not saving our parents?'

Natalie cocked an eyebrow, with an obvious disapproval for Luke written all over her face.

'Don't say it …' Jordi closed the van's sliding door, then climbed in, started her van, and lowered the driver's window. 'I'll text you from Elsie Creek and at the resorts on the itinerary. Pass on my congratulations to Mitchell over the job.' She punched the large button for the automatic roller doors to rumble open, where daylight barely broke in the salmon-pink sky. 'And congratulations on the baby, I'm thrilled for you, Nat.' But she wasn't thrilled about the rest of the news.

Thirty

Almost fifty sleek barra boats rested on trailers that lined up under the spotlights beside the towering two-storey pub. Nearby a band played in the beer garden, where a crowd of sports fishermen in their fishing caps and team shirts mingled with cowboys in Akubras and denim jeans, and the miners with their high-vis shirts and steel-capped boots, all discussing the day's events over beer and roast beef, as the judges tallied the scores for day one of the Elsie Creek Barra Classic.

In the kitchen, Jordi helped Lenny with the stream of orders that had been constant from the second she'd stepped inside. Wrapping up takeaway meals, plating salads, in between packing and unpacking the dishwasher. She'd never worked so hard or fast, up to her elbows in suds and water, she gazed through the kitchen window to catch the last of the sunset.

Sadly, there was no Luke to watch while he worked in the bottle shop. He was at the Lodge, watching over Esther where the mood was heavy either from the pending test results or the pressure to perform well at tomorrow's final full day of fishing for the Classic, with the million-dollar barra still swimming free.

'Is it time?' With his fancy felt fedora pushed back on his head, Billy carried a stack of dirty plates into the kitchen.

'For what?' Lenny checked over his board full of meal orders while flipping burgers and steaks on the grill.

'The pirate podcast?'

'I'll take them from you, Billy.' Jordi took his pile of dishes.

'You're a good sort, aren't you little miss Flower Girl?' Billy tipped his hat to her, then fiddled with the speakers that sat on the shelf. 'Shh, it's on.'

The radio speakers boomed out some cheesy music introducing the show known as *Dramas from the Dinghy*, where the pub's front bar became eerily silent.

'Today, being day one of our tiny town's Barra Classic, the pub's no doubt full of menacing land lubbers who've come from all over to share their tall tales of the fish that got away. And we all know that classic story where the fish gets bigger and bigger every time they tell the tale. So, here's hoping you've got your ears glued like you do to your favourite fish finder, and listen in on this week's fish reports,' started the husky voice of the reel rascal, River Ron, with Tidal Tom chuckling in the background.

They breezed through the expected tides, then talked about how the full moon, expected tomorrow, would affect the water and the brains of fishermen. Then it was on to lures, reels, and all things to do with fishing. Jordi zoned out as she unpacked the dishwasher, piling up porcelain like a deck of cards.

Waitresses rushed in carrying dirty plates from the outdoor spit roast, while Lenny continued cooking for the truckers' usual Friday home-time rush. The front bar was full, and the restaurant booked out for tonight. Yet Lenny executed dish after dish, order after order and still found the time to show Jordi how to make the most delicate lotus flower out of a lush green kiwi fruit. She had to keep admiring it on the windowsill above the sinks.

'And now we pull the bung outta the boat for the Alpha Angler of the week, Dom, and his pretty black boat, the Barra Wrangler, for doing an unwarranted rooster wave over the flower girl.'

Billy looked up from his dinner to point his forkful of cauliflower, at Jordi. 'Oi, that's you.'

'Not again.' She rolled her eyes, turning her back on them to scrub at the pot in the sink, yet she couldn't stop listening to River Ron over the speakers.

'According to the fellas enjoying a cool frothy ale on a warm day from the top deck of the Sandfly Saloon, the flower girl had just made the Virgins' Board and was showing off her masterful first fish—a whopping thirty-two kilo barra.'

'Whoa!' Tidal Tom chimed in, but the same word seemed to echo from down the corridor of the pub.

'Then she was forced to swallow a face full of river water, thanks to that coastal cowboy, Dom.' River Ron wasn't happy.

'Listen fellas, we all share the same river this weekend,' said Tidal Tom. *'Can we please keep our heads cool and not interfere with other boats and their passengers? We're fishing with crocodiles. Man-eating mothers! And we all know how big, bad, and fugly the crocs are around Sandfly.'*

'But as a change of subject, congratulations to all those fishing virgins who became a part of the Elsie Creek fishing tradition, getting their mugshots on the Sandfly Saloon's wall of fishing virgins. And to the flower girl for scoring that big barra. We saw that photo. It was a beauty.'

'Too right it was. So, the myth of women being bad on boats is busted—unless you're one of those fellas who like to use that myth to keep the little women at home.' Tidal Tom chuckled, with Billy and Lenny doing the same in the kitchen.

'Whichever way you throw your lures this weekend, peoples, be sure to kiss the little man or woman on the cheek as you leave home, pat the billy lids on the head, and tell 'em you love 'em. Most of all, fishos, be safe in the waters, and may the best fisherperson win this year's Elsie Creek Classic.'

This week it didn't bother Jordi that her nickname was mentioned on the radio, not like it had last week. But then going back to the city where no one knew her, or had even heard of Elsie Creek, helped. Or was she getting a thicker skin for being recognised in this small town?

Today, while doing her deliveries, with Esther hijacking the passenger seat of her van, people waved to her as she drove through town. Esther introduced her to the women who worked in the supermarket where she put out her displays. Then it was across the road to the post office for Esther to collect her mail, where the owner of the craft store, that was part of the post office, hit her up to do classes on floral arrangements. Her! The girl who hid. Ha!

But then walking with Esther back to her van to complete her deliveries, men tipped their wide-brimmed hats to them along the main street and asked about Luke. A few of them even congratulated Jordi on her first fish.

And for a moment, it was like she was a part of something, with that sense of belonging to a community that cared.

But she didn't live in Elsie Creek, and Jordi had no idea what her future might hold. Not after the massive cannonball pounding of information overload from her sister this morning, it left Jordi with an overwhelming blend of fear, from the fear of change, the fear of loss, the fear of rejection and loneliness, and the fear of her family leaving her. All those combined fears sent waves of panic rising in her chest, overwhelming her with the need to hide, freeze, or flee. She had to talk about something else.

'What's a rooster wave?' Jordi asked Billy, who was using a bread roll to sop up the gravy on his dinner plate.

'It's when they tilt the outboard engine propeller to push up a wave of water that's shaped like one of those long and curvy feathers on a rooster's tail. Is that what happened to you?'

'Yep. I got doused. Big time.' And lost the lotus flower Luke had given her.

'I used to play rooster wars with my brother in our dinghies, all the time. But back then, crocodiles were being hunted, and they'd run for cover at the sound of a boat. Now, as a protected species, them smart buggers just sit around waiting for us fisherman to jag a barra, and reel it in, so they can steal it from us.'

'Luke warned me that could happen.'

'They do it all the time, the mongrels.'

'So how big was this fish?' Lenny asked Jordi. 'Tell me

Luke took a photo.'

'He did.' She swiped through her phone to the photo of her holding her fish. 'Here.'

'Wow, what a whopper! And your first catch, too. Luke's gonna win the Classic for sure.' Lenny passed the phone to Billy.

'Luke is the local favourite to win. How come you're not going with him?' Billy handed the phone back to Jordi. 'Everyone knows you two are seeing each other.'

She felt the heat brush her cheeks. 'I'm helping with Esther.'

'I saw Walden in town the other day,' said Billy. 'He's a good sort. Shame, what happened to their crops. The Bennetts grew decent bananas. But I've been on some great hunting trips with Walden, he had this knack for reading animal tracks like he was reading a newspaper. Luke's got the same deadeye for shooting, like his ancestor, Bison-eye Bennett. All of them Bennetts are lethal and cunning when it comes to hunting their prey, so my money's on Luke winning this weekend.'

'Oi, I've still got a shot at the title, you know.' Lenny patted down his white chef's shirt, wearing a cheesy grin.

'As if. You won't even roll outta bed until lunchtime, just in time to turn on the grill.'

'That's my job. You go do yours and leave me and my little cake crumb alone.'

With Billy chased out of the kitchen, Jordi went back to washing dishes, when the screen door opened and a bunch of flowers were thrust into her face.

She stepped back, with a smile growing, expecting to see Luke.

But it wasn't Luke that held them, it was Dom.

'What are you doing?'

Dom removed his white cowboy hat and held out the flowers. 'I wanted to apologise for doing the rooster wave over you last weekend.'

'That was rude.'

'I know.' He dropped his chin, holding his hat over his heart, with his big blue eyes filled with remorse. 'I'm sorry you got caught in the middle of our war. I never meant to hurt you, or ruin your celebrations on your first fish. It was a great catch, by the way. You look cute in the photo on Sandfly's wall.'

Wow, Dom was being really sweet for a bad guy.

'If you ever want to go fishing with a proper professional, I'll gladly take you out.' Sliding on his big cowboy hat, he flashed a grin full of cocky confidence.

It was the look of a player, that her father had warned her about in one of his many valuable life lessons. But normally nobody saw her, and certainly not to give her flowers.

'Oi!' Lenny swished his spatula in the air like a sword. 'You leave the flower girl alone. That's Luke's lady now.'

'Here, take them.' Dom pushed the flowers into her hands.

'You know I made these, right?'

'I know. And I bought the last bunch so you can enjoy them.' Dom winked at her and was out the door, leaving her to hold her first bunch of *sorry* flowers, which weren't from the guy she was seeing.

Was she really Luke's girl?

She'd trusted her instincts over Dom being a player. And she'd always thought of Luke as a hustler. So now that Luke had gotten over his guilt, and once this weekend competition was over to end her granny-sitting duties, what then of their future? Did they have a future—when she struggled to see one for herself.

Thirty-one

L uke hadn't been able to sleep. The excitement and the pressure to perform well today were getting to him.

Yesterday, he'd had a huge haul that put him well in front of the other competitors in the Elsie Creek Classic. But today, he had to be sneaky and super smart, to keep ahead in the game. Every move had to be calculated and recalculated with a laser-like focus that was exhausting. It had him grinding his teeth with that desire to win, especially when he was just a small-time local going up against the professional anglers who did this for a living.

At four in the morning, he was out of bed, and showered. With the billy boiling in the background, Luke walked around his boat, checking for the hundredth time that his fishing rods, reels, and lures were all in place, as the large moon hung like a round globe in the night sky.

'Nervous?' Jordi stood in the bedroom doorway, rubbing the sleep from her eyes. She was breathtaking with her hair down, wearing his shirt with the hem brushing her soft thighs.

'You should be back in bed.' He kissed her forehead, inhaling her floral aroma.

'I'm used to being up early.' She headed for the small kitchen area and made herself a cuppa. 'When do you head out?'

'Soon. I want to beat the rush for the boat ramp this morning. I found an AirTag under the boat seat last night.' It's why he was inspecting the boat's hull. Again.

'A what?'

He held up the large metallic button. 'It's a magnetic GPS tracker.' These dirty tactics were ruining the fun of fishing — especially when the Elsie Creek Classic used to be a spot of fun for the locals.

Her cute nose crinkled, highlighting her freckles that weren't freckles. 'Are you saying you're being followed? Over a fishing competition. For real?'

'Angelfish, there's a million dollars up for grabs. You bet its big business.' And he had a lot to prove this weekend.

'I didn't think fishing was such a big thing. Please don't be offended by that, when we both know I caught my first fish just last week.'

'All good.' Luke took her coffee, kissing her cheek. He liked being near her. Fully understanding what an honour and a privilege it was to hold her hand or stroke her soft hair, when she didn't like anyone touching her. Plus, he'd never slept better than whenever he had her in his bed — except when there was a million dollars on the line and a chance to prove himself if he wanted to start a fishing charter business.

As the glowing full moon hovered over the sleeping outback, they sat by the bench and faced his boat. His pride and joy. And again, he went over his mental checklist for the thousandth time.

'How big is sports fishing?'

'Huge. My tackle box has close to fifteen thousand dollars' worth in lures.' A special tackle box he strapped to the floor of his boat so it would never be flung overboard.

'No way.'

'It's not hard to accumulate, when you pick up a lure here and there. A lot were given to me.'

'Like sponsorship?'

'Mainly it's Christmas, birthdays, as a prize in bets, or in a barter deal.' But he loved fishing and his boat. But with so much on the line, it felt like a job filled with all this pressure to beat the clock. '*The Barra Bandit* is a second-hand boat, but you saw some of those anglers' boats last night at the pub.'

'Some of them are very fancy.'

'The cheapest would be worth about twenty grand. But the real anglers' boats, the professional game fishing boat—'

'Like Dom's boat? What's that called?'

He frowned at that mention of that cretin's name. '*Barra Wrangler.* With all its trimmings, it'd be worth a cool hundred grand.'

'Wow.' Her eyebrows lifted over the rim of her coffee cup.

'Hey, why did Dom give you those flowers?' Luke nodded at the flowers sitting in a large pickle jar on the workbench. No one should be giving Jordi flowers—except him.

'I told you last night, Dom gave them to me to say *sorry* for hitting me with that rooster wave at Sandfly.'

'Why did you bring them home? I don't like that prick.' Luke still owed Dom a punch in the mouth for doing that to Jordi.

'You're not jealous, are you?' She pursed her lips in disbelief.

'I don't want you near Dom, and I'm sorry you got caught in our war, but he's only doing that to get back at me.'

'Funny, Dom said the same thing.'

Didn't that make his frown deepen as his hands curled into fists. Luke was going to pummel Dom for playing mind games, not only with him, but with his sweet, sensitive Jordi—who'd come so far in such a short amount of time. He wasn't going to let anyone mess with that or her.

'Don't worry, Lenny chased him out of the kitchen.' Jordi flippantly waved her hand.

'You should've thrown those flowers in the bin.'

She plonked her cup onto the bench. 'I made that flower posy. And I was planning on giving them to Esther this morning, even though she'll probably throw them onto the lawn to feed Cecil.'

He chuckled. 'Yeah, sorry, you can't keep flowers around here for long. Not with Cecil. He's known for breaking fences and trampling over obstacles for a decent feed of flowers.

We've had to reinforce our veggie patch and only grow certain things because of Cecil.'

'My sister's had an offer to buy the house.'

'Eh?' Luke blinked at the abrupt change in conversation.

'And we've had an offer for the store.'

His jaw dropped, knowing the reason Jordi was working at the pub was to save up to help her buy out her sister's share of the florist shop.

'Also, Natalie's asked me to go down south, to Adelaide, with them.'

Oh, no! 'So your brother-in-law got the job?'

She nodded. 'And they're pregnant …'

Oh, he was wide awake now!

Jordi traced her finger over the aluminium bench. 'It seems my new profession is to be a sitter for grandmothers and future nieces or nephews.'

'Why didn't you say anything sooner?'

'My sister sprung all of this on me yesterday morning as I was leaving, and I've been digesting it.'

'It's a lot …' *It was too much.* Running his fingers through his hair as if to get a grip.

'And before you ask, I don't know what I'm doing—but I'm fully aware that this weekend is a big deal for you. So, what are the chances of someone catching that fish?'

'A million to one.'

'And if you land it?'

He gave her a lopsided grin. 'Look at you using the fishing lingo.'

'Hanging out with you it's bound to rub off.' She rolled her pretty aqua eyes.

'And that's a good thing, Angelfish.' He leaned over and kissed her forehead as his phone's alarm beeped. 'It's showtime.'

'Can I help?'

'Could you grab me an extra bottle of insect repellent from my room? With the full moon, it'll bring out the midges, which is good for the fish, but not so good on the ankles.

There should be some repellent in the shopping bag on my desk somewhere. I'll load up the ice.'

It was as if hot strips of lead lay across his shoulders, with the anxiety swirling deep in the pit of his guts at the thought of Jordi leaving. But he had to focus on today, then tonight he'd talk to Jordi to find out what she wanted, because he didn't want to lose her. Not now.

Thirty-two

Inside Luke's large bedroom, a few closed doors made up the far wall, where she searched for a shopping bag. Among the fishing lines and lures there was no shopping bag or insect repellent on his desk, but she did find a red box hidden under some paperwork.

The stiff lid on the flat jeweller's box creaked as she opened it. Inside, lying on a bed of black velvet was a circular bronze medal containing the Commonwealth's coat of arms, attached to a ribbon made of alternating red and magenta stripes. It was the bravery medal she'd heard about. Loose in the box was a smaller medal for valour from the fire department, and other commendation bars similar to the ones her father had worn on his police uniform.

Hearing about the accident from Luke's point of view had been both harrowing yet illuminating. He'd been able to answer the many questions she'd always wanted to ask, but her sister would cry every time Jordi asked, so she stopped asking.

Still in a coma, Jordi had missed the policeman's funeral they gave her father, buried alongside her mother. Stuck in the hospital and then the house, due to an incredibly high risk of infection simply for going out in public, she couldn't go to the coroner's inquest.

But now with her sister preparing for her next journey in life, and with Luke ready to start his next grand adventure, where did that leave her?

She slammed the lid down on the box and rummaged

around for the repellent. She shifted around the desk, bumping into the side door it cracked open.

Was this the door to the armoury? Surely Luke wouldn't leave it open?

Curious to see what a professional hunter's armoury looked like, she found the light panel.

As the overhead light flickered on, her eyes widened.

It was a small room, with special padding along its walls and ceiling. Recording equipment and a pair of microphones sat on two desks facing each other, where a plastic shopping bag sat containing the insect repellent. Next to that lay a notepad, where the blue ink read:

Angelfish's flowers of the week:

-Pamela Hopkins' birthday, teacher at the school, dating a cowboy (not Cowboy Freaking Craig)

-John Frazier's sorry flowers for his wife Eliza

-Marie Pederson does twenty years at the council office

The list went on …

-Alex sends Verily flowers to celebrate Baby Elsie's first month after heart surgery

-Tony Wright sends flowers to Kelly-Anne for thirtieth wedding anniversary

Page after page of the same handwriting, recording every floral delivery Jordi had made to Elsie Creek these past few months.

Her frown deepened as she read the whiteboard's big fat headline: *Dramas from the Dinghy publishing schedule.*

'Is this where I'm supposed to come up with something profound?' Luke stood in the doorway, rubbing the back of his neck.

'What is this?'

'What do you want me to say? It's pretty obvious what it is.'

'You're that podcast? The *Dramas from the Dinghy*?'

He nodded.

'How? It doesn't sound like you.'

'We use an AI filter to disguise our voices.'

'Who's we?'

'Porter and me.'

'Which one is Porter? Because I've heard that podcast tease the police.' And Porter was a policeman.

'Porter is Tidal Tom, and I'm ...'

'River Ron.' She rubbed her forehead. 'You hustled me. No—you used me.'

'No, I didn't.'

'Yes, you did.' She held up the wad of notes. 'This is a list of my deliveries for who knows how many months?'

'It's not a secret, is it? Because every customer who drives through the bottle shop brags about their fishing trips, tides, who caught what and where.'

'I asked for directions, not fishing tips. I know I didn't give out too many details, just addresses for places I couldn't find ... Did Esther tell you?'

'Some.'

'But that was only two trips.' She flicked through the names on the sheets. 'This is months' worth of customers names ...' All those times Luke had loaded her esky and peeked into the back of her van, he wasn't checking out the flowers, he was checking out names and messages written on the cards.

But then she saw the name for baby Elsie and waved the notes at him. 'Hey, I told you not to say anything about Baby Elsie and her flowers for heart surgery when we spoke on the phone. I know I did.'

He hung his head low.

'My family, we may not have some sworn oath like the

police or firemen do, but customer confidentiality is important to us. We don't share personal details about a customer's order without the customer's explicit consent.'

'You asked me for directions, to find the people you were delivering flowers to.'

'Because *I trusted you!*' But then she had also told him more than she'd normally would because she'd been so stupidly attracted to him and so desperate to keep a conversation. 'I didn't expect you to turn it into gossip and blab about it all over the airwaves.' She fisted the notes tight, tempted to throw them at him. 'This is my family's business and professional reputation.'

'What do you want me to say? Sorry? When I don't get why you're so upset over this. It's just harmless gossip. Besides, I'd never expected you to listen to the show in the first place, especially when you don't fish or live out here.'

'Lenny and Billy play that podcast in the kitchen.'

'Damn, I forgot about that.' He dropped his head with hands on hips.

'So, I was never meant to know.' She narrowed her eyes at him, clenching her teeth.

'No one is. Except Porter and me.'

She exhaled heavily, trying to be reasonable about all of this, because her policeman father had taught her that there were always two sides to every story, offering him a chance to explain themselves. 'Why? What do you have to hide?'

All he could offer was a shrug. 'I know you hide, when you shouldn't.'

Whoa! Her eyes widened as she staggered back. Where did that come from? But she hid for a reason—and that was to stop herself from getting hurt. Case in point.

'Arsehole!' She shook with fury. Storming past him, she scooped up her overnight bag and dumped it on the bed.

'Hey, I didn't mean to say that, Jordi. I'm sorry.'

'Me too.' Her sister was right, she shouldn't be committing her future or anything to anyone, especially when they'd just started dating—*if* you could call it dating.

Because it was just a deal for Luke to have her granny-sit so he could go fishing.

The thing is she'd do anything for Luke. Absolutely anything. And that's what scared her. She cared for him so much more than she'd realised. And after losing her parents, that sting of losing someone she loved still hurt. She had to stop this. Right here. Right now.

'Where are you going?'

She wriggled into her jeans and T-shirt, dumping his shirt on the bed. 'To the Lodge. Don't worry, I'll still perform my duties as your granny-sitter just for today—but that's for Esther, not for you. You can go do whatever the hell you want.' Even though the humiliation of being used burned her chest in a whole new way. A new type of scalding stabbed at her heart like a thousand hot pokers. She'd been played by the hustler.

But she also had to play the hustler by pushing him away.

'Aw, come on, Jordi, the podcast was just a joke.'

'A joke, huh? And I nothing more than a joke to you, too?'

'No. Never.'

Or was she just a tool he used to stop that guilt he'd put on himself over his parent's accident—especially when it wasn't his fault.

'We only did it to blow off steam, and as a distraction when Porter was trying to get over. Tess. Hanging around the bottle shop, Porter heard the customers eagerly tell us where they went fishing, and who caught what, while I'd load up their eskies with booze and ice.'

'But I never spoke to Porter, and I never spoke to you about fishing—I just asked for directions!' Even though it hurt to do this, she needed to fight this feeling she had for him, livid at herself for daring to fall for a guy and stabbed her finger at him. 'Yet you broadcast my list of customers, my deliveries. On. The. Air.'

How had she been so blind to not see this? She'd recognised the names broadcasted over the air, while washing dishes in the pub's kitchen. At the time, she'd been surprised that she knew the names, because she didn't know many people in town, only the title on the cards that she delivered to strangers. Those fleeting moments where she got to peek into people's personal lives, that would make her customers happy, that in turn made her feel happy. Now, she felt like she'd betrayed them all.

'Jordi, I never meant to hurt you. The podcast was just something Porter and I did while hanging at home watching over Gran. We didn't think anyone would find our podcast to listen, or that it'd take off as fast as it did when the local radio station started broadcasting it. I only meant it as a joke, scribbling down a script in between serving customers in the bottle shop. We weren't serious about it.'

'Serious, huh?' She pointed back to the room. 'Your recording equipment and publishing schedule looks pretty serious to me.' But was he serious about her?

She zipped up her bag and threw it over her shoulder. For once she didn't let the pain of her pinching scars win. 'Why do you hide behind fake names and fake voices?'

'Because I don't like airing my business, Bennett business in public.'

'Ha! Says the front man running a pirate podcast, gossiping about everyone else's lives. Me included, as the famous flower girl!' The sarcasm hung from her words as she headed out the door.

'Oh, come on, baby, let me explain. We can—'

'Go. You have a competition to win. After all, that's why I'm here—as the granny-sitter.'

'It's not like that.' He grabbed her arm.

'Don't touch me!' She pulled her arm away and stared him down.

'Easy …' He held his hands up in surrender. 'I'd never hurt you; you know that.'

Not physically, that she believed. But it's what he was doing to her emotionally that hurt more. He was already too deep into her heart, she had to push him away.

'You know you're much more than a granny-sitter. I only

asked for your help because I want to keep my grandmother safe. So sue me for being overprotective in wanting to keep my family safe.'

'I'm all for keeping family safe. Believe me, after losing half of mine, I get it.' Boy did she get it, that pain of losing not one but two people she loved, was unforgettable. And she cared too deeply for Luke as it was, that this had to end now. 'But there's a big difference between being overprotective and being obsessive—and you are obsessed about keeping Esther safe.' The she winced, raising her open palm. 'I'm sorry, I take that back—' Fully aware he was waiting on Esther's test results. And she adored Esther. 'You know what? No, I don't. You've put cameras inside her house when she's a grown woman who gets into trouble *outside* of the place.'

His frown was filthy.

And she deserved that for hitting with a low blow.

But he'd lied to her, too. For an entire year she'd been visiting him at the Bottleshop and not once did he tell her about being her rescuer! So if he could hide that from her for a year, what else was he hiding?

She swiped her bunch of flowers off the bench, then waved them in Luke's face. 'At least your mate, Dom, was man enough to bring me flowers when he told me he was sorry. And I happen to believe him more than I believe you right now.' She stormed off to the Lodge with hot tears were trailing down her cheeks, and never looked back.

Thirty-three

It was the fishing trip from hell. First arguing with Jordi, who was too angry to even listen to him, Luke had decided to let her cool down and head out. Only for the boat trailer to get a flamin' flat tyre beside one of those towering roadside signs on the way into town.

Covered in dirt, Luke finally arrived at the boat ramp where he had to wait an hour before he could put his boat in the water, with a group of boats waiting to follow him.

He then had to deal with the stupid bow waves caused by the other boats trolling too fast, which made his boat rock. There was a constant flow of river traffic, blocking exits and entrances to creeks, congesting the eddies and sandbars. He was surprised there were any fish still swimming in the region.

Yet Luke persisted, trolling to the mouth and back.

He'd caught a few smaller barramundi, as well as some nice threadfin salmon for the esky to take home. Nothing that would earn him serious points for this fishing competition, not if he wanted to win and make a reputation for himself.

He'd taken date-stamped photographs to prove he'd caught each fish, measuring them against the unique measuring tape they supplied each competitor, before releasing them back into the water, then went on the hunt for more. But with the sense of urgency dogging him so hard, he couldn't relax—when the reason he enjoyed fishing in the first place was it made him relax. But not today.

He steered his boat around a sweeping bend on the river

where Porter waved him down from the police boat.

Coming alongside, Luke tossed a mooring line to Porter, who loosely wrapped it around the horn-shaped cleat, allowing their boats to drift side by side.

Porter rested his sunglasses on the brim of his police cap, then pulled a bottle of water from the icebox, tossing it across to Luke. 'How's it going?'

'Lousy. I should have stayed home.' Luke guzzled on the water. If he'd stayed in bed, Jordi would have never found the recording studio, giving him more time to explain it to her gently. He'd always planned to; he just never found the right time. 'Jordi found the recording studio this morning.'

'From the way you look, I'm guessing she didn't take it too well.'

'She's not happy.' Understatement. Jordi was ticked, and he'd been the idiot that upset her, when all he wanted to do was make her happy and—dare he say it—keep her safe.

Was he obsessed over Gran's and Jordi's safety?

'We may have to cool it for a bit. The podcast thing was fun, but the pressure with its popularity isn't for me, mate.'

'Come on, Porter, you're a natural at it.' When they made those recording sessions, they had fun. They'd never planned for anyone to get hurt, least of all himself. 'You're the star of the show.'

'Yeah, well, stars fall …' Porter's Adam's apple bobbed up and down as he drank from his water bottle. 'But you've got talent as the producer, writer, and editor. Me, I'm just a bloke having a beer with a mate after work, but with microphones, that ended up being part of a two-man show.'

'Which explains why I'm sucking at this sport today—I've got no partner in crime.' He pointed to the empty first mate's seat, that Porter usually sat in. The last person who'd had that seat was Jordi.

Again, his heart squeezed at the thought of the hurt he'd seen written all over her face—and that he'd done that to her.

'I get now why you've given up on dating.' This emotional stuff sucked. He'd always had a soft spot for Jordi, but was that because of the guilt for failing her, or pity for the pain she'd endured? Or was it something more?

The heightened level of bliss he'd felt with her was gone. She took that when she turned her back on him. And with her sister moving, it might be best for Jordi if she went too, because if he was smarting like this now, did he dare risk going deeper?

Porter frowned, grabbing the boat's mooring rope and pulling their boats together. 'Listen, mate. I gave it my best shot, big time, before I gave up on Tess. I changed myself for that woman. I quit smoking for her. I shaved off my beard, and I forced myself to read her favourite books that were this mushy historical romance, dude.' Porter shuddered. 'I was there every night helping Tess work in that damned post office, bringing her flowers, coffees, and freaking cupcakes, and she still wouldn't go out with me. You know how hard I tried, even asking your grandmother for tips.'

'But you've dated no one else since. When there's plenty of fish out there—they're just not jumping on my line today.' He frowned over the river, reflecting clear skies. Normally he didn't care if he didn't catch a fish, he'd still enjoy the cruise along the river. Yet, this competition had changed all that—or was that because of his argument with Jordi, messing with his head and his heart?

Porter crossed his arms over his chest as their boats slowly drifted apart. 'I'm not interested anymore. I'm done with that. Career comes first, now. But you like Jordi, you've cared about her for a very long time. Mate, you drove all the way to the city, just see her when she was in the hospital.'

'Dude, I kind of stalked her while she was in a coma.'

Porter chuckled, the prick. 'You were checking to see if she was okay. You'd rescued her, travelled with her. And sure, you may still see yourself as her rescuer, trying to protect her, but you care for her, too.'

'I'm not obsessed with her, am I?'

Porter grinned, holding back the laugh. 'Mate, you have this goofy smile whenever Jordi texts you, and you get into this cuddly bear mode whenever you're near her.'

'Pull your head in.'

'Hey, I was the same with Tess. At least you got to date Jordi, and she wants to be with you. You're luckier than you realise, mate.'

'So, can I ask you something really left field?'

Porter nodded.

'Do you think I'm obsessed about keeping Gran safe?'

Porter didn't answer for a long time, only to eventually share a serious, slow nod.

Luke leaned his back against the console at the realisation. 'Really?'

'I think it began after that accident. By not being able to save Jordi's parents, and with Jordi so severely hurt, and you getting hurt yourself. You quit your job after that, and with your folks not being around to share the responsibilities, it's understandable that you're so protective over Esther, who's the only one at home—in a house that used to be filled with people.' Porter sighed, gripping the overhead bar of the police boat's canopy. 'But come on, mate, Esther is eighty-four. She may be a handful, but she's old enough to take responsibility for her own actions.'

'Gran is deteriorating, I think …' No, he knew there was a reason to foolproof the house and lock up the keys. 'I mean …' Luke scrubbed his hands hard over his face as if to get rid of the reality he was being made to face. 'Gran's being tested for dementia.'

'That explains a lot.'

'Am I capable of taking care of her? When Jordi thinks I'm only with her so she'll granny-sit and for the guilt of not saving her parents.'

'Are you?'

Luke scowled at his best mate, who shrugged with his straight-shooting question.

'I'm going to give you some advice that this smart-arse who works in the bottle shop would tell me …' Porter let loose another cheeky grin.

Luke arched an eyebrow. 'You mean you actually listened to me for once?'

'Didn't want to. But it kind of rattled around in my head like some silly song stuck on the same chorus over and over again.'

'That bad, was it?'

'Like that eighties commercial jingle you turned into our podcast's theme song. Cheesy.' Their laughter echoed over the surrounding water.

'Go on, out with it,' said Luke, cleaning his sunglasses on his shirt. 'What wise words of wisdom did I dare to spout from my mouth?' That he was pretty sure Jordi wanted to slap this morning.

'What do you want that'll make you happy?'

Didn't that wipe the smile off his face. 'Are *you* happy?' Because Tess had broken the man's heart.

Porter narrowed his eyes as he gazed over the water, then nodded. 'I like living in this town, and its people. I get to go hunting and fishing with a mate—when we're not making the podcast, which has been a lot of laughs. And I like my job.' Porter winced over the water.

'You don't look happy about it. And you were stressing big time when your boss decided to take a long honeymoon without any warning.' It had practically turned Porter's hair grey.

'Marcus dumping his job on me was a tough lesson learned. Now I know what to expect, it's given me something to work towards. Dude, I'm cruising on a police boat, watching over a fishing competition as part of my day job. There aren't too many officers I know who get to do that.'

'True ...' It had Luke wondering if he going to be a bottle shop manager for the rest of his life.

He could just picture his mother lecturing him to go back to being a fireman, with his dad on his case about doing something productive with the land at Anaborro Downs. Luckily, his gran supported him no matter what he did, as long as he was happy. And he was trying to keep her happy by letting her stay at her home. But was that the right thing to do for both their sakes?

'What's the traffic like upriver?' After all, he was here to win the Classic for his future.

'Congested. A lot of them are hanging around Goat Island's bend where the aroma of Sandfly's barbecues is incredible. Now that the Sandfly's gone legit, I had two steak sangers yesterday. I highly recommend it. I might check it out for morning smoko.' Porter grinned, brushing off some lint from his police shirt.

'I'll check it out on my way home.' Hopefully Jordi was still there, so he could talk to her too. 'Have you seen anything worth my time?'

'A nice school of bait fish passed me not that long ago, just by the billabong's breach we liked to hit. It's nicely hidden by the mangroves that the tourists have missed, so far.' Porter slid on his sunglasses and grinned widely, with a nod from one local to another.

'Thanks for the tip, officer.' He dragged in his mooring line, then tapped the brim of his fishing cap as he sat behind the helm. 'Might troll on my way up there. I found a top spot on the flats last week.' With the thick rain clouds on the distant horizon, he pointed the boat's nose towards the spot where Jordi had caught her first fish.

If he got through today's leg of the competition, and if he jagged that million-dollar fish, he could then plan a future worth fighting for. Right now, it was time to hunt.

Thirty-four

'How did you talk me into this?' Jordi whined to Esther, who stood on the other side of the beefy water buffalo.

'Stop complaining, you like it and so does Cecil.' The buffalo was getting a brush down while Esther handfed him breakfast.

Then Jordi dressed up his thick horns and tail in ribbons she normally kept in the van for floral emergencies. 'I'm used to wrapping up flower arrangements in ribbons, not a set of buffalo horns.'

'But doesn't he look beautiful? I've never seen him look so gorgeous.' Esther kissed Cecil's large forehead, then hugged him around the neck. 'Off you go, my boy. Have a fabulous day.'

Cecil took a few steps, then turned around and lowered his head in front of Jordi.

Jordi tried to sidestep past the buffalo, but he blocked her. A whopping big water buffalo, wearing pale pink and white ribbons wrapped around his wide horns like they were flower stems in a bridal bouquet.

'Is there something wrong with his headdress?' Jordi checked the large peony and willowy soft chrysanthemums made from the florist's crepe paper and silk ribbon. She'd made them this morning, sitting in the open door of her van, while waiting for Esther to wake up. They became part of the largest headdress she'd ever made, securely attached to the crown of a water buffalo.

Again, Jordi took another sidestep to get past the gigantic animal.

But Cecil blocked her, swishing his tail that was beautifully laced with both pink and white satin ribbons, better than any fancy horse presented in a dressage competition.

'What's he doing? Cecil won't let me pass.'

Esther giggled, her tiara sparkling under the early morning light. 'Cecil wants you to hug him.'

Jordi huffed at the buffalo who stared at her with big dark eyes.

'You're kidding.'

'No, I'm not.'

Hands on her hips, she faced the buffalo. 'Listen up, Cecil, I dressed you, handfed you flowers that were given to me as a present, and I handmade those flowers in the headdress you're now wearing.' She wagged her finger at the buffalo. 'And those silk flowers are only created for the mother of a bride for their corsages or hats. And we both know you're no bride. So, that's enough. Off you go and do what you do.'

But Cecil refused to move.

'He won't leave until the job is done.' Esther dragged Jordi to Cecil's large side. 'Put one arm over his neck like that to hold him and listen to his heart.'

At first, she remained tense as his coarse hair brushed her cheek, tickling her ear, while being forced to hug-it-out with a water buffalo. It was weird.

But then the big beast sighed, releasing a slow warm hum that travelled from his chest. A wave of goosebumps spread across her skin, that somehow brought a comforting sensation deep inside her soul. She sighed, just as heavily as he did, feeling the tension in her shoulders loosen.

'Thank you, Cecil.' He'd been a fabulous distraction from her argument with Luke this morning.

Cecil gave a nod, as if he understood.

'Now, off you go, my darling boy.' Esther waved at her pet buffalo waddling his big black rump, with his ribbons shifting in the breeze, all dressed up to go play flower girl at an outback wedding.

'Come along, petal, it's our turn to start the day.' Esther hooked her arm through Jordi's and escorted her into the grand colonial house known as the Lodge. 'Why didn't you go fishing with Luke?'

'I'm here with you.'

'I don't need a babysitter.'

'I know that. I'm just your companion. A friend.' Jordi headed for the kitchen sink, where the last of her flowers from Dom sat, the ones Cecil didn't eat. 'Can I use that teapot as a vase for these flowers? I like how you did that with the flowers for your birthday.'

'Sure, here …' Esther brought down the teapot from the cupboard displaying her many colourful jars of preserved fruits and vegetables.

The crunch and pop of gravel alerted them to a car slowly driving towards the house. 'Who is that?' Esther squinted through the windows, then headed for the front doors.

'Hello?' the driver called out from the car. *'Yoo-hoo, I'm looking for the lady of the Lodge!'*

'That'd be me.' Esther stood warily on the steps of her verandah.

'Hi, Felix.'

'Hey, Jordi. I'm assuming that's your doing dressing up that buffalo in ribbons.' Felix pointed to the front driveway. 'I'd recognise a decent floral ribbon flower anywhere. And the way that buffalo looks, Cecil's either off to be in a wedding or he's about to be sacrificed to some pagan god.'

Jordi giggled with Felix. 'I can't believe my finest work is about to get covered in buffalo dust.'

'Who are you, again?' Esther frowned with suspicion.

'The new neighbour. I'm Coco's daddy.' Felix opened the back door of his car, where the cream-coloured pug yapped as it eagerly bounded up the steps.

'Oh, it's the rat.' That leapt into Esther's open arms.

'Coco.'

'Rat's better.'

'Coco is French for *darling* and after Coco Chanel.' Felix stood firm, with hands on hips. 'Please show some respect to the designer of chic feminine style who started her career as a cabaret singer.'

'I like their perfume.'

'Me too.'

'Hmmm …' Esther narrowed her eyes at Felix.

'Would you like a cup of tea or something, Felix?' Jordi was hoping to broker the peace between the neighbours. Even though Luke and Jordi told Felix that Esther had become quite attached to the pug, they had chosen *not* to explain the whole story to Felix about what happened to Coco, because they didn't want to upset him.

She shut her eyes, as the wave of realisation washed over her. Luke didn't tell her that he knew her for a year to protect her—to not upset her. Because he cared.

Ugh, she was such an idiot, who had been so cruel to Luke in what she'd said to him this morning, too.

'I'd love to stay. I truly would,' said Felix. 'But I must run to work.'

'So why the visit?'

'I'd like you to dog-sit for me while this fishing thingy is on. With my partner, Reggie, busy with my club—'

'What kind of club?' 'Esther arched her eyebrows at Felix.

'Nightclub. Where we put on these amazing drag shows and cabaret nights, which I dearly miss. But I spoke with the owner at the Peddler palace, my bestie, Wren, who said I can pick you up to sing at the Sandfly Saloon.'

'I can't do the steps from the boat. Grandson won't let me.'

Jordi dropped her head, desperate to stop her frown at that comment over Luke and his obsession with Esther's safety. She knew it was for a reason, and it was admirable; it also hadn't been right for her to snap at him for caring.

Felix continued, 'I meant by land.'

'No one goes to Sandfly by land. That's Peddler's

property only. You get shot and fed to the crocodiles if you do, everyone knows that.'

'Are you for real?' Jordi's eyes widened. How wild was this country?

'Not if you stick with me, princess.'

'Puhleese.' Adjusting her tiara, Esther said, 'I'm a queen.'

'I can see that. Which is why I'm happy to escort you to the blues and jazz nights at the Sandfly.'

'What's the catch?'

Felix popped a hand on his hip and lifted his chin. 'You have to audition first. The other week Luke played at the Sandfly and passed with flying colours. That boy plays a mean piano.'

'He should. I taught him.'

'So I was told. Two-dollar Darryl also said you can sing. But, as I choose all the talent acts for my cabaret shows, you'll have to get past *moi*. I'm the saloon's entertainment manager.' Felix poked at his chest, then plucked off a dog hair from his fine linen shirt, to catch the time on his watch. 'Who is late for their job! I'm so not used to commuting. I've only been driving for a month.' He playfully giggled as the excitement rose in his voice. 'We're doing another brilliant balcony barbecue for the many fishermen at the Sandfly. We sold out so fast yesterday, so I'd better scoot to make the morning smoko rush. I'll pick up Coco later.' Felix pulled a fancy doggy backpack from the back seat of the car. 'If you need me, my number is on Coco's collar, or radio the Sandfly. Here is Coco's lead, his treats, his toys, filtered bottled water that flips out to a darling doggy dish, plus his rug, all inside his doggy day-bag.'

'I didn't say yes.' Even though Esther was hugging the pug like she owned it.

'Esther,' Jordi whispered under her breath to the stubborn woman in a tiara, 'you were stealing Felix's dog every day.'

'Listen, ladies, it'll give me peace of mind to know someone is caring for Coco.' Felix handed the doggy day-bag to Jordi.

'Do this often, eh?' Esther arched a disapproving eyebrow at the bag.

'When I was at the club, Coco was with us all day and night for the company. But at the Sandfly, I'm scared he'll end up as croc bait. So now the poor thing is lonely, home alone all day.' He tenderly patted Coco's head and adjusted its collar. 'So, pretty-please look after my baby. I'll name a cocktail after you and I'm happy to pay for doggy day care fees.'

'Esther will do it. And she likes her cocktails at sunset.' Jordi slung the bag over her shoulder, nodding at Esther. 'Thank you, Felix, for offering such an amazing opportunity for Esther.'

'Thank you and tootles.' Felix blew an air kiss before rushing back to the car. 'See you at sunset, then. I like your tiara, Esther. I should bring mine over some time.'

Jordi giggled as she waved off Felix in his car, leaving Esther gobsmacked on the verandah holding the pug.

'Now you've got me into trouble, rat. Cecil might get jealous when he gets home from town.' Esther put down the pug. It ran in a circle, its tail wagging before skittering into the kitchen, with Esther following to put out his dish of water. 'No filtered water here, rat. Rainwater is better. You should wear a tiara today, petal. It'll make you feel better.'

Jordi narrowed her eyes at Esther, who had exceptionally good hearing. Did she overhear the argument Jordi had with Luke this morning?

Never had she been so angry with anyone, like she had been with Luke. And she'd never argued with anyone like that—except her sister—and never with anyone outside of the family. But a lot of harsh words were spoken. And she'd done most of that to push him away.

But if it was meant to be for her own good, then why did it hurt so much?

Esther opened a cupboard in the small hall between the kitchen and the sitting room and removed a dark tiara. 'This one will suit you.'

'I'm good.'

'No, you're magnificent. Come here and let me put it on.' Leaving Jordi with no choice, Esther placed the dark tiara laced with fine rose-gold leaves, black roses, and obsidian that sparkled like black diamonds. 'I've never worn this one. It never suited me. But it suits you.' Esther gently tucked it into Jordi's hair, then gave a nod of approval.

'It's not heavy like I thought it would be.' And it didn't irritate the scars hidden by her hair.

'But our invisible crowns are heavy, and they only get heavier with time. But no matter how bad the world may be, we get up, adjust our crowns and smile, and that's what makes us queens.' Esther cupped Jordi's cheek and shared a soft all-knowing smile, as if to see through those layers she'd created to hide from the world.

'Why tiaras?'

'Because the world will judge you, no matter what you wear. And when people see a tiara, they only see a pretty crown. They forget they're made of iron, forged from fire to rise from the ashes to shine. You, petal, are precious. And if we don't treat ourselves like royalty, no one else will.' Esther turned Jordi around to face the large mirror. 'There, see.' Esther pointed to their reflections. 'There's a young queen, standing right there, who is a lot stronger than she realises.'

Jordi swallowed down the lump in her tight throat. She lifted her eyes to face herself in the mirror, which she'd always avoided doing, especially since the accident.

'Just remember, my darling, a queen always takes care of herself and her happiness. After all, the queen is all about the *Happily Ever After.*' Esther wandered into the kitchen, leaving Jordi alone to face herself.

Was she really a queen? With all her beastly scars.

She wanted to tear the tiara off her head, feeling silly wearing it.

Reaching out to close the cupboard, to hide the mirror, she discovered it had shelves full of tiaras, from large crowns to dainty head pieces. A lifetime's worth.

In the kitchen, Esther filled up the kettle at the kitchen sink. Her large tiara, fit for a queen, sent small rainbows across the polished floorboards.

'Queen, huh?' Jordi forced herself to stare at the face in the mirror. She wrinkled her nose, where the burn scars that Luke called freckles blended and shifted. No longer seeing the scars on her chin or on her ears, she poked out her tongue like a child. She didn't feel like a queen, yet, wearing the silly thing unearthed the long-forgotten playfulness of a child.

It reminded her of a time when she'd played with her sister, wearing tulle skirts that shifted as they danced around the garden, waving their wands, while wearing wings and crowns. All those times she'd lie on the living-room floor beside her sister, to eagerly watch *Cinderella,* and even *Beauty and the Beast,* dreaming of being the belle of the ball.

Now she was an adult who'd never worn a ball gown. Yet, Esther had dozens she'd wear weekly just to read to children, and she chose a tiara to wear every day like a queen.

Esther was right. The world did judge people for how they looked. Jordi should know.

And Jordi was her harshest critic. The scars were there, but only she could see them, and Luke was right, she had nothing to be ashamed of. She had to stop looking at herself like the burned beast when she deserved to find her own happily ever after.

That argument with Luke may have hurt her, but it could also be a blessing in disguise. Why wait for Luke to rescue her like some prince, when she was quite capable of rescuing herself.

With her shoulders back, chin raised, she smiled at the tiara that sparkled. Let the play date begin.

Thirty-five

With a lightness to her step, Jordi entered the kitchen to arrange the last of Dom's flower inside the teapot waiting at the sinks. 'Why do you have a pet buffalo? Considering your family were buffalo hunters.'

The microwave dinged, and Esther removed a jar of milk, screwing on a lid. 'Can you shake this for me? It's the old-fashioned way of frothing milk.'

'Sure.' The warm milk sloshed around in the jar, warming the glass sides, as she shook it to form bubbles like a milkshake.

Esther pulled down a silver tray and set out two delicate teacups with matching saucers. 'Cecil was special from the moment I found him. That's enough shaking, petal.'

'Where was that?' Jordi poured the frothy milk into the matching milk jug that Esther placed on the tray.

'At the place where my husband had his accident with a buffalo.' Esther spooned some Earl Grey tea leaves into another teapot, added hot water from the steaming kettle, and a dash of syrup from a small glass bottle and stirred.

'What's that?' It looked like Esther had poured whisky into their tea.

'It's homemade lavender syrup.'

'In tea?'

'We're having the London Lavender Fog. It's perfect for our tea party.'

'Tea party, huh?'

'Petal, you're wearing a tiara, so let's make our tea a little posh, eh.' Esther winked, carrying the tray to the table and poured the dark rich tea into their cups. Warm fluffy milk was spooned on top like a cappuccino, and she finished it off with a sprinkle of dried lavender.

Esther scooped up the dog and let him settle into her lap. 'Where were we ...' She tapped on her chin. 'Oh, yes, how I found Cecil. Well, it was on the anniversary of my husband's passing. I was so sad then ...' She sighed heavily as if the joy leached out of her. 'Walden had closed the Lodge to visitors, so no more parties. My husband was gone, and I was so terribly lonely. I'd driven out to the site of my husband's accident to put down some flowers, and there was this baby buffalo. He would have been a day old, if that. All alone. He was only a wee thing. So, I scooped him up and brought him home.' She giggled, patting the pug. 'You should have heard Walden carry on. And Violet! She was worse, arguing about having a baby buffalo in the house, because Cecil followed me everywhere. But Luke loved him. Back then, I could pick up both boys at once, they were so little.' She rubbed her nose against Coco's and then settled him into her lap.

'How old is Cecil?' Jordi put the flowers dressing up the teapot on the table.

'Almost thirty.' Esther reached across the table to lean a white business envelope against the vase. It was addressed: *To Esther Bennett from Iris Rosewood.*

'How long do buffaloes survive?'

'The average is ten to fifteen years in the wild. Cecil is considered an old man in buffalo years.'

'I didn't realise.'

'Cecil has been wandering Elsie Creek's roads for a long time.'

'And you dress him in ribbons every day.'

'Not as fancy as you did it this morning.' She smiled, lifting her teacup, and sipped. 'It was Walden who first put the ribbons on Cecil.'

'Luke's dad?' She couldn't picture the burly, bearded buffalo hunter even holding a ribbon.

'Walden pinched them from Violet's dresser, thinking she wouldn't miss them. But she was so angry, complaining they were from some special Sydney what-not store. But Walden ignored her, wrapping this fancy red ribbon around Cecil's horns as a signal to the other buffalo hunters that Cecil was a pet.'

'I get that Cecil's an escape artist, I do. But why would he want to leave when he has a fancy bed indoors? He gets brushed and bathed daily and can have all the food and water he could want right here. I don't know of any other buffalo who'd get that sort of treatment.'

'It's my fault Cecil is so spoiled. He was so young, I had to bottle feed him, so he came to school with me. When he was too big for the back seat, I used the old cattle ramp in the yard to get Cecil to climb into the back of the ute. Now we tow him in the trailer Luke and his father made specially for Cecil so he could come to school, otherwise he'd follow me.'

'So it was bring-your-pet-to-work day every day, was it?'

'Something like that. Oh, how Cecil loved going to school. He just didn't understand why he couldn't go to school every day—you couldn't explain to a buffalo what school holidays were.'

'I lived for summer holidays as a kid.'

'Didn't we all? Even teachers.' Esther giggled as she tickled the chin of the dog in her lap. 'But my Cecil is a smart boy. He soon learned that school days happened when that big yellow school bus drove past our front gate. You should have seen all the children waving at him from the bus when I drove him to work. He was like this big dog with his head in the wind, smile on his face, with his ribbons flapping, as he stood on the back of the trailer going to work.'

'What did Cecil do for holidays?'

'He'd wallow in our old dam among the wild lotus and sulk.'

Jordi grinned behind her cup where the steam curled, releasing the deliciously rich fragrance of the Earl Grey tea, with the warm milk turning the dark tea into the colour of fog. The addition of the vanilla-lavender syrup truly enhanced the flavour of the slightly citrus black tea. She licked her lips and stared at her teacup.

'It's nice, yes?'

'It's divine.' Jordi took another sip, settling back into her chair, just breathing in the aroma from her teacup. 'Is that how Cecil became a walking billboard?'

'I had a lot of students who came from the outlying cattle stations who didn't cope very well being stuck inside a classroom. So, I'd take my entire class outside and I used Cecil as my chalkboard for lessons. Cecil would happily stand there all day and let these little kids draw on his coat. And they all passed my English classes with flying colours. We even received a few awards at our tiny little bush school for excellence in reading and writing.'

'I wish my school had a buffalo as a teaching tool.' Jordi took another sip of the scrumptious tea. Esther was right, it was the perfect bit of fancy.

'And then one day, someone in the pub wrote something about a mate's birthday. Then those rascals, who play cards in the hardware store, drew on his back about a sale for stockfeed. Soon the supermarket wrote down their specials, the craft store advertised classes, and the coach would add the scores of the softball match. It became Cecil's job. Cecil knows what school days are by watching for the yellow school bus as his signal to stroll down the road to our lovely new neighbour, Que, who paints these fun quotes on his back. And then he'll roam the streets before coming home at sunset.'

'But today is Saturday.'

'Well, with the town buzzing over the fishing competition, Cecil will be gone all day, like Luke.' Esther smiled at the pug sleeping in her lap, but there was a deep level of sadness behind her smile. 'I love my Cecil, I truly do, but he belongs to the town more than me.'

Jordi gently patted Esther's frail hand. 'Cecil still sees you as his mother. I saw how much he missed you when you were in the hospital, he wouldn't leave his bed beside your chair because he was waiting for you to come home. Cecil may be a part of this town, Esther, but this is his home, because he comes home to you.'

'That marvellous buffalo does keep me going. Animals are such wonderful companions.' Esther stroked the pug's furry coat.

After finishing their tea, there was plenty more in the large pot.

'Shall we have another cup?' It was yum.

'We can save it for later. Would you mind driving me somewhere?' Esther scooped up the teapot filled with flowers. 'We'll take these flowers you brought home for a drive, shall we?'

Jordi winced at how this household tortured their cut flowers—well, those that survived after being sacrificed to the water buffalo. 'Where to?'

'You'll see when we get there.' Esther passed the teapot of flowers to Jordi. 'I'll put this Earl Grey mix in the fridge. We'll make cocktails for sunset with that mix, you'll love it. It'll keep you up all night if you have too many, but they're perfect to kickstart the festivities.' Esther winked as she closed the fridge door. 'Come on, rat, we'll go pinch some more flowers along the road.'

'That's illegal, you know.'

'Who's going to arrest an eighty-four-year-old for picking flowers? You can drive, Jordi. Them pesky policemen stole my licence and Luke's hidden the keys to anything with an engine. But I've got this rascally young ringer selling me his esky.'

'Why? You've got a stack of coolers and iceboxes in Luke's shed.'

'This one has a motor on it. No keys, no fuel, just charge up the battery and it'll be enough to drive me to town and back. Let's see that Porter and his beefcake Sergeant arrest me for that!'

After meeting Esther when she was being escorted home

by the police, while riding a lawnmower, Jordi could clearly picture the mischievous octogenarian riding an esky like some child's toy tractor, in her ball gown and gumboots with her tiara sparkling under the sun. Should she warn Luke?

'I've got to get something first. Meet you at the van. I'm sure you know the best way to wrap flowers for transporting them.'

Jordi grinned at Esther's tinkling laugh, catching her reflection in the window, reminding her about the tiara. She wasn't going to wear that in public.

At the far end of the kitchen, Esther pointed at Jordi. 'Don't you dare take off that tiara. Not until the sun goes down. It's yours now.'

'I, ah …'

'It's the rules. Come along, rat. We should find a tiara for you too.' The pug yapped as it happily followed Esther down the corridor.

Jordi rolled her eyes at her reflection in the window, then grinned, adjusting her tiara. She could play queen for a day, too. Not.

Thirty-six

Coco the pug pranced on his lead beside Esther, who was shading them with her parasol. While Jordi brought up the rear with her arms full of assorted native flower arrangements, as they traipsed through the outback graveyard.

From the side of the small hill the entire town spread below them; the pub stood tall at the far end, with the train line and highway running north. Beyond that, there was nothing but a whole load of country, reminding her how remote they were. 'Why are we here?'

'For family. We'll start putting out the flower arrangements from here.' Esther's tiara sparkled, as she pointed to the plots bearing the name *Bennett*, while the pug eagerly sniffed around. 'Manners, rat. We'll have none of that leg lifting around here, thank you.'

'I'm guessing the one with the marble buffalo statue is your father?'

'Grandfather. The original buffalo hunter. We'll start there.' Esther took a small flower arrangement from Jordi's stash of many.

The trip to town had been an adventure, with Esther showing Jordi pockets of paradise. It started by driving to the back of Anaborro Downs, then alongside the road in their hunt for flowers.

They'd gathered assorted grey-leafed eucalyptus and needle-like linear leaves from various melaleucas. Rich yellow pompoms from the acacia, fiery red bottlebrushes, and pink gumnut clusters complete with hardwood shells grew in abundance, along with pink mulla-mullas, to the fine spiral curls of the feathery grevillea.

Fallen leaves and flower heads were scattered throughout Jordi's van, but the excursion had been a welcome distraction. They'd discussed the meanings of flowers while sitting under the shade of a large flame tree, creating marvellous native floral arrangements, that would only get better as they dried. Perfect for a place like this.

'So, Luke has you babysitting me today.' Esther placed the floral arrangement at the base of another headstone for Ebony-Rae Bennett. Esther's mother.

'Granny-sitting.' She peered around at the silent resting place with dates going back to the late 1800s, as guilt washed over her for avoiding her own family's graves.

'I don't need it.'

'I think you do.'

'Eh?'

'What I'm trying to say is that you might want to consider getting a companion, someone who can drive you to see your friends more often. Someone you can talk to more regularly because you have this amazing personality that loves to entertain. I just disagree with Luke's methods.'

'How so?'

'I told Luke off about those granny cams.' But she understood why he was adamant about caring for Esther. And, in all honesty, it really wasn't her place to say anything.

Esther coyly grinned as she tucked a posy into a pair of old workboots that made up the headstone. 'My uncle. My son, Walden, did those boots. He used to bring some rum and have a drink with them …' She sighed softly as she artfully arranged the native flowers into the weather-worn boots. 'I'm being tested for Dementia. I'm pretty sure what the results will be, I just haven't told Walden. But Luke knows.'

'I'm so sorry.' She was sorry for Esther, the beautiful woman she was, and for Luke.

Esther tenderly squeezed her hand, sharing a giving

smile. 'And I know Walden and Luke put the Granny cams in the house for my safety. Do you know where?'

'No.' Jordi followed, holding out the next floral arrangement to Esther to place beside the various plots that made up the Bennett family.

Jordi had visited her parent's resting place only once. Even then she couldn't stand there for more than a few minutes before rushing back to the car. The reality of their names etched in stone made it all-too real that they were gone. But it was also the sun savagely biting into her raw skin, still covered in gauze and tape, that forced her to leave.

Lifting her face to greet the sun, she'd come a long way since that day.

'If I didn't love those two men,' said Esther, 'I'd have them for intruding on my privacy with those cameras.'

Jordi frowned at Luke for using their private conversations for public use, on a radio show that everyone in town listened to!

Esther grinned, leaning closer to whisper, 'I know where they are.'

'You do?'

'Pfft.' Esther plonked a hand on her hip and gave a single shoulder shrug. 'Petal, I have lived in that house all my life. You don't think I'd notice?' She then wagged her plump finger. 'But we won't tell those boys anything. Let them think they're smarter than us girls.'

Jordi could only laugh.

As Esther laid assorted flowers at various graves, she spoke of her family, her mother, her father, uncles, and brothers—who had all been bachelors.

Esther took the large trailing wreath from Jordi, leaving one posy.

It was the floral arrangement Dom had given Jordi, that upset Luke. The same flowers she'd tried to give to Esther, who'd fed half to Cecil, and dragged the rest out here. It'd have to be the most well-used second-hand bunch of flowers in Elsie Creek history.

'That's my plot, next to my husband. Terrence was a good man.' Esther's fingertips tenderly smoothed over the top of the headstone as if brushing the shoulders of the man himself. She then draped the long wreath of flowering gumnut seeds that blended with the soft willowy native grasses over it.

Giving Esther a moment, Jordi climbed the hill as a group of magpie geese flew overhead in an impressive V-shaped formation. On the distant horizon, large cotton flower clouds were gathering.

A trickle of sweat ran down the side of her forehead. It didn't bother her that her shirt stuck to the scars on her back, but the weather was changing.

Summer was coming.

It's why the flowers were blooming in their final push from a long dry spell as a good sign of the rains to come. It was a signal that the tourist season was ending, and where the resorts would become ghost towns. With her sister leaving and the changes in the shop, was this her final outback floral run?

On her left lay the town's outback airstrip. Beside it the highway rolled like a black ribbon disappearing in the haze of heat towards central Australia. Nearby was the river, glistening like the scales of a snake, winding its way behind the tall gum trees and native bamboos that lined the banks.

She truly hoped Luke was having a good day and achieving his goal for the future. Luke was a smart man who could do anything.

It had been stupid to think they'd be a couple. Now that she'd forgiven him for something that was never his fault, Luke had no reason to see her anymore. It was for the best that they stopped seeing each other, because she'd only be a reminder of the trauma they'd suffered.

She didn't need or want his pity.

Even though her heart was heavy over their argument, which seemed pretty petty while standing in a graveyard, it was done. She couldn't do anything now. But she still had a deal to keep, and that was to take care of Esther—who was on the move.

A few stones tumbled and dust stirred as Jordi skipped down the hill to catch up with Esther, who was heading for the far side of the small-town cemetery. 'Where are you going?'

'To visit Iris.' Esther took the last bunch of flowers from Jordi, as the pug pranced along with his cream tail curled high, and his shiny black nose lifting just as high. 'I haven't been here since her funeral.' There was no tombstone yet, so she laid the flowers down on the plot. 'Do me a favour, petal, and read this for me?' From her carpetbag, Esther pulled out the envelope that had been sitting on the kitchen table for ages.

'Are you sure?'

'Yes. I want Iris to know I got it, and I want to do it here so I can shout at her if she's filled it full of codswallop.'

From the sheath clipped to her jeans, Jordi removed the pocketknife Luke had given her. He'd called it a *fisherman's friend,* when it should be named the *florist's friend* because its blade had quite the workout today, proving to be perfect for cutting at the woody stems, in their hunt for native flowers.

She sliced open the flap of the envelope and removed a sheet of paper and read aloud:

> To my fun-loving, colourful, and dear friend, Esther.
>
> What a joy you have been to me, from the day we met when you were that fearless ten-year-old, in a fluffy pink fairy dress with matching tiara. I always wished I had the courage like you did, to never stop wearing ball gowns and tiaras. Like the way you'd tell us we were queens, raising our cocktail glasses to the sunset to celebrate another day we got to walk this earth.
>
> I was always grateful for my neighbour who became part of my family, like a sister, when I

Now don't be feeling guilty because you lost your driver's licence and couldn't visit me in the hospital as much as you'd wanted to. The lovely ranger, Alice, kept me company, sneaking in her wallaby for me to play with, while hiding it from the doctor.

But I was grateful when you did visit. Your thirst for life was a blessing to be around. Unlike the others who'd also retired, where the men would grumble about weather and politics, and there you were trying to decide what tiara we should wear for the day, what tunes should we dance to, and who should we visit, or how many wallabies we could save travelling in your car? What marvellous adventures we had.

So allow me to start you on the next one …

As you know, I sold the farm, and I don't blame you for wanting to shoot that real estate manager. I'd never recommend him again. But I sold the property to a wonderful young man named Felix. He loves cabaret, show tunes, and cocktails. I think you two will get along swimmingly, so please play nice and don't start any wars with the neighbours.

'You're only telling me that now!' Esther rolled her eyes, rummaging through her carpetbag for her hipflask and took a swig.

Jordi arched an eyebrow. 'How long did you leave this letter sitting, unopened, on your kitchen table?'

'Keep going, petal, the school bell hasn't rung yet.' Esther motioned with her hand, as if shooing away an annoying fly.

With the sale of the farm, I gave those funds to the fabulous Ranger, Alice. She's been a wonderful friend who is building an animal refuge for brumbies.

'Bah!' Esther rolled her eyes.

> I can practically hear you scoffing like your father
> would about brumbies.

Jordi's laugh had her squeezing her ribs, trying to contain it.

'You made that bit up?'

'No, it's written here.' Jordi showed her the page. 'Here, you can finish reading this letter.'

'Nope.' Esther lifted her chin, facing the other direction. 'Didn't bring my reading glasses, so you have to keep reading.'

> As for you, Esther ...

Jordi peeked over the letter she was reading aloud.

> You were like a sister, so you deserve something
> special.
>
> When the mining company paid me that
> settlement for losing my son and grandson in their
> accidental deaths, you were there that day I got
> that big lump of a cheque.

'Biggest cheque I'd ever seen in my entire life. It'd make your eyes bulge, rat.' Esther leaned down to pat the pug.

As much as Jordi wanted to ask how much, she kept reading aloud:

> It was you who bundled me up into your car to
> visit my two boys at their graves to share flowers,

spill champagne and celebrate. You said it was a gift, to ensure I was well taken care of.

And I most certainly was.

Living alone, I needed very little. So I put that big whopping cheque to use by investing it, while trying to think of what to do with it.

And now, here I am, stuck in this stupid room at the hospital and I think I've found the perfect solution.

I want you to spend it.

'How?' Esther asked Jordi, reading the letter.

If I had to hazard a guess, I'd say you would have taken your sweet time to read this letter—

'Sorry,' muttered Esther

—you are forgiven. And as we both know you love a good hunt, you need to go visit Otis. Just don't visit him during the times when his favourite soap is playing on the tellie. We all know he won't answer the door.

So let the adventure begin …

Iris.

'What? That's it?' Esther snatched the letter from Jordi and squinted at the white page with pursed lips.

'Who's Otis?'

'The lawyer who gave me this letter in the first place. At the will reading Otis put Luke to sleep with his droning hypnotic voice.' Esther peeked at her watch. 'If we're lucky, we'll catch Otis before he sits down and binge-watches *Days of Our Lives*. The man is obsessed with that show.'

'Excuse me?'

'Otis hasn't missed an episode in ten years, and lately he binge-watches the reruns on weekends. Everyone knows that.' With her eyes sparkling, she folded her parasol and raised it like a sword to the sky. 'Come along, petal, we're going on a hunt.'

Thirty-seven

'Why don't you just rack off, mate?' Luke shouted at Dom, who was following him in his barra boat along the river.

'It's not your river, I have every right to be here like you.' Dom tipped his white cowboy hat with that white-toothed smile Luke wanted to pummel with his fists.

Luke had been powering upstream, around bends, ducking trees, taking detours to get rid of the prick that kept following him. But Dom just stuck to his bow waves like a teen on a boogie board.

When Luke came around the sweeping bed of a large creek that was an intersection to three smaller creeks, it looked like a good spot to fish. He killed the engine, tossing a mooring line with a buoy, over a branch as a form of loose anchoring that allowed him to float further into the current, marking his turf, but also allowing for the ease of leaving in a hurry if needed.

Dom slowed down, thankfully enough for his bow wave to not bother Luke.

It was time for Luke to get his head back in the game and to stop playing chasey with Dom.

He assessed the run-off coming from the three stem creeks where the water collided, curled, and twisted as it blended to become a part of the wide stream that was clear and deep, to then flow into the main river.

He pulled open the deep drawers of his tackle box, searching for the perfect lure to match this creek's conditions.

The choice was his hard-bodied, hand-painted, fluorescent orange and green paddle prawn with its lethal haul of treble hooks so laser sharp they didn't need barbs. It was a beast. And it was his very own invention, which had never failed yet.

Using his favourite fishing rod, he attached his lure onto the swivel clip, checked the drag on his casting reel, adjusting the spool's tension against the weight of the fishing lure. As habit, he glanced around for any potential snagging spots where he might lose his lure, spotting Dom the dick, keenly watching from his boat a few metres back. Well, within casting distance. 'Look, there's a tree out there working very hard to produce oxygen so that you can breathe, so stop stealing mine.'

'Touchy, aren't you?'

'Dude, you're like that first slice of bread in the packet that everyone touches, but no one wants to eat. So move out of my strike zone or I'll be dragging out your teeth when I cast.' He flicked the rod and let the lure fly. It whizzed over the top of Dom's boat, making him duck.

'Fine. I'll be over this side of the river, and you can have that side.'

'I'm already anchored, moron.' Luke scowled at Dom, in his fancy boat gliding as if on ice to flow to a delicate stop on the right side of their wide stream, directly opposite Luke.

Ignoring him, Luke lightly gripped his casting rod and, with a well-practised flick of his wrist, sent the fishing lure flying to land in the water, where he let it float with the current, counting down the seconds.

The lure was designed to not sink or float, but to imitate the bait fish he'd studied over the years, and he allowed it to sit still. The trick was to not let it sit there too long or it'd look like the bit of floating wood it was. It was all about creating an illusion for the attention of the mighty fighting barramundi.

Luke slowly wound up the reel, giving the line the *fish twitch* by creating erratic pulses, allowing the lure to wriggle and imitate live bait the way he'd designed it. He'd reel it back to the boat, checked the lure's hooks were free from debris, then cast it out again.

Opposite him, the cretin was doing the same.

Sure, Luke had done this with Porter in the past, in order to tackle both sides of a stream. They'd taken turns casting, always keeping a lure in the water, timing it perfectly to never cross their lines—but not with Dom. Dom was a prize dick.

With another flick of the wrist, the lure flew, the reel whirled, and Luke's fishing line freely spooled to land in the same shady edge where the water's depth dropped from the three creeks to smoothly level into one current, allowing the lure to float downstream. Then he'd reel it back to the boat, imitating the bait fish twitch, then flick it back into the water.

It was almost hypnotic with its rhythm when WHACK!

'I'm on.' Luke's rod bent and the line whirled, as the reel sang. It took two hands on the rod to control the beast under the water.

'Me too.' Dom's line also bent over, their lines crossing.

'Oi, that's my fish. Reel in your line, we're crossing, dumbass.'

'No, moron, that's my fish.'

Their lines wound around each other, but Luke wasn't letting go. That fish was his.

A beautiful, fully mature barramundi glistened like silver as it leapt free from the water in the space between the two boats. It had a pointed head and concave forehead, its large jaw open, and just behind its sharp dorsal fin, it wore a long, skinny red tag.

'It's the million-dollar barra.'

'That sucker's mine!' Luke gritted his teeth and reeled it in as fast as he could, but the fish fought hard.

What made matters worse, Dom was fighting for the fish too and his line became entangled with Luke's. The faster they reeled in their lines, the more it drew their boats together.

'Cut your line, Dom. That's my fish.'

'No. You lose your line, mate.' Both struggled to reel in the fish.

From the leather sheath clipped to his belt, Luke whipped out his pocketknife and sliced the foreign line, then dragged the barramundi onto the boat, landing flat on his back with the fish flinging around him. Scales and spiky spinal fins stabbed at his skin as he struggled to contain it, then something hit the boat's hull.

Luke struggled to his feet, gripping the fish. 'Rack off, Dom. It's my fish.'

Dom's boat thumped into the side of Luke's boat, and with a mooring rope in hand, Dom jumped on board.

'Get off my boat.'

'When I get my fish. That's my lure.'

'It's my lure in its mouth, mate. An original hard-body lure I made! Your lure is barely sticking to the fin on its side. Now get off my freaking boat.' He shouldered Dom.

A fist slammed into his face.

Anger exploded, and Luke swung back, his knuckles connecting with the drongo's jaw. But Dom's uppercut had him seeing stars. So he struck back with his right elbow, unleashing with his left fist to pummel Dom's nose. Blood flew, fists hit flesh, the fish flapped, the boat rocked, and the fight for the million-dollar barramundi was on.

When something slammed hard into the boat, both men stopped.

'What was that?' In the scuffle, Dom had lost the rope to his boat, that was slowly floating downstream.

'Dunno.' But it wasn't right.

Then there was another thud so hard it made the boat rock. They both crouched to catch the side of the hull to gain their balance.

'What is that?' Dom craned his neck to peer over the hull, as something ran under the boat, the way a kid dragged a stick along the wooden slats of a picket fence.

'No way!' Luke pointed to the enormous shadow gliding

under the water. His eyes widened when it turned and raced directly towards them. *'Move!'* He pushed Dom aside as a tremendous splash came from a massive crocodile leaping free from the water, slamming its scaly body onto the floor of the boat. With its gigantic tail still in the water, its sheer weight flipped Luke's boat onto its side, sending both men flying through the air to land heavily in the river!

Never in his life had Luke swum so fast. His lungs burned and his legs kicked, aiming for the closest point of safety—the dead tree in the middle of the waterway.

Arm over arm, with legs scissoring, and his heart hammering with the scream of terror itching to free itself from his throat, he swam until his fingers slapped against the trunk, and he dragged himself out of the water.

Splinters stabbed into his skin, the bark broke away tearing his fingernails as branches snapped, forcing him back. Gritting his teeth, his toes dug into the slippery trunk, and he leapt higher, desperately climbing, until he'd pulled himself free from the water. 'DOM?'

'Help me, man.' Dom was frantically swimming towards him.

'Gimme your hand.' Luke reached down and dragged Dom free. 'Get your legs up now.'

The jaws of a massive crocodile opened wide, its teeth gleaming, giving them the perfect view of its open throat as the monster rose from the water, unleashing the spine-tingling stench of death on the crocodile's breath. Its powerful jaws slammed shut louder than any shotgun, it had his ears ringing, before the crocodile crashed back into the water, causing another wave of terror to wash over him.

Luke strained, his muscles burning, as he hauled Dom along with him, desperate to get higher up the tree. 'Climb, Dom. Keep climbing.' His hands scrambled for a hold, as they climbed for safety in the single dead tree in the middle of the wide stream.

When the tree creaked, sending a tremor of icy fear through Luke's body, his teeth began to chatter. 'STOP,

DOM.' Pressing his palm to the trunk, the strained creak made his skin crawl, but the crack was somewhere inside the trunk, right beneath them. 'It's our weight. We're too top-heavy for this trunk.'

It was an old tree leaning over the water. If the tree snapped, they were back in the water. If it bent over, they would be within snapping distance with that man-eating crocodile directly below them, with more crocodiles swimming towards them from all directions, with their boats now on the far side of the stream. 'We're surrounded.'

'Where did they come from?'

'It's breeding season. There must be a nest nearby. The one that jumped the boat must be the bull, and the rest of the crocodiles are his harem.' And it was a big bask of about eight fully mature saltwater crocodiles. Prehistoric creatures who were at the top of the food chain, making them the ultimate hunters. And right now, Luke and Dom were the prey.

The tree wasn't stable, as another crack made the hair on the back of his neck rise. They had to offload some weight that would allow them to climb higher, hoping to minimise the strain on the tree.

He searched for a solution — that's when he saw it.

'You didn't?' He scowled at Dom, who was holding the silver barramundi with its long red tag, catching the sun. 'You brought the fish?'

'My fish.' The fishing line, holding the barramundi, was wrapped tightly around Dom's hand.

But the fish flapped against the tree, signalling to the predators below. The blood from Luke and Dom's noses, cuts and scrapes dripped into the water, spreading like oil across the surface where now over a dozen crocodiles had surrounded them.

'We're going to die.'

Thirty-eight

'That was awful.' Jordi shuddered behind the wheel of her van, as they drove onto the tarmac road, making a change from the dust that had been billowing out behind them these past ten minutes.

'What was awful? That you got to see Otis in his tighty-whities.' Esther cackled from the passenger seat, hugging the pugdog.

Jordi gagged as if tasting something foul, from seeing a balding, lily white, bandy-legged, elderly man in his underwear. She struggled to erase the image permanently imprinted in her memory. 'Why couldn't he get dressed?'

'We didn't have an appointment, petal. And I think Otis does that to deter people from banging on his door, demanding to see the lawyer.' Esther frowned. 'But that pompous twit knew all about the second letter. Why he didn't tell me when I came with Luke for the reading of the will, and just hand me both letters at the same time.'

'Otis said it was what Iris wanted.'

'Have you ever seen that many zeros?' Esther held out the note scribbled in Otis's extremely neat handwriting, detailing the sum of fifteen million dollars sitting in a trust for Esther to spend on a secret sister project. Fifteen million—to spend!

'What do you think Iris wanted you to spend it on?'

'No idea. She was a clever cookie, good with numbers.' Esther re-read the second letter:

Hi, Esther

You did it. Or should I say: it took you long enough.

Now don't get mad at Otis. He's been told that you would enjoy the game. I just hope you remembered not to barge in on his tellie-time, we all know how he hates people interrupting him.

'Where was the warning about Otis in his undies!' Again, Jordi shuddered behind the wheel as she steered them down the road.

So, Otis's job is to show you the trust account.

I never realised how much it had grown when I'd invested that big whopping cheque and let it grow over the decades. The stock market was better than a day at the races. Buy. Sell. Hold. It was addictive.

Otis and his accountant friend had a real struggle converting all that cryptocurrency into one lump sum.

So how are you going to spend it?

To find out, take a quick trip back to town to the Elsie Creek Hospital. There, look for Jenny, the adorable head nursing sister. She'll have the next letter for you, and she's happy for you to visit her anytime, day or night.

Please tell Luke it will be the last letter, so he won't be driving you around forever. And you'd better not be driving something illegal, Esther!

'Is this where we talk about your motorised cooler-scooter?' Jordi butted in with her eyes on the road. Her heart twinging a little over the mention of Luke's name.

Esther coyly grinned as she read the last of the letter:

Let the adventure continue, because I promise

you it will make you smile.

Iris

Esther folded up the letter and slid it into her carpetbag. The corners of her lips curled into a soft smile, but there was a glimmer in her eyes, a sparkle as bright as her tiara, that Jordi had never seen before. Was it excitement? Or was Esther finally coming out from under the heavy cloud of grief?

'Were you aware that Iris played the stock exchange?'

'Oh, yes. Iris didn't tell too many people; it was a secret.'

'Why not?'

'Because back in the day women weren't allowed near the stock exchange. But Iris learned from her father.'

'Excuse me?' Jordi blinked, wondering if she'd heard right.

'For ages, Iris used to invest under her husband's name. I mean, back in the seventies a woman couldn't even open a bank account without a male co-signer. And I was almost forty before I had my very first bank account just in my name.'

'I didn't know that.' Jordi shook her head, never realising how much freedom she took for granted as a female.

'But once we got that upgraded internet thingy it became Iris's hobby—until the new ranger, Alice, started helping Iris become a wildlife carer for wallabies. And they'd share romance novels, too. Iris found a real passion for reading smutty books that came with content warnings. She couldn't get enough of them.'

The laugh expelled from Jordi's chest was only amplified by the enclosed van. It had the dog looking at her like she was an alien.

'I told you, Iris was smart as a whip, right up to the end. Hey, how come they have decent roadside signs on this side of town?' She pointed out the passenger window. 'The ones near home are so dull looking. They're advertising a business, they should have more pizzazz.' Then Esther pointed at the road ahead on the sweeping bend. 'What is that? A fire?'

A plume of grey smoke rose into the air as if trapped in a bag and suddenly set free.

Coco the pug started barking. Not yapping. But a terrified bark full of urgency as they came across debris littered over the road. It came from the broken body of a caravan with only its trailer still attached to the car that was tipped on its side.

'Jordi, we have to help them.'

'Call the police.' She pulled on the handbrake and handed Esther her phone, hoping that one teeny tiny bar was enough to get a phone signal. 'You know where we are and can tell them what road we're on.'

'Take your fire extinguisher and help them.' Esther pushed Jordi's shoulder.

'I-I can't.' She was quite safe inside the van.

'Yes, you can. Or I will.' Esther struggled to unclip her seatbelt.

'No. I'll go. You stay here.' Jordi opened the van's side door for the tiny fire extinguisher and approached the caravan lying on its side in the grass.

A potent chill of icy fear washed over her as the flames flickered in the grass. She stopped breathing and couldn't move, her eyes glued to those vivid orange flames, the crackle all too fresh in her memory.

Esther bustled towards Jordi. 'The fire brigade is on the way. Here, give me that.' Esther snatched the fire extinguisher, pulled the pin, aimed the nozzle at the flames and squeezed the trigger, releasing a white power. In a matter of moments, the small brush fire was gone.

'I'm impressed.'

'You can't live with a fireman without picking up a trick of two.' With no parasol, Esther shaded her eyes with her hand. 'Where are the passengers? The driver?'

'Esther, don't.' She pulled on Esther's sleeve, as she walked back from the edge of the road, well away from the car attached to the caravan where its squashed fuel drums were spilling into the surrounding grasses.

'COOEEE!' Esther's voice echoed like a sonic boom. It made Jordi jump in fright.

'HELP. *We're in the car, we're trapped. Please, help.*' It was a man and a woman calling for help.

'Jordi, do something.' Esther pushed on Jordi's shoulder.

The caravan had been stripped free of all its walls, scattering debris everywhere. Leaving only the trailer, attached to the vehicle, twisting the car onto the driver's side, where it had slid to a stop in the dry grass, exposing the entire underbelly of the car with its axle spinning, and the exhaust spewing smoke, with various liquids dripping onto the dead grass pooling around the running vehicle. *'Turn the car off.'*

As the car wheels kept spinning, the driver's rear tyre rims hit against the rocks, causing sparks, as the smell of fuel hung thick in the air. 'Turn. Off. The. Car.'

'I can't,' called out the male driver.

Dead grass brushed against the knees of her jeans as Jordi pushed through to the front of the car, where the passenger's window reflected the sky.

Through the front windscreen, she found an elderly couple tangled around the steering wheel of the car. They were fighting with the airbags that had burst like balloons, covering the steering wheel and dashboard.

'I'll use a rock. Prepare yourself.' Jordi grabbed a nearby rock and smashed at the front window, but it only cracked.

The car's wheels kept turning, sparking, with more fuel spilling out of the car as she bashed at the window. But it did nothing.

She picked up a heavier rock and used it like a hammer. But all it did was make the crack bigger. 'Come on.'

'Hurry, Jordi, the caravan is on fire.' Esther shouted from the road, pointing to the rear of the car.

There was an explosion, and large flames shot high in the sky.

Jordi flinched, crouching down to cover her head and ears

from the blast as a plume of smoke led to an angry ball of fire.

Oh no, Esther was out there!

'Get back in the van, Esther.' She waved at Esther. 'Reverse the van back down the road. Move. Now.'

For once Esther did as she was told, jumping back into the van, and reversed well away from the danger.

Jordi then hoisted the rock over her head. 'You will not die on me today.' And it was as if an army of hands forcefully pushed behind her, to drive that rock through the windscreen, where it cracked like ice. With her sleeves over her hands, she peeled back the glass like a sheet of sharp plastic and dragged the middle-aged woman from the car. 'Run to the road and stand by my van.'

'I can't leave my husband. Barry?' Blood trickled down one cheek from a gash on her temple.

'Don't worry, Norma. I'm right behind you, luv.'

'Go, I'll get Barry. Just go.' Jordi dragged away the airbag's nylon materials that were wound around the steering wheel. 'We need to turn off the engine. Now.'

Barry struggled behind the steering wheel, trying to free the airbag's waste.

Jordi saw the keys and ripped them straight from the ignition. It silenced the engine, and the wheels stopped spinning. Only to reveal the spine-tingling crackle and snap, the hiss and sizzle, as the beginning of a guttural growl built into a roar. It was fire!

'We've got to go. NOW.' She tugged on Barry's arm, as a thick black smoke swirled around her, cutting her view from the road. 'Why can't you get out?'

'The seatbelt's jammed.'

With a deep breath, Jordi did the most daring thing in her life and jumped inside the vehicle. The acrid stench of fuel and burning plastics was overpowering and she gagged for air, tugging on the belt's clip, but it wouldn't budge. She pulled out her pocketknife, her gift from Luke. Using the blade, the seatbelt fell away.

But the driver was still stuck.

'I'm trapped. My boot is stuck under the pedals. Go, save yourself.'

The smoke stung her eyes, as terror had her scars stinging from the horrendous heat as the angry, nasty, deadly fire surrounded them. 'No. I will not leave you behind.' The acid bile of fear scalded her throat so tight it was hard to breathe the ferociously hot air. With watery eyes, she reached for the pedals and hacked at Barry's bootlaces, to drag his foot free. 'Let's go.'

'Where?'

Because when she looked up through the hole in the windscreen, she discovered a thick wall of flames had completely surrounded them.

Thirty-nine

There was now a float of thirteen crocodiles surrounding Dom and Luke as they clung to a dead tree in the middle of a wide stream that made up part of the remote outback's river system.

'Got an EPIRB on you?' Dom asked, hugging the million-dollar-fish. It had stopped fighting for survival a while ago.

'On the boat.' Both of their boats had floated along the current and were now well out of sight.

'Got a phone?'

'On the boat.' Luke tapped his pockets to discover he had his fisherman's friend still in its sheath. But bringing a pocketknife to a crocodile fight was like holding up a toothpick against these prehistoric monsters.

Not even midday and the horrendous outback sun beamed down, only to reflect off the water. There was no escaping it. He'd kill for a glass of cold water while standing on dry land.

But land was a good twenty-metre swim in either direction, while they were stuck in the middle of a causeway that connected three different creek run-offs.

In the wet season, this area would be underwater. Right now, this old tree was all they had. A tree struggling to keep upright under their weight.

'Let go of the fish, Dom.'

'No.'

'Hey, I don't want to—'

'I'm not going to throw away a million dollars.'

Sure, that fish would solve a ton of problems, but they had to do something about saving today. 'If you let go of the fish, and throw it to the top dog, he'll take it and his family will follow.'

'Yeah, right. Is that when we'll learn how to run on water, too?'

'Well have you got any suggestions you'd like to share with the group?'

Another crocodile leapt at them from the water.

Dom screamed, as Luke stabbed at the air with his pocketknife. 'Get back, you mongrel.'

The crocodile landed back with barely a splash as another twelve sets of beady eyes remained ready to take their shot at the prize.

'You won't hurt it with that pocketknife. They're bulletproof.'

'They are *not* bulletproof. They're like any animal, they have their weaknesses.' Luke searched for a solution. Snapping off a sturdy branch, he wedged himself in the fork and he wrapped his legs around the trunk the way Jordi had hugged her legs around him. What he'd give to be on land right now, with Jordi in his arms.

'What are you doing?'

With the small blade he sliced off pieces of wood at the tip. 'Making spears.'

'I'm sure they'd be about the right size for my sister's Barbie doll collection, but for crocodiles?'

'Those pricks are going to keep coming for us. We're nothing but sport to them, especially while you're holding that fish.'

'Coming from a family who hunts for sport, that's rich.'

'We haven't done commercial hunting for years, we only do it for meat or if they're a danger to man.' Like the thirteen sets of beady eyes watching him with evil intent. He pulled on another stick, a much longer and thicker one, the cracking sound like a shot in the air.

'Don't break our tree, man.'

'I'm not. It we stay close to the trunk, it won't snap.' He hoped.

'What are you doing?'

He frowned at Dom and at this entire stupid situation. 'Should I have brought my crayons to draw you a diagram of stick figures to explain what this stick will do with that crocodile—'

'Dude!'

'What?' Because this was all Dom's fault.

'All I see and hear are those things looking at me like lunch.' Dom nodded down at the crocodiles staring at them with the cold eyes filled with deadly predatory intent.

Luke recognised them as the eyes of a hunter. 'Here, take this stick.'

'I can't.' Dom was hugging the fish and the tree, with sweat pouring down his red face.

'Lose the fish.'

'No.'

'Lose the damned fish or we're both croc bait. If you don't drop it, we won't survive to spend any of that money. Drop the fish and it'll make us thirty kilos lighter, so we can climb higher and get into a better position to defend ourselves.'

'Look man, I get the speech. I just can't.'

'You can.'

'No, I can't. The fishing line has made my hand numb, and my fingers are throbbing something fierce. I move, I fall.'

'Dammit.' Luke carefully shifted around the trunk as if sitting on a sheet of glass. He peered down to discover the tight fishing line was turning Dom's hand blue. If Dom lost that grip, he was gone. And if Dom grabbed onto Luke in a panic, he'd drag them both down, potentially snapping their tree's top off. His homemade fishing lure had snagged that fish good.

'I'll lean down.' As he did, another crocodile leapt up. It was much smaller, but it leapt higher, snapping into his face.

'Arsehole.' Dom kicked out at it as Luke tried to stab at it.

'They're going for the fish.' With his pocketknife, he

leaned over. Even if it broke his heart, he cut the red-tagged fish free.

His breath hitched, and it was as if the entire world slowed down to a torturous slow motion to watch as a million dollars fell into the open jaws of a monster.

Damn.

He could only blink, as it disappeared under the churn of muddy river water. And everything, all his hopes and dreams went with it.

'Help, dude.'

'I've got you.' Luke helped Dom scramble up the tree, where they could tuck their feet safely away from the rest of the crocodiles waiting below.

Luke snapped off another branch and started whittling the end into a point. 'If we make enough of them, we could create a barrier around the trunk.'

'Dude, they're sticks.'

'That'll be sharp enough to spear their open mouths and give them a toothache.'

Dom wiped the blood off his face with his fishing shirt, which was saturated in sweat. 'You should just hit them with the uppercut you gave me. I think you've chipped a tooth.'

'You gave me an earache, to go with my shiner.' Because his cheek and left eye were pounding, the tight swelling only magnified by the sun's heat and sweat.

'I think I'd better grab some sticks to defend myself from you.' Dom leaned back to reach for some lower branches and the tree creaked as loudly as a cracking stockwhip.

'*Stop.*' Luke dragged Dom back by the shirtfront. 'You lean back any further and the weight of this tree will shift, and it'll crack, right below you.'

'Gotcha.'

'Here, you can sharpen the ends.'

'How?'

'Rub it against the trunk.'

'I'm not going to start any fires, rubbing on that wood?'

'This tree is sitting in water, there's no way it'd burn. But we need to keep busy making weapons.'

'Why?'

'That way, we're not tempted to punch each other in the mouth—or panic.' They were literally staring into the jaws of death as another crocodile leapt at them, and this time he threw his stick like a spear. 'You mongrel.'

'You got him.' Dom pointed at the stick in the crocodile's mouth. It groaned in pain as it fell back with a mighty splash, and swam away fast. The flurry of its exit somehow warned the others who floated backwards, as if to stand back and regroup for their next plan of attack.

'I see now what you're doing. I'll sharpen the tips.' Dom rubbed the tip of a stick against the trunk.

Luke grabbed another stick and started whittling the end into a sharp tip. 'What were you going to do with a million dollars? You're rich now as it is.'

'I'm not rich.'

'You've got that flash car and boat.'

'I'm in debt up to my eyeballs because of that car and boat. It was either buy a house or buy a boat. When my girlfriend left me, the answer was simple: I bought a boat.' He grinned.

'You know what the word boat stands for …'

'Bring on another thousand.' They said in unison, even sharing a slight grin in a grim situation.

'I thought you were some rich cattleman with that white cowboy hat.' That was nowhere in sight, like his own hat. Leaving them both unprotected from the harsh outback sun.

'No. I'm a carpenter.'

'Eh?' Luke cocked an eyebrow. 'You're a chippy?'

'And you're a bottle shop attendant.'

'Pays the mortgage, mate.'

'Pays for my toys.'

'I thought you must have been a ringer, or a helicopter muster pilot.' Luke shaped the end of a stick into a spear tip, passing it to Dom to sharpen it against the tree trunk, while he searched for another branch.

'No. Just a chippy. Came up here with my girlfriend for a holiday. I fell in love with the fishing, and my girlfriend fell in love with my best mate. Where's your girlfriend?'

'I'm not sure she is anymore ...' Luke wiped at the sweat from around his eyes. Damn, he missed her.

'What do you mean by that?'

'We had a big barney this morning. It was stupid, really.' He should have stayed home with Jordi and sorted out their mess.

'About you fishing in the Classic?'

'No. Jordi found out I was running the *Dramas from the Dinghy* podcast.' Luke blew off the sawdust and splinters from the stick's tip, before handing it to Dom to finish.

Dom's brow ruffled in disbelief. 'No way that's you. I've heard that podcast, it's funny. But it got me into trouble with that scary bar manager, Mean Rene, over doing a rooster wave over the flower girl.'

Crack! Luke snapped back another stick. 'I owe you a punch in the mouth for that. As for those flowers, don't mess with Jordi like that, leave her out of our beef. You hear me.'

'Hey, okay, chill, dude.' Dom held up a hand. 'I swear to you those flowers I gave Jordi had no ulterior motive to them. I was being genuine when I said sorry to her—I felt bad when I found out I'd ruined her celebrations for her first fish. I hadn't meant to douse her; I was aiming for you.' Dom rubbed his red jaw where a bruise was forming. 'Besides, I don't think my jaw will handle another punch from you, or I'll be sucking my meals through a straw for a month.' He went back to sharpening the stick point against the tree's trunk into a lethal spear.

Luke studied Dom for a moment, trying to cool his temper, but in this heat, it was a struggle. To distract himself he went to work whittling on the end of another thick stick.

'Why was your girlfriend upset over the podcast? Hey, it can't be you.' Dom waved his stick at Luke. 'Those guys would have to be in their late fifties.'

'Real-time voice filters. We could sound like schoolgirls if we wanted to.' He'd done that with Porter when they first started, laughing so hard, they fell off their chairs. For a week, they couldn't look at Cecil in his schoolgirl ribbons without it reminding them.

What he'd give for Porter to come putting around the corner in his police boat.

'Why did you choose to use fake voices? Old men at that?'

'Wouldn't you rather listen to some old man of the sea than a bloke like me?'

'Yeah, I guess. I was listening for their tips, too. Where did you learn all of that?'

'The customers who'd come through the bottle shop. And, as a kid I learned a lot from those visitors who'd come to the Lodge for their next great hunting adventure.' And here he was in a tree being hunted.

'When this is over, can you take me hunting?'

'Haven't been for a while.'

'Why not?'

'I've been busy working, looking after my gran ...' Avoiding all those things that reminded him of being with family, like the times spent with his dad hunting. 'I'd given up a lot of things.'

'Time spent with the girlfriend would eat into hunting weekends. My ex got sick of me going fishing.'

'It's got nothing to do with Jordi.' Or was it? 'You see, I pulled my girl out of a burning car. And until a few weeks ago, I was living with the guilt for failing her, until she forgave me.'

'For what?'

Luke was surprised he'd said anything, but he had nowhere to hide, stuck in a tree in the middle of a river, surrounded by crocodiles, dying of thirst and sunburn under a midday sun. Oh, and he'd lost his boat, his girl, and a million dollars. Was this his penance for being a prick?

'For not saving her parents.' What Jordi had done for him, by forgiving him, had unleashed that blissful feeling he only felt with Jordi. Every time he talked to Jordi, or was near

Jordi, he felt that incredible feeling of bliss, like she was his home.

From the treetop, beyond the river there were nothing but an ocean of trees spreading in all directions. Would he ever see Jordi, Esther and the Lodge again?

'I should have been up-front with her and not have been so sneaky.' For the podcast and for not telling her how he knew her. 'And I shouldn't have climbed into the boat this morning.' He glared down at the crocodiles lying like logs in the water.

'I agree with you on that one …' Dom shook his head, while working on his mini spear. 'If your girl forgave you over the accident—which is huge, dude. There are very few people who'd run into a burning car, they're usually running the other way. I'm sure she'll forgive you for mucking up.'

Keeping busy, talking nonsense, stopped them from panicking—but for a guy who'd been told to never air any Bennett business in public, he needed to change the subject. 'You're not superstitious, are you?'

'I've got a lucky fishing hat. Wish I had that on me now.' Using his hand to shade his eyes from the sun, Dom peered around. Licking his lips, he looked down at the water. 'All that water and we can't drink any of it.'

'Not unless you want to be the main ingredient in a crocodile's cocktail.'

'True …' Dom went back to sharpening the tips against the trunk. 'Are you superstitious?'

'Well, this morning I argued with Jordi, got a flat tyre on the boat trailer, lost my girl, lost my boat, and now this …' This morning he thought it was the fishing trip from hell. Now, staring down at the mob of man-eaters, it was the stuff of nightmares.

'Don't forget you lost my million-dollar barra, too.'

He'd lost everything except the air in his lungs. But with the crocodiles gathering below them Luke didn't know how much longer they had left. As the water rushed down from the floodplains where pregnant clouds were gathering, and with the Northern Territory's king tide a whopping nine metre swing expected to turn at sunset, the water level would rise within this tidal river, all in favour of the ultimate hunters who were at their fiercest in the dark.

Forty

'What do we do?' The grey-haired Barry, wearing only one shoe, leaned against Jordi, while they were trapped beside the car as walls of ferocious flames surrounded them.

Jordi couldn't see beyond the horrendous heat and flames leaping high in the sky. The deafening crackle and the smell of fumes had opened a door allowing the memories to rush back. All of them.

She remembered waking up to her parent's car spinning out of control. Then the deafening noise and the jolt of landing on the roof of the car as glass chips flew everywhere, leaving her dangling upside down. Her father shouting at her to get out, her mother unconscious, while Jordi struggled to get her seatbelt undone.

She remembered a set of black boots crushing the grass as they rushed to the car. The first flicker of flames and how they crawled like ghosts across the car's ceiling, burning her bag, her shirt's sleeves, her hair. That was when Luke kicked in the window, climbed inside, and cut her seatbelt free, to then drag her out.

She fought against Luke to get to her father, but the steering wheel had him pinned, crushing his chest. Yet her dad had the strength to tell her he loved her.

In that moment, all she wanted to do was save her parents, but Luke had dragged her away. Then the car exploded, and she woke up a month later with no hair, covered in skin grafts, staring at a hospital floor because nothing could touch her back, and she was all alone …

But she wasn't alone now, even if she was facing her worst nightmare.

'We have to make a break for it, Barry, or we'll die.' And she was not going to die today.

Jordi leaned over to the back seat and dragged out a car blanket and used it to beat back the flames. 'I'll try to create a path that we can leap through.'

'I can't run. I've sprained my ankle.'

'You have to, and you will.' He was too heavy to carry, with her scars stinging with the memory of how they came to be, suddenly unleashing a new terror inside that made her want to scream.

Gritting her teeth, she slapped the blanket against the flames, not only fighting the horrendous heat, but her fear, the memory of the accident, and of the past that had kept her trapped from daring to live.

'Hold on to my hips, keep your head down and we'll hide under this blanket and try to use it as a shield. Just don't fall.' If one of them did, they'd both go down.

She bashed back the flames, creating a small hole, and with a helluva lot of hope, she flung the blanket over them like a cloak. Barry gripped her shoulders that burned from his touch, forcing her forwards, she gritted her teeth, and roared. 'AURGHHH.'

The flames lashed at her arms, stinging like whips, as she shouldered through the wall of fire that felt like it went on forever.

Behind them was an explosion, sending a gust of wind to push the flames flat. She saw her break and dragged Barry behind her to roll in the dry grass.

Jordi scrambled to her feet, dragging off her shirt, which was on fire. 'Roll, Barry, roll. You'll put out the fire on your shirt if you roll.' She pushed Barry, rolling him across the dry dirt as she slapped at the flames on his shirt and trousers, when a huge plume of water washed over them.

She was blinded. Gasping for air.

But it was water. Glorious cold water.

On her knees, Jordi cried for joy, as she willingly surrendered to the rural fire brigade's bushfire unit dousing them with water.

Jax, the local fire chief, rushed towards her. 'Jordi? Are you okay?'

'Am I glad to see you!' She didn't care if it was the wrong or right thing to do, but she hugged Jax in his thick yellow fire coat. Wishing it was Luke. Now wishing that she'd hugged Luke that very first time they'd met when he'd pulled her free from the flames, so he didn't feel the burden he'd been carrying all this time.

'Come on, let's get you both to safety.' Jax threw Barry over his shoulders in a classic fireman's lift, and they scrambled up to the road. A second bushfire unit moved in and worked on dousing the fire as the sound of more screaming sirens rushed towards them.

As they attended to Barry's and Norma's wounds, Jordi staggered away to lie back on the road in the shadow of a gum tree and took deep breaths. The asphalt's stones irritated her skin as she lay on the road in her jeans and sports bra, but she could still feel the tiara in her hair. She didn't care, as she stared up at the blue sky and closed her eyes. She'd survived the worst.

That's right, she was a *survivor!*

Firefighter crews busily ran around her as Jax gave out orders, when something started licking her face.

'What the?' She winced and came face to face with the pug. 'Coco.'

'There you are. I've been so worried about you.' Esther pulled Jordi off the road and into her arms for a massive hug.

'I'm okay.' And she believed it.

Forty-one

'What will happen if we stay here all night?' Dom asked Luke, each straddling a thick branch, high in a dead tree in the middle of a crocodile-infested waterway. Armed with needle-sharp spearheads aimed and ready to stab like thorns as their only defence.

'Do you want the truth?'

Dom shrugged.

Honestly, Luke didn't want to say it either. But what choice did they have? Maybe they could come up with a solution. 'Hopefully the worst of it is being eaten by the midges and mosquitoes.' They were already snacking on his ankles.

Dom nodded at the crocodiles as he, too, scratched his ankles. 'But ...'

'We've got to fight the dehydration ...' Luke wiped at his dry mouth. 'We might get dizzy, or suffer headaches, maybe even faint. Mostly the fatigue will set in where we'll want to fall asleep so deeply that we'll forget where we are.'

'We could tie ourselves to the trunk.'

'I thought about that, too.'

'What's the issue?'

'This tree isn't stable.'

'We're sitting in it aren't we?'

'Sure. But if one of those hunkering lumps of meat gets smart enough to realise this trunk is top heavy, they'll throw themselves at the trunk we're strapped to.'

'We'll topple over.' Dom stared wide-eyed at the water.

'At least being free, we might get a shot at swimming away.'

'What are our chances of surviving that swim?'

With over a dozen crocodiles below them? 'None. All we can do is hang up here and wait for help.'

'How long do you reckon that'll take?'

'There's the fishing marshals and the police boat patrolling this river, plus over eighty boats competing in the Classic. As soon as they find two unmanned boats floating downstream, they'll organise a search party.'

'Most of the other competitors are upstream on the other side of the boat ramp.'

'There was a large group headed for the mouth. They'll be heading back soon for the nightly check in.' He glanced at his watch. For five hours they'd been clinging to this trunk, roasting, from high noon to where the sun now hung low on the horizon.

They held their sticks, sharpened to a narrow and deadly point, while slapping at mozzies buzzing around their sunburnt skin as the sweat saturated their fishing shirts.

The shimmery surface of the water reflected their sad and sorry position. And that jagged crack in the tree trunk was bigger than he thought.

Luke pointed at their reflections. 'You being a chippy—'

'I see it.' Dom shuffled closer along his branch to wrap his legs around the tree. 'We stick close to the trunk and no more leaning back.'

'You'll have no complaints from me.' Even if he was closer than he wanted to be to the guy he'd always hated.

'Hey? Where did all those crocodiles go?'

Luke pointed to the banks. 'Some are sitting on the banks, the rest will be sitting at the bottom of the river watching us. Don't worry, they won't be going too far.'

'How long can they stay underwater like that?'

'Up to an hour. They reduce their heart rate right down and just lie there like a dead log and wait.'

'How come you know so much about them?'

'Grew up here.'

'If we survive, you're taking me hunting.'

'If we survive, I'm parking up my boat for a while.'

'To do what?'

Luke shrugged. 'With that million-dollar barra, I was planning to start a fishing tour business.'

'I heard.'

'And you wanted to start a helicopter fishing business? Can you fly a helicopter?'

'I've been having lessons. You?'

'Not my thing. I don't enjoy flying.'

'You're kidding.'

'Nope. My parents keep asking me to fly over for Christmas, but I won't do it.'

'Go figure.' Dom grinned.

'Are you going to be a dick about it?'

'Nope. I don't like balloons.'

'Hot air balloons?'

'Any kind of balloon.' Dom shrugged, then used the pointy end of the stick to scratch his back. 'Since I was a kid, balloons have always freaked me out. I don't know if it's that bang when they burst, or that rubbing noise from their plastic skin, but they freak me out.'

Luke grinned. 'You know a bursting balloon is as loud as a gunshot and you want to go hunting?'

'Believe me, balloons have a distinct sound. It's called globophobia—the uncommon fear of balloons.'

'Are you for real?'

'Look it up when you find your phone.' Dom used the heel of his palm to wipe the sweat off his sunburnt brow. 'Balloons give me a freaking panic attack. I'm no good at kids' birthday parties.'

Luke arched an eyebrow. He had never heard of such a thing.

'You won't say anything?'

'Nah, man. We're good. What happens in this tree stays in this tree.' Luke patted the tree's trunk like an old mate.

'Unless you start being a dick again.'

'We're good, dude. What do you say we make peace with the feud?' Dom held out his hand.

'Yeah, we're good.' They shook hands in the tree.

'You know, I can't even remember how this barney between us started.'

'Me neither.' It seemed so stupid, now they were fighting for their lives. 'But I'd spend all week thinking of something smart to say to you, because you kept coming back.'

Dom grinned. 'You did come up with some pearlers. I've used a few on the worksite … Did you hate me because you were jealous of me? Thinking I'm the rich guy.'

Luke shrugged. 'You just rubbed me the wrong way. Talking down to me like you were better than me. It was the same way some of the guests at the Lodge used to speak to me, calling me *boy*, back when I had to carry their bags, fetch this and that, load bullets into their guns and carry their hunted geese like an underpaid golf caddie.'

'I didn't know that. Well, I won't call you boy again.'

'Mate, we're about the same age. I'm thirty-one.'

'The boat was my present for hitting my dirty-thirties.' Dom raked fingers through his sweaty hair. 'And if this is my last confession—'

'Don't say that.'

'I'm sorry for being a drongo. But you dished out too, buttercup.'

'Yeah, I'm sorry too. Cretin.'

'Tosser.'

'Ijit.'

They grinned at each as they hugged a tree trunk shared between them.

'Hey …' Dom sat taller. The tree creaked.

Luke gripped Dom's shirt. 'Don't lean back, man.'

'What is that?' He pointed to a group of diamond-like shadows shifting upstream. 'It's too wide to be a fish or a crocodile. There's a few of them.'

With narrowed eyes Luke peered past the shimmering

surface in the direction Dom was pointing. 'Oh, please be real.'

'Is that floating paper?'

'Whiprays.' Half a dozen crocodiles were now sunning themselves on the banks. The other half of their group floated like logs, surrounding the tree, completely ignoring the school of whiprays swimming beneath them as they headed upstream.

'Why aren't the crocodiles chasing after those whiprays?'

'Why would they go for a gritty disc full of bones and tough as boot leather, when there are two beefy blokes already frying in a tree as part of their afternoon's menu?'

'I knew I was hot.'

'You're such a dick.' But this time they chuckled, watching the freshwater whiprays float like angels in the water. 'Remember when you asked me if I was superstitious?'

'Yeah? I told you about my lucky fishing hat.'

'Well, those whiprays are my good-luck charm. I swear, it's like I'd rub the side of some magic lamp and wish to catch more fish, that's what those whiprays do for me.'

'Every time?'

'Every time. Jordi caught that whopper as her first fish after seeing those whiprays. But right now, I'm wishing hard to be rescued ...' He'd never needed to be rescued before. Maybe he did need rescuing in other ways—like how Jordi had helped him in her own sweet way.

What he'd give to hold Jordi again. He imagined them floating in a shady pool of ice water while drinking an ice-cold beer.

'No freaking way.' Dom tapped Luke's shoulder, snapping him out of his daydream. 'I think those whiprays will become my good-luck charms, too.'

'Why?' He peered over his shoulder in the direction that Dom was pointing, and spotted a boat slowly coming around the corner.

It was the park ranger's boat.

'Ranger! Over here. Over here.' Luke and Dom shouted as

they vigorously waved from the tree.

The blond-haired passenger, who Luke recognised as Doctor Mannen, pointed as he spoke to the local park ranger who steered her boat towards them like the queen of their small ocean.

'Am I glad to see you, Alice. Doc.'

'Hey, Luke. How many crocodiles have you got fighting for their meal?' Alice grinned at him from behind the helm with Stewart, who the local women had nicknamed the Hot Doc, chuckling beside her.

'Thirteen,' replied Luke. 'And one big bull who rugby tackled my boat.'

'Well, you are in his breeding grounds. His ladies have their crocodile nests all through this area.'

'I can see that now.' He could see the world from high in his tree.

'Where?' Dom asked Luke.

'That tall floating grass is croc grass. They nest in that.' And they were smack bang in the middle of a whopping field of the stuff that covered the banks. He just hadn't wanted to scare Dom into a lifetime of therapy.

'Sit tight, you two.' Alice pulled back the throttle. The twin engines on her boat churned the water as her boat floated backwards.

'Where is she going?' Don asked. 'We're here, not over there.'

'If we climb down, those crocs are going to lunge at us. They're not scared of boats. Relax, this isn't the ranger's first rodeo. Alice catches crocodiles for a living.'

'Is she single?' Don grinned at the woman with red hair in a long thick braid.

'That's her partner on the boat, Doctor Stewart Mannen. Why would she go for a chippy when she has a doctor to go home to?' Would Jordi be at home waiting for him with Gran? He hoped so. With everything inside, he hoped she was there so he could tell her he was sorry for being an idiot and would do anything to make it up to her.

But she'd let him go, too. Or did she push him away?

Either way, he'd walked away, instead of sorting out their differences for this …

He peered around at the water in a place that was meant to be a big part of his grand plans for taking tourists fishing. Was that what he really wanted to do? Did he want to deal with the pressure of catching fish while being responsible for the welfare of strangers?

He loved fishing. But this weekend's competition, and the pressure to perform, had turned his hobby into a chore. Would turning it into a job mean he'd lose that passion? When right now he cared more for family.

As for his obsession?

Hell, yeah, he was obsessive over their safety. Damned straight! Because that was his family, and he loved his family, and he would do anything for them — which included Jordi.

Alice threw a black ball into the water. *'Fire in the hole!'* She put her fingers to her ears, the doctor doing the same, both hunkering down behind the console.

A few seconds later, the water imploded with a loud bang as they clung to the tree that creaked as the crocodiles fled in all directions.

'What the heck was that?' shouted Dom.

'Concussion grenades. I know a bloke from the special forces who gave me some. He said it worked quicker than waiting for crocs to take some bait while getting poachers out of a tree. Don't worry, it won't hurt them, it just scares them off for a bit.' Alice then nudged the nose of the boat against the tree. 'You can come down now, gentlemen.'

'I've got you, Dom.' Luke helped Dom scramble down. He quickly followed to the safety of the boat. There, both men, covered in scratches, sunburn, and bruises from their own fight faced each other. They may have started this day out as foes, but they hugged each other like brothers.

Forty-two

Jordi steered her van down the thin laneway she'd been avoiding for over a year. Yet, for the second time today she was visiting a graveyard, this one a hundred times larger than the one at Elsie Creek.

'Hi, Mum, Dad.' Jordi stood before their headstones without a single flower in her hand. Nothing.

With Esther's blessings, Jordi had driven straight here. Even if Jax wanted her to get checked for smoke inhalation, she needed to do this today. Helping Esther hustle a lift to town with the fire chief, where she was going to chase up the final letter from Iris.

'I'm sorry I didn't come sooner.' Tears trickled down her cheeks as she ran fingers through her filthy hair, the smell of smoke clinging to her clothes. She didn't want to put it off any longer or find another excuse—not when life was so fragile it could extinguish like a flame if you weren't careful. Especially when life was like a fire that needed fuel to breathe life into the flame, it needed soul.

And today she'd found it.

'I saved these two people today. They had an accident in their caravan, and there was a bit of a fire …' *A bit? Ha!*

She wiped the tears off her grimy cheeks. 'That couple are both fine, at the hospital being checked out, and I'm fine, too. Actually, I'm better than fine.'

She heaved in a shaky breath. 'I also remembered the accident, ours, and where you told me you loved me, and in your own way, said your goodbyes.'

She dropped to her knees in the soft, trimmed grass, wiping at her hot tears. 'Dad, remember when you'd tell us to face our fears like you did almost every day on the job? You said sometimes you didn't think, you just acted or reacted. Well, I did that. I faced that fire and stared down that demon—while freaking terrified! But, instead of freezing, or running and hiding, like I normally do, I helped those two people survive.' She grinned, feeling a little foolish as she hugged herself and said in a whisper, 'I felt like a freaking hero wearing this car blanket for a cape.' She giggled behind her hand, peering around to make sure no one else heard.

'But I'm going to be okay. I'm ready to get on with my life. So …'

She exhaled long and slow. 'Natalie's pregnant, and Mitchell just got this promotion and they're so happy like one of those romantic Christmas movies you loved, Mum … And well, I want that too.'

She shuffled back onto her feet, fidgeting with her fingers as she spoke to a silent world where not even a bird sang. 'I know I won't get that hiding out the back of a florist shop. And I won't find it hiding behind the flowers I deliver, living life on the outer edge of other people's happiness, while watching their celebratory moments, instead of finding my own reasons for celebrating. It's my turn to get out there and not be so scared to find my brand of happiness.' She wiped her tears with the back of her sleeve, and for the first time, willingly rolled her sleeves up, exposing the burn marks. Some looked like birthmarks, freckles perhaps, but she had nothing to hide. Not anymore.

'My scars are my signs of survival telling me I may have been kicked and beaten once, but I'm not down and out for the count. And I understand that it's okay to be scared. But I'm tired of being scared when I want more.' She pointed at her chest and said, 'So, I'm here to make a promise to stop being so afraid, to not let my fears hold me back, and to take a chance and find my own kind of happiness.' She inhaled deeply, finding that courage to stand tall.

'I guess this is goodbye for a bit because I'll be getting busy. But know you'll always be in my heart, no matter where I go.' She pressed her fingertips against her lips to kiss them, then placed them against her parents' headstone. 'I love you, Mum. I love you, Dad.'

With a soft, teary smile, Jordi headed back to the van and dialled a number.

'Hey, is everything alright?' Natalie asked over the phone.

Even though the butterflies were swirling in her tummy she recognised it wasn't from fear, it was from excitement. 'I'm ready to talk about the sale of the house and the store, because I want to make a fresh start, too.'

Forty-three

Inside the small bush hospital's emergency room, Luke was being fitted with an IV. He had a splitting headache from dehydration, sunburn, and a black eye. Various types of insect bites covered his lower legs, along with a vast collection of scratches across his skin from hugging a tree, but by God he was alive.

Dom sat on the examination bed beside Luke's, holding an icepack to his fat lip, with black eyes from his swollen nose, along with the same insect bites, sunburn, and scratches as Luke.

But they were both still smiling.

Luke shifted his arm where they'd attached it to a tube. 'You can let me out, Doctor.'

'Ditto to that, dude.' Dom nodded, giving a thumbs up. 'We could do with a beer.'

'Now I'm hearing you.'

'Not on my watch, you pair of cowboys.' Doctor Mannen Senior pushed back his white doctor's coat to put his hands on his hips. 'Get comfortable. You'll be staying here with those drips in to replace the fluids you've lost. The pain medications should relieve you of those headaches while the nurse gets the ointment for those itchy insect bites.' The grey-haired doctor Luke had known since he was a boy, glanced at his phone. 'I've got a message from my son to say they've found your boats and that they're being towed back by the police.'

'Alright.' Which meant his best mate, Porter, was on the

job.

Luke lay back on the cool sheets to stare at the dumb dots on the ceiling. The cool air conditioning was a relief as it brushed over his burnt skin. 'Reckon we do the ice-bucket challenge and just sit in a tub of ice.'

'Now that sounds like a plan.' Dom nodded eagerly.

'I could call the pub and have Billy bring over a couple of ice bags from the bottle shop—'

'*Where is my grandson?*' Esther's voice echoed through the halls, as she came barrelling down the corridor, wearing her tiara, like a woman on a mission.

'Over here, Gran.' Luke waved from the far end of the room.

'Oh, my boy. Please tell me you're going to be okay.'

'I'm fine.'

'Hmm ...' She brushed back his hair, exposing his bruises, then glanced over at Dom in the neighbouring bed and his various technicolour bruises. 'Were you two boys being boys?'

'We sorted it out.' Luke smirked at Dom.

Esther chewed on her bottom lip, the worry deepening the creases around her eyes.

'We're fine, Gran.' He gave her hands a reassuring squeeze. 'We're just a bit dehydrated and sunburnt, that's all.'

'You know, your uncle was in a similar predicament, his boat sprung a leak and he clung to a tree all night. He wouldn't go near the river, not even the dam in the back, for a year after that.'

'Don't blame him.' Luke peered past her shoulder to the doors. 'Where's Jordi?'

'Gone.'

'What?' His heart fell as he raised himself onto his elbows. 'Where?'

'Jordi went with my blessing, and I want to tell you I don't need a granny-sitter, Luke.'

'But—'

'Jordi and I had a good talk about my um...' She

swallowed. 'My condition.'

'Have you got the results?' He pushed up from his bed.

'Not yet.' She sighed. 'But I know what it'll be. And Jordi mentioned that I could get a companion.'

'Did she?' He arched his eyebrow.

'Yes. Someone to drive me around to not bother you.'

'I just want you safe, Gran.'

'I get that. But you can take down those silly cameras.'

'I agree.'

'You do?'

'I hated putting them in. I kept telling Dad it wasn't right. But I'll gladly disconnect them when we get home.'

'Good.' Gran gave a satisfied nod, peeking back at the doors. 'I'm waiting for Jenny, the head nurse. She's bringing me the last letter from Iris. I've had quite a day with Jordi.'

'And where is Jordi?' He sat higher, but a piercing pain stabbed behind his eyes. It forced him back onto the pillow, placing the icepack over his eyes as the migraine pounded.

'Don't worry, Jordi is safe. She texted me earlier to tell me she's safe at home with her sister. See, I used my phone.'

'About time you turned that thing on.' *Oh, no. She's gone ...* The realisation that Jordi was back in the city had him slumping back in defeat.

'Oh, my poor boy. We can fix this.' Gran tenderly stroked his cheek, but with the sunburn it felt like sandpaper.

He cracked an eyelid open. 'Did Jordi tell you what happened?'

'Not in so many words. But you would have been so proud of Jordi. She was quite the hero, saving this couple from the fire—'

'What did you say?' Pushing through the pain, he sat upright.

Esther dropped her carpetbag on the bed, and the pug poked its head out.

'Tell me you didn't steal that dog, *again*.'

'Felix dropped off the rat on his way to work this morning. He's paying me to puppy-sit.'

'Can we skip to the part about the fire and Jordi?' Was that why Jordi raced back to her sister's? He shifted his legs to get off the bed, but his grandmother pushed him back.

'You, young man, lie back.' She was serious, too. 'Oh, I just realised something, it's me now telling you to stay in the hospital bed.' Bobbing her eyebrows up and down, highly amused.

'About time you started playing the grown-up,' he mumbled.

'Now that I have your undivided attention, young man, allow me to tell you about my marvellous day with Jordi …' Esther regaled him with her tale, her eyes sparkling in ways he hadn't seen for a long time. His grandmother had found her spark again, as well as that smile.

'And then there was this accident. This whopping big fire, and Jordi …' As Esther explained the road accident, Luke forgot his pain and was ready to rip out the drip line and race after Jordi.

'No, you don't! Stop that.' Esther slapped at his hands, pushing him back onto the bed. 'You're just like your father. Walden couldn't keep still either when he was in hospital.'

'When was Dad in here?'

'When the old bull catcher tipped over, Walden got some stitches and a broken rib. He was only twelve, being a lunatic like you were at that age. It's why your father put in seatbelts in the buffalo catchers when you started to drive. You were how old?'

'Eight, nine?' Luke shrugged.

'Dude, I didn't drive my first car until I was of legal age,' called out Dom from the other bed. 'Did you even do a driving test?'

'Here we are, Esther …' Jenny, the head nursing sister, approached with an envelope.

'Oh, it's here.' Esther, in her eagerness, slapped Luke's arm.

'Oi, watch the sunburn, Gran.' How was it that the more he rested, the more he ached? At least the painkillers were working against the headache.

'It's the letter.' His spritely grandmother practically slid across the floor to meet the nursing sister. 'Thank you, Jenny.'

'Come and see me when you're ready, Esther.' Jenny walked away with a smile as if she knew some inside joke.

'Here, you read this.'

Luke took the envelope addressed to his grandmother. 'Why is Iris making you go on a wild goose chase?'

'Because we used to have these driving excursions—back before that pesky policeman stole my licence—to visit people or for her wallaby rescuing. Oh, and Iris wants me to spend fifteen million dollars.'

'*What?*' Dom sat up from his bed.

'Are you for real, Gran?'

'It's why we saw Otis in his undies, to see the trust account.'

Luke cringed. 'Can we please stop talking about Otis that way?'

'Who is Otis?' asked Dom.

'Town lawyer. He'd be in his sixties.'

'He's nearly seventy. And seeing Otis in his tighty-whities is something you can never unsee. Just ask Jordi.'

'Gran.' Luke wanted to ask Jordi. He wanted her here.

'In your big voice please, so the rest of the class can hear you.' Esther fluffed up Dom's pillows for him to sit up.

Luke cleared his throat and began reading Iris's letter.

Dear Esther

So this is where the party begins …

By now you should have learned about the trust I want you to spend. It's the perfect task for you, my friend, because I want you to create a place for the local elderly population. A home.

According to my research, there is enough money in the trust to either build or renovate a place for Elsie Creek's elderly and set up an endowment. I want you to create a home for our friends where we can sing along with you as we gather around your grand piano. A place where we can share stories on the verandah as we watch the sunsets and storm clouds shift across the horizon.

Somewhere close enough for us to visit our friends in hospital, or stroll through town to have tea at the train station, instead of waiting for someone to drive us.

I want you to create a place for the retired stockmen who have no family, but whose spirits would shrivel to dust if stuck in suburbia. They'd love it if you found a place where they were close enough to go and admire a sea of cattle backs at the train station, hear the deep rumbling sounds of a road train coming down the highway, while having a beer at the pub with old mates.

Esther, I'm also giving you permission to create a safe space where that great big lump of a buffalo can sleep beside you like he does, as we both know he's getting on in age.

Jenny, Elsie Creek Hospital's wonderful head nurse, explained what such a place would need and can help with ideas for its long-term future. The lawyer has the funds waiting to begin as soon as you find the perfect space to build.

But don't use that real estate manager again—the one you tried to shoot. Talk to Bea and Frank's niece, Kat, Kathryn Jones. I've been told that she's the lady to talk to about properties and interior decorating or was that interior designing. I could never remember which one it was, but do talk to Kat.

'Do you know this Kat?' Esther interrupted Luke, now sitting on the end of his bed, the pug keeping Dom company.

'Not much. She drives Frank's old Ford ute around town.

I know her husband, Kyle, he owns the local garage. Good bloke. You'd know his brother, Jimmy, Caveman, king of the Billabong Barbie Bake-off.'

'I do,' she said with a nod. 'Well, go on.' Esther waved her hand at him like the ex-schoolteacher she was, urging her student to read before the class.

> But it's all up to you, my friend. You are the one who must give the green light on this project, because you'll be the advocate for all of the retiring Elsie Creek residents.

'No way! That's too much ...' Again, Esther interrupted, gripping her throat at the enormity of the task.

Luke squeezed her hand as he continued to read Iris's letter.

> Don't worry, my friend, there are plenty of professionals willing to help you with the business side. Talk to Kat and Jenny, who are part of the outback sisterhood, who are all willing to help. I want you to oversee the fun stuff, making it a home for our friends the way the Lodge used to be. I can already picture you planning tiara-making contests, cabaret nights, and birthdays that everyone gets to enjoy from breakfast.

> And don't you dare think for a second that we should leave it to some big-wig city consultant to create a home for the mature people we are— that's why I want you to put in your honest feedback on this project. You know Elsie Creek, and how we like things done, because you've lived its history right alongside me.

> And as we both know your memory is failing, and because I understand you feel like a burden to your grandson, Luke, who tries so hard to keep you happy at home, too. So, as my gift to you, dear Esther, let's build the perfect retirement

home for our friends, a place where I would have been delighted to spend my last days with you.

Ever your sister in style, raising my last cocktail glass to the sunset, may we never stop wearing our crowns as queens and may we meet again,

Iris

'Smart as a whip she was, right to the end.' Esther dabbed at her tears as Luke handed her the letter.

'What do you think?'

'Hmm, it's a lot.'

'I agree.' Luke couldn't see Esther leaving the house she'd grown up in. She loved the Lodge as a proud member of the Bennett family.

'But now I get why Iris had us traipsing around the countryside. Good thing, too. Who knows what condition that couple would have been in if Jordi didn't climb into their burning car and rescue them.'

Didn't that make his chest spike with worry for Jordi. 'Gran, give me your phone, please.'

'Why?'

'I want to call Jordi.' That fire would have brought up all sorts of issues for Jordi.

Luke selected Jordi's number, praying she'd pick up. But it went straight to her pre-recorded message.

'This is Jordi. Leave a message.'

'Angelfish, please call me. Gran told me what happened today and I need to know you're okay.' He stared at the phone, willing it to ring back. But it didn't.

'So, I'm guessing that's another fish that got away today,' said Dom from his bed.

'What fish?' Gran asked.

'We lost the million-dollar barra,' said Dom.

But this felt far worse than letting all that money slip through his fingers. 'Jordi is worth more than that.' And Luke wasn't going to let her get away from him that easily.

Forty-four

The overhead doorbell tinkled as Luke entered the city store where cool air and assorted floral aromas washed over him, reminding him of Jordi. The front window displayed gift baskets, silk flower arrangements, with the name *Stalks and Stems Floristry* stretched in gold letters across the window.

It was like he'd stepped into a vintage store with its black-and-white-chequered floor, tin buckets filled with fragrant flowers, and various wreaths decoratively hanging from a wooden ladder.

'Can I help you?' Behind the counter was a woman who looked like Jordi, just shorter, blonder, and older. Wearing the same style of business shirt Jordi wore on her deliveries, with *Stalks and Stems* embroidered on the pocket.

'Are you Natalie?'

'I am.' She smiled the same way Jordi did, but it wasn't Jordi's smile. Jordi's smile would have him smiling alongside her, and the ache he had in his chest would be replaced with that feeling of bliss he only got with Jordi.

Damn, he missed her. 'I'm looking for Jordi.'

'You are?'

'Luke.' He stretched his neck to peek around the back in hope of finding Jordi, who had been avoiding his calls all week. He just had to see her.

Natalie's smile was swapped for a scowl as she crossed her arms over her chest. 'What do you want?'

'I'd like to speak to Jordi. Is your sister out the back?'

'No. She's not here. So off you go, don't let the door hit you on the way out.'

'I want to see Jordi. Please. She's not answering my calls or messages or—'

'You should have thought about that before you gossiped about our customers.' She wagged her finger at him. 'I heard your podcast. I know exactly what you said about our customers.' Natalie then leaned over the counter, her voice hushed but still full of anger. 'You're lucky the new owners didn't hear about it—you could have cost us the sale of this store.'

'You sold it.'

With a smug look on her face, she lifted her chin. 'We signed the contracts this morning for both the store *and* the house.'

Wasn't that a kick in the guts, making his ribs ache with the emptiness of an endless pit. 'You're leaving?'

'Just like you are, out that door.'

'But—'

'Door. There. Walk. Now.' Natalie pointed to the door.

'I'm not leaving until I speak to Jordi.' Not if the sisters were selling everything. It was his last shot. He walked around the shop's large counter, knowing Jordi lived in the back.

'*Mitchell!*' Natalie's voice was as shrill as his grandmother's. 'Oi, you can't go back there.'

'I just want to speak to Jordi.'

'What's going on?' Mitchell was a big guy. With a pen tucked behind one ear, he was busily taping the bottom of a large removalist's box, letting it rest with the others. 'You're Luke, aren't you?'

'I am.'

'And he won't leave.'

'All right, sweetheart, take a breath. I've got this. Go and finish your fancy milk tea you had me fetch.'

'But—'

'Go on.' Mitchell gently held Natalie's shoulders and

turned her around to face the door to the shopfront.

'Oh, hey, congratulations on the baby.'

'Thank you.' The pair of expectant parents smiled at Natalie's flat stomach, just like his mate Alex and Verily did when they'd first announced they were having a baby.

The tender moment didn't last long before Natalie's frown returned. 'Don't you try and sweet-talk us. I'm not telling you where Jordi is.' Her wagging finger was lethal.

Luke held his hands up in surrender, backing away from the pregnant woman.

'Nat. Babe. Let me handle it.' Mitchell guided her back into the store, and soon returned. 'We'll talk out here.' He led Luke through the back shed area. It was bigger than expected, with a fancy kitchenette and a lounge area set up like a staffroom. No wonder Jordi was comfortable in his shed. Yet this place was cleaner, and nicer. But there was no van or any sign of Jordi anywhere, just a lot of packing boxes.

Mitchell opened the back door to the small alleyway where the smell of garbage and Chinese takeaway blended with the fumes from a passing delivery truck.

'Can you tell me where Jordi is?' Because he'd just been shown the back door.

'I honestly couldn't tell you where Jordi is. But I remember you.' Mitchell rubbed his chin, as if sizing up Luke. 'You were in a fireman's uniform.'

'When was that?' Because he hadn't worn it in a long time.

'I was at the hospital with Natalie, waiting for them to bring Jordi in ...' He crossed his arms and leaned his back against the wall. 'The police had told us a fireman was hurt alongside Jordi and both were being medevaced. I was in the corridor when the ambulance arrived from the airport. You were holding Jordi's hand as they rolled her through to the ER, and I saw your shoulder all bandaged up from your own burns, but you didn't let Jordi's hand go. I admired that.'

'Nothing admirable about it.' Luke leaned back against the wall beside Mitchell.

'I get it.' Mitchell sighed. 'It was a crappy time. Nat's parents were the best. Nat takes after their mother, all fire and passion, and is very protective. Jordi's like her dad, who was a good man. Poor Nat went through hell over losing her parents, and so scared she'd lost Jordi when she was in that coma. And, hey, I'm protective of Jordi too. She's like my little sister.'

'So why aren't you giving me the lecture? Or telling me to get nicked?'

'Why? Do you want me to call my wife back and let her give you another tongue-lashing?' Mitchell chuckled.

'I'm good, thanks. That was enough.'

Mitchell glanced back at the store, then narrowed his eyes at Luke. 'But I do know Jordi's going to be okay now. Last Saturday, she came back from your place different.'

'How? Did Jordi tell you about the car accident, the fire?'

'Me, yes. Nat, no. And we never told Nat, to not worry her while she's pregnant. My wife has been through enough.' Mitchell glanced back at the door. 'But I can tell you that you made Jordi smile again. After the hell that Jordi went through, Nat and I were both glad to see it. Jordi would come back and share her stories of fishing trips, and the Lodge, your grandmother, and that buffalo. Jordi loved every minute out there, even working with Lenny doing the dishes in the pub's kitchen. But in all of her stories, it was obvious how deeply she cared about you. And I can see you care for Jordi. But what I liked was when Jordi told me how much you care for your grandmother, not many blokes would bother. But it's something I would do because my grandmother bought me up.'

They shared a nod. Grandson to grandson.

'I don't want her leaving until I can talk to her.'

'I get that. Look, I understand you two met under extreme circumstances ...'

'Extreme alright.' It'd been life changing.

'If Nat and Jordi's mother were alive, she'd tell you it's more than a coincidence. She'd tell you it was fate.'

'Eh?'

'Come on, they're florists working in a family florist shop—they brought those girls up on romance. So I'm going to tell you what Nat's father told me ...' Mitchell leaned closer, with his finger pointed at Luke's chest. 'If you want to win over one of the Watkins sisters, you'll need to do something big to get Jordi's attention. And if it's big enough, you might even win Natalie's approval too. Because, mate, this store was a part of their home and you upset both girls.'

'I'm sorry about sharing their customer's stuff on the air. I honestly didn't think it was such a big deal.'

'This store was started by their parents and they named it *Stalks and Stems* after their two daughters. With their dad working night shifts, those girls spent a lot of time here— weekends, after school, school holidays—more than they did at home. It's filled with fond memories, so they hate anyone threatening their livelihood, when they treated their customers like friends, some like extended family.'

'So, I stuffed up.'

'Big time. This store, it's a part of their legacy. I'm actually surprised they signed the sale contract this morning. But they did, and we're packing to go.'

'When do you leave? And congrats on the promotion.'

Mitchell grinned and nodded. 'Cheers. I'm on leave now, helping with the move. I want to get Nat settled in Adelaide quickly, so we can get ready for the baby.'

'Is there any way I can see Jordi? Before she ...' He couldn't say it. 'I have to say sorry.'

'You look sorry enough.'

He scrubbed his hand roughly over his face. 'I haven't been able to sleep ...'

'You're in deep, aren't you?'

Luke shrugged, not sure what to say.

Grabbing the pen tucked behind his ear, Mitchell

scribbled on the back of a business card. 'Well, here's hoping you two kiss and make up, because I'd love to go on a fishing trip. I'm going to miss the Territory's mud crabs.'

'I'm on a fishing hiatus for a bit.'

Mitchell passed a copy of the florist shop's business card to Luke. 'Well, that's my number, and the details for Jordi's last delivery run, which is tomorrow.'

That didn't leave him much time. 'Do you know what Jordi is doing? With the shop being sold?'

'I know Nat wants Jordi to come with us to Adelaide.'

'I wasn't asking about Natalie.'

'Good answer.' Mitchell nodded with approval. 'Honestly, as much as I love Jordi like a sister, and I'd kick anyone's arse who'd hurt her—' he said with a blunt warning, 'Jordi's finding her own path.'

'What do you mean by that?'

'Did she ever tell you about the plans she had with her dad before the accident?'

He nodded.

'Jordi is determined to do what'll make her happy. And now you have to ask yourself, will you be able to help her?'

'I'm here, aren't I. But what can I do if she's sold the business and is avoiding my calls? I know she's avoiding me. And I think she pushed me away on purpose. What do you think?' He couldn't believe he was asking a stranger, but he was desperate to find her.

'Well, you should know that they didn't sell all of the business.'

'What do you mean?'

'The new owner wasn't interested in the rural run.'

'Fuel costs, and it's the rural area, I get it. It's costly.' Because Jordi had been working at the pub for extra cash.

'You'd think.' Mitchell gave a coy grin. 'But that rural run has become a very profitable sideline for this store.'

'Hey, all I know is that Jordi loved doing that run.'

'We know. You see, Jordi created the entire rural run for one reason only.'

'Yeah, what's that?'

'Because that little flower girl had a crush on this guy so badly, she hustled hard to build an entire business around him, just so she'd see this guy she only knew as *the Bottle Shop Boy*.'

Forty-five

Storm clouds hovered like white carnation clusters just off the horizon, casting long shadows over red soil plains, where the long black road spilled like a spool of silk ribbon under the sun.

Jordi gripped the steering wheel, gazing at the long road with fondness.

The shop was sold, the house was sold, now just waiting on the paperwork, with her sister busily packing to move down south and do some serious baby shopping. Her world was changing.

But just for a moment she could admire the beauty that surrounded her. Jordi had missed this place, this town, and the vibrant and ever-changing Northern Territory outback that surrounded them, with its rustic reds and sunburnt ochres through to the mix of black soil planes, dotted with gigantic ant mounds and clusters of boulders so smooth they looked like giant dinosaur eggs.

But it was also the stunning range of gums, banksias, and other flourishing native trees, highlighted by an abundant display of wildflowers dotting the area like paint across a canvas. Her seasonal rural run always cleared her mind as the outback unveiled itself around each sweeping turn along the asphalt road. Even though she'd been tempted to avoid this trip, she'd started this rural run, and now she wanted to complete it.

Jordi shifted in the driver's seat as she approached the first of the usual road signs that announced her approach to

Elsie Creek.

It reminded her of the conversations she'd had with Esther hijacking her front seat. She grinned at how Esther used to complain about how those dusty billboards weren't bright enough or bold enough in their advertising for the local supermarket. They needed some pizzazz—whatever pizzazz was. Esther would question why the publican only chose that brand of beer to advertise the pub. She'd explain how there was more to the hardware store than tools and camping supplies, and how it had a drive-thru feed store attached to it, too.

She missed Esther and Cecil. Especially Luke. And even the small outback town of Elsie Creek, that started with this string of roadside billboards.

Jordi had passed the same signs so many times, she didn't really see them anymore. Displaying how far away from Elsie Creek she was: *fifteen kilometres. Ten kilometres. Five kilometres.*

In the past, with each passing sign, she'd swallow with nervous anticipation, fighting her desire to see Luke, to talk to Luke, to ask him for directions.

But she hadn't spoken to Luke all week. She'd been avoiding all his calls, but she needed to get all of her plans sorted before she could talk to Luke.

She leaned over the steering wheel as she approached the first sign. It was supposed to be the one advertising the supermarket. But someone had covered it with large sheets, to splash massive black letters across the billboard that read:

TO THE FLOWER GIRL ...

A little further down the lonely outback highway, where the heat washed over the road, the next road sign said:

I'M SORRY.

The big black letters took up the entire billboard, big enough to be seen from miles away. But it wasn't the biggest sign.

Gripping the steering wheel, she swallowed nervously as

her eyes flicked to the side mirrors to check she was the only vehicle on the road as she approached the third billboard, which normally advertised the pub.

It was also covered over, leaving an eight-word message that read:

PLEASE FORGIVE ME

**From the BOTTLE SHOP
BOY**

'No way ...' Jordi slowed down her van as she approached the final sign. The one that normally read: *'Welcome to Elsie Creek.'*

But all it showed was a black arrow that pointed to Cecil, the water buffalo, wearing bright pink ribbons wrapped around his horns and tail, tied to the billboard's post, with words written across his side that said:

**FLOWER GIRL, PLEASE
TAKE ME HOME**

Forty-six

On the front verandah of the Lodge, Luke paced backwards and forwards, watching the road where fine swirls of red dust shifted as the heat rose to greet the sun. 'Jordi is not going to do it, Gran. What's stopping her from untying Cecil and letting him walk through town like he normally does.'

Gran sat in her wicker chair, with Coco the pug resting in her lap. 'Be patient.'

'I should have driven into town.'

'And find her where? Don't worry, she'll be here.'

'This sucks.' He paced back and forth, raking fingers through his hair. 'Everyone in town is going to read those signs. I can't believe you talked me into this.'

'You said you needed something big to make up for being such an idiot. What's bigger than a billboard?'

'I thought you were on my side.'

'I am. But I understand why she's angry at you, and why she won't answer your calls.'

'I know.' With the florist shop and house sold, this was his last chance. Jordi had to take the bait, or it was over for good. 'You know what, I don't care who sees those signs. I should have written on all of them, just so Jordi knows I'm sorry.'

When he saw the roof of the van, it was moving slowly along the road, but then so was the pace of the ageing water buffalo following the trail of flowers.

'I told you.' Esther got up from her chair and playfully

thumped his arm. 'I told you.'

'What do I do?' Suddenly he was drawing a complete blank. Everything he had planned to say had disappeared from his mind. There was just too much on the line if he stuffed this up.

'Go and talk to her, or you'll regret it for the rest of your life. I'll be inside making a tiara for Coco. Come along, rat.' The dog yapped as it followed Esther, leaving Luke to meet his fate.

The van pulled up in the drive, and the door opened like the first time she'd come to Anaborro Downs. This time, Jordi wasn't being pushed against the side of the van to get licked in the face by a water buffalo. This time, she held out a bunch of daisies to feed Cecil, when before Luke had held her hand to show her how.

What he'd give to hold her hand now.

'I never did pay you for the flowers you made for Gran's birthday, or those daisies we fed to Cecil.'

'No, but that's okay...' Jordi took a shuddering breath, her eyes were filled with remorse. 'Are you okay? I'd heard you'd lost the million-dollar barra and got stuck up a tree. It made front page news.'

He rolled his eyes. 'I blame Dom for spilling that story.'

'I'm really sorry, I know what that money would have—'

'It wasn't the most important thing I lost that day.' Not when his greatest fear was losing her.

'Excuse me?'

He licked his lips, taking a deep breath. It was now or never.

Crossing the distance, which felt wider than a canyon, he stood before her, his heart beating louder as if recognising its better half, to fill that gaping hole in his chest that missed her. 'You are worth more to me than some fishing competition.'

'It was worth a million dollars.'

'Hanging on to a dead tree in a life-and-death situation, you tend to look at things differently.'

'I get that.'

'Obviously, if you've agreed to sell the store.'

'And I've got a deadline—'

He pushed shut her driver's door to stop her leaving. 'I may have let go of a million-dollar fish, but I'm not letting you go, not until I explain myself. Please? You owe me that, at least.' Because he'd been searching for her for a week.

'Please look at me, Jordi.'

Slowly she turned, and lifted her head, but there was a hurt in her eyes, and he'd done that to her.

'I'm sorry for being an idiot, for not being up-front with you about the podcast and the notes about your deliveries, and for not telling you who I was. You see, when you drove into the bottle shop that first time, I was so over the moon I wanted to hug you right then and there. But you were so shy, that I was scared I'd never see you again if I told you who I was. At first, I just wanted to keep you talking, get you to open up because I was just so freaking happy to see you. Every single time. But you only came out of your shell when you talked about the flower deliveries, so I encouraged it. I wasn't trying to use you for information, I swear it. And I honestly didn't think there was any harm in using that information.'

'I shouldn't have told you all those details—that's my fault. Not yours. I only did it because I wanted to talk to you, too. I-I—'

He cut her off, because he didn't like her tone, scared she was breaking up with him. 'Jordi, last Saturday night, after I got back from fishing the Barra Classic, I was going to tell you I wanted to plan a future with you—but it all went pear-shaped, and I never got that chance. And what I wanted to tell you is that you are a prize catch for a guy like me. So, I want to make you a business deal that'll make you happy.'

She only frowned at him.

'I'm offering you the Lodge, and all of the land and equipment at Anaborro Downs, including the services of a guy who is an excellent, well-trained farmhand, so you can grow your commercial crop of flowers.'

'What?' Her face dropped in sheer surprise.

'I have the equipment just sitting there. And I can help you.'

'But this is Esther's house. And it's home to a fence-destroying, flower-eating water buffalo.' She pointed at Cecil, who lifted his head from devouring a posy, with daisy petals dusting his lips.

'Gran is moving out with Cecil.'

'To where?'

'To the *new* Lodge. In town.'

'Where's that?'

'They're building a retirement home for Gran and her friends, complete with a stable for Cecil, where the old ranger's station used to be. Right down the road from the hospital in town. It was what Iris wanted in her last letter.'

'That's why Esther was told to go back to the hospital?'

'To speak with Jenny.'

'And Esther agreed?'

He nodded. 'She's got early signs of dementia.'

'I'm so sorry. What are you planning?'

'We've got her a companion to help out, until the new Lodge is built.'

'But Esther won't leave.'

'I thought so, too. But Gran reckons she's old enough to finally move out of home.'

'But Esther loves the Lodge. She's always telling me a Bennett must stay at Anaborro Downs.'

'Which is why you need that farmhand—me—to work as your land slave.' He lowered his head to meet her gaze, giving her his best suck-up smile yet. 'Gran's excited about it, wishing they'd have it built already.'

But where was Jordi's excitement?

'Angelfish ...' He took a step closer, his fingers tenderly clasped hers until he had a hold of her small hand and gave it a gentle squeeze. 'I don't want you going to Adelaide. I want you here, where you can grow your commercial crops of flowers, just the way you'd always planned. I'll rebuild the dam, and fill it full of wild lotus, where we can both fish free from any crocodiles.'

'Are you done with fishing? And what about your fishing tours?'

He shrugged. 'I'm in no hurry to get back on the water.'

'But you love fishing.'

'I did. But there's no life without you.'

She gasped, blinking at him.

He stepped closer, holding her small hand to his chest so she could feel his heart that beat only for her. 'I want to share your afternoon coffee breaks, where you'd laugh with me at the back of the pub when you took your break from the kitchen. I also want to share those mornings with you, where I get to see your sleepy eyes and hear your dream-drenched voice asking for *five more minutes sleep, babe*. But I also want your Friday afternoon smile that feels like I'm drinking straight from the sun, when you steer that white van into the bottle shop as the start of my weekend. And I want all of that to be a part of my every day.'

He tenderly brushed back her hair, tucking it behind her ear to then lift her chin.

'Jordi, I want to be there to hold your hand on the bad days, to hug you in your sleep and tell you it's okay as you fight with your nightmares—because you do that for me, so now it's my turn to do that for you, because I want to be a part of your every day in every way for the rest of my life.' And hoped with everything she was hearing him, feeling everything he was feeling for her.

Forty-seven

Jordi gasped, stepping back from Luke, but the van was stopping her. Never had anyone spoken to her like this. She was too stunned to speak.

'Jordi, this, between us, it's the real deal. It's why I held your hand to fly across the Territory, and why I drove every few days, to the city to just sit in the corridor while you were in the coma. It wasn't out of pity.'

She narrowed her eyes at him and tried to shake him off. 'I don't want your pity or anyone's pity.' She'd had enough of that while recovering. She was over it.

Stepping in closer he made her look at him and all she saw, felt, smelt was him, trapped by the earnest spell of his eyes. 'Don't you dare ever think that. I thought you were fragile, but I was wrong. You are the strongest person I've ever met, Jordi. You became my hero from the moment we met. And somehow you became my everything. I can't and I won't let you go, because my mission in life is to see you happy.'

'So, what will you do that'll make you happy? Fishing?'

'No. I'm not doing fishing tours. But I'm hoping my new landlady will let me move in with her, and I'll help her manage the crops. I like farming. I'm good at it. Of course, I'll keep working in the bottle shop for a few nights a week for cashflow. And maybe I'll go speak with Jax at the fire station, but I'll consult with my partner first to fit in with her.' He then shared his lopsided grin.

She was desperate to not smile back. 'I didn't say yes.'

'You're here, aren't you?'

'Only because the water buffalo asked me. Did you do the signs?'

'Gran said I needed a grand gesture.'

And there was nothing bigger than a billboard that had her attention. 'You do realise that everyone would've seen them. And you've always said not to air any Bennett business—'

'I don't care. Sure, my dirty laundry may be in the open, but I stuffed up, and I needed to get your attention to tell you how sorry I am, because you weren't answering any of my calls.'

'I didn't want you talking me into something I didn't want to do. Not when I wasn't sure what I wanted myself. But I know now.'

He grinned.

She grinned back, couldn't help it, especially when she spotted that surge of hope flaring in his eyes that somehow had her heart doing warming flips of joy.

'What do you want to do, Angelfish?'

She shrugged.

'Come on.' He frowned at her.

That made her giggle, she had to stop teasing him and raised her chin to proudly announce her master plan. 'With the store sold, I've been busy going through my own business plans. I've been ringing all my florist contacts down south to keep them informed as future customers. I've been searching for suitable properties to start farming flowers. And because I didn't sell the rural run, I'm in the process of renaming it under my own business name. Which meant a lot of late nights filling out paperwork, talking to accountants and the banks. I've been busy.' As the inner pride filled in her chest, she pushed her shoulders back to stand taller. 'I'm doing it. I'm finally following my original dream.' The excitement just buzzing inside her chest, she wanted to do some dance in the dust like a toddler high on sugar.

'I know. I'm proud of you.'

'Did my sister tell you what I was doing?'

'No. Your brother-in-law. Didn't he tell you?'

'No. Which is rare.' She narrowed her eyes at him. 'What else did he tell you?' Because Mitchell had been on her back all week about calling Luke, just so he could go mud crabbing before he moved to Adelaide. She'd never realised they'd actually spoken.

'Your brother-in-law told me about the crush you had for me and built a business just to see me.'

'Oh no.' Her cheeks were suddenly burning with heat. She ducked her head.

'Hey, listen, Jordi...' He lifted her chin to make her look at him. 'I don't just have a crush on you: I love you.'

Her eyes widened and she blinked. Did she hear right?

'There, I said it.' He stepped back tossing his hands in the air. 'That huge long-winded speech really comes down to three words—I. Love. You. Jordin Watkins. Just as you are.' He then stepped in close with his palms cupping her cheeks, and pressed his lips against hers, and kissed her. Cupping her jaw, he took her mouth and greedily kissed her as if she was the air he needed to breathe.

But it ignited something inside her, what she'd been denying all along, what had been stopping her from living a life worth living, was love. That wonderful blissful feeling of deep, soul-igniting love.

He brushed a thumb over her lips, plump and wet from his kiss, her heart hammering, with her breath as ragged as his.

'I can't let you run away to Adelaide when I want you here, at Anaborro Downs.' His hoarse voice. 'Let me help you start that business, while we create our own family, right here, and we'll make it our home. So, what do you say, Jordi? Will you come and live with me?'

She wrapped her arms over his broad shoulders and gently pressed her forehead against his. 'If you keep kissing me like, we may just have a deal, Bottle Shop Boy.'

Forty-eight

Never in her life had Jordi been so nervous. She tugged at her tight collar, then pushed down her shirt's sleeves to hide her hands.

'Stop that. Breathe, Angelfish, we've got this.' Luke took her hand in his and gave it an encouraging squeeze as they stood in matching uniforms on the side of a small stage in front of the entire town. 'It'll be all over soon. Remember, this was your idea.'

'No, Esther talked us both into this.' Where she now suffered from stage fright. 'How long will this guy keep talking for?'

The mayor continued to prattle over the microphone, reading out a speech that no one was listening to.

'This town rarely gets official ceremonies like this, so, hopefully, not too long.' Luke looked at his grandmother, who rolled her eyes while the mayor talked, and talked, and talked.

'And now,' said the mayor, 'our Fire Chief, Jackson Turner, will finally get to officially present firefighter Luke Bennett with that Commonwealth Bravery Medal he received a while back. Fire Chief Turner will also be presenting the NT Bravery Award to Luke's fiancée, volunteer firewoman and local floriculturist, Jordin Watkins, for saving two passengers from a fire.'

'That's our cue, Angelfish.' Under the shade of the large parking bay area Luke and Jordi were awarded their bravery medals in front of the entire town.

'My turn, Mayor, you waffle on too much.' Esther, in her blue ball gown, snatched the microphone from the mayor. She adjusted her sparkly tiara, as Cecil stood beside her wearing matching blue ribbons and a massive silk-flower headdress.

'On behalf of my fabulous old neighbour, friend and sister, Iris, Cecil and I would like to thank all those who helped make this dream a reality and to welcome everyone to Elsie Creek's retirement home's opening day, a place we like to call *The Lodge*. Please come and join us for the festivities in the sunroom. You can't miss it, it's the one with the grand piano. Luke, can you help me.' She motioned him forwards.

With a pair of scissors Luke and Esther cut the red ribbon, officially opening the new Lodge to a round of applause and camera flashes.

As Esther proudly showed people inside, laughter and jazz music drifted out the main doors, all the makings of a party where Esther was ecstatic to host.

'You don't regret moving in with me?' Luke slipped his arm around Jordi's shoulders.

'Not for a minute. Say *peonies*.' Jordi held up her phone, taking a selfie. She took them all the time, printing them out for their own virgin's board at home as a reminder to celebrate those precious moments in life. It held images of the first time she'd volunteered at the fire station, the day Luke had officially returned to the job as a fireman—and Jax took off fishing for a few days.

Their board included photos of her first piano lesson, her first driving lesson on the tractor, and when they planted their very first commercial crop of gingers, heliconias, and various other tropical varieties. There were images of her first hunting trip with Walden, Porter, and Dom, where they transported a small herd of banteng, to allow the near-extinct animal to live safely at Alice's wildlife sanctuary.

As for the *Dramas from the Dinghy* podcast, Porter and Luke stopped hiding behind an AI-filter to use their authentic voices. Now famous as the guy who'd lost the million-dollar-fish to a crocodile—and lived to tell the tale—their small podcast received lots of sponsorship and advertising requests, courtesy of their neighbour, Felix, who had a flair for marketing.

Even though Luke wasn't signing up to do any more fishing competitions, he'd signed up with Porter to be on his police boat to help the punters, along with microphone in hand to interview those fishing while on the water for the show. But when Luke did go fishing, he preferred going with a friend, where he didn't care if he caught a fish or not, it was just the idea of getting out there and living in the moment that made the adventure.

But being the hustler he was, Luke was busily preparing the launch of his perfect fishing lure—the one that caught the million-dollar barra—and was about to sell it to the masses.

As for Jordi, instead of hiding herself, she took photos to record their life together, making Anaborro Downs their home. From the renovation of turning Luke's bedroom back into an office, the old slaughter shed became the new flower shed, where they cut flowers, trimmed stalks and stems, boxing their native flowers to meet the mail plane at the Elsie Creek airfield at daybreak, just in time to share breakfast with Esther and Cecil across the road.

Jordi continued her weekly rural run, making it a standard date for Esther to hijack the passenger seat in her van, where Esther talked her into running a class for the local craft store.

Esther never got her motorised esky, but she still chose her tiara of the day and dressed up in her ball gowns once a week to read at the school with Cecil beside her. Esther loved being the lady of the New Lodge, with no two days the same, and where she only had to walk across the road to visit Luke when he was on duty at the fire station.

But it was the quiet moments that Luke most loved

sharing with Jordi at Anaborro Downs. They'd lie back on plush cushions on the floor of their rowboat, drinking wine under the stars, while floating among a sea of giant lotus lilies that Jordi could hold in two hands, in their private dam that was a place free from crocodiles.

Luke kissed Jordi's cheek as she played with her phone. 'Are you texting those photos to your sister?'

'I am. Nat just texted me that Mitchell has confirmed he's got the time off, so Nat's booked their flights with my fabulous new niece. And Mitchell's put in a request for a big feed of mud crabs and fish.'

'Mitchell can catch them himself when he gets here. But I think your niece needs a cousin. Lots and lots of cousins because there must always be a Bennett at Anaborro Downs,' he said nuzzling her ear. 'How soon before we can go home?' He gently pulled her closer, his lips meeting hers. They never got tired of kissing each other.

A big black nose sniffed against Jordi's hair, and a short blast of hot air hit their ears making them cringe, as Cecil licked at their faces. 'Aww yuck, Cecil.'

'I think you've just been summoned.' Porter, dressed in full police uniform for the occasion, chuckled with Esther beside him. 'And there are all these old fellas who want to share their fishing stories with us.'

'Come on, you two, we can't party without you.' Esther hooked her arms through Luke's and Jordi's and escorted them back inside.

Cecil's black ears flickered, and with a swish of his tail ribbons he faced the road where the sun slowly sank like an orange ball of fire to disappear beyond the outback's never-ending horizon.

His black nose twitched at the slight breeze carrying the scents of dust, cattle, and the warmth of summer. Nearby, happy excited voices filled the air, followed by the laughter of people, young and old. It was the voices of a small town.

As his shadow stretched across the red dirt, his hoofs shifted stirring up the dust that brushed over his buffalo hide. Facing the road that led to the never-wherever of Northern Australia, he nodded at the road he usually followed home. Instead, he strolled into his new home that was right in the heart of Elsie Creek that was a place that may just be a speck on the map, but it was a place that always promised its residents a happily ever after no matter who, what, or how old they were because it was home to all.

THE END

For now ...

I have a gift for YOU!

Learn the secrets of

ELSIE CREEK

Exclusive to Elsie Creek Readers!

Simply go to:

https://melarowe.com/elsie-creeks-secrets/

Did you like the story?

If so, your opinion matters to me!

It's true.

A good reader's review is worth a lot to this author.

So, if you enjoyed this book, please leave a review and

recommend it to your friends.

I'd appreciate it.

With much gratitude,

A. ROWE

ACKNOWLEDGEMENTS

Thank you

My grandfather was diagnosed with Alzheimer's. And I was in awe of how hard my grandmother worked to keep him at home on the farm. When he was eventually moved into a residential facility, she'd visit every day to share lunch with him, and they were married for over sixty years. Although I've dedicated the entire *Elsie Creek Series* to my father, *Buffalo Dust* is dedicated to the memory of my amazing grandparents, Ron and Grace Schmidt.

Growing up, my grandmother grew flowers on the farm to surround the old hills hoist clothesline as her view from the kitchen window. I had aunts who took turns making flower arrangements for church on Sunday. My great-aunt was a florist who grew flowers amongst their vast orchards, where I got to accompany my uncle on his rural flower deliveries as a kid. With fleeting dreams of becoming a florist, I worked in a large inner-city florist that made posies for the supermarkets. Sadly, my hay fever wouldn't allow me to continue with this profession, yet I still grow a decent crop of tropical flowers, and enjoyed the fond memories unearthed while writing this story.

I'd also like to spare a thought for those neighbours who suffered under the Banana Freckle debacle. In the Top End, most of us had bananas plants somewhere on our properties, to then have strangers peeking over fences or traipsing through our yards to rip up perfectly healthy plants, and then poison the soils, was heart-breaking for many. So next time you shop for bananas, remember those farmers who've worked so hard to bounce back from that challenging time.

Thank goodness for the fishing that is a big part of the lifestyle (besides avoiding water buffaloes) where many will tell tales of that mighty fighting barra that got stolen by a some sneaky saltie. Not to spin too long a yarn, I'd like to thank my old skippers who've mentored me over the years especially Gary Fein and Peter 'Pedro' Hunter who helped me get my skippers tickets and commercial fishing tour operators licenses. Yes, I know how to float a boat and enjoyed my many adventures on the waters that I gleefully *(*grins*)* shared in this story.

I'd also like to thank the real podcast pirates known for the best fishing gossip in the Northern Territory, the ABC's iconic *Tales from the Tinny*. Sadly, at the same time that this book is published, they will be broadcasting their final episode, ending 17 years on the airwaves. You guys will be missed.

As always, I'd like to thank the Handbrake for playing co-pilot on my many adventures, except for boats, we know you hate them. Thank you to the incredible editing Deb team at DP Plus who I torture with my grammar. Thank you to the Fabulous First Readers team for their amazing support; I am truly blessed to have you all join me on my writing journey.

Lastly, to you, dear reader, thank you for taking the time to read this story. It means the world to me, as I look forward to sharing more with you in that *'Escape to Happily Ever After'*.

Until next time,

A. ROWE

ABOUT THE AUTHOR

Australian bestselling author, Mel A ROWE, creates romantic escapes for today's busy women to enjoy from the comfort of their home.

Delivering stories with a dash of drama, witty humour and quirky family units, Mel is known for reinventing romantic versions of home, taking her common characters on uncommon journeys that lead from boardrooms to billabongs as they try to find their own HAPPILY EVER AFTER.

Living in Australia's Northern Territory, Mel enjoys random outback road trips, fumbling with her camera, annoying her family with her bad singing, and making new friends in the middle of nowhere—except for water buffalos. She's been chased by a few.

Find Mel at

MelAROWE.com

Receive exclusive insights, book gifts, news
of upcoming releases by joining:
https://melarowe.com/newsletter/

Also by MEL A ROWE

ELSIE CREEK SERIES:

The ART of DUST

DIAMOND in the DUST

CAKED in DUST

XMAS DUST

MUSTER in the DUST

ROLLED in DUST

WRITTEN in DUST

DOCTORING DUST

BUFFALO DUST

OASIS OF THE OUTBACK DUOLOGY:

The Station, Volume One

The Station, Volume Two

STANDALONE STORIES:

Avoiding the Pity Party

Unplanned Party

The Football Whisperer

Winter's Walk

Run Beautiful Run

The Sister Trip

For story exclusives & more visit MelAROWE.com